THE CAMOMILE LAWN

Mary Wesley was born near Windsor in 1912. Her education took her to the London School of Economics and during the War she worked in the War Office. Although she initially fulfilled her parent's expectations in marrying an aristocrat she then scandalised them when she divorced him in 1945 and moved in with the great love of her life, Eric Siepmann. The couple married in 1952, once his wife had finally been persuaded to divorce him.

She used to comment that her 'chief claim to fame is arrested development, getting my first novel [*Jumping the Queue*] published at the age of seventy'. She went on to write a further nine novels, three of which were adapted for television, including the best-selling *The Camomile Lawn*. Mary Wesley was awarded the CBE in the 1995 New Year's honour list and died in 2002.

ALSO BY MARY WESLEY

Jumping the Queue
Harnessing Peacocks
The Vacillations of Poppy Carew
Not That Sort of Girl
Second Fiddle
A Sensible Life
A Dubious Legacy
An Imaginative Experience
Part of the Furniture

MARY WESLEY

The Camomile Lawn

VINTAGE

3 5 7 9 10 8 6 4

Vintage
20 Vauxhall Bridge Road,
London SW1V 2SA

Vintage Classics is part of the Penguin Random House
group of companies whose addresses can be found at
global.penguinrandomhouse.com

Penguin
Random House
UK

Copyright © Mary Wesley 1984

Mary Wesley has asserted her right to be identified as the
author of this Work in accordance with the Copyright,
Designs and Patents Act 1988

First published in Great Britain by Macmillan in 1984

A CIP catalogue record for this book is available from the
British Library

ISBN 9781784871284

Printed and bound by Clays Ltd, Elcograf S.p.A

Penguin Random House is committed to a sustainable future
for our business, our readers and our planet. This book is made
from Forest Stewardship Council® certified paper.

MIX
Paper from
responsible sources
FSC
www.fsc.org   FSC® C018179

to James Hale

1

Helena Cuthbertson picked up the crumpled *Times* by her sleeping husband and went to the flower room to iron it.

When she had suggested they should buy two copies of the paper, so that each could enjoy it in its pristine state, Richard had flared into rage and his accusations of extravagance had gone on for weeks, made worse when she had pointed out that it was her money that paid the paper bill.

Ironing the paper, a self-imposed task, she inclined to regret her period of widowhood after the war when she had read *The Times* whenever she pleased and not had to wait. Replacing the sheets in their proper order, she considered it ironic that any man could take so long reading the leaders and the Hatch, Match and Dispatches and reduce the paper to hopeless disorder. She looked round the flower room; it was far from tidy. Something should be done about it, but not now. Helena let herself into the garden, walked round to the camomile lawn, sat down in a deck chair and settled to read the paper. Richard would sleep for another hour before fussing as to whether he or she should meet the evening train, and to which bedrooms his nephews and nieces should be assigned, as though they did not always decide for themselves. Richard attributed his temper and fussiness to being gassed in the trenches. Turning the pages of the paper, Helena rather wondered. She laid the paper down and, closing her eyes, lifted her face to the sun. There was no good news these days and although Richard had touching faith in Mr Chamberlain it looked as though Calypso, Walter, Polly and Oliver were in for the next bout of gas. Sophy, too, of course. She tended to forget Sophy, so small, so quiet, so young compared with the ebullient others. Helena knew she should make an effort about Sophy. She had never had a child of her own, neither had Richard. Calypso, Walter, Polly and Oliver were Richard's siblings' children. Calypso was the only child of Richard's elder brother John Cuthbertson, a dim country solicitor with a vapidly pretty wife. Polly and Walter were the children of his younger brother Martin Cuthbertson, a surgeon and rising star, and Oliver only child of Sarah, his elder sister, married to George Anstey, a prominent civil servant.

Richard resented clever Martin's success, felt contempt for John, and was not only rather afraid of his sister Sarah but also jealous. Poor little Sophy was his half-sister's child, an error which had killed the half-sister, leaving Sophy solo. Helena admitted to herself that had she known about Sophy when Richard had pressed her to marry him she would have thought twice. The others were all older and only came for visits, whereas Sophy of necessity was always there, though thank God fairly invisible.

Lying on her stomach along the branch of the Ilex tree overhanging the camomile lawn, Sophy looked down on her aunt. She was trapped until Helena chose to move. She had a foreshortened view of Helena, relaxed, legs apart, cotton dress riding up her thighs, lolling. A perfect view across the lawn to the cliff running down to the cove, and of the path winding along the contours of the coast a few feet from the drop to the sea, calm this hot August day. She wondered whether Oliver would have the Terror Run as he had for the last three summers and whether she would be old enough to join in. The Terror Run was run by moonlight along the path from the headland below the coastguard station. The first year Walter had sprained an ankle and last year Polly had been badly scratched by brambles. Oliver so far held the record. Calypso always came in unscathed, her exquisite face no pinker than usual, her breath only lifting breasts the better for the boys to gaze at. As Sophy watched the coastguard walk along the cliff path, going on duty, she wondered what it would be like to have breasts, what it would be like to be loved as Calypso was loved. Aunt Helena's breasts were packed into a garment called a bust bodice which made Calypso and Polly laugh. They wore Kestos brassières.

The coastguard reached his station. Uncle Richard limped through the French windows saying 'Ah, there you are' in a surprised voice, as though his wife never sat on the lawn. Helena pulled down her skirt.

'Would you like some tea?' She wished he would not limp so obviously. There was no need.

'Yes indeed, why not? Shall I ask Betty?'

'It's Betty's day out. I will get it, it's all ready.'

Helena sighed and rose to her feet. Above them Sophy edged backwards along the branch to her window.

'I'd get it if it weren't for my leg.' Richard Cuthbertson always said this. The leg was somewhere in Flanders, a place he talked about with nervous affection.

'You rest it.' Helena always said this. Oliver had once been heard to say: 'When I drove through the battlefields of Flanders with Mother the thought of Uncle's leg double-trenched among the beet made me give up sugar with my tea.' That Helena had overheard him he was unaware. Calypso had laughed her chuckling laugh.

'Imagine in bed! Poor Helena! I mean, as they, well – as they – there it is, the false one, propped against the wall, as often as not still in his trousers. I couldn't, I simply couldn't.'

Oliver and Walter had laughed too and increased their laughter when Calypso had added: 'They don't, of course. It was twin beds and now he sleeps in the dressing room.'

When Sophy asked, 'Don't what?' Walter had cried: 'Sweet innocence of youth', and Sophy had angrily blushed.

3

As Sophy eased herself over the sill into her room she saw Jack from the post office pop up the path leading to the lawn.

'Telegram, Major, for you.' She watched Uncle Richard tear the envelope with his thumb, read, then glare at Jack. 'Damn the boy!' he exclaimed, staring at Jack, who retreated a couple of steps and asked: 'Any answer, sir?'

'No, no thank you. Damned inconsiderate.'

Jack disappeared down the path to his bicycle.

Uncle Richard shouted, 'Helena, Helena, I say.'

'What is it?' Helena came through the French windows, pulling a trolley. 'I thought tea out here would be nice. What is it?' she asked, bringing the trolley up to the deck chair. 'I'll get another chair,' she added, as her husband sat in the one she had vacated.

'It's Oliver. Has an appointment in Harley Street, isn't arriving until the midnight train. He is inconsiderate. It's inconvenient, means meeting two trains. I ask you.'

'Calypso can meet him, she can drive.'

'Not my car.' Uncle Richard helped himself to a scone. 'Any cream?'

'On your left.' Helena poured tea. 'She can take mine, then.' Helena passed her husband his cup. She seldom allowed herself to refer to the fact that not only the car but the house and nearly all their possessions were hers. It was a pity Army pensions were so small, a good thing her first husband had left her well off.

'Oliver has been wounded in Spain. I expect George wants to make sure he is all right.'

'George is a fool. Why did he allow the boy to get mixed up with those dagos?'

'I don't suppose Oliver asked, he just went. They are lucky he has come back. The Turnbulls' son has been killed.'

'At least he was fighting on the right side.'

'Do you mean right or Right?' Helena spread jam on her scone.

'If you are going to start up again with that attitude I

4

refuse to discuss this – this scuffle in Spain. Where is that child Sophy? Should she not be here for tea? Sophy?' He raised his voice to shout as he would have liked to shout at his wife if he had not been afraid of her.

'Coming.' Sophy wiped the tear she had spilled in disappointment, combed her hair and called again, 'Coming.' Perhaps Calypso would let her go to meet Oliver, although it was all too probable that she would be sent to bed long before midnight. That she loved Oliver with all her heart and always would was Sophy's burden.

2

Helena met the London train, taking Sophy, who seemed quieter than usual. Sophy was small, ten, and her appearance had a touch of the Orient, not what Richard would call the Tarbrush, but the Orient. Her cheekbones could be called Slav but not her eyes. Helena hoped that she would improve. She had never enquired precisely what and who Richard's half-sister had been up to with or where.

The London train snaked into Penzance. Calypso, Walter and Polly sprang from it with zest, kissing Helena, hugging Sophy and crying, 'Well, well, how are you? Isn't this lovely? Isn't this wonderful? What air after London! Let's grab the luggage, find a porter. Where's the car? How's Uncle Richard? How's his leg?' Their anxiety always seemed to be addressed to the artificial limb, which indeed went wrong oftener than the active member.

Calypso was breathtaking. Helena was freshly surprised. At nineteen she was still gangly. Her dreadful red mouth and nails and excess face powder could not spoil her beauty. Walter at eighteen had broadened. He was a dark version of his father and uncle except for his nose, which he had broken when small. Polly, on the other hand, favoured her mother with a square jaw and startling green eyes with long lashes. Her teeth slightly out of kilter, like a false step in a chorus line, gave her smile a particular gaiety. At nineteen there was already beauty.

'Did you hear about Oliver?'

'Oliver is coming on the late train.' Helena watched the young people pile into the car. 'And nobody is to mention General Franco.' She settled herself at the wheel.

'Oh, Aunt Helena, you spoilsport. Here, Sophy, sit on my knee.' Calypso clasped Sophy round the waist and kissed the back of her neck. 'Nice to see you.' She squeezed the child. 'Come and meet Olly with me? May I meet him, Aunt?'

'If you like, but Sophy should be in bed.'

'Oh, Aunt, just this once.'

'She's a growing child, she needs her sleep. She can see Oliver tomorrow.'

'Mother talked to Uncle George and he said Oliver had a near miss. The bullet grazed the side of his head.' In the back with Polly, Walter leant forward to talk to his aunt, who was driving recklessly. 'What do you think of the war, Aunt?'

'Which?' Helena jammed on the brakes to avoid a van. 'What your uncle calls "the scuffle in Spain" or the coming one?'

'The coming one. I shall join the Navy.'

'But you are always sick.' Polly closed her eyes as Helena increased speed. 'Even in a dinghy.'

'I shall get into submarines. You can't be sick under water.'

'You are too young,' said Helena.

'I am eighteen, I've left school.'

'What about Oxford?' Helena changed down and set the car up the steep hill out of the town.

'Either it will have been destroyed or it will wait. Besides, I haven't got a place like Oliver. I wonder whether he will go now.'

'Uncle George didn't at all like him using his waiting year to fight in Spain. He wanted him to learn German.'

'He wouldn't have liked Germany. I was there at Easter. It was vile. All those *Sieg Heils* and *Juden verbotens*. A filthy Brownshirt was rude to me in Munich because I was wearing shorts.' Calypso flinched

8

as Helena rasped the gears at the top of the hill.

'Let's not discuss politics or war. This may be our last summer holiday ever.' Polly spoke with urgency. 'We can't stop it now.'

'Your uncle does not think there will be a war. I would rather you did not discuss it in front of him.'

'Oh, Aunt, really!' Calypso threw back her head and laughed, then, seeing Helena's face, stopped abruptly.

'He wants the last one all to himself,' Polly muttered to Walter, 'and Aunt lost her first husband completely not just a leg and an eyeful of gas.'

'Here we are.' Helena swung the car into the drive, which led to the back of the house and the entrance protected from the prevailing wind. 'When you've seen Richard will you choose your rooms?'

'Shall you get full up with evacuees, Aunt?' Walter hefted the suitcases.

'Uncle's leg will prevent that.' Polly slid out of the car. 'Oh damn, I've laddered my stocking.'

'Polly, please –' Helena felt inclined to slap.

'Sorry, sorry, Aunt. Hullo, Uncle Richard, how are you? Father and Mother sent their love.'

Polly and Calypso kissed their uncle. Walter held out his hand, too old now to kiss and comment on whether or not his uncle had halitosis.

Waiting for the midnight train, which was late, Calypso shivered as she walked along the platform. She remembered Polly's suggestion that this might be their last holiday. She and her cousins had been coming every summer for ten years, ever since Helena married Richard and bought the house, square and ugly but in a marvellous position.

Every August since she was Sophy's age she had come with Polly, Walter and Oliver to bathe, climb cliffs and over-eat at Helena's expense, treating the house as their own, then vanish like a flock of starlings, leaving the house for Uncle Richard and Helena and, for the whole year, Sophy, who could speak of winter storms and

9

violent seas, of driving rain, wind she could not stand up against and fog. Calypso hugged her cardigan close and hopped from one foot to another. 'Come on, train, come on, Oliver.' Would he be changed? Would beautiful funny Oliver, who planned all the games, be the same? What had he seen and done in Spain in this war people felt so passionately about?

Oliver stepped stiffly from the train and looked about him. Calypso ran.

'Oliver, darling, how brown you are! You look like Suzanne Lenglen. Does it hurt?' His head looked strange bandaged. Oliver put his arm round her shoulder. It was all exactly the same, nothing changed, same porters, same ticket collector, same cab rank, harbour, water lapping at high tide, tired train.

'Does it hurt?' she repeated.

'No, I can take the dressing off tomorrow. Are you driving? Where's the car?'

'Usual place.'

'D'you think there'd be a pub open?'

'It's far too late. Have you taken to drink?'

'Just wanted to delay arriving.'

'Why?'

'All the questions.'

'There won't be many. Helena says we are not to talk about Spain or the war. How soon will it be, Oliver? How long have we got? They are all in bed by now.'

'Could we stop on the cliff before we get to the house?'

'Of course.' Calypso, vaguely embarrassed, drove fast through the sleeping town on to the cliff road. 'Will this do?' She stopped the car. Oliver got out, walked across the rough ground and stood looking down at the sea. He seemed to have forgotten Calypso, who sat in the car watching him. He did not move so she joined him.

'The Terror Run.' She pointed to the cliff path. 'Shall we run it this year? Polly says this may be our last holiday.'

'May I fuck you? Now, at once? Calypso, I want to marry you.' She said nothing. 'Well?' Oliver looked down at the sea. 'Well, can I?'

'No, darling. I'm a virgin. I'd have a baby. I can't marry you. I want to marry somebody rich, you know that.'

'To keep you in the state to which you wish to become accustomed?'

'Yes. I do love you, Oliver, you know that. Besides, we are only nineteen.'

'Nineteen!'

'Nineteen is too young for a man to marry. You have to go to Oxford.'

'Oxford, Christ –'

'Don't spoil our holiday.'

'All right, we will have the Terror Run.' He walked back to the car. 'God, I'm tired.' Calypso got in beside him. 'The smell. I can't tell you what it's like.'

'What smell?' She started the engine.

'Death.'

'Bits of people, like Uncle's leg?'

'Exactly. The poor sod, and we mock him.'

'You have changed.' She tried to speak lightly.

'I've only come out of my shell, woken up, grown up.'

'Here we are.' Calypso stopped the car by the house. 'I'm so sorry, Oliver.'

'Goodnight. Which room am I in?'

'The red room.'

'Thanks.' Oliver went up the stairs without looking back and into his room. He undressed without putting on the light, pulled on pyjamas, crossed to the window to pull back the curtains, found Sophy.

'Sophy, what are you doing here?'

'Aunt Helena wouldn't let me meet you. Calypso wanted to take me to the station.'

'She did?'

'Yes, she suggested it, but Aunt Helena said I must go to bed and could see you in the morning. Are you cross?'

'No. You are cold. Come here.' He picked her up. 'Let me warm you.' He carried the shivering child to his bed. 'Let's warm each other. Get in with me.'

'Does your head hurt? How did you get shot?'

11

'No, it doesn't. Lie quiet. Perhaps we can hear the sea.'

'Oliver, you are crying.' She touched his wet face. He held her close in her Viyella pyjamas. She smelt of soap.

'Just let me cry –' He wept for the horrors in Spain and Calypso's rebuff.

3

'May we ask the twins over?' Walter addressed his aunt. 'Of course.' Helena glanced fleetingly at her husband's fingers and balding top, which was all she could see behind the outspread *Times*. She watched the fingers tighten their grip. 'Ask them to lunch tomorrow or Friday.'

'I am out on those days.' Richard Cuthbertson doubled up the paper with a sweep of his arms, tearing the top sheet. Helena winced and Walter and Polly exchanged a smile.

'Telephone and ask them.' Helena spoke towards Polly without moving her head. 'Such nice boys.'

'Extraordinary, considering their father. The fellow's a conchie. I hear he's filled the Rectory with Germans. What's he going to get away with next?'

'Actually, the Erstweilers are Austrian. He played the organ quite beautifully on Sunday, even though it needs repairing. It was so nice of him.'

'Playing for his supper, that's all. The fellow's a Jew, I hear.'

'Presumably that's why they are here.' Walter helped himself to more butter than he needed.

Polly reached for the toast. 'Are there any young Erstweilers, Aunt?'

'One, in a camp. The Floyers say the Erstweilers are worried stiff.'

'Brace him up, do him good. The General says they are splendid places. His friend at the Embassy offered to show him round one when he was over there. Of course he knows it's all propaganda.'

13

'What's propaganda?' Calypso came sleepily into the room. 'Forgive me coming down in a dressing gown, Aunt. Good morning, Uncle.'

'Concentration camps.' Walter swallowed his toast.

'Father says General Peachum is the most gullible man he's ever come across. Any kedgeree?'

'I ate it.' Polly got up from the table.

'All of it?' Calypso whispered.

'There wasn't much. Sorry.'

'That's all right. I'll eat an egg.' Calypso sat beside her uncle. 'I didn't think it worth dressing as I intend spending all day in the sun. Oliver's marvellously brown.'

'We are going to ask the Rectory twins to lunch tomorrow,' said Walter.

'If they are conchies like their father I won't have them in my house,' said Richard aggressively.

'It's Aunt Helena's house, Uncle, and Father says we should all admire people like Mr Floyer. If there had been more like him in 1914 we should all be living in a better world.'

'Walter,' said Helena quietly. 'Stop it. He will wreck *The Times* if you tease like that!' The three young people gave a whoop of laughter. Helena suppressed a smile. Richard Cuthbertson left the room.

'Aunt Helena, he's worse than ever.' Calypso laid a hand on her aunt's.

'He doesn't want another war.' Helena patted Calypso's hand. 'He won't admit it's coming. Here's Oliver. You are up early, that's not like you.' Oliver came in through the French windows carrying a towel.

'I've developed new habits, Aunt. Not all of them good. I've been swimming in the cove with the twins. Is there any coffee left for us?'

'Come in, twins, we were talking about you. We were going to ask you to lunch.' Polly went to pour coffee. 'Don't just stand there.'

David and Paul came in shyly, muttering 'good morning', 'thank you' and 'hullo'. Tall, with startling yellow hair and brown eyes, indistinguishable, they sat down, their eyes fixed on Calypso, by whom they were fascinated.

'Uncle was suggesting you will be conchies if there's a war.' Polly handed them coffee.

'No, no,' they said. 'Not this war. One should fight for the Jews.'

'Two should.' Calypso, aware of their eyes, mocked them.

'Two will,' said David.

'Two are joining up at the end of the holidays,' added Paul.

'Oh,' said Walter eagerly, 'what in?'

'Air Force,' they said.

'Long distance killing.' Oliver looked at them. 'Heard of Guernica?'

'Of course we have. Picasso.'

'Just as awful as close to. I shall go into the Navy as soon as they will take me.' Walter spoke eagerly.

'Oh!' cried Helena, rising from the table. 'Do stop, children. There may not be a war. It may not happen. All that over again. I can't bear it.' She left the room, closing the door.

'Poor Aunt Helena.' Oliver buttered his toast. 'She will not face the fact that in all of us, even in her, there is the person who is capable of killing, you, you and you.' He pointed round the table with his knife. 'Every one of us is capable of killing other human beings. Let's have that game for this year. As well as the Terror Run we will have the Killing. What do you say? Draw straws? Not afraid, are you? Let's have a killing, to take any form you choose. We'll include Sophy. That makes seven of us.'

'You are mad, Oliver.' Calypso was looking excited.

'It's a mad world. Are you on?'

'I'm on.' Calypso smiled across the table at Oliver. 'I'm on.'

Nobody else spoke until Sophy, who had followed Oliver and the twins into the room, said: 'What does it matter if there's going to be a war, anyway?'

15

'Out of the mouths –' said the Floyer boys in a tone of relief and Walter said: 'All right, let's make it that the killers kill within a time limit of five years. That should include us all. Sophy doesn't really count.'

'But I do. I do count, don't I, Oliver?' Sophy screamed suddenly at Oliver.

'Yes, yes, you count,' Oliver said soothingly, not taking his eyes off Calypso. Calypso stared back, remembering the coarseness of his words the night before, her hasty refusal more from habit than inclination. Oliver back from Spain had a new dimension.

4

Richard Cuthbertson smoothed his hair with the ivory brushes Helena had given him when they married, brushing the grey hair along the sides of his head. He laid the brushes in exact alignment with the bottle of hair oil in symmetry with the matching clothes brushes, and glanced as he always did at the photograph of his first wife Diana, posed looking away from him, her arm round her dog, a sensible smooth fox terrier, not one of those rough-haired things one saw nowadays with oblong snouts and trembling legs. He had no dog now that his retriever had died. Helena had objected to the smells when it farted and the hair shed on the carpets. She was happier without a dog. She would not prevent him replacing his old companion but difficulties would be made, hints dropped. Two can play at that game, he thought. 'It would be good for Sophy.' His eyes travelled past his first wife's photograph – had she really looked like that? – to the group photographs of his fellow officers, a splendid lot, mostly dead. He ran over their names, a familiar litany. They looked so young. Peter a stockbroker now, Hugh a brewer, Bunty secretary to a golf club, Andrew farming, their commanding officer now retired a general, chairman of the local bench of magistrates, Master of Hounds, rich.

'And I live on my wife's money and have one leg.' Richard looked closer at the regimental group of 1913, young men without fear. He wiped a tear from his right eye with a fastidious handkerchief, a perpetual tear due to gassing just before the loss of his leg, an

17

embarrassment and a nuisance. He would get a dog, to hell with Helena. He settled his tweed jacket squarely on his shoulders, tweaked his trouser crease into correct line down his artificial leg and turned to leave the room. As he did so he glanced out of the window and caught sight of his nephews and nieces running from the house across the lawn, carrying towels and bathing suits and accompanied by the parson's twins.

'Wait for me!' Sophy's high-pitched scream halted Oliver, who with Calypso made the tail end of the processsion. 'Wait, wait!' Irritating child. He watched Oliver pause and noticed with a frown that he and Calypso were holding hands. Oliver had taken off the ridiculous bandage he had worn at breakfast, showing off, of course. Oliver dropped Calypso's hand and, catching hold of the child, swung her on to his shoulders to sit astride. The child's gingham dress flew up and Richard saw that she was wearing no knickers, bloody little bastard exposing her bum.

'Helena?' Richard shouted, limping downstairs. 'Helena, where are you?'

'Here.'

'Helena, I don't often interfere in your department, but this time I must insist –'

'What?' Helena was in the drawing room, putting roses in a bowl he had won at polo before the war. She did not look round.

'That bowl needs cleaning.'

'If we polished the silver according to your directions there wouldn't be a silver mark left. What is it, Richard?'

'That child Sophy is wearing no knickers.'

'How on earth do you know?' Anxiety showed in Helena's eyes.

'I saw Oliver pick her up.'

'Is that all?'

'All?' He was nonplussed. 'It's indecent. I ask you.'

'Richard,' Helena laughed, 'she's only ten, she never wears knickers if it's hot. What are you fussing about? She's gone bathing with the others. A little girl of

Sophy's age can't be indecent.'

Helena's laughter infuriated Richard.

'Your friend the General wants you to ring him.' Helena always referred to the General as 'your friend'.

'What about, did he say?'

'He's going to put the hounds down, thought you ought to know as you are on the Hunt committee.'

'Good God!'

'He says if it's war it's total. No more hunting.'

'Good God! So he thinks there will be a war?' Richard was shaken.

'Yes, my dear, he does.'

'Helena –' he took the hand she held out to him. 'Helena, I am useless, useless.'

'Nonsense, Richard. There will be masses of things for you to do.'

'Such as what?'

'Organizations, A.R.P., things like that.'

'Answering the telephone? I ask you. I'm not a bloody clerk.'

'Ring the General. Have a talk with him, he will be in the thick of things.'

'I have only one leg.'

'You don't answer the telephone with your legs,' Helena said brutally. 'Now I must get on, if Cook and I are to feed your army of relations.'

'What about Sophy's knickers?'

'There's going to be a war. What the hell do Sophy's knickers matter? If you are interested I don't wear knickers in very hot weather. Knickers are a Victorian innovation.' Helena picked up the flower scissors, brushed stalk ends into the wastepaper-basket and left the room. Oh, why must I be so awful to Richard? she asked herself. If Anthony had only lost a leg instead of being lost altogether would I be so beastly to him? Getting no answer to her hypothetical question Helena dismissed her first husband, whose bones lay some-where in France, from her mind, and went to discuss meals in the kitchen. It was amazing what a lot of food

19

Calypso, Walter, Polly and Oliver consumed; not only breakfast, lunch, tea and dinner, but continual snacks from the larder. Remembering the last war she speculated on the return of food rationing, one of the chief topics of conversation among her friends and relations of that time. The shortage of potatoes. The occasion when one of her aunts had had her butter ration stolen on a bus, blown up into an epic, treated as a tragedy almost equal to the loss of a dear one in the trenches. Helena stood in the doorway leading to the kitchen, remembering the telegraph boy bringing the news, 'killed in action', and the physical shock in her chest. 'Now all's to do again.'

'What, Madam?' said Cook.

'Oh, nothing, Cook. I was just thinking. What shall we feed the Major's crowd on?'

'Something filling.' Cook said this every August. Helena was horribly aware of the end of the life to which she had grown used, afraid of what a drastic change might do to her uncertain equilibrium. Women entering what is euphemistically called 'the change of life' were not famous for making the passage of others' lives pleasant.

I must, she told herself, speak to Mildred, she is a rock, and she smiled at Cook as she thought of Mildred Floyer, barely five feet tall but with the strength required to cope with a High Church parson husband in a parish which was essentially Chapel and Low.

'Poor Mrs Floyer has two sons,' she said.

'Coming to lunch, are they?'

'Going to war.'

'Then we must see that they get a good lunch,' said Cook, who had the talent of living in the moment.

5

'When is the full moon?' Polly, lying on the rocks beside Oliver, watched him watching Calypso swim out from the cove with Walter. Oliver closed his eyes and lay back.

'Thinking of the Run?'

'Yes. Shall we let Sophy do it? She does so want to.'

'I don't see why not, if she practises a bit first.'

'Will you tell her? It will fill her cup of happiness.'

'A full moon ago,' said Oliver, 'I was on the Ebro.' Polly said nothing.

'One of my friends, a Czech, was killed, never made a sound, shot through the jugular. He and his friends burned a priest, made a bonfire and burnt him. What good did that do? The joke was it turned out he was one of us, or had been.'

'Joke?'

'Atrocities are jokes, you can't survive otherwise. We all committed atrocities, their side and ours, made this pit, built a fire in it and pushed them in to frizzle.'

'You did?'

'I stood by. It comes to the same thing. I don't remember whether I actually pushed anybody in but I think I helped.'

'Think?'

'We were all drunk, Polly. If it wasn't wine it was fear or rage or just wanting some action. There's an awful lot of waiting about. To fill the time you burn, rape, pillage.'

'Rape?'

'Yes. Well, actually she was more than willing and later I thought, oh God, I may get clap.'

21

'Did you?'

'No, I was lucky. I didn't.'

'Just the once?'

'No, sweet, every time I got the chance.' Oliver laughed.

'So that's why you say we are all capable of killing. You've changed.'

'Who would you like to kill?' Oliver leant on one elbow, looking at Polly stretched beside him, her body nearly as beautiful as Calypso's.

Looking down her nose at the bobbing heads in the cove, Polly said, 'I don't think I know anyone I want to kill, but I'd like to have the power to make people suffer,' she lied, speaking lightly, for there were times when it would be nice to have Calypso out of the way. 'What's your killing game to be?'

'It's just an idea. I must plan it. Look how far out the twins are. They've got Sophy with them.'

'They won't drown her. D'you know, Olly, their father was a stretcher-bearer in the war?'

'Jolly brave. He's never talked about it. He's not a war bore.'

'Poor Uncle. I hope none of us will become like him.'

'The Somme, the Marne, Wipers, the B.E.F., General Haig, General French, trenches, conchies, war profiteers, yankees, comradeship and what does it produce? Cotton poppies and two minutes' silence. Christ Almighty!'

'I don't feel, somehow,' Polly was laughing, 'that he'd call you officer material if he heard you now.'

'Too true. I'm for the ranks.'

'Really? After all that O.T.C. at school?' Polly was intrigued. 'I should have thought you'd go straight into the Guards as an officer.'

'Not after the International Brigade.'

'I suppose not. Was there comradeship there?'

'Lots of comradeship.'

'Making bonfires?'

'Yes, yes, yes. Now let's plan the new game. Sophy!'

Oliver shouted through cupped hands towards the twins who were swimming to shore, Sophy between them, a hand on each twin's shoulder. 'Like to join the Terror Run this year?'

'What?' The child scrambled up the rocks. 'What did you say?'

'I said would you like to join the Terror Run this year?'

'Yes, please.'

'You'll have to practise.'

'I know the path. I know it better than any of you.'

'Not in the dark, not by moonlight.'

'Yes, I do.'

'Well, you must let me see you run it so that I'm sure.'

'I'm sure. There's a man with a snake on it. Will you watch the whole way?'

'Yes. We'll watch both ends and the middle and see how you do.'

'Oh, thanks, Oliver.'

'See what it is to give happiness.'

Calypso sat beside the twins, who watched Oliver, who watched the drops of water run down her legs into her groin.

'Will you run?' Polly invited the twins.

'Yes,' they said. 'When is it?'

'Full moon, whenever that is.'

'And the Killing Game?' Calypso looked round. 'You both in on that?'

'Yes,' they said, surprising the cousins.

'That makes six of us,' said Walter.

'Seven,' said Sophy. 'It's me, too.'

'Oh, Sophy, you're too small to kill anyone.'

'Oliver said, he said.' Sophy looked from face to face, distressed. 'Besides, I shall grow up.'

'Oh, let her.' Calypso wiped the salt water from her arms with fastidious movements. 'I think we should include Aunt Helena and Uncle and Betty and Cook and the Rector; make it more of a lottery.'

'Not Father,' said the twins.

'All right. Aunt and Uncle then, not Betty or Cook.'

'Why not? Because they're village, not our class?' Walter jabbed at Oliver. 'I thought all you Comrades were classless.'

'Far from it,' said Oliver, laughing, 'as you'd know if you'd been there. No, Betty and Cook might get ideas.'

'Above their station?'

'No, you fool. They might easily go full tilt, might take it seriously.'

'Go to the police?' Polly grinned.

'Oh, forget it. Just don't include them.'

'I thought the whole idea was that it is serious.' Calypso stared at Oliver maliciously. 'Wasn't it?'

'May I do my practice run soon? Will you watch me?' Sophy put her pale face close to Oliver's so that he squinted into her large black eyes. He put up a hand and pushed back her hair, black too like a cat's and silky.

'Puss.' He caressed her as he would an animal. Calypso and Polly watched, amused.

'Why not this afternoon? How would that be?' Oliver patted the pale cheek dismissively.

'We shall have to see that she doesn't cheat.' Walter stretched his arms to the sky.

'It's so hot.' Polly turned over on to her stomach.

'It won't be hot if we line along the top of the cliffs. We will get the breeze. It's Sophy who will get hot.' Calypso closed her eyes, lifting her face to the sun. 'Is my nose getting red?'

'Put a leaf over it.' The twins spoke in chorus.

'Clever. Find me one.' Calypso lay with a leaf shading her nose while they all cooked gently on the rocks.

The only flaw in her looks, thought Polly, observing her cousin, was that both sides of her face were symmetrical, her expression masklike. Most people had two sides to a varying degree, good and evil, happy and sad. Walter was particularly varied, as though he had been sat on at birth, and she herself had a slightly bent nose, while Oliver had the trace of a squint.

They lined the cliff that afternoon, Walter and Polly starting Sophy off from the headland under the

24

coastguard station, the twins stationed above the path half-way along the course, Calypso and Oliver waiting at the finish. For most of the course Sophy would be visible, only out of sight where the path ran through dense thorn or at one point just above the sea, where it twisted sharply round high granite boulders.

Up on the cliff that afternoon the twins sat with their backs to the fence which prevented straying cattle from falling over.

'She's off. Walter's unleashed her.' They looked down at Sophy leaving Walter at a run to tear along the path.

'I wonder what it will look like from the air.'

'We've never flown. D'you think they will let us keep together?'

'Surely they won't separate us?' Paul looked at David aghast.

'It may happen.'

'My God, I hope not.'

'Death may.'

'Not us. We shan't get killed.'

'Hi, we've forgotten Sophy. I can't see her.'

'She must be among the thorns.'

'Or the boulders. She was going lickety spit. You don't really think we can get split up, do you?'

'Father says the authorities are bound to. He may be right. Think of the confusion at school.'

The other twin laughed. 'Whatever happens we've had fun.'

'If you die, I die.'

'Oh, gloom! It hasn't started yet. Where the hell is Sophy?'

'She may have hurt herself. We'd better follow her. Remember Walter's ankle.'

They scrambled down through the gorse and heather to the path, unusually tall young men, loose-limbed as puppies, their maize-coloured hair flopping over brown eyes fringed with feathery lashes, their looks the more noticeable because duplicated. They brushed their hair back from brows untouched by experience and ambled along the path.

'Where are Walter and Polly?'

'They must have gone back by the short cut.'

At the finish Calypso sat with Oliver, holding his hand.

'I tell you what, Olly, even if I won't marry you I'll sleep with you. Have you ever done it?'

'Yes, I have.'

'Is it nice?'

'Nice.' Oliver looked at Calypso and repeated 'nice'. How could 'nice' be a word applied to Calypso? 'I want to have you to myself. I'll wait.'

'If there's a war I'll sleep with you before you get killed. That's what maidens did in books and I am a maiden.'

'How you carry on about your virginity. Virginity's nothing. You can lose it riding a bicycle.'

'I never knew that. I must be careful. I'm going to ride a bicycle in London. Pa says petrol will be rationed.'

'And virginity not. How shall you find your rich prince from a bicycle? It's so bourgeois.'

'I will find him. If you want something hard enough you get it, and I want a very rich husband, always have.'

'Oh, Calypso, don't.' Oliver put his arms round her. 'Oh, my love, I will get rich, very rich. Then you will marry me.'

'What's that?' Calypso drew away from him and sprang up. 'Somebody screamed. Sophy.'

'Something's wrong.' They ran down the path to meet Sophy, who approached them in a rush, hurling herself into Calypso's arms, sobbing wildly.

'What is it? What happened? Are you hurt? What's the matter? Stop it, Sophy, stop it.' But Sophy, clinging to Calypso, could not stop. Her sobs turned to screams, her fingers dug painfully into Calypso's neck.

'Sophy, you are hurting.' Oliver pulled the child away and smacked her face. 'Stop, Sophy. What happened?'

Through white lips the child said, gasping, 'Pink, pink snake.'

'What?' Oliver stared at the child, her tears splashing white cheeks. 'Speak up.' But Sophy neither could nor would.

26

'Did it bite you? She said "snake".' Calypso looked anxiously at Oliver. Sophy, silent now, said no more.

'Our word, you made good time. What's happened?' The twins came trotting up the cliff path out of breath, flushed.

'She's been frightened, something about a snake. Did you see anything?'

'No,' they said. 'Let's see if she has been bitten.' The twins examined Sophy's legs as she lay across Oliver's lap, giving an occasional exhausted hiccup. 'Nothing, not even scratched. Let's see your arms.' They examined the child. 'Surely you ought to wear knickers,' they said, pulling down her skirt.

'Oh, leave her alone. She's been scared by something and she's not going to tell us.' Calypso stood above Oliver and the twins. 'Come on, Sophy, it's over now, time for tea.' Her voice was adult, she held out her hand, Sophy took it, letting go of Oliver.

'Sorry.' The child looked round at their kind faces. 'I'm sorry.'

'You did the run jolly fast,' said the twins.

'Record time.' Oliver smacked the child's bottom in friendly fashion as he stood up.

'Did I really?'

'Yes, I shall have to look to my laurels.'

'Oh, good. I'm even quicker by moonlight.' She sprang away from them towards the house.

'Something happened.' Oliver watched her go. 'I wonder what.'

'Well, she's not going to tell.' Calypso put a full stop to the incident, feeling that Sophy wished to draw attention to herself.

6

On the evening of the Terror Run Helena invited Max Erstweiler and his wife Monika to supper. They walked with the twins across the stubble on the top of the cliff.

'So peaceful,' Monika said. 'A year ago in the country at harvest time we were full of fear.'

'We are full of fear still. But not for ourselves any more.'

'I find it worse to be safe and Pauli not, he must follow us. God will help us and our friends.'

'*Gott mit uns*? Don't be ridiculous,' Max sneered.

'Father says we must not lose God,' said David, walking beside Monika, 'but we already have. We lost him when we slipped our cartilages playing rugger. We lost the match as well. We really had prayed.'

'How old were you?' Monika smiled.

'Twelve,' said Paul, laughing.

'And you dropped him just like that?'

'We've never told Father,' said David gravely.

'Your father is a saint,' said Max. 'I say this in case there are saints, though personally I doubt it.'

'You go to Father's church, you play the organ for him.'

'That is the least I can do for your father and mother. Also you boys are fortunate.'

'We are,' said the twins, grieving for the Erstweilers' anxiety. 'It will be all right, Monika, you wait and see. We are going to fight for him.'

'How?'

'The Air Force. We are off at the end of the month to

join up, fight for all you people. We will get your son for you.'

'In a casket,' said Erstweiler bitterly. 'They send you a casket. Our son is a musician, you cannot play the piano in a casket.' The twins fell silent, showing their awkwardness by stiffening their legs as they walked.

'What is this game you play?' Monika felt the hurt in their silence.

'We race along the cliff path. Oliver called it the Terror Run because he is afraid of heights. It is a bit scary in places but even Sophy can do it now. It's an institution. We run by the light of the moon.'

'May we watch?'

'Of course. The elders sit on the camomile lawn and gossip while we run.'

'And this new game? Did you not say there is another game?' asked Max.

'Yes, a secret, a dare. We are going to draw lots, you and Monika too, if you want.'

'Even if we don't know what for?'

'Yes. We know and the cousins and if any of us draws the card we shall know what to do but if you and Monika join in it makes it more exciting for us. There are only three marked cards so it's much better if you and the Major and Mrs Cuthbertson join in. That makes eight blanks.'

'And the result is secret?'

'Yes.'

'It sounds like life,' Max said grimly as he rang the bell in the Cuthbertson porch.

Walter came to the door. 'Come in,' he said, 'come through the house. We've persuaded Aunt to let us dine on the lawn.' He led the way. 'Look,' he said, 'isn't it terrific?'

'Ach!' exclaimed Monika. 'So schön.'

The cousins had carried out the dining table and chairs. The table was set with a white cloth on the camomile lawn, the setting sun and the sea a backdrop.

'Isn't this fun?' Calypso came to greet them.

'Lovely,' the twins admired, 'brilliant idea.'

'It was my idea.' Calypso led Monika up to her uncle.

'Uncle Richard, this is Monika Erstweiler and Max Erstweiler, who are staying at the Rectory.'

'We met briefly in church.' Richard limped forward to shake hands. 'My wife allows my nephews and nieces a very free rein. May I offer you a drink?'

Helena came out wearing a long dress which gave her dumpy figure dignity. She admired Monika's looks and was struck by Max's charm. 'This is a party we have every year,' she said. 'It may be the last. When the war starts we shall have to black out our windows, show no lights.'

'Every year out of doors?'

'Never before, but tonight it seemed safe. It's fun for the children.'

'The children are talking of fighting, are they not men?'

'I suppose they are.' Helena looked at the twins, at Oliver, at Walter. 'Men –' her voice trailed.

'You have a son,' Richard broke the silence heartily, 'in a camp, I believe. My friend the General says they are doing all these people a power of good.'

Max Erstweiler gasped and uttered a word which sounded alien on the lawn above the English channel – 'Unerhört –'

All the cousins started talking at once and Helena said: 'Shall we start dinner? The sun is almost set. Light the candles, somebody. Mrs Erstweiler, will you sit here, and you beside me, Mr Erstweiler.'

'What did the fellow say?' Richard hissed at his wife, who had kicked his good shin painfully. 'Can't understand his accent.'

'It's what you said.' Helena spoke from the corner of her mouth.

'Oh, did I drop a brick?'

Helena was already chattering to Max, and the agony passed as they ate and talked while the sun slid into the sea and the light from the candles lit their faces so that

31

eyes shone from mysterious sockets. The girls grew more beautiful and Sophy, sitting still beside Oliver, who held Calypso's hand on his other side under the table, registered the scene in her mind.

When the moon came up like an outrageous balloon they fell silent, watching her rise red, gold then silver into a taffeta sky.

'The moon.' Oliver held his glass high.

'And absent friends.' Richard rose, steady on his good leg, smiling down at Monika. 'Absent friends,' he repeated as they all drank.

He can be splendid, thought Helena. I must encourage him and not crush.

'Thank you.' Monika smiled at Richard, her eyes wet. He is a sensitive man, she thought, noticing the tear in his eye, and one can't deny these Semites have looks, thought Richard, wiping the tear with his habitual flick.

'Shall we draw lots before or after the Run?' Polly enquired.

'Let's do it now.' Calypso let go of Oliver's hand. His was dry, hers growing sticky.

'Uncle Richard, shuffle the pack.'

'Very well.' He picked up the cards. The Cuthbertsons, the Erstweilers, the nephews and nieces and the twins all drew, Sophy last. 'Whoever draws a marked card keeps it secret.'

They looked at the cards and threw them back into the bowl.

'That's done,' said Oliver. 'Now for the Run. Bags I go first.'

'Me next,' said Calypso. 'Will you time us, Uncle Richard?'

'Very well. Got your torches?'

'Yes.'

'Right. Same rules, I take it – flash the torch when you start?'

'Yes.'

'Off you go, then.' Richard settled in a chair beside Monika.

32

The young people moved off.

'Isn't Sophy rather small?' asked Monika.

'She is running with the twins keeping an eye on her. She'll be all right,' said Helena.

'And this other game for which we have drawn lots?' asked Max.

'I have no idea. Oliver dreams up something new every year. It's no good asking, they won't tell us.'

'So we do not really take part?'

'Possibly, but not consciously.' Helena laughed.

'It sounds like a gamble.'

'Yes.'

'Our son is involved in this sort of game. He was to follow us but the Brownshirts came to the University and took every fourth boy. It is terrible being a mother.'

'I have always regretted missing out on that experience.' Helena sought to comfort Monika.

'Personally I think you've been spared a lot of bother,' said Richard. 'Think what the Virgin Mary went through.'

Helena burst out laughing. Max looked puzzled and muttered to his wife, '*Herrlicher Humor?*' Before coming to England he had heard much of this English trait and wished to cultivate it himself.

'They have reached the start.' Helena pointed. 'See their torches.'

Across on the headland the Cuthbertsons and Erstweilers could make out the group of young people above the sea, the rocks black and stark, the moon now quite high. Below the cliffs a calm sea and at the top of the cliffs the coastguard station white and functional.

'Isn't it dangerous? I can see no path.' Monika was interested.

'They all know it very well.' Richard was lighting a pipe. 'If I had my leg I would think nothing of it.'

Helena guarded her tongue.

'Where is the finish?' Max filled the brief silence.

'Below us, out of sight. We hear them shout when they reach it. I time them. I have my stop watch and my word is final.'

'Oliver is starting.' Helena pointed. A torch flashed three times and Richard started his watch. They saw Oliver bound down the cliff, running hard along the narrow path which twisted through the bracken and heather, then close to the cliff edge past clumps of thrift and sea campion, through short grass which in spring was full of squills, past gorse still in flower, mixing its sweet smell with the heather.

Oliver ran feeling exhilarating fear. If he ran fast enough he would outstrip terror. He had never let the others know the extent of his fear of heights, of the vertigo which would paralyse him if he looked down. He ran a race against his weakness.

As he doubled and jumped past the rocks he thought briefly of Sophy's snake, then his feet pounded on grass and the scent of Lady's Tresses came sweetly up and he knew it was over.

'*Spiranthes autumnalis*,' he cried, exulting, flashed his torch and sat down panting to wait for Calypso.

Within minutes she had run the course straight into his arms.

'Was I fast, Olly? Shout for Uncle Richard, I have no breath left.'

Oliver held her close and they stood face to face, he holding her against him so that he felt the rise and fall of her breasts as her breathing steadied.

'Who is next?'

'Sophy, then twin, twin, Polly and Walter last.'

Oliver stroked her hair then ran his hand down her back, holding her close.

'Oliver, what's that?'

'What?'

'This.' She touched him.

'Me. My cock.'

'Oliver!'

'What is it?'

'It's enormous.'

'It's quite ordinary. I've got an erection.'

'A *what*?'

34

'An erection. I want to poke it up you. Have you never seen a man with an erection?'

'No.' She turned in his arms and stood with her back to him. His hands covered her breasts.

'So you really are intacta.'

'What does that mean?'

'Virgin. I didn't believe you.'

'You embarrass me.' Calypso leant back against him, covering his hands with her own. 'Is it true? Wouldn't it hurt me frightfully?'

'No, you stretch. After all, you must stretch to let a baby's head get out. You know how babies are born, or don't you?'

'Of course I do.' Calypso closed her eyes against the moon.

'I love you.' He kissed her neck. 'I always shall.'

'I don't think you will.' Sophy arrived beside them, scrambling up the last slope silently. 'What time did I take? Flash the torch for me and shout, please.'

Calypso raised her voice in a long cry, then said: 'Why won't he love me for ever?' But Sophy knew better than to answer when Calypso used that tone of voice. They waited, flashing the torch and shouting up the cliff towards the lawn as Paul, David, Polly and Walter joined them. Then they sat for a while looking at the moon-path on the water.

'Never again,' said Polly. 'This time next year where shall we all be?'

'Under the sod,' Walter grunted.

'Lying in some distant field for ever England,' misquoted Oliver, 'like Uncle's leg. I hate that poem. I prefer the one "and is there honey still for tea and crumpets with my strumpet". Three of us had a bowdlerizing competition in a ditch a few months ago.'

'Who drew spots and who drew blanks?' Sophy, thinking of the new game to distract her mind from Oliver and Calypso, tried to catch them napping.

'That would be telling.' Walter rolled her over on the grass. 'There were eleven of us, so eight will be innocent

35

and most of the eleven wouldn't know what to do if they did draw a black spot.'

'Makes it very exciting. Did you say five years for a time limit, Oliver? That's rather short for something so important.'

'Make it ten,' said Oliver grandly, 'then Sophy, if she's drawn a spot, can wait till she's twenty.'

'The war will be over by then.'

'Or we shall be dead. Come on, up, up the cliff. Like a ride on my shoulders, Sophy?'

'No, thank you.'

'What will the old people do in the war!' Polly climbed beside the twins.

'Compare it with theirs,' said Walter over his shoulder.

'Watch and wait,' said the twins, thinking of Pauli Erstweiler trapped in his concentration camp.

'Mourn,' said Calypso. 'They know how to.'

'No doubt we shall learn,' said Oliver drily.

'Uncle Richard wants a dog,' Sophy exclaimed, apropos of nothing.

'How do you know?'

'He is mourning old Farticus.'

'Then we shall find him one. Helena won't be pleased.'

'It's about time we stopped always considering Helena,' said Polly. 'She gave him a pretty hefty kick before dinner.'

'He deserved it, he and his General. Down with all Generals, I say.'

'And especially Franco.'

'That's right.'

'It's going to be awkward for the General,' said David.

'Why?' asked Polly sharply.

'Because when he was invited to the Nuremberg Rally, and introduced to Hitler by his Nazi friends, he came back to tell us it's all a damn good show which puts a bit of backbone into the youth of the nation. He was full of it last year after Munich.'

'The General told my father it would be a good show if the pansy youth of England were put into the Hitler

Jugend.' Calypso laughed. 'That was because he thought all you boys needed a haircut and Oliver's suede shoes got up his nose.'

'He's being very patriotic now,' said Polly. 'I hear he's organizing air raid precautions and urging all his tenants to join up.'

'Oh, blow,' said Walter, 'you put me off. When I'm in my submarine it won't be for his sake, not bloody likely.'

'It will be for the Pauli Erstweilers of this world, I know.' Polly turned to Calypso. 'What shall you do?'

'Find a glamorous job where there are lots of rich men.'

'I really think she means it,' said the twins, laughing. 'Won't you comfort the troops?'

'I shall do that, too.' Calypso smiled sweetly. 'Impartially,' she added, looking sidelong at the twins and Walter. Did they too get erections? She must consult with Polly, who knew about sex since she had access to her father's gynaecological books, without if possible betraying her own sexual ignorance.

As they reached the lawn Polly called out: 'Did Oliver win, as usual?' but the elders were in the drawing room, an anxious group talking in low voices. Helena stood in the doorway white-faced.

'It was your father,' she said to Walter and Polly. 'His hospital is to be evacuated tomorrow.'

'War,' said Polly. Nobody contradicted her.

The fear in the room was tangible. Monika reached for her husband's hand. Helena found herself exchanging a glance of despair with Max. Looking round at the young people she read on their faces fear mixed with a sexual combustion she was to remember later. Walter's eyes were clouded. Polly stared questioningly at the twins, who held her gaze. Calypso looked up at Oliver.

'Well?'

Sophy tugged at Oliver's hand: 'What about the new game?'

'Scrub it.' He stared at Calypso, ignoring the child. 'We've all drawn marked cards now.'

Sophy muttered mutinously. Oliver shook his hand free.

Richard limped into the hall to tap the barometer. 'Weather's set fair,' he said cheerfully. The tableau melted.

'We should be going,' Monika said gently.

The Erstweilers said polite goodbyes. The cousins and the twins went and sat on the lawn, staring out at the sea. Helena called from the house: 'Sophy, go to bed. It's long past your bedtime.' The child trailed into the house without saying goodnight.

'Shall we try and get through to Mother?' Walter and Polly went to telephone.

'We'd better go.' The twins left sadly. 'Shall we tell them tonight or wait till the morning?' They considered their parents.

'We've had a good time there.' David looked back at the house standing square to the winds. 'What an ugly house. I suggest we let them sleep and tell them in the morning,' said David, feeling protective towards the innocence of good people. 'They are as vulnerable as Sophy.'

'Differently.' The brothers exchanged a glance, each seeing his concern for their parents mirrored in the other, and their joint fear.

7

Helena undressed, brushed her hair, cleaned her teeth, rubbed cream into her face, then sat on the edge of her bed listening to Richard going through his familiar routine in the dressing room.

'Richard.'

'Yes, my dear? A good party. Thank you for your trouble.'

'It's no trouble.'

'Sorry I dropped a brick with those Jews.'

'You made up for it. Richard, I don't think I can sleep. Could we talk a bit?'

'What about?' Her husband stood in his shirt and trousers, his braces hanging down at the back.

'The war.'

He said violently: 'It's another false alarm. There isn't going to be a war.'

'The hospitals and doctors are being evacuated and the children too. Martin knows –'

'It's just another exercise. The General says –'

'The General is killing the hounds.'

'He hasn't done it yet. Good God, Helena, there won't be a war. Don't be so panicky.' Richard's face grew scarlet.

'I can't talk to you.' Helena was filled with bile.

'What do you mean?'

'I can't. If you deny what is happening how can I talk to you? All those children will be in it, all the horrors will happen again, only worse. Richard, I can't stand your head-in-the-sand attitude. I'm going to London.'

'What on earth for?'

Helena looked at him helplessly, unable to say 'To get away from you', which was her uppermost feeling. She said: 'To do some shopping.'

Richard closed the door of the dressing room. She heard him get out of his trousers, prop his leg against a chair, hop to the bed, scrabble into it, and the wheeze of the mattress as he lay down.

Oh God! Helena changed her clothes, packed a case and left the house. This is the most terrible row we've ever had and nothing said. She carried her case to the car, got in and drove down the hill. When she reached the level road at the bottom of the hill the engine coughed, choked, moaned. She had forgotten to fill up with petrol. She laid her arms across the steering wheel, her head on her arms, and wept with frustration.

In the warmth of the late summer night Oliver and Calypso lay on the scented lawn. Oliver held Calypso's hand, lying on his back with his free arm across his eyes.

'*Now* will you marry me?'

'No, no, no.'

'But war changes everything.'

'Does it?'

'Of course it does. I must have you if I am to fight.'

'You could get a safe job. They say there's no need for so many men in this war. There are to be reserved occupations.'

'I've got to fight. I'm committed.'

'Who to?'

'Myself, you.'

'I'm not asking you to fight. I didn't ask you to rush off to Spain in that silly way. I'm not asking you to fight for the Jews.'

'Against Fascism, against the Nazis.'

'Oh, that. It's just a tag. Some of them are awfully nice. All that lot we met skiing. I loved that lot in Kitzbühel.'

'They liked you, I remember. Did you kiss them?'

'One or two.'

'Calypso, look at me. I'm serious. Will you marry me?

At least let us be engaged.'

'If I've said no once I've said it a hundred times. No. I will comfort you, as they say, but marriage, no. I'd only make you unhappy,' Calypso snapped.

'I'd risk that. I'm unhappy already.'

'Well, then, you've a taste of what it would be like.' Calypso stood up yawning. 'I'm so sleepy, Goodnight, Olly.'

'I'll hold you to the comfort bit.'

'You do that.' Calypso drifted into the house.

Oliver rolled over and lay on his face. Above him Sophy edged backwards along the branch, her pyjama trousers rucking round her waist.

'Sophy, were you listening?'

'Yes.'

'You shouldn't eavesdrop.'

'I happened to be here. I often am.'

'Come down. I'll catch you.' He held out his arms, catching the child as she jumped.

'There. Let's just sit for a while.'

They sat with their backs to the tree, listening to the sea slapping against the rocks.

'It's high tide,' she said.

'War tide.'

'I'm frightened, are you?'

'Yes, very.'

'Worse than the Terror Run?'

'Oh much, much worse. This is real.'

'In what way?'

'The noise, the smell, the filth.'

'I shall run again in your honour.'

'Funny little thing. You should be in bed.'

'Let me stay a bit.'

Oliver sat, his arm round the child. In the east the false dawn. He kissed the top of her head. 'I'm going, Sophy.'

'When?' She was startled.

'Now. The sooner the better. There's nothing for me here. The war's waiting.'

41

Sophy looked at him, tears on her cheeks. She longed to say, 'I am here, I am not nothing.' She followed him into the house, watched him push his clothes into his rucksack, followed him downstairs and out of the door, hopping beside him barefoot across the garden. At the gate he stopped.

'Say goodbye now and pop back to bed.'

'I would comfort you,' Sophy cried passionately.

Oliver laughed and bent to kiss her.

Sophy flung her arms round his neck. 'Will you come back? Promise.'

'Perhaps. Let me go now.' She dropped her arms and watched him lope down the road, the pack on his back turning him into a monster. The first seagull of the day set up its wailing. She was cold in her pyjamas and wanted to pee. Her desolation was great.

At the bottom of the hill Oliver found Helena in the car, asleep with her head on her arms.

'Are you all right?' He wondered what she was doing at this hour.

'I've run out of petrol.'

'I'll walk on and get you some. The garages will be opening soon.'

'Leave your pack with me.' She asked no questions.

He returned carrying a can. 'Where are you going?' he asked.

'London.'

'Me too.'

'I can drive you there, we can take turns.'

'All right.' He got in beside his aunt.

'Are you staying with Mother?'

'I hadn't thought.'

'She'll be glad to put you up. If we stop for breakfast in Truro I will ring her up.'

'Thank you, Oliver.'

Forty-five years later, driving down the surgical motorway, Helena remembered with nostalgia the journey she and Oliver made. Breakfast at the Red Lion in Truro,

42

bacon and eggs and marmalade eaten in silence in an empty dining room, reading the papers. Then on through central Cornwall, catching glimpses of the sea on the north coast, through Bodmin on to Bodmin Moor, past Jamaica Inn to stop in Launceston for a drink at the White Hart before lunching at the Arundel Arms at Lifton, where the talk at neighbouring tables was of the state of the river and the prospect of catching a fish. On through Somerset where farmers were cutting the corn, the machines clattering behind plodding horses, past Ilchester and Ilminster along the road bordered by stately elms, the late summer foliage dark green, to Mere where they stopped to dine at the Old Ship. Then the last hundred miles over Salisbury Plain, watching the moon swing into a cloudless sky as they came down into Hampshire where the corn stood waiting for the reaper. On through Andover and Camberley, past the Cricketers' Arms at Bagshot, past Virginia Water and Egham, to be caught in a jam of traffic in Staines until at long last they reached the street where Oliver's parents lived, within easy reach of Harrods and Peter Jones. What had they talked about that long day, she and Oliver? Speeding down the motorway Helena could not remember. What had they discussed? Not Richard, not Calypso. War? Books? Music, perhaps? Travel, very likely. She remembered describing Greece. Swimming in warm seas and clambering over rocky hills in autumn where yellow crocus sprang from the rock itself and pink cyclamen.

They had also remembered the villages decorated with flags all the way from London to Penzance only two years before, when a party of them in different mood had fled London and the King's Coronation crowds, driving through the night along deserted roads. That was a happy night she remembered, thinking. Of course he was happy, he was not in love with Calypso then.

'You must be exhausted,' Oliver's mother called down to them from the balcony, leaning over the trailing pink geraniums. 'I'm coming down.'

Oliver lifted Helena's case from the car. Sarah Anstey put her arms round Helena and kissed her.

'Sarah, I had to come up. I hope you don't mind. I can go to an hotel.'

'Don't be absurd. George will be in soon. They've hustled him into the Admiralty, he's terribly busy, over-worked already. I am glad to see you.'

'I can't make up my mind in Cornwall. I never can.'

'No, of course not. I understand.'

Had Sarah understood? Of course she had not. She was fortunate, in love with George, always would be; worried of course about Oliver and the war, but how could a woman like Sarah, who always got everything right, understand Helena, whose talent was to get things wrong?

She remembered, speeding down the motorway, Sarah had put her in the spare room on the floor above her own, had sent her maid, who later became something rather grand in the Wrens and called them all by their Christian names, to help her unpack, turn down the bed and make a welcoming fuss. Helena remembered a long soak in a hot bath and the relief of getting into a bed out of earshot of Richard.

'I should have been ashamed,' said Helena, speeding down the M4.

'Ashamed of what?' The driver of the car kept an eye on the road, driving in the fast lane.

'Ashamed of myself,' said Helena recollecting, 'but I wasn't. It was such a relief to be in London.'

'When was that then?'

'At the outbreak of war.'

'Oh.' He accelerated, overtaking a Lancia, making it swerve. 'Pity about the elm disease,' he said, making conversation as she appeared to be awake. 'Must have been lovely once, this countryside.'

'No, I wasn't ashamed, I was just bloody relieved.' Helena hoped to shock her driver and succeeded. 'Oliver thought I was past it then,' she added.

'When?'

'Forty years ago – more.'

But she had been ashamed, for it was shame as well as pity for the animal which had caused her to buy Richard a puppy in Harrods' pet shop a few days later.

'How Sarah laughed.'

'Who was Sarah?'

'Sarah was Oliver's mother.'

'Oliver Anstey?'

'Yes.'

'He was quite well known. I didn't know you knew him.'

'He's still alive, very much so.'

'Oh. I didn't know. I've read his books, of course. Always seems to be looking for something, doesn't know what it is.'

'You are very perceptive. Would you mind not driving quite so fast? I am not afraid of death but I am afraid of being mangled in a pile-up,' and the driver, who had offered a lift from kindness of heart, reduced speed, regretting his soft-heartedness. Another time he would know better, though on second thoughts his passenger looked frail and might not have many more times.

'I thought you might be in a hurry to get there.'

'Oh, no. I have never been in a hurry. Indeed at one time I came close to leaving altogether.'

'Oh really, when was that?'

'Mind your own business.'

Helena's driver pressed his foot on the accelerator.

8

'Sarah.' Helena sat with Oliver's mother at the kitchen table that September Sunday morning. 'I am thinking of leaving Richard.'

'I thought as much.' Sarah felt no surprise. 'Why did you marry him? We've always wondered.'

'I don't really know. Could it have been because he had known Anthony? Because I needed someone to look after? Because I was lonely? Pity? Because he was lumbered with orphan Sophy? It wasn't love.'

'Not love, of course not.' Sarah went on peeling potatoes. The world might be about to end but her husband expected Sunday lunch. 'I am so unused to cooking,' she muttered, peering into the oven at the joint of beef. 'Do you think it's doing all right?'

'I expect so.' Helena looked up at the feet passing by the area railing. 'He had a fine war record. That seemed to matter. Shall I do the greens? I know how.'

'Yes, please, be an angel. Here's a knife.'

Helena picked up the knife and a handful of spinach. 'I've suddenly realized why I married Richard.'

'Why?'

'His leg, it was his leg.'

'But surely that's why you are leaving him.' Sarah's eyes, brilliant as Oliver's, caught Helena's worried ones. Both women burst out laughing, an outburst of hilarity which filled the kitchen. George's voice shouting down the stairs was drowned. He repeated himself, running down the stone steps followed by Oliver.

'What did you say, darling?' Sarah wiped her eyes.

47

'You missed the announcement.' George looked at the laughing women. 'We are at war.'

'Bother, I'd meant to listen to that jackass.'

'In a way it's a relief.' Helena had stopped laughing, drew in her breath. Sarah and George had a son. 'Oh God,' she said, 'dear God.'

'I thought you didn't believe any more,' Oliver pounced on her.

'In time of stress –' If she had been able to say more Helena would not have been heard. The first siren of the war started its whoop. They went up to the balcony to look at the sky, standing in a row behind the geranium-filled flower-boxes.

'Take cover, get your gas masks,' a hurrying warden shouted up at them.

The calm of a London Sunday continued. An owl hooted some distance away in Thurloe Square. 'Must have been woken by that filthy noise. Nobody seems to be taking cover.' George thrust his chin forward to ease his neck. He had been changing while listening to Chamberlain and tied his tie too tight. He felt half throttled.

'Loosen your tie, darling, you will choke. Oh, look!'

A taxi. Calypso's head craned out of the window, looking up at the sky. Calypso, Polly and the twins got out.

'Any bombs?' shouted Polly.

'Gas?' called the twins. 'Any gas?'

'Seven and six,' said the taximan.

'Want to take cover?' George called down from the balcony.

'Nah. Thanks all the same.'

'Let them in, Oliver.' Sarah looked up at the sky, innocently blue.

'Where's Walter?' Helena leant over the balcony.

'Got off at Plymouth to join the Navy. Marvellous smell of beef.'

'Oh, my God, the joint!' Sarah fled down to the kitchen to switch off the oven.

It was later, while they ate an overcooked lunch, that Oliver told them he had enlisted in the Army. 'I'm in the

48

ranks but having been in the O.T.C. helped a bit. I fixed myself up before I went down to Cornwall.'

'What about Spain?' asked a twin.

'They didn't ask, so I didn't tell.'

'We must hurry. I wonder where we go. Any idea?' They looked at George.

'Try the Air Ministry.' George was preoccupied.

'There will be posters, let's go and look. Our country needs us.'

'Where are you all staying?' Sarah looked round the table.

'With me,' said Polly. 'Mother and Father have got rooms near the hospital in the country. They said Calypso could stay and the twins until they are fixed up.'

'What are you girls going to do?'

'Jobs? Any ideas, Uncle George?' Calypso looked beguiling.

'I can give you some introductions, I suppose.'

'I've got a job,' said Polly. 'I fixed myself up months ago.'

'Oh, lucky you. Is it glamorous?'

'I hardly think so, just War Office.'

Richard telephoned that night. When was Helena coming home?

'I must do my shopping.' How lame that sounded. 'There will be shortages. I am going to stock up.' This sounded reasonable.

'It's very inconvenient without the car.'

'Get the General to drive you.'

'He's very busy organizing things.'

'Get him to give you a job. You will be needed now.'

'Helena, he put the hounds down, can you believe it? I ask –'

'Poor Richard. What do you feel?'

'You may be right about Hitler.'

'Richard, are you all right?'

'Of course I am. The General thinks so too.'

'Thinks what?'

'Thinks Hitler's a jumped-up cad, only a ranker could behave like that.'

'Richard, that's the best joke you've ever made.'

'I wasn't joking.'

Helena heard him replace the receiver, cutting her off.

'Are you going back?' Sarah looked troubled.

'Not yet. I have to think.'

'What about? Sophy?'

'Sophy is what a lot of it's about. It's not altogether the leg, it's Sophy too. Sarah, I don't like Sophy –'

'I know,' said Sarah. 'I know. Why don't you send her to school?'

'In war time?'

'Helena, life's not stopping, it's going on, war or not. Find the child a school, send her away, you will both be much happier.'

'Do you think so?' Helena respected Sarah.

'Ask Polly. She was quite happy at her school. They might take Sophy. Calypso's wouldn't do, she was expelled, supposed to have flirted with the gardener.'

'But Polly's was near Cambridge –'

'There are such things as trains. Ask Polly and check with her mother. They will help you. Why don't you make a list? Start it with Leg, then Sophy, then your shopping. You can cross out Leg straight away since there's nothing you can do about it.' Anxiety made Sarah sarcastic.

'I knew you would help.' Helena reached for a piece of paper and wrote on it 'List', which she underlined, then underneath she wrote 'Leg' and ticked it, followed by 'Sophy? Food and clothes'. 'What shall we run short of?' she asked, but Sarah was busy and left her.

It was the following day after an exhaustive spree in Harrods that, taking a short cut through the pet department, she bought a dachshund puppy. Her attempt to get the price reduced on the grounds that it was German met with contempt. She was, though, able to make arrangements to have it sent to Richard by train. 'I was mindful of your carpets,' she told Sarah.

'Carpets aren't going to matter much. I have

50

telphoned Polly's mother about Sophy for you.'

'And what did she say?'

'Said it's a good school, send the child and she can stay with Polly when she has to pass through London or for half terms.'

'You've done my job for me.' Helena was huffed.

'You can visit the school, here's the address. Telephone tonight. Get it done, Helena.'

'You are rushing me.'

'There is a rush. Being hated at Sophy's age isn't right.'

'I never said I hated her.'

'But you do.'

Helena went to visit the school. When she got back to London she found a message from Richard to ring him urgently. 'Something has happened to Sophy,' said Sarah.

'What?'

'He won't or can't say. He sounds desperate.'

'All right, I'll go.' Helena gave in.

This time alone, Helena had an unpleasant drive down the winding roads. From now on, she thought, petrol rationing would restrict what freedom the car gave her.

Richard came out to meet her, carrying the dachshund puppy in his arms.

'So you got my present.'

'It chews everything, it's eaten my best cardigan.'

'Where is Sophy?'

'In bed at the Rectory.'

'Why? What happened?'

'Child won't or can't speak. The Rectory offered. It seemed better for her to be with a woman. I can't do much with my leg. Monika Erstweiler sits with her. The doctor said to keep her quiet.'

'But what happened, for God's sake?'

'Don't know.' Richard put the puppy down on the grass and watched it make a puddle. 'Good little chap. Nice thought of yours.'

'What happened to Sophy?' Helena felt furious impatience.

'Went out for a walk. You know how she wanders. I don't know where. I've been stuck here with my leg –'

'Damn your leg!'

'Yes.' Richard looked at his wife with sympathy. 'Must be as trying for you as it is for me. Sorry. Must ignore it. I hear there's a chap with no legs who flies, chap called Bader trying to get back into the Air Force with no legs, I ask you.'

'Sophy?'

'The Rector found her wandering on the cliff road. Thought she looked odd, offered her a lift and she passed out in his car. She hasn't spoken, just lies there. It's unnerving.'

'Any bumps or bruises?'

'Nothing, had some sort of fit, I'd say.'

'Rubbish.'

'Well, yes. The doctor says shock, but round here, it's ridiculous, how could she get a shock?'

'We'd better go to her.' Helena opened the car door and Richard got in holding the puppy.

'Doesn't even respond to the puppy. You'd think she'd like it.'

'Did the doctor say, I mean has he –' Helena hesitated.

'Not interfered with. Nothing. Can't have seen anything of Penrose either. Wrong place, wrong time.'

'Penrose? Who is Penrose?'

'Coastguard chap, you know him. The Army are wiring off the path against invaders, I ask you. Hitler's not going to invade up perpendicular cliffs. Of course with my leg I never walk along it. Oh, sorry, mentioned it again.'

'It doesn't matter.' Helena drew up at the Rectory. 'What about Penrose?'

'Fell over the cliff. Drunk, I suppose, or suicide, moody fellow his wife says. Anyway the Army found him, saw him floating. The police are being quite active, gives them something to do. If I had my leg I'd –'

Helena got out of the car and rang the Rectory bell.

52

The Rector opened the door. Helena kissed him on the cheek.

'Like to go straight up? Monika's with her. The room at the top on the left. Mildred had to go out.'

Sophy lay propped on pillows, eyes dark in a face no paler than usual. Monika sat by the open window sewing.

'Hullo, darling.' I never call her darling, thought Helena, feeling embarrassed. 'Hullo, Sophy, I've come home. How are you?'

Sophy did not answer; her eyes looked at some point other than Helena.

'While I was in London I bought that puppy and I bought you a lot of clothes, too.' No response. Helena looked at Monika, who smiled encouragingly and pointed at a chair near the bed. Helena sat.

'Polly's got a war job and Calypso is looking for one. Walter is joining the Navy, the twins the Air Force. Oliver has got into the Army, in the ranks, he doesn't want to be an officer.' The child lay limp, eyes unblinking, disconcerting. Helena felt her sense of exasperation rise. Why couldn't the child answer? She looked at Monika for comfort.

'Aunt Sarah and I thought you might like to go away to school, so I went and saw Polly's old school near Cambridge. I think you will like it.' Monika nodded approval. 'There will be children of your age, games, and so on. Polly says you can stay with her on your way through London. What's that noise?' Monika was looking out of the window.

'Police,' said Monika Erstweiler. 'Police.'

'Oh, yes.' Helena dropped her voice to a whisper, which Sophy heard perfectly but Monika not, since she was leaning out of the window. 'I hear there was an accident to a coastguard, so unfortunate.'

'For us.' Monika turned back into the room, white-faced. 'Not the coastguard,' she said. 'Your kind brother-in-law warned us. We are to be interned. We are enemy aliens.'

'How totally absurd,' said Helena, speaking loudly from anger.

'I must find my husband.' Monika came close to Sophy. 'Be brave, my child.' She bent and kissed her. 'These are English police not the Gestapo.'

Sophy sat up abruptly. 'We will get you out, write to our Member of Parliament, write to *The Times*.' She scrambled out of bed. Helena and Monika, taken aback by this adult attitude, began to laugh.

'Sophy, I love you.' Monika put her arms round Sophy and hugged her.

It would make my life easier if I did, thought Helena, watching them.

'Uncle Richard can write the letters.' Sophy had run down the stairs calling loudly, 'Uncle Richard, Uncle Richard, please!'

'And he did write,' said Helena to her driver. 'He wrote to *The Times*, to all the Members of Parliament he could think of, he became very passionate about it.'

'About what?' Her driver overtook a large lorry, causing Helena to wince.

'About the wrong aliens getting interned.'

'Like Arthur Koestler?'

'Yes. He was well known, but the Erstweilers were hardly known in those days. He wrote to Calypso's husband, got him interested. He was quite helpful, very helpful really.'

'My father?'

'I'm sorry, I'd forgotten for a moment that Calypso is your mother.'

'That's quite all right.'

'It gave Richard something to do, made him forget his leg.'

'What was wrong with it?'

'He lost it in Flanders.'

'Wouldn't have stopped him writing, surely?'

'It didn't. The injustice gave him a lift.'

'Did he get them out?'

'Yes, eventually.'

'Then he remembered his leg.' Helena's driver considered himself a student of psychology.

'Yes, yes, he did.' Helena sighed. 'He remembered the bloody thing.'

Helena's driver, Calypso's son, raised his eyebrows. In his book middle-class old ladies did not swear, not in their eighties.

'Of course, looking back, being among the first to be interned was a great help to Max.'

'How was that?'

'His name became familiar in the papers, favourably compared with Furtwängler who had stayed in Germany. He wasn't Jewish, of course, like Max, and very pro-Hitler. Monika and Max were released just when all the others were gathered in. He got a head start professionally.'

'Became famous in this country.'

'I've always believed it was the General's doing.'

'What General?'

'General Peachum, a friend of your great-uncle's, a neighbour, loathed Jews, an admirer of Hitler and Ribbentrop, rather a silly man, Master of Hounds, urged the local police and coastguards to watch for spies, a typical "country gentleman", a good man. They do a lot of harm.'

9

Calypso's marriage to Hector Grant, during the early days of the war, when for months nothing happened except a tremendous freeze, came as welcome entertainment. One day she was working in the glamorous secret job she had found for herself and the next inviting everybody to her wedding at Caxton Hall.

Hector Grant, a tall, elegant Member of Parliament for a Scottish constituency, had been married before with no issue and was extremely rich, with a house in Westminster and a castle in the Highlands. The trouble in the eyes of Calypso's parents was that he was the same age as Calypso's father; indeed it was he who had introduced them.

'How could John have been so stupid?' cried Sarah, on hearing the news.

'I don't suppose it occurred to him,' replied George. 'The man is supposed to be uncatchable. How was John to know the advent of war made Hector determined to beget a son and heir?'

'But he's had a wife.'

'Who wouldn't or couldn't oblige.'

'Perhaps Hector can't.'

'We shall see, won't we?' And George had gone gloomily off to his office, leaving Sarah to telephone what she called the Cornish Contingent, Helena and Richard.

Richard refused Calypso's invitation, excusing himself on the grounds of pressure of work. 'I've written to Hector of course about the Erstweilers, knew him in the

57

war, splendid chap, got a very good D.S.O.' Richard had received no decoration for losing his leg. Sarah suspected that Richard resented this. She asked to speak to Helena, putting this point to her.

'Don't be absurd, Sarah,' Helena had said briskly. 'His leg blew off when he had his back to the enemy and was drinking a mug of tea. He remembers it perfectly. He never expected a medal. He really is busy.'

'Will you come, then? Stay with us.'

'I'd love to. I've never been to a registry office wedding.'

'The reception is at the Ritz.'

'I daresay he can afford it. I gather he's paying for all of us to have lunch.'

'Yes. He won't allow Calypso's parents to spend a penny.'

'They have no pennies, that's their trouble. Calypso wants money.'

'Helena, you will bring Sophy, won't you?'

'She's at school.'

'They might let her come. Try.'

'I'll have to see.'

See that she doesn't, Sarah thought, but did not say, and Sophy did not come. In the event George, too, was too busy. Sarah and Helena sat with Calypso's mother, watching a stony-faced John give his only child to Hector, magnificent in a morning suit with hardly a grey hair in his thick thatch, his black eyebrows like moths' wings meeting above his nose.

Calypso shone triumphant in a white coat and skirt, satin shirt, a wreath of gardenias on her sleek head.

'I've never seen anyone look so smug,' one twin in Air Force uniform whispered to the other. Polly, overhearing, grinned. Walter arrived in time for the luncheon, a scrubbed and healthy Able Seaman. Oliver came late but in time to kiss the bride, hugging her against his rough khaki uniform.

'How prickly you are.'

'Am I still to get my comforts?'

'Oh, that!'

'I may claim them soon. I am hoping to get to Finland.'
'Hector says that's all collapsing.'
'There will be other campaigns.'
'I wish you joy of them –' She looked at him with fear.
'Well, you've got what you wanted.' Oliver made no effort to lower his voice. He turned away, caught Walter by the arm, 'Come on, old sod, let's go and get drunk.'

Hector raised eyebrows, murmuring, 'He seems half-way to his goal,' and, holding Calypso's arm, steered her away.

'Come and meet some of my friends from the House. Then we must go, if we are to catch our train.'

'Even you were young once,' Calypso said brightly, thus setting the tone of their future relations. 'I'll keep my word if you'll keep yours,' she whispered up at his darkening face.

'How fond she is of him.' The wife of a junior minister tried to open a conversation with Helena, who was watching.

'Fond? Oh yes, fond.' Helena, who had drunk more champagne than she should, let the conversation abort.

Later that evening Polly steered the twins to the York Minster in Soho, where they found Oliver and Walter sunk in alcoholic gloom, and amazed them by leading them on to the Gargoyle, a haunt Oliver had heard of but never visited, where Polly appeared to be quite well known. Amused by their dazed expressions she said: 'I have not been letting the grass grow. I work for half the literati in London in my dump.' Oliver grew sober as she pointed out Cyril Connolly, Philip Toynbee, Erica Mann, Robert Newton, Brian Howard and various other figures of the older generation.

'My bosses know them, I don't,' she tried to console Oliver. 'When's your train?'

'Midnight, Paddington.'

'Walter, too. We'll put you on it. The twins are staying until tomorrow.'

'She's quite a girl, your sister,' Oliver gasped when he and Walter had struggled on to the train, pushing their

59

way into an overcrowded carriage.

'Not stupid,' agreed Walter.

'Very pretty, really – pity old Sophy couldn't make it.'

'That's the most uncomfortable wedding I've ever been to.' Sarah climbed into bed with George that night. 'I've never seen so many unhappy faces. Oh, my poor Oliver.'

'Lucky escape, if you ask me.'

'Perhaps. I wonder what's going on in the night train to Inverness.'

'Night of the long knives, by the bride's looks.'

But George was wrong. Hector had whisked Calypso off to the Savoy, where her joy at finding a telephone by the lavatory seat had set the tone for an enjoyable wedding night.

'I did appreciate that,' she said at last. 'I can't tell you how I was dreading it.'

'I thought as much.' Hector was pleased. 'Would you like some oysters?'

'In the middle of the night?'

'Why not?'

'Build up our strength for your Highlands? I'm dreading them, too.'

'Wait till you see them.'

'All right, I will. They'd better be good.'

'You are driving too fast again.' Helena, sitting ancient in the bucket seat, turned her head to look at Hamish, watching his mouth tighten with annoyance as he obediently reduced speed. 'You are very like your mother.'

'Oh, am I? I'm glad to hear it. I thought I took after my father.'

'You do, but you often have your mother's expression.' Helena undid her safety belt, letting it wind back, to Hamish's alarm.

'You really should wear that belt, Great-aunt. She must have been very beautiful.'

'Not if you drive at a reasonable speed. Of course she was beautiful. She still is. Much improved since her stroke.'

'What could you mean?'

'Calypso's face was too regular, both sides were the same. Since her stroke she looks human, lopsided. I don't suppose it's changed her character.'

'She seems to have made a good recovery except for her face. She drags a foot sometimes. How well did you know her when she was young?'

'My dear, I was just an onlooker. She and the others came every summer. All the men were in love with her; she took it as a matter of course, as far as one could see.'

'How far was that?'

'I don't know.' Helena turned to watch the landscape flashing past. 'She never made any bones about what she wanted.'

'Oh?'

'She got it, too. Money, a good time, nice houses, clothes, jewels, yes, she got what she wanted.'

'Did she want me?'

'Of course she did.' In her eighties Helena's voice was better than it had been in her forties. 'Of course she wanted you,' she repeated. Was he not part of the bargain? 'I don't believe she wanted more than you. She had a bad time when you were born.'

'So she always says.'

'Well, it wasn't your fault, my dear. She would insist on staying in London. Air raids and childbirth are not compatible, but you don't want to hear about the war.'

'Why did she have me in London?'

'She loathed Scotland, that was a flaw in her marriage. Your father wanted her to have you in Edinburgh.'

'He adored Scotland. I do, too.'

'He took her up there on their honeymoon. She found it cold. How she complained when she got back! The train got stuck in a snowdrift.'

'I expect they had a sleeper.' Hamish tried to visualize Calypso young and beautiful in a sleeper with his father. 'I suppose they had sleepers in the war?'

'Oh yes. Paddington to Penzance. Euston to Inverness.

61

We had them when we could get them. Your father, being an M.P., had priority.'

'My mother must have liked that.' Hamish drove faster.

Helena resigned herself, closing her eyes. 'I don't believe it made up for the cold.'

'So you don't think I was conceived in a sleeping car?'

'Not until much later, my dear. At this speed we shall arrive early.'

'We can have a drink or two.'

'Yes, of course.'

'I don't take after my father in that.'

'I wasn't suggesting you did.'

'Do you think he got drunk in the sleeper?'

'I wouldn't know,' said Helena, who had often wondered the same thing.

10

Getting no nearer Finland than a brief interview in London, Oliver went to his parents' house for a bath. The house was empty; in the bitter cold the water either turned off or frozen. After wandering round the empty rooms he telephoned Calypso, writing her name in the dust as he waited.

'I am in London for the night. Any chance of seeing you?'

'We are going out, you just caught us. Hector's already on the doorstep, we are due at a party.' She sounded breathless.

'Can't I come too?'

'It's not your sort of party, so sorry. Another time give us some notice. There are so many parties. London's great fun.'

'My camp isn't.'

'I suppose not. Why don't you try Polly? Coming, Hector, coming.' She rang off.

Oliver walked through the snow to Polly's and rang the bell, stamping his feet in their heavy boots.

The door flew open.

'Oliver!'

'Sophy, what are you doing here? I thought you were at school.'

'I've got a week off because I've had German measles. Polly's out with the twins. Come in, don't let the ice indoors.'

'You've grown. D'you think I could have a bath?'

'Of course.'

'Anything to drink?'

'There's some gin in the kitchen. I was just going to have my supper. The twins are up for the night.'

'I'll take you out to supper when I've had a bath.' The child looked peaky. Helping himself to gin, Oliver tried to remember what his mother had told him. Something had happened to Sophy. What?

'Any news of the Erstweilers?'

'Uncle Richard is trying to get them out. I had a letter from Monika. It was censored. Isn't it stupid?' Sophy flushed.

'The whole bloody war is stupid.' Oliver swallowed his gin. 'Boring, too. Polly shouldn't leave you alone in the house, there might be an air raid.'

'I'm all right. I'm used to being alone. There have been no raids.'

'There will be.' Oliver had a bath and emerged feeling better.

'Where shall we have dinner?' The child looked a waif with her black silky hair unbecomingly cut, eyes wary.

'Anywhere.'

'I'll take you to the Savoy. I'd like a good dinner.'

'I've never been anywhere in London.'

He took her to the Savoy. 'My father used to give me lunch here at half term. Why didn't you go back to Cornwall?'

'Aunt Helena said it was too far for such a short time.'

'Do you mind?'

'Not really.' Sophy looked evasive.

'Do you like school?'

'It's all right.'

'Not like Cornwall?'

'Not a bit. What's it like being a soldier?'

Oliver tried to tell her, watching her eat, gradually relax after drinking a glass of wine.

'You weren't at Calypso's wedding.'

'Aunt Helena didn't want me to miss school.'

'I see. Going back to Cornwall for the holidays?'

'Yes. Perhaps Uncle Richard will have got the Erstweilers out by then. She said they are hoping in their letter.'

Oliver refilled her glass. 'Drink up.'

'Won't I get tipsy?'

'I'll look after you.'

Sophy drank. 'I don't like it much but it makes me feel warm.' She pressed her flat chest then, leaning towards Oliver, she whispered: 'I ran the Terror Run.'

'What?'

'It's wired off now but I ran it the day before they put the wire along it to prevent the Germans invading.'

'Oh, the Terror Run. I'd forgotten. Seems a long time ago. What was the other thing going to be? Something idiotic. We drew lots, a killing, wasn't it?'

'Yes,' she said slowly, 'but you cancelled it.'

'What's the matter, Sophy? You look funny. Seen something in the woodshed? Did the Terror Run frighten you?'

'Fear lent me wings. I met, I mean I saw, I -' Sophy stared at Oliver, who stared back, thinking, She's going to be lovely one day with those eyes. What did she see that day? 'Yes?' he said.

Sophy drew a deep breath. 'I met the Rector, he was very kind and took me home.' She rearranged the knife and fork by her plate. 'Oh, look,' she said, looking across the restaurant. 'There's Calypso.'

There indeed was Calypso, dining with a man in naval uniform, not Hector. By the look of their table, they had reached the brandy stage. They had been there some time.

'Bloody, bloody bitch – "London's great fun". How long have you known she was there, Sophy?'

'I saw her when we came in. I'm not a bloody bitch.'

'I meant Calypso, not you. Waiter, my bill, please.' She did see something in the woodshed and she's not going to tell me, Oliver thought as, choked with jealousy of the unknown naval man, he paid his bill and led Sophy out past Calypso who, deep in talk, had not seen them. 'Comforts for you, old chap?' He addressed the stranger, who looked startled, as he pushed Sophy on ahead. Calypso laughed. In the Strand the cold bit deep. Oliver took

Sophy by the hand. 'Let's go for a walk.'

All her life whenever there was a full moon Sophy remembered walking the empty streets, her hand in Oliver's greatcoat pocket, their feet crunching the snow, a full moon casting black shadows from tall buildings, the frozen air painful to breathe, walking in silence all the way to St Paul's, where they stood looking up at the dome and listened to the starlings fighting for roosting places on the cathedral, whistling, high-pitched, aggressive.

How long had they stood there? Long enough for Oliver to regain his composure, long enough for Sophy to get thoroughly chilled, long enough for a solitary policeman to get interested and pace slowly towards them.

'Monika said the police were not the Gestapo when they came to fetch Max and her. I hope they get out soon.' She shivered in the snow.

'Sophy, you are freezing, why didn't you say.'

'I'm all right.' Her hand at least had been warm, held in his pocket. That, too, she would remember.

'The Erstweilers will be released. Come on, I must get you back to Polly. We never left a note, she will think you have vanished.'

'She's out with David and Paul.'

'They may be back by now.' In later years Oliver was to wonder why the whistle of starlings always gave him a sensation of sexual jealousy. He quite forgot St Paul's by the light of the moon before the bombing.

The twins and Polly had been dining more modestly at the Royal Court. Polly had pointed out Augustus John at the bar. They looked older, more confident, more alike than ever in uniform. Oliver wondered whether he had chosen the wrong service.

'How's it going, Oliver?' Polly, too, had aged. Her face had thinned so that her eyes seemed larger, her lashes longer, mouth wider.

'It's going nowhere. I've been trying to get in on the Finnish war but they say it's nearly over. I'm bloody bored and cold in my camp. You look fine.'

'I'm busy. I think I'm doing something useful.'

'Secret?'

'Not so that you'd notice. Well, it is really.'

The twins laughed, watching her.

'We saw Calypso,' said Oliver to test them.

'We've rather gone off her.' David glanced at his brother for confirmation. 'She's become grand and social, not too keen on old friends – has other fish to fry.'

'She was dining with one tonight.' Oliver was still angry. 'She said she was going out with Hector when I telephoned.'

'He's in the House most nights, she can't be expected to sit at home alone.' Polly came to Calypso's defence.

'No need for her to lie.'

'Well, that's Calypso. She will be free another time. Try again, you may have better luck.'

'She's no Penelope.' David exchanged a glance with Polly. 'We went to her house last time we were up. Have you been there?'

'No.' Oliver noticed the change in the twins' attitude. 'You two used to sit there drooling. She loved it.'

'You did too. She liked you better than us.'

'Or Walter,' Polly remarked. Then, noticing Oliver's expression: 'She's married, got money, a lovely house, she entertains, is the wife of Hector Grant, she isn't one of us any more.'

'Is she happy?'

'I think so. Next time you get leave give her notice. The twins did.'

'How did you get on?' Oliver looked from Paul to David. 'Was she glad to see you?'

'I suspect she prefers officers.' David was ironic.

'You'll get commissions. Tell me about yourselves.' Oliver suddenly wanted to drop the subject. 'Where are you stationed? What are you doing?'

'We are near Cambridge at the moment. We are escorting Sophy back to school tomorrow. We tried to get into bombers but they are training us for fighters.

67

We could have been together in bombers, we thought in our innocence.'

'How long before you are trained?'

'Another month, less.'

'And I am kicking my heels square bashing. God!'

'Walter's full of grumbles, too. They won't have him in submarines. He says the Navy are sadists, that he'll spend the war being sick.' Polly yawned. 'I've got to work tomorrow. I'm off to bed. If I'm gone in the morning before you wake don't worry, come again whenever you like. There's plenty of room. I'm in Mum and Dad's room, the twins have got the spare room, you can have Walter's. Sophy's in mine. Goodnight.'

Oliver looked after her. 'It's not only Calypso who's changed.'

'We all have,' the twins said. 'Who would have thought a year ago we'd all be sitting round a kitchen table in fancy dress, the camomile lawn days over?'

'You know I still can't tell you two apart, can you, Sophy?'

'No.' Sophy grinned. 'Nor can Polly.'

'Nor the R.A.F. It's like school. Perhaps the war will make some distinction.'

Sophy looked at the twins across the table, troubled. 'Wound.' She spoke in her clear voice. 'Or kill.'

The twins looked at her. 'You never know,' they cried cheerfully. 'Anything left to drink?'

'There's someone at the front door.' Oliver stood up. 'Who, at this hour?'

'Go and see. Don't wake Polly, she really works very hard.'

Oliver opened the front door, peering out. 'Good Lord, Uncle Richard! What are you doing here?'

'Looking for shelter.' Richard limped indoors. 'Got lost in the bloody blackout, difficult to see the numbers, what do they want a blackout for with a full moon, I ask you?'

Oliver shut the door. 'We are in the kitchen. Polly's gone to bed.'

'Went to your house, found it shut up, nobody there. What happened to your maid?'

'Joined the Wrens.'

'Women in uniform, I ask you.'

'Lots are. Why are you here, Uncle? Come down and have a drink or something. The twins are here and Sophy.'

'What's she doing here? Run away from school? No, don't tell me, half term.'

'German measles, actually.' Oliver led his uncle down to the kitchen. The twins stood up politely.

'Hullo, hullo, not conchies, then? Nice to see you. What's this about measles?'

'German.' Sophy pecked his cheek. 'Why are you in London? Aunt Helena never said –'

'Germans, child. Well, they say they are Austrian but it's all the same thing. Enemy aliens, I ask you, it's ridiculous. Quiet respectable violinist, law-abiding. I told them. Cut your bloody red tape, I said, and let them out, costing the taxpayer a packet. The Rector and I will take care of them. What's this? Gin? Oh, all right, if it's all you've got. Been at the Home Office all the afternoon, absolutely bloody people, positive Huns in their methods, wound in red tape, can't tell a simple violinist who can play the organ and wouldn't hurt a fly – they've called up Tompkins, by the way, so we need him – from an enemy agent. Any more gin? Thanks. Not taking your last, I hope? Well, I got nowhere at the Home Office, didn't do my leg any good, they passed me from one buffoon to another. Why aren't they in the forces, I asked them. They didn't like that, I can tell you. Go and lose a leg as I did, I told them. In the last war we didn't sit on our bums in the Home Office, we fought. I saw six of the buggers. I ask you. Got nowhere, absolutely bloody nowhere. What are you all laughing at?'

'Nothing, sir.'

'Well, where was I? Oh yes, nowhere, so I didn't give up, I'm not German, not that they've given up but they will, mark my words. I went along to the House of Commons and found that chap Calypso married and two friends of his. Good bar they've got there, by the way, and bingo, what do you think? This fellow, member for some Home County or other, tells me the Erstweilers are being released and arriving in London the day after tomorrow and none of those fellows sitting on their arses wound in red tape had heard, I ask you, what is the country coming to? Any more of that gin?'

Oliver poured the last of the gin into the outstretched glass. 'So you've got the Erstweilers out?'

'That's what I said, made myself clear, didn't I? I may have lost my leg but not my wits. Can't see what's so funny. Can't think why you are all laughing.' Putting his empty glass carefully onto the table, Richard Cuthbertson leant back, slid from the kitchen chair onto the floor and lay prone.

'Mind the leg.' Sophy hopped behind Oliver and the twins as they carried the unconscious figure up to bed.

11

'Try and relax.' The lady doctor smiled down at Polly.

'That was my idea in coming here.' Polly lay on the couch.

The lady doctor stood warming her hands. 'There, my hands are warm. I have always thought touching patients with cold hands the height of cruelty.'

'Our doctor always made us jump as children.'

'A man, I suppose.'

'Yes. He gave us disgusting medicines, too.'

'There, my dear, how's that? Feel comfortable?'

'Will it stay in?'

'Goodness, yes. Now try it yourself, don't hurry, remember what I said.'

Polly tried. 'That right?'

'Perfect. Do it again to make sure. I don't want you getting home and panicking.'

'I don't think I'll panic.'

'I expect not. How old did you say you are?'

'Nineteen.'

'Are your parents pleased?'

'I haven't told them yet. My father's a doctor. He's been evacuated with his hospital, Mother's with him.'

'You seem the sort of girl who knows her own mind.'

'I am.'

'I hope you will both be very happy. It's two people's job to make a success of it.'

'I realize that.' Polly got off the couch. 'Thank you very much.' She smiled warmly. 'The war doesn't help,' she added.

'The war shouldn't be allowed to destroy values.' Seeing Polly's face, the doctor added, 'That's my only bromide.'

'I'm hanging on to my values.' Polly held out her hand. 'Thank you very much for your help.'

The older woman looked thoughtfully at Polly's green eyes, bright hair. They shook hands. Her values are not the usual run of the mill, the doctor thought. She rang for the next patient. While she waited she watched Polly skip down the steps into the street and run a few yards before crossing the road. Rather a monkey, that one. She wondered what Polly was really up to. She had not seen any reason to tell her that she had trained with Martin. Any child of Martin Cuthbertson's would be likely to manage her own business.

Polly went alone to see *The Wizard of Oz* and was singing 'Somewhere over the Rainbow' when she let herself into her parents' house. She shut the street door and fumbled her way round the house, drawing the blackout curtains before switching on lights. A musty smell of tobacco and alcohol seeped down from the floor above her parents' room, which she had made her own since there was a telephone beside the bed. She cursed Oliver and the twins who had disturbed her on their way up the night before. She had left without waking them that morning. She ran up to Walter's room to fling open a window. A bitter wind blew in then sucked out the sour air. A lump on one of the beds groaned. Polly spun round. Unable to see, she tripped over an obstacle wrapped in cloth and fell full length on the floor.

'Curse it!'

'Who is that?' A grumpy voice she recognized as her Uncle Richard's emanated from the bed. Polly disentangled herself from his trousers, drew the curtains and switched on the light.

'Uncle Richard, what are you doing here? I fell over your leg.'

'Arrived last night. Must have overslept. What time is it?'

72

'Sevenish.'

'I'll be up for breakfast.'

'Supper. It's seven in the evening.'

'Oh.' Her uncle dragged himself into a sitting position. Polly had never seen him grey and unshaven.

'We were celebrating. I remember that. I wonder how I got here?'

'I heard Oliver and the twins making an awful noise going to bed. I suppose they were putting you away.'

'Where's Sophy?'

'The twins took her back to school this morning. That was their plan. They were all asleep when I went out.'

'She was pleased about the Erstweilers.'

'What about them?'

'They are out, getting out. What day is it?'

'Wednesday.'

'Tomorrow they get to London.'

'How thrilling! Did you do it?'

'Pulled strings, made a fuss, got drunk, I remember now, brandy with Calypso's Hector, gin when I got here, haven't been drunk since 1918, not like that, what will Helena say, I ask you?'

'No need to tell her. Why don't you have a bath? I'll see what I can find for supper. There's a razor of father's somewhere.'

'Feel woeful.' Richard Cuthbertson lay back with a groan. 'Woe, woe.'

'I'll mix you some Alka Seltzer. When you've had a bath come down and have supper. I live in the kitchen nowadays.' Polly went for Alka Seltzer and stood over her uncle as he drank it.

'My God, how disgusting.'

'It helps.' Polly waited while he drained the glass.

'I remember now, I had a few whiskies before going to the Home Office. You won't tell Helena?'

'Of course not.'

'They all laughed last night when I told them what I'd said to those bureaucrats, found it funny. Helena finds me funny too, can't think why, I never make jokes, do you find me funny?'

'Not at the moment. Come down when you're ready, Uncle. I'll make some soup.' Polly left him.

In the kitchen she laid places for two and started preparing a meal, humming Judy Garland's tune as she worked. She was disturbed by a ring at the front door. She called up the area steps: 'Who is it?'

'It's me, Calypso. Can I come in?'

'Of course.'

Calypso felt her way down the area steps.

'We are far more likely to break our necks doing this than get bombed. I've laddered my stockings tripping over the kerb.'

'That's not like you. Come in. What's the matter?' Polly looked at her cousin. Something was wrong. 'What's up?'

'Just felt I'd like to see you. Hector's in the House, thought a chat would be nice. I've hardly seen you since I married.'

'What with your marriage and my job it's not easy. What's wrong?'

'Nothing. Oh, are you expecting somebody?' Calypso looked at the table. 'I don't want to butt in. Shall I go?'

'It's only Uncle Richard. He's got the hell of a hangover, he seems to have been boozing with Hector. He's in London getting the Erstweilers out from the Isle of Man. I found him in bed when I came in. Last night Oliver and the twins who were here put him away. I only just found him.'

'Are they here now?'

'No, they took Sophy back to school on their way to their station and Oliver had to be back in his camp.'

'What fun. I wish I'd seen them all.' Calypso sounded wistful. Polly made no comment.

'The twins did come one evening and Olly rang up but I was doing something else. What a pity.'

'They can always come here. I'm alone. I've given them keys. Walter has his, of course.'

'Polly –' Calypso took a deep breath. 'I've got to tell somebody.'

'Fire away. Stay to supper, won't you?' Calypso looked awful, hunted, her normal bright confidence gone.

Richard came into the kitchen. 'Hullo, girls.' He kissed Calypso's proffered cheek. The girls exchanged glances, the moment for confidences passed. During supper Richard told them all he had done for the Erstweilers, finishing his account with a compliment. 'Damn good chap, your Hector. Couldn't have managed without him, you're a lucky girl.'

'Yes,' said Calypso. 'Yes, of course.'

Helena telephoned from Cornwall. Polly called Richard to speak to her. The girls listened.

'Yes, of course I'm here, couldn't get in at Sarah's house, they've shut it up. What? Tomorrow I'm meeting the Erstweilers and will bring them down with me, tell the Rector. What? When? Who? How ridiculous. One of those buggers must have done it to annoy, sitting there swathed in red tape – I told them – what? Not till tomorrow week? How did you find out? They telephoned Floyer? Why not me? I'm the one who's on the spot. I'm the one who's made all the running, well, not running, not with my leg, how could I? Polly fell over it. What? Oh all right, I'll come home. Yes, tonight. I –' He turned to the girls. 'Cut off, goddammit. They aren't getting out until tomorrow week and travelling via Bristol, I ask you. They get a train pass. Helena seems to want me home, didn't know where I'd got to. I'd better catch the night train.' He spoke forlornly.

Polly said, 'It's only one more week, Uncle, you've done marvels. It's thanks to you they are getting out.'

'I'll take you to Paddington. I've got Hector's car round the corner,' Calypso offered.

'What about –' Polly began to speak but Calypso shook her head. 'It was nothing, nothing important.'

Presently Polly watched Calypso, driving Hector's Lagonda, their uncle beside her, vanish in the blackout.

'Poor Calypso,' said Polly out loud in the freezing street. She had never felt sorry for her cousin before. 'I wonder!' Indoors she went to the telephone and dialled thoughtfully.

'Sorry I couldn't ring before. I found my uncle here in bed.' The telephone crackled. 'Not my bed, one of the spares.' She listened, then, 'Well, I'm rather depressed. I came in full of zeal, went to see *The Wizard of Oz*, was all cheerful and relaxed, but not only was there Uncle Richard, you know who I mean, one leg, I tripped and fell over it. How? In the dark. No, not particularly funny, no, it just wasn't. Then Calypso came along, yes, the beautiful cousin you want to meet. No, she was not at her best, she looked terrible, well, worried, fraught. She was just going to confide when Uncle interrupted us so we couldn't talk. No, she clammed up. No, I can't imagine what it is, she's got everything. Well, I know she's not got you. Yes, I promise you shall meet her, blast you. Yes. No, what I'm trying to say is not tonight. Because I'm feeling sad. Oh, really – do you think so? Cheer me up? Does it? All right, then, come along. I see I've got a lot to learn. Don't forget I've got to clock in at my office at nine. All right, all right. No, I'm not joking. I can't see it as funny.'

But forty years later, on her way to the funeral, Polly laughed out loud and her daughter in the back seat asked: 'What's the joke, Ma?'

'Only something in my distant past. You wouldn't find it amusing, just something I learned.'

'You always said you were dead bored at lessons.'

'Not on that occasion.' Stifling her laughter, Polly snorted like a horse.

12

When Calypso had her stroke in 1979 she was completely paralysed for two days, unable to speak but able to see and hear. Bored by what she heard – everyone within earshot was cagey – and only able to see part of the room where she lay, she nerved herself to think back while she could and remember what had happened. She had long been aware of self-deception and wilful forgetfulness, a self-preserving double standard. As a convert to Catholicism, she was aware of her deceptions even in the confessional, of making her sins sound droll, therefore less serious. She was always angry when the priest could not share her view. Now, convinced she was dying, she cast her mind back to the moment she had realized that she had grown up and must manage by herself. When she made a rapid recovery her first words addressed to Hamish, who was sitting by her bed, were: 'It was the night I put Uncle Richard on the night train. I got him a seat but I couldn't get him a sleeper.' Her speech was only slightly slurred and that left her after a few days. All that remained was a slight stiffening on one side of her face and a small limp.

'I'm not dying,' she had added, watching Hamish's expression. 'It takes three.' Hamish, at a loss, had said: 'Three what?' looking at his mother with pity. Calypso answered 'Strokes', and drifted into a healing sleep.

It was a struggle to get Richard on the train, carrying his overnight bag in one hand, holding on to his arm with the other. The station swarmed with soldiers, sailors,

77

airmen, a large proportion drunk. They overwhelmed the civilians and smelled different. Calypso supposed the materials their uniforms were made of absorbed the smells of beer and tobacco differently from civilians. She dragged her uncle along to the First Class carriages. 'Get in here, Uncle Richard, I'll find you a seat.' She pushed and shoved, popping her head in and out of carriage doors. 'Is there room for my uncle? He's lost a leg, he can't possibly stand all the way to Penzance.'

Taken aback by her beauty, made to feel guilty about the leg, a competition took place to surrender hard-won or booked seats. Calypso thrust Richard into a corner seat, crying: 'Thank you, thank you, how kind of you. He's not feeling very well, so it's specially kind. Come and see me when you're in London, won't you? Oh, I am grateful.' She kissed Richard, hissing in his ear, 'Don't you dare give them my address. Goodbye, Uncle Richard, goodbye,' and leapt from the train as the guard blew his whistle. Watching the overladen train snake away into the dark she stood feeling totally alone, frightened but defiant. Now, she had thought, and remembered it all those years later, now I must live.

And if Uncle Richard hadn't interrupted us and I'd asked Polly's advice and taken it my life might have been entirely different. She thought, recovering from her stroke, that it was better that she had made her own decisions. There was nobody to blame but herself. Waking, she saw that Hamish still sat beside her bed. He must be anxious. He was also easily bored, taking after her.

'Why don't you read a book?'

'Wouldn't you mind?' He hated the twist in her lovely face.

'Why should I mind?'

'Seems a bit insensitive.'

'I'm not sensitive but I keep my promises.'

'Of course. Don't tire yourself talking.'

'It's wonderful to find I can. You are a promise.'

'What?'

'Glad I made it.' His mother's eyes smiled. He felt closer to her than he ever had. Perhaps she was dying? Hamish bent and kissed her.

'Not dying yet.' Her twisted mouth smiled. 'Not this time.'

She had gone home after putting her uncle on the train, taking the Underground from Paddington to St James's Park, then walking through the dark streets. She put her key in the door and pushed it open. Hector was standing in the hall.

'I thought you were visiting your constituency.' Calypso was suddenly very tired.

'I decided to go tomorrow instead.'

'Oh.' Calypso walked past him and up the stairs.

'I wanted to say I'm sorry.'

She stood on the stairs looking down. 'Do you behave like that often?'

'I thought you'd walked out on me.'

'Do you behave like that often?'

'Not very often. Darling, I wanted to say I'm sorry.'

'Now you've said it.' She started on up the stairs.

'Calypso, I've said I'm sorry. Will you forgive me?'

'No.'

'Calypso, I'm sorry, darling, I'm sorry.'

'Why didn't you warn me?'

'If I had you wouldn't have married me.'

'Oh yes I would.'

'Why?'

'For your money.'

'Bitch.' Hatred stretched between them, tangible, horrible. They stared at one another across the chasm. 'It's my fault,' he said.

'Mine too, now.' Infinitely tired, Calypso held the banister. 'I've been putting Uncle Richard on the night train.'

'Oh my God, it started with him, stupid man trapped me in the bar.'

'So I gather.' Coldly she spoke, she felt numb with misery. 'I'm cold, I'm tired.'

'It won't –'

'Oh yes it will. I may be only nineteen but I know it happens again and again. I know that much – I'm twenty next week.'

'Twenty. Oh God, Calypso, don't leave me.'

'I'm not leaving you.'

'Why not?' He stood in the hall looking up at her, eyes strange under the thick eyebrows. 'Daphne left.'

'I'm not Daphne.'

'I didn't love Daphne. I do love you.'

'It doesn't matter whether you do or not. I'm not in love with you. To be honest, I don't think I'm the sort of girl who can love. I married you for your money and to give you an heir. That's the deal, whatever way you wrap it up. I'll keep my word and I hope you won't get drunk and violent too often. I promise I'll keep it. I only hope he's not a sod like you.'

'We'll make a fine pair of parents,' Hector shouted up the stairs. Then – 'What the hell are you laughing at?'

'I left your – Oh Hector, I left your precious car at Paddington. I took it to go and see Polly then I took Uncle Richard to Paddington in it. Oh!' she wailed. 'Your precious car. I came home by Underground, forgot I'd had the car. Oh!' She gave a whoop of laughter. 'It's by Platform One.'

'And the keys are in the ignition, I suppose?'

'Yes, they are. Why are you laughing?'

'Because you are so funny. I'll ring the police about it, then I'm coming to bed.'

'Not with me, you're not. I'm not keeping that promise tonight.'

'I wouldn't ask you to. I'm too bloody tired. I've been working like a dog all day with the most diabolical hangover.'

'And bad conscience.'

'That, too.'

'It was months later,' Calypso whispered to Hamish.

'What was? Don't tire yourself.'

'Months later I kept my promise. I never let him promise, it would have been too humiliating.'

'What would have been humiliating?' Hamish wondered whether her mind was affected by her stroke.

'Never mind,' she said and reached for his hand. 'Look, I can move my arm. I shall get well.'

13

Oliver telephoned. 'Can you have dinner with me?'

'When?' Calypso lay on the sofa.

'Tonight. Please. I'm going away.'

'Where?'

'I'll tell you when I see you. I'll come round at once.'

She met him at the door. 'Darling Olly.' She hugged him.

'I'm going to Norway.'

'Oh, my God! Hector says it's ill-fated. Why you?'

'They want people who know mountains. They are even flying chaps from India who've done mountain warfare. I'm being given a commission.'

'What about your principles?'

'No commission no action, so I take it. I've been so bored doing nothing, it's demoralizing.'

'Where shall we go? Hector's in the House, won't be back till late.'

'Berkeley?'

'Fine. I'll dress.'

'No, don't waste time.'

'Talk to me while I tidy, then.'

Oliver followed her to her bedroom. 'You do live in style.'

'Nice, isn't it? I'm changing the house quite a lot. Hector doesn't mind what I do here as long as I don't interfere in Scotland.'

'What's that like? Antlers and kilts?'

'It's Hector's place,' she said drily.

He watched her brush her hair, touch up her face, put

on a coat, move about the room. He kept his eyes away from the bed. Hector's bed, her rich husband.

'Polly's got a bigger one.' She stared at him from the mirror, a finger smoothing her eyebrows.

'Bigger what?' She'd noticed.

'Bigger bed. She's moved into her mum's room to have the telephone near her. It's not so high up if she gets bombed.'

'I suppose there will be raids sometime. Hurry up, Calypso, I'm starving.'

'I must just telephone.'

Oliver waited impatiently. Calypso appeared to be breaking an engagement. She rang off.

'Who was that?'

'Just someone I was having dinner with tonight. I can go out with him any time.'

'Like that sailor?'

'He was only in London for a night.'

'Like me.'

'I didn't know him like you. Did you take Sophy out faute de mieux?'

'Polly left her alone.'

'I bet she enjoyed it. Sophy is going to be a beauty. She adores you.'

'She loves us all because we are so much older.'

'We represent glamour.'

They walked along the street. Oliver held Calypso's arm. She wore an expensive fur coat, smelled of scent, clipped along in high heels. He remembered holding her on the cliff, the feel of her breasts. He stopped a taxi. They got in.

'You smell different.'

'So will you when you get your new uniform.'

They sat side by side in the restaurant. Calypso knew people at other tables. She waved.

'Tell me about your rich husband.'

'He's busy. He's clever. He's ambitious. He's doing well. He will do better. He visits his constituency. He lets me do what I want, within reason.'

'Are you happy?'

'I've got what I want.'

'That's not the same thing.'

'When do you go to Norway?'

'I wouldn't be allowed to tell you if I knew. I leave London tomorrow, tonight, really, at dawn.'

'I see.'

'What about my comforts? You swore you'd sleep with me.'

'Did I?'

'You know you did. I'm off to war.'

'I keep my promises. Where shall we go?'

'I'm not staying anywhere. I telephoned from the station. Not your house.'

'Where, then?'

'Mine? My parents are away. I have the key. Let's go there.'

'All right.' She was docile. They drove to his home. The house was dark, the flower-boxes on the balcony empty. Oliver put his key in the lock and pushed. A bit of newspaper rustled in the hall. No light came on when he pressed the switch.

'It's empty. They've moved the furniture. You knew?' He held her arm.

'Aunt Sarah told me. They've taken a house in Bath near your father's war job, moved everything there.'

'You bloody bitch. I shall fuck you on the floor.'

'Not in this coat you won't. Hector said if I bought mink I must make it last.'

'Damn and blast Hector.'

'Oh, well.'

'Come in. They may have left something, a sofa, a bed, a carpet.' He pulled her into the house, slamming the door. Holding hands they climbed the stairs, their feet loud on uncarpeted boards. They stood in the drawing room, empty, the long windows black, the trellised balcony just visible.

'How damnable.'

'You explore. I'm afraid of breaking a leg. I won't run

85

away.' She listened to him walking about the house, his feet stamping in their Army boots. He came back.

'You can lie on my uniform.'

'That scratchy thing!'

'I'm randy as hell.'

'I'm not. I'm cold.'

'You promised.'

'I know I did. Let's go to Polly's, see if she's in.' She took his hand. 'Come on, Olly, have some sense.' He pressed himself against her, pushing her against the wall.

'Not a tuppenny upright!'

'All right, we'll go to Polly's. I bet she's out or having a party. This is bloody hell.' He slammed the door. They were out in the street walking.

'I've got a large sofa.'

'I don't want a sofa or your rich husband's bed.'

'You are hoity-toity.'

'No I'm not. I suggested the floor.'

'And I refused.' They walked along, he holding her arm. 'It's not that I'm unwilling, Olly, it's just, well, I do like a bit of comfort when I make love.'

'You don't know what love is.'

'I don't think I do.'

'This is the street, isn't it?'

'Yes.' They stood and rang the bell, looking up at the blacked-out windows.

'She's very particular about her blackout is Polly.' He could see her neck as she looked up at the house white against the black mink collar. 'But she doesn't answer the bell. Polly's out.'

'What's the time?'

'One-thirty. What about an hotel?'

'I haven't got enough money.'

'I've got money.'

'I don't want your rich husband's money.'

'My sofa?'

'Your husband will be back.'

'Probably, but he'll be asleep.'

86

Oliver put his arms round her, holding her close to him. 'You used to smell of camomile and salt.'

'Oh Olly, dear Olly, that was so long ago.'

'Last August.' He kissed her hard. 'I'll walk you home. I'm not randy any more.'

When they reached her street she felt very tired. Her feet were hurting. 'Better luck next time.'

'I may not come back.'

'We'll arrange it better. Take care of yourself. Of course you'll come back.'

Oliver gave her a push and watched her until she reached her door and let a shaft of light escape as she opened it. Then it closed and he began a long walk to the station, to the train, to the camp, to the war which for him was beginning at last.

Calypso got into bed beside Hector, who sleepily put an arm round her.

'Where have you been?'

'Having dinner with Oliver. He's off to Norway.'

'Poor devil. It's a crazy mission.'

'He's got a commission.'

'So have I.'

'What?' She sat up.

'Lie down, you are letting the cold in. Snuggle up.' He smelt of cigars.

'I hate cigars. What did you say?'

'Got a commission, it came through today. In the Guards. Can't leave it all to the young boys. It's a nice surprise for you.'

'Oh, no!'

'Aren't you pleased?'

'No, I'm not. You'll go away.'

'You won't mind.'

'Yes, I shall.'

'You'll get used to it, sweetie. I'm forty-four. I don't suppose they'll let me do anything dangerous. If I'm sent overseas I'll send you up to Scotland where you'll be safe.'

'Oh no you won't. I'm staying here, whatever happens.

I'm quite fond of you,' she said, snuggling up. 'How nice and warm this is.' She thought of Oliver and sighed. Hector slept, turning away from her.

Oliver sat, crushed among others, sleepless in the train taking him back to camp. Soldiers sang in the next compartment. Wryly Oliver thought how bad their songs were compared to the last war's.

14

When the Erstweilers reappeared from internment the Rectory was full of evacuees. Helena, using Richard's leg as a pretext, had escaped her quota of unwilling London children but was glad to welcome Monika and Max as paying guests. In camp the Erstweilers had not been idle. In a way they had rather enjoyed it. While Max found friends with similar interests, Monika discovered a cousin in international banking who was prepared to chance his arm and help them financially. They were no longer humiliatingly penniless. Max, using introductions from musical friends, started a cat's cradle of correspondence which was to lead first to employment in orchestras up and down the country and soon to playing solo in London.

Helena, tone deaf and uninterested in the arts, had not realized the Erstweilers' former position in Vienna, Prague and other European cities and found herself playing second fiddle to Richard, who emerged in the guise of a lover of music, a taste she had never suspected he had. His knowledge of the subject was, she discovered to her annoyance, considerable.

Max's English was poor. Richard made himself busy translating his mittel-European letters into plain English, bought a typewriter and became Max's secretary and adviser.

With Monika's help Helena adjusted to the changes brought about by the war. Her first hurdle was the disappearance of domestic staff. It had never occurred to her to manage the house on the cliff with less than three servants. Daisy, the parlour maid, was the first to defect, giving in her notice and going home to her parents' farm to become a land-girl. Janey, who had housemaided for years without complaint, left to join the A.T.S. When Max and Monika arrived Helena was managing alone with Cook, a placid woman fond of Helena, agreeable to Richard, devoted to Sophy and exhilarated by the annual visits of the nephews and nieces. Whereas Helena was relieved to be spared the threat of evacuee children by the advent of the Erstweilers, she was not prepared for their effect on Cook.

Monika, eager to make herself useful, helped in the house, proving better and quicker at sweeping, dusting and polishing than Helena, clever at ironing, quick to make labour-saving, comfort-enhancing suggestions which Helena would never have thought of. It was when she moved into the realm of food that clouds gathered.

It began on the two women's walks together. Monika picked herbs and berries and brought them home. She acquired a clove of garlic and showed Helena how to grow it.

'If you grow herbs and garlic, darlink, we will transform the rations.'

'Richard won't eat garlic, he hates it.'

'Do not tell him, he will not know. I will tell Cook.'

'Do you think that wise?'

'Helena, she must learn. I find her throwing away sour milk.'

'Well, if it was sour –'

'She must make cheese! She must use it for cooking.'

'I don't want to upset her.'

Monika smiled. 'All right,' she said, 'don't worry, I am going to the woods. Also yoghourt!' she called over her shoulder as she set off inland with Richard's dachshund, sadly in need of exercise. Helena waved and called after her, 'Yoghourt.'

'Helena is learning German.' Richard looked up from the letter he was translating.

'It is food.' Max's brow was furrowed. 'I need a music

stand, a piano and a stool. I cannot work without.'

'I'll ring the General. He had a piano at one time, his mother's.'

The General refused to part with the piano. 'I'm not lending it to the enemy.'

'Look here, old boy, he's not the enemy. He's a refugee working for us, I ask you.'

'Call that work? Why doesn't he join the Home Guard, not that they'd have him. Chap's a spy, making a fool of you. Get him to do something useful. You heard what's happened to the hounds.'

'You put them down.'

'So I did, but the farmers have collected others, formed their own pack, not going to be done out of their fun. It's mutiny.' The General laughed. 'Rather enterprising. Showed the proper spirit, even had the nerve to ask me for a subscription.'

'Did you give them one?'

'Said I'd think about it. I'm rather in favour of a mounted Home Guard.'

'What for?'

'Get an allowance of corn. Be able to keep my horses. Damn good idea, if you ask me.'

'What about that piano? It's in a good cause.'

'What good cause?'

'Entertaining the troops, boost morale. Let me bring Erstweiler over to look at it. You never use it, it just sits in your house. There's a war on, I ask you.'

'Oh, very well,' the General grumbled.

Max got the piano and had it tuned. The Rector found a music stand. Monika returned from the woods full of hope for the autumn crop of fungi to enrich their diet, but long before the autumn Cook left. Monika was making yoghourt. Cook went to Birmingham to work in a factory, a move she had been planning for months. Helena wrung her hands while Monika moved smoothly into the kitchen to produce Continental meals both delicious and nutritious and still found time to accompany Max on the piano when needed.

'She's taken over everything,' Helena wailed down the telephone to Sarah in Bath. 'I'm left with nothing but the shopping and driving the car.'

'You should be thankful,' said Sarah. 'You hate cleaning and can't cook. Consider yourself lucky. I wish I had some Erstweilers.'

'But the drawing room's become a music studio. I can't go in without appearing to interrupt.'

'You will find some solace. Our three minutes are up.' Sarah, with no news of Oliver in Norway, had little sympathy for Helena. Where was Oliver? Dead or alive? News gleaned from the wireless was of retreat. Desperately anxious, she telephoned Calypso. Could Hector get news?

'No, Aunt Sarah, he knows no more than you. Try Polly.'

'What good would she be?'

'She works in an office which is in the know –'

'But she's not allowed to tell.'

'There is that. If I hear a whisper from any quarter I'll give you a ring.'

'If there's any news he'll get it to you, he loves you.'

'I did get a letter,' Calypso admitted.

'What did it say? Quick, tell me.' The line from Bath was faint but Sarah's anxiety strongly conveyed.

'Nothing much. It was censored. He just said, "This is worse than the Terror Run".'

'That game you all played? What does it mean, for God's sake?'

'I don't know. Don't worry, he'll be back safe.' Calypso knew well enough what the message meant. Oliver was afraid. She telephoned Polly. 'Polly, Aunt Sarah's having kittens about Oliver. Have you any tit-bit of news in your office?'

'Nothing good.' Polly was cagey.

'The radio says they are retreating and Hector is pretty glum about it.'

'I can't tell you anything, it's no use asking me. I don't know and if I did I couldn't tell you.'

'Damn and blast!'

'Come round and have supper. Are you doing anything?'

'Twiddling my thumbs.'

'Come to supper. I've got a friend here who wants to meet you.'

'Would I like him?' Calypso was doubtful.

'Yes. Light entertainment. Just the job.'

'All right,' said Calypso, 'but I can't stay late, Hector said he'd be back tonight.'

'There you are, she's coming.' Polly turned to the man beside her. 'I promised you should meet her, didn't I?'

'You did.' He grinned.

'Mind you are nice to her.'

'I always am, surely.' He looked pleased.

'You can take her home after supper. I want an early night.'

'But Polly –'

'But Polly's had enough, so off you go.'

'Are you giving me my congé?'

'Yes. That was the arrangement. It's worked very well, now it's over. Thanks a million and all that.'

'You are a cold-blooded bitch.'

'No, no,' said Polly, laughing, 'just practical.'

'I've grown very fond of you. You've used me.'

'Yes,' said Polly, 'I have. You've been an investment, a tutor.'

'You've behaved like a young man in a brothel!'

'Any why not?' said Polly who was ahead of her time.

'Polly was ahead of her time,' Helena said to Hamish years later, driving down the motorway. 'And if you go on driving as fast as this you will cut your time short.'

'She must have been a very attractive girl.' Hamish slowed down a little. 'Irritating, too,' he added, knowing that Helena liked to gossip.

'Yes, she could be irritating to some people but only if they were too pleased with themselves, got too big for their boots.'

'Like me?'

'I daresay yours fit a bit tight, you are your mother's child.'

'Was she pleased with herself?'

'I wouldn't say that. She just knew, how could she not, that she was the most lovely girl around.'

'I bet she gave a lot of pleasure. Did she ever suffer? I've often wondered.' Calypso's son probed.

'I wouldn't know, my dear. Your mother is as proud as she is beautiful.' Helena closed her eyes. I must pretend to doze, she thought, else I will be disloyal to Calypso and damage her child. She never really loved, so how could she suffer? 'I stood on the sidelines and watched.' Helena glanced at Calypso's son. 'They were all so young. Mine was the older generation. Not that I was altogether idle,' she added, half to herself, and Hamish wondered what so ancient and shrunken a creature could have been like when his mother was twenty.

'She was twenty when I was born.'

'About that. She got her figure back instantly, I remember. Slim, she was.'

'She still is.'

'I was plump.' Helena thought back to the days when Hamish was born. 'Some men like women plump. I was the same age as your father, of course, not that he ever looked at me,' she added as the car swerved slightly. 'A very attractive man, your father. He liked slim girls.'

'Who liked them plump?' Hamish played along with reminiscence. 'Apart from Great-uncle Richard, I mean.'

'Poor Richard. He knew a lot about music, or so he thought.'

'You are using my father as a red herring,' said Hamish, using guesswork.

'You are not stupid.' Helena was amused in her eighties, remembering what she had gained when she lost her drawing room. It had not occurred to her, until she found herself on her back in the daffodil field, to consider Max Erstweiler as a lover. Having been married so long to Richard she had thought herself past that sort of thing.

15

Sophy and other girls crossing London at the end of term were escorted to Liverpool Street by a mistress who handed them over to their relatives. Helena informed Polly of the times of arrival and expected her to meet Sophy, keep her for as long as necessary and put her on the next convenient train to Cornwall. Helena ignored the fact that Polly worked and might not be able to take time off.

To overcome this difficulty Polly had given Sophy instructions to pretend to recognize anyone who approached her with glad cries of 'Sophy, how are you?' so that any suspicious mistress would be deceived. 'If I can't come myself, ducks, I'll send a friend.' Rather apprehensive to begin with, Sophy learned to enjoy the variety of her escorts, in the event mostly men. She was met by soldiers, sailors, airmen, Free French, Dutch, Poles, on one occasion a turbanned Sikh and latterly by Americans. It never occurred to her to wonder how these strangers recognized her. If she had thought she might have supposed Polly had shown a snapshot. She never knew that Polly's orders were, 'Look for a thin chinky child with black hair and slant eyes who looks like a Siamese cat. She stands out among the goosey English.'

At half term in 1940 she was met by the twins, who greeted her with cries of 'Hullo, Soph-ophy-ophy, give us a kiss. You're not to go home, you're to spend half term with us.'

'Oh, goody, where?'

'With Polly. We are building her a shelter. You can help,' said Paul.

'She says she'll never go down to a shelter so we are reinforcing her bed.'

'When are these raids, then?' Sophy had learned to be sceptical.

'They will come, never fear,' said the twins, bundling her into a very old car they had bought for five pounds. 'We can't have our Polly in more danger than she need be.'

'She hasn't noticed,' said David to Paul. 'She hasn't noticed our elevation, have you, Sophy?'

'What?' said Sophy.

'You haven't noticed us.'

'You look exactly the same, more so than ever. Oh, I see,' she exclaimed. 'You've become officers. How grand!'

'What else?'

'Wings. Oh gosh, you've got wings!'

'Pilot Officers with wings on leave. We're posted. We've been home, now we've got three days in London.'

'Any news of Oliver?' Sophy did not want to ask but did.

'No,' they said soberly. 'No. He'll be all right, bound to be.'

They showed her the shelter, a corrugated iron canopy above Polly's bed, strongly supported by struts and stays. 'A wartime four-poster.'

'Is she pleased?'

'She doesn't know. You can paint it while we finish it off. We could only get moss green; it doesn't look too bad. We want to get it finished before she gets back from her office.'

Sophy enjoyed that hot June day making sandwiches, answering the telephone when Polly called to find out whether she had arrived and later telephoning Calypso, asking her to come round and see the twins.

'I can't. I'm in bed with a throat, can hardly speak. Give them my love.'

The twins opened the windows to lessen the smell of paint and sent Sophy to Harrods to buy ribbon. As children they had built a tree house in the Rectory garden; reinforcing the bed recaptured for a day their childhood delight. When Polly came home the canopy was overhanging the bed, the struts bound around with pink and yellow ribbons. She said: 'Oh, twins!' She put her arms round them. 'You darlings! I love it and I love you.'

'We must have you safe,' they said, hugging her.

'Christ Almighty! What is going on?' Walter, carrying a bottle of gin, appeared from nowhere.

'Walter, I thought you were in Portsmouth.' Polly hugged him.

'I was. I'm on my way to Plymouth to another bloody destroyer. It's total hell, sadistic bastards.'

'Who?'

'The Admiralty. Can I stay the night? I'll take you all out to dinner.'

'It's your home as much as mine.' Polly was indignant.

'I keep meeting people who've stayed the night. I just wondered whether there was a bed.'

'They are often your friends.'

'Let's go out while the smell blows away. Sophy, you've grown.'

Sophy felt happy with Polly, the twins and Walter with his squashy face. She was glad Calypso couldn't come, glad a sore throat kept her away.

Walter rang her up. 'Says not to come near her, she feels rotten. Must be, she's missing some do she was going to with Hector. She had been looking forward to it, says she hopes he'll be all right on his own. Quite the little wife, our Calypso.'

'Yes,' said Polly, 'er – yes.' Then, 'Come on, Sophy, put on a pretty dress, I'm going to.'

Calypso answered the telephone in a husky croak when it rang beside her bed.

'Can I speak to Calypso?'

'Oliver! We all think you're dead, it's months –'

97

'I'm not. I got back a while ago but I've only just got to London. What's this sexy voice?'

'I'm very ill – tonsillitis. Nearly dead.'

'Coming to dinner with me? You promised.'

'I can't. I'm in bed. Doctor's orders.'

'Oh come on, I've booked a table.'

'I'm very ill. Hector's had to go to a party without me.'

'Good.'

'And I couldn't go out with Walter, Polly and the twins. They're all there with Sophy. I'm stuck in bed.'

'Get up and come out. Dinner with me won't kill you.'

'I mustn't. The doctor says –'

'You bloody well must –'

'I've got a temperature.'

'I don't care. Meet you in half an hour at the Berkeley.'

'Feeling rich?'

'Nothing to spend my pay on in Norway. Half an hour. Look sharp.' Oliver rang off.

They held hands through dinner. Calypso felt ill. Oliver refused to talk about Norway except to say it was 'awful, bloody awful. If the War Office hadn't interfered all the time we might have managed something.' He was bitter.

'How long have you been back?'

'Several weeks. I've been in bed, too.'

'Wounded?'

'Very slight. The trouble was fatigue. Retreating, as they call running away, is tiring.'

Calypso said nothing. This was another Oliver, very different from the Oliver who had come back from Spain. That man had been furious but intact. She said: 'If you hadn't been retreating in Norway you might have been in France. Incredible how many got back. Hector was sent down to Dover to meet them.'

'How nice for them. Being met by Hector would be the last straw.'

'Now, now.'

'Norway's forgotten now. All I hear about is heroic Dunkirk. Paddle steamers and dinghies helping the British Navy. Was Walter there?'

'Polly says he was. He rang up to say he hadn't been sick because it was calm. I haven't seen him because I'm so ill.'

'He's obsessed with seasickness. Wasn't he terrified by the bombing?'

'Polly didn't say. She was just glad he was all right.'

'Like me.'

'More cheerful than you. He wanted me to go out tonight, he sounded quite normal, said he was passing through London – like you – just tonight. I'm glad I'm not in Paris, it must be horrible. You wouldn't think anything had happened if you'd been in London lying in bed trying to swallow – ' Calypso rather wished she was back in bed. Oliver was poor company. He looked strained. Shell-shock was a state she had read about but never seen. She said: 'Were you, I mean, are you shell-shocked?'

Oliver laughed, his taut expression relaxing. 'Only demoralized. I've got a room in Half Moon Street, let's go there for a sex shock.'

'What, now?'

'Yes. I'm not hungry. You're not eating anything, either.'

'I can't swallow.'

'That won't prevent –'

'Oliver, I can't, I'm infectious.'

'Try not to be silly, stop prevaricating.'

'Have you told your mother you are back?'

'Not yet.'

'You must, she's in agonies of anxiety.'

'I will. Soon.'

'Do it now. Then I'll come with you to your room.' She led him to the telephone. 'I'll get the number for you.' Calypso watched Oliver's strained face as she got through to Sarah in Bath. 'Aunt Sarah? It's me, Calypso. No, only tonsillitis. Aunt Sarah, Oliver is here – ' She handed the receiver to Oliver, who listened a moment.

'Yes, I'm all right. Yes, I'll come down tomorrow. No, don't. I'm quite recovered, it wasn't serious. Tell Father

99

I got a medal, he'll like that. What for? What medal? Oh, an M.C. for being the last to leave. Couldn't run as fast as the others. See you tomorrow.' He rang off. 'Why do mothers cry?'

'It's relief.' Calypso held his hand as they walked along the street. 'I wonder whether I shall cry for my child?'

'Are you pregnant?'

'Not yet. I've put it off. I shall put my mind to it soon. I promised Hector.'

'You promised me my comforts long before you met Hector. Here we are.'

'Why didn't you tell me you'd got a medal?'

'I was looking forward to this.' He led Calypso into his room. 'Hope you don't mind, it's the only room I could get at short notice. Landlady's a tough old bird.' Oliver took off his coat and helped Calypso out of her dress. 'Come on, my love, hurry up.'

'The zip's stuck.' Calypso stood with her arms above her head. 'Not down, you fool. Pull it up and start again.'

'I believe you are doing this on purpose.'

'No I'm not. Oh God!' Calypso gave a yelp of pain as the zip pinched flesh. At the same moment the howl of the air raid siren began. 'Oh my God, an air raid! Hector will kill me if I get caught out in this.' She pulled the dress down and stood looking at Oliver with her hair tousled, mouth open. A heavy hand banged the door.

'Let me in, sir, there's a raid.'

'I know. I can hear.'

'I've got to see that the blackout is all right.'

'It is,' shouted Oliver, drawing the curtains.

'I must see for myself and in the bathroom. Let me in,' the angry voice cried. 'Our warden's a terror.'

Calypso stepped swiftly into a hanging cupboard. Oliver opened the door. 'I was just going to bed,' he said angrily.

'You alone? I thought I heard voices. I don't allow my lodgers to bring ladies in.'

'Just fix the blackout and push off.'

'Aren't you going to take cover?'

'No! All well now? Had a good peek round? Goodnight, then. Have a good raid.' He closed the door after her and pulled Calypso out of the cupboard. 'What d'you want to hide in there for?'

'It's Hector.'

'It was my nosy landlady.'

'I have to be careful because of Hector. If he found out he'd kill me. Oh, look at my hair.' She began to comb it. 'Goodness, I feel ill. Will you take me home, Olly, please. I don't think I can be of much comfort –'

'You do sound a bit hoarse, now I come to listen.'

As they walked across Green Park towards Westminster the All Clear sounded.

'I don't think the Furies want me comforted.'

'It's midsummer night. Do hurry, Oliver. It won't be all clear unless Hector comes home to find me safely in bed. I don't want to get myself divorced.'

'Don't fuss, it's not late. What's midsummer night got to do with us?'

'Nothing. I just thought – well, Hector said this morning that it's midsummer day and we've had the most wondrous summer so far. Hector loves hot weather.'

'Damn and blast Hector, may he fry in hell.'

'I forgot to tell you. He's in the Army now, got a commission in the Guards.'

'I hope he gets killed. Here's your street.'

'Oh good, he went in the car and it's not back. We don't seem to be very lucky, do we?' She put her arms round Oliver's neck and kissed him. 'I'd better run or he'll be back before I am in bed.' She fled down the street. Oliver watched, leaning against a lamp post, until some time later the Lagonda drew up and, resplendent in Blues, Hector stepped out, locked the car and let himself into the house. Unwilling to go back to Half Moon Street, Oliver walked across the park and down Knightsbridge until he found himself outside his aunt's house. Looking down the area steps he saw a chink of light and heard laughter. He ran down. Round the kitchen table sat Polly, Walter, Sophy and the twins.

'Oliver!' they cried, surprised and joyous. Oliver sat down at the table, rested his head on his arms and wept. Sophy came to stand by him, he put out a hand and she held it between hers.

On her way to the funeral years later, Polly remembered that night. 'What a fool Oliver was,' she said aloud. 'Such a fool.'

'I should have thought that was the last thing one could say about him,' said her son, who was one of Oliver's admirers.

'I'm entitled to my opinion,' said Polly, 'he was a fool.'

Then, sensing her son's disagreement, she spoke with the irritation she had felt all those years before. 'He was obsessed – crazed.'

'About what?'

'Calypso.'

'Well, I never!' said Iris, Polly's daughter. 'She's so artificial.'

'That's because she had a stroke, idiot,' said her brother.

'No, it was a face-lift,' said Iris, knowing best.

'She's had both a lift and a stroke,' James persisted, knowing better still.

'Stop wrangling, you two,' Polly flared up. 'How horrible you are.' She switched on the car radio to drown their voices and drove faster. She shouted above the pop music – 'She is honest.' Polly's son and daughter, sitting on the back seat so that Polly's mongrel could sit beside her, looked at one another in an effort to deduce what exactly their mother meant by honest in relation to Calypso.

16

Max Erstweiler was so excited by the success of his first wartime concert that he was unable to sleep. He telephoned Helena, who was staying with Polly. 'I want you to come out with me, I am restless.'

'But Max, I am just going to bed. Polly has made us a hot drink, we are tired.'

'You must walk with me. You do not know the musical soul.'

'Can't you walk alone?'

'Don't be feeble, Aunt,' Polly whispered in her ear.

'If I am stopped I might be interrogated. I must have you to translate. I need to find calm by walking. I come at once.' He rang off.

'Aunt Helena,' said Polly, rinsing her cup at the sink, 'that man is making use of you.'

'He needs me. He is an alien.'

'I quite see he needs moral support, but dragging you out now! We've been to his concert, we all clapped until our hands were sore! Why didn't Monika come?'

'She is afraid of the air raids.'

'Aren't we all. There's no raid tonight. She could have come. Lots of us live with them, work through them. Why is she so terrified?'

'She just is. He will be round in a moment.'

'But you're tired, Aunt.'

'Not really, no.'

'He's treating you as though you were his mistress. Oh!' Polly caught Helena's expression. 'Are you?'

'Don't be ridiculous.' Helena was blushing.

'Oho, I see.'

'No, you don't.' Helena was quick to deny a situation which was already established but which she was not prepared to discuss with Richard's niece. 'The poor man is highly strung, he needs –'

'An audience. I shall go to bed. I have to be up early.' Polly kissed her aunt.

'I suppose you realize it's two in the morning.' She opened the door to Max.

'What about it?' Max came in. He did not at that time much like Polly, who resisted his charm. 'I like to see cities in their sleep. Come, Helena,' he called down the kitchen stairs and Helena obediently called back, 'Coming, Max.'

Polly got into bed resolving to telephone Calypso next day, for Calypso, watching Helena helping with the preparations for the concert, had said: 'Aunt Helena is having a canter with Max Erstweiler.'

Polly had mocked this theory on the grounds that their aunt was too old.

'She is a year younger than Hector,' Calypso had said.

'But he is a man, that's different.'

'I bet you I am right. I wonder how it began? If Sophy had not been sent to school she would know.'

'She wouldn't necessarily tell us.'

'She would if we asked her indirectly.'

Remembering this conversation Polly curled up under the corrugated iron canopy and slept, so tired that she did not hear the siren wail to alert London to attack. There had been no news of Walter for weeks, and no sight of the twins since the beginning of what was later known as the Battle of Britain. All she knew was that each had been shot down once and survived. For all their cheerfulness when they telephoned, they sounded tired and frightened. That Helena should be having an affair with Max Erstweiler afforded light relief in a world of black anxiety.

* * *

'The war was very romantic,' said Helena all those years later, driving down the motorway with Calypso's son Hamish.

'Surely not, Great-aunt.'

'Surely yes. Why, Max and I went to Covent Garden at dawn and he bought flowers as they were unloaded from lorries. He filled a taxi with roses and carnations. He was exhilarated by his first concert in London. What a success! Those flowers! I can remember the smell now. We drove back as it grew light to Polly's house, where I was staying. It wasn't so romantic when we got there.'

'Not enough flower vases?'

'No. Someone had just woken Polly to tell her her parents had been killed by a stray bomb. They were somewhere near Godalming, near the hospital. Her father was a doctor, you know.'

'I didn't know.'

'They can't have known anything about it, but it was sad for Max after his concert.'

'Did he know them? Worse for Polly, surely.'

'No, but think of the embarrassment of all those flowers, and Polly so upset.'

'What happened to the flowers?'

'We told the taxi driver to take them to a hospital, but I expect he sold them. I kept some roses for Polly.'

'Not so romantic, then.'

'It was when he bought them. It is those moments one remembers. Oh, yes.'

'Nice to look back.' Hamish knew old people lived in the past. He was glad poor old Helena found it enjoyable.

'Nicer to think of him extravagantly buying flowers than to be on our way to his funeral. I'm not sending any flowers.'

'Have I done the wrong thing? I ordered a wreath,' said Hamish.

'Wrong? Right? You must do as you please. If it helps you to order a wreath, do. It can't help Max. A wreath isn't a lifebelt.'

Hamish resented his passenger's snappy tone. In an

effort to remain agreeable he said: 'Max Erstweiler must have loved you very much.'

'I suited him. He grew to rely on me. I taught him English manners and customs. I don't know about love. I loved him, I don't know whether he loved me as much.'

'What happened to his wife?'

'Monika? She worried, grew very thin. Max liked women plump. I was plump. Yes.'

'What was she worried about? You?'

'Oh no, no, no. Monika was quite used to Max's ways. She used to say he was worse than Furtwängler. Monika worried about their son.'

'Oh. Should I know him?'

'He was in a concentration camp. Pauli. You must have heard of him.'

'Oh dear. Yes.'

'News filtered through from Switzerland and poor Monika simply faded. Made no fuss, but she nearly died of anxiety.'

'Poor woman.'

'Well, it didn't help Max. Or suit him,' Helena added. 'No.'

'But you did.' Hamish's tone was congratulatory.

Helena smiled. 'Yes,' she said, looking back. 'Mind you, musical souls – you will remember he called himself "a musical soul"?'

'Yes, I remember, like Thomas Mann.'

'They can be extremely boring.'

'To the non-musical,' Hamish teased.

'To anybody. Those mittel-European tantrums. I never stood for them. I used to clap my hands and say, "Stop that, Erstweiler", and he did. Over-excitement made him play badly, not that I would have noticed, but that's what I was told, so I stopped him when I saw him working himself up. I'd say "Stop it, I say, stop it!" and he would laugh and call me his "Kleine British Phlegm".'

Helena laughed in ancient reminiscence.

'Not a very endearing pet name – Phlegm. I never heard him call you that. Nobody ever mentioned it.'

'It was private. He used it in bed, too.'

'Oh.' Hamish ruminated, allowing a motorcycle to overtake him. 'Why in bed, Great-aunt?'

'Does nobody ever tell you to stop?' enquired Helena with asperity.

'Sometimes,' said Hamish, laughing.

'Well, then.' Helena smiled, pressing her lips together, a habit she had formed when forced to have false teeth.

'It's very interesting to have you for a great-aunt,' said Hamish, seeing her face in the driving mirror, 'a great, a famous man's - er - '

'Mistress,' said Helena. 'No need to be coy, everybody knew then and now. Yes.'

'Now we are on our way to his funeral.'

'It's a bit thick.' Helena used a colloquialism of her period.

'What is?'

'To be the last of my lot. It's a bore. Yes.'

'You bear it very well.'

'Not inside,' said Helena, rummaging in her bag for a flask. 'D'you think you could slow down while I have a swig? Max envied me this flask, it was my first husband's.'

'Great-uncle Richard?'

'No, dear boy, I was married to a man with two legs, he was killed in 1916. You must get your facts right. Richard came next. He rather envied this flask, too. I shan't offer you any as you are driving.' Helena tipped the flask and swallowed. 'That's better.'

Hamish accelerated, moving smoothly down the M4. 'What was your first husband called?'

'Anthony. He was beautiful. I never had to tell him to stop. No.'

Hamish tried to imagine dried-up Helena as a sex object. Perhaps his mother or Polly had photographs. He must ask them.

'He was stopped almost before we began. Girls should comfort their men before they go to war.' Helena's voice sank to a mutter.

'What did you say? I didn't hear.'

'I said "however uncomfortable".' Helena put the silver flask back in her bag. 'Whatever the discomfort of comforting to the comforter. I did not fail there. No.'

'I'm sure you never failed.'

'Ho!' Helena laughed, exposing her teeth. 'Of course I failed. I was not expert like your mother.'

'My mother?' Hamish looked sidelong. Helena's face was wrinkled, like a Cox's Orange Pippin in January.

'I think if you don't mind stopping I shall buy some flowers, after all, when we get to Penzance. There's a good shop in Causeway Head.'

'It's a very narrow street.'

'But it has the best flower shop.' She would go no further about Calypso.

17

It was during the bombing in the autumn of 1940 that Helena bought two adjacent houses in Enderby Street. The price was low, the owners anxious to get away from London.

'You must be mad,' Richard yelled on the telephone from Cornwall.

'I am using my own money.'

'Throwing it away!'

'They are convenient for Harrods and Peter Jones.'

'They will be bombed, I ask you.'

'Not necessarily. No.'

'The General says you should see a psychiatrist.'

'So do my lawyer and my bank.'

'Why can't you stay in Sarah and George's house?'

'They have moved to Bath.'

'With Polly, then, as you are doing now? Buying houses in London is lunacy. That street is jerry-built. Not even solid. I ask you.'

'The houses are an investment. Our three minutes are up. Goodbye.' Helena turned to Polly. 'What's so funny?'

'You and Uncle Richard. Your three minutes were not up.'

'He was too cross to notice.'

'I know why you are buying those houses. Shall you have a communicating door?'

'What a good idea. Do you know a reasonable builder?'

'We can find one. You know, Aunt, you can always stay here.'

'Thank you, but this house is for the young. I want my own house. I shall enjoy furnishing it.'

'Why stop at a door? The two front rooms knocked together would make room for a grand piano. You can have musical soirées.'

'I think not. He's ruined my drawing room for me in Cornwall. Monika bangs away for him, it's no longer mine. Richard encouraged it. Oh no.'

'Then where will Max have a piano?'

'He has the use of a piano in Pont Street. He can go on using that, it's only a minute away.'

'You are tough.'

'Pont Street won't get bombed.'

'Why not?'

'It's too ugly. I refuse to have a piano in my house. No.'

Helena moved fast, finding a builder who was willing to decorate and plumb. By the end of October her houses were ready, sparsely furnished but comfortable. The communicating door was disguised as a bookcase. Monika, should she overcome her fears, could stay with Max with propriety.

On the evening when Calypso visited Polly, arriving on her bicycle before air raid time, she found Helena and Polly discussing furniture.

'What have you bought so far?' Calypso was interested.

'Beds,' said Helena, 'the best from Heals.'

'Very important. Hector had a frightful thing. He had slept in it with Daphne. It sagged in the middle. I bought a new one.'

'I thought they weren't close.'

'They weren't. Hector slept in his dressing room. Daphne's Great Dane slept with her. That's what Hector says, one can't be sure.'

'I shall collect furniture from damaged houses. Prices will be astronomical if we survive the war. I shall pick up antiques.'

The girls looked at one another, amused. 'Rather a gamble,' suggested Calypso.

'Worth taking,' said Helena. 'Goodnight, girls.'

'There's a lot more in Aunt Helena than I'd thought possible,' said Polly. 'What do you think Max is like in bed?'

'Better than Uncle Richard. By the way, I told Tony he could pick me up here when he comes off duty at eight. Is that all right?'

'Perfectly,' said Polly coolly. 'He seems to enjoy being a fireman. Who would have thought it?'

'You don't mind?'

'Why should I? He doesn't belong to me.'

'I rather thought he did.'

'I introduced you, didn't I?' Polly said equably.

'So you did, but I rather thought, well –'

'Only for a short time. Just long enough, actually.'

'Long enough?'

'Yes. Darling, do you imagine if he were mine that I'd allow you to meet?'

'Tony says he doesn't understand you.'

'Of course he does.'

'D' you think that's him? There's someone at the door. Are you expecting anybody else?'

'No.'

'He can see me home.'

'Is Hector away?'

'Yes, Aldershot. I haven't seen him for a week. I'll let him in, shall I?'

'Don't show a light.' Polly tidied the kitchen as Calypso ran upstairs to open the front door. She heard her exclaim and men's voices. Then Calypso came in, looking rather pink, followed by Tony and Oliver.

'Can you house me for a couple of days? I'm on embarkation leave.' Oliver kissed Polly.

'Of course.' Polly looked over his shoulder at Calypso. 'Did you meet Tony on the steps? Tony's a fireman. Are you going on duty or coming off, Tony?' Her smile showed her slanting teeth.

'Coming off,' said Tony, eyeing the girls, his expression conveying the words 'as well you know'. He said: 'I

111

saw your bicycle, Calypso. Someone might fall over it out there in the street.'

'Yes. Well, I'm just leaving.'

'I'll see you home,' said Oliver.

'My bicycle.'

'I'll wheel it, or run beside you.'

'Oh Olly, like a faithful dog.'

'Shall we go?'

Polly and Tony listened to them leave.

'Did she know he was coming?' he asked suspiciously.

'No, Tony and nor did I.'

Tony laughed. 'I shall have to wait till his leave is over.'

'I suppose so. Would you like to meet our aunt?'

'Your aunt? Not particularly.'

'Helena. Max Erstweiler's chum.'

'That aunt. Yes, I would. Is she here?'

'Just gone upstairs. She's bought two houses near here. She's – well, you'd better meet her.'

'I saw her at his concert. She didn't look musical. A dumpy figure.'

'She isn't, but she's learning all sorts of tricks.'

'How do you know?'

'Not bed tricks, tricks of speech. She's taken to ending her sentences with yes or no, like *Ja* and *Nein*. Her life, once so dull, is now far from it.'

'Lead me to her.'

'Tony Wood became a great friend of Helena's,' Polly later told Iris and James as she drove them to the funeral.

'Really? Tony Wood? How did that come about? Isn't he homosexual?'

Polly took a hand off the wheel to stroke her mongrel dog. The dog continued to gaze ahead without acknowledgement. 'Well, he is, but at one time he was a great one for the girls. I'd call him ambidextrous.'

'Was he a friend of yours or Calypso's?'

'I introduced him to Calypso. We all shared him.

112

Hector found him amusing. Walter liked him, even Oliver grew to like him, I believe, later, but it was Helena who really caught his fancy. He was older than us, just that much nearer to Helena. She made use of his sophistication, he taught her a lot, it helped with Max.'

'I should have thought,' said James, 'that in the war, with the bombing and so on, there wasn't much time for private life.'

'That's where you are wrong,' said Polly. 'We all lived intensely. We did things we would never have done otherwise. It was a very happy time.'

'What about fear? What about anxiety for your loved ones?' Iris leaned from the back seat to speak to her mother.

'I was frightened and anxious all the time, but it made the delights all the more so, the surprises more surprising. People like Oliver, Walter, David and Paul appeared and disappeared, it was wonderful that they were still alive. My parents were killed. I thought they were safe in Godalming. In London I survived. Calypso survived. If we were in love it was acute. We had fun. I know Calypso did. I did and Helena, who had never had fun, grabbed it. Tony, who was in London all the war, watched us, was amused by us and in his way loved us. All the other men came and went but Tony was always around.'

'What about Oliver?'

'I saw him towards the end of 1940. Calypso had come to see me. He walked her home pushing her bicycle. She had a bicycle.'

Holding Calypso by one hand, Oliver pushed the bicycle with the other. Calypso used her torch with care. 'The wardens get awfully ratty if one flashes it about.'

'Is Hector in London?' Oliver asked stiffly.

'No. He may turn up but I don't think so. I haven't seen him for weeks. I'm alone. I'd come round to see Polly and find out what Aunt Helena is up to.'

'Who is that man?'

'Tony Wood. Friend of Polly's.'

113

Oliver, holding Calypso's arm, now said: 'I'm on embarkation leave.'

'Again? Where are you going this time?'

'I don't know. Not supposed to tell.'

'Egypt, I bet.'

'How do you know?'

'Hector and his friends talk. He was at Dunkirk, you know.'

'You said Dover last time I saw you.'

'Well, he went across to collect the French from Dunkirk, then further along to Cherbourg. Some of them are awfully jolly.'

'Jollier than me?'

'Much.' Calypso chuckled as they walked in the dark. 'One of them, a buddy of Hector's, rowed himself across to Dover, then got sent back to France only to have to bunk again. Lots of bunking, isn't there? Look at you in Norway.'

'Is this your street?'

'Yes.' Calypso was silent as they reached her house. 'Would you bring the bicycle into the hall?'

Oliver propped the machine against a radiator and took Calypso in his arms, kissing her neck gently. 'My darling.'

'Darling Olly. Nice sofa. Come.' She led him to her drawing room. 'I must pull the curtains. Take off your scratchy uniform. Oh, it isn't, I'd forgotten you'd become an officer, but take it off, I hate being squashed against buttons. Hector's make quite a pattern in groups of three, or is it four?'

'Being snobby about buttons won't put me off. You'd better unzip yourself this time –'

Calypso laughed, kicking off her shoes. Oliver watched her undress, then walk naked across the room to put logs on the fire. 'One of my luxuries, having a log fire. We get the logs from a friend of Hector's in Berkshire.'

'Stop talking. Come here.'

'I'm nervous.'

114

'No, you're not. Here. There.' He held her, stroking her back. 'Relax. Remember the camomile lawn – magic.'

'Helena planted it for our games, our plots.'

'Hush, pay attention.'

'Oh, Oliver, Oliver.'

'You didn't enjoy it. My God, you didn't enjoy it. Oh, damn and hell and blast.'

'I didn't say –'

'You didn't need to.' Oliver was collecting his clothes, pulling on his trousers, buttoning his shirt, tucking it into his trousers, putting on his tie, putting on socks and shoes in bitter concentration.

Calypso sat naked on the sofa watching him, her eyes in her pale face thoughtful. Below them the street door opened with a bang, then slammed shut. There was a clatter of collision with the bicycle, a man's voice: 'Whoops!'

Calypso snatched her dress, pulling it over her head, zipping it up. 'Hector.' She pushed her underclothes behind a cushion.

'Whoops-a-daisy.' The bicycle clattered again. Hector broke into song: 'And when I'm dead don't bury me at all.' He kicked the bicycle. 'Out of my way, weighy! Just pickle my bones in alcohol.'

Calypso, who had been listening intently, grinned. 'He's in a good temper. Thank God.'

'Is he often drunk?'

'Sometimes.' She was evasive.

'Violent?'

'I think you'd better go.' She went out on the landing and leaned over the banisters, looking down. Hector lay entangled with the bicycle. 'He's passing out,' she whispered.

'Shall I help you put him to bed?'

'No, no. I'll see you out from the kitchen, he's blocking the front door. Come on,' she said impatiently.

'Are you sure? Surely I can –'

'No. Please, Olly, go.' She took his hand, leading him

down to the basement, through the kitchen, up the area steps.

In the street he took her shoulders, looking into her face. 'Goodbye.'

'It was small comfort, I'm afraid. Better than none, I hope.'

Almost, Oliver thought, she minded. 'Better to know.' His voice was neutral. He kissed her lightly and was gone, his steps diminishing fast in the quiet street.

Calypso noticed the Lagonda at an angle to the pavement, its lights still on. She parked the car properly, switched off the lights. Back in the house she disentangled Hector's legs from the bicycle, fetched cushions to prop his head and blankets from the dressing room bed, making him as comfortable as possible, unbuttoning his tunic.

'What a pattern of buttons!' The affection in her voice surprised her. Hector opened his eyes, focusing carefully, squinting up.

'I'm drunk.'

'I know. Come to bed when you can.'

'I'm not. I'm not-er-er-what do I want to say? Calypso, don't leave me, stay here.'

She lay down beside him. He put an arm round her while she pulled the blankets up to cover herself.

'Come close.'

'Your buttons hurt.'

'Never mind.'

'I'm terribly uncomfortable.'

'Go to sleep.'

'D' you think you could get up to bed?'

'All fours.'

'I'll help you. Come on, try.'

'So drunk.'

'Yes. Try harder.'

Hector suddenly reared to his feet and headed up the stairs at a run. As she propped the bicycle against the wall she heard a crash and Hector laughing. She helped him undress, levering him out of his trousers. 'There, lie still.'

116

'The room's going round and round and it comes out here.'

'I'll make us some coffee.'

When she came back with the coffee Hector was asleep. Calypso drank coffee, watching Hector. He looked vulnerable, eyes closed under his thick eyebrows. She smoothed them gently with a finger and then ran it along his lips, which were slightly rough. Outside the All Clear sounded. She had not realized there was an alert. She put the light out and drew the curtains to look down at the street. Was it possible Oliver was still there? The street was empty.

As she stood looking down a special constable strolled round the corner. He was joined by an air raid warden. She saw them laughing. They walked along to Hector's car and admired it. The warden patted the bonnet as though it were the nose of a horse. Calypso turned to look at Hector whose eyes were open watching her.

'Hector?'

He pulled her down. 'Does my breath smell?'

'No.' She sniffed. 'Yes.'

'Get in with me. Would you mind?'

'No. What's the matter?' She slipped her dress over her head and got in beside him. 'What's the matter?'

'I'm on embarkation leave.'

'You too?'

'Who else?'

'Oliver.'

'Was he here?'

'Yes, he walked me home from Polly's.'

'He's in love with you.'

'He *thinks* he is.'

'And you?'

'No. I like all those boys. They are cousins, might be brothers.'

'There's incest.'

'Not for me.'

'I might be your father.'

'My father never behaved like you. Wild.'

117

'Ah me. Do you think there's any Alka Seltzer?'

'Yes. And coffee.' She brought him coffee. He drank and lay back with his arm round her shoulders.

'Will you go to Scotland? Stay there?'

'Oh *no!*'

'Would be safe.'

'But lonely. I hate it. I'd die of melancholy. When are you off?'

'Two weeks. Put my affairs in order. Get lightweight uniform.'

'Egypt?'

'Probably. I must do a dash north, will you come with me?'

'Of course I will, just for a day or two, not more.'

'I wish you'd stay there, safe out of London.'

'If London gets too bad I'll go to Cornwall. I'll take care of myself.'

'Promise?'

'Yes.'

'That man Tony Wood is in love with you too.'

'It isn't love, it's lust.'

'Do you know the difference?'

'I know lust. I don't think I know love.' Calypso leant her head back, closing her eyes.

'Lucky you, oh lucky, lucky you.'

'Why? I thought I was missing something.'

'You are, you certainly are.'

'What then?'

'Pain, lots of pain.'

'You do talk rubbish.' Calypso chuckled.

'If you say so,' said Hector dryly.

'I don't even know anyone who is in love. I don't think it exists.'

'Quite apart from me, it's under your lovely nose.'

'Who, for God's sake?'

'Helena, Polly, Sophy.'

'What a buffoon you are. Perhaps that's why I put up with you, apart from your money.'

'That reminds me, I must make my will.'

118

'What filthy bad taste.'

'I'm a hard-headed Scot.'

'You hurt me.'

'Good. Another time,' Hector's voice was turning nasty, 'please leave your bicycle where I won't fall over it.' They laughed together, relaxing.

'My mother says she and my father used to laugh together,' Hamish said conversationally to his passenger.

'Yes, they did. Calypso had very little humour, but then she had no love either, poor girl.'

'They say my father had humour.'

'He also had love.'

'Did he love my mother?'

'He adored her and he knew her.'

'What do you mean? You sound a bit,' Hamish hesitated, 'a bit, well, as though you didn't like my mother.'

'I like her, she's always been very nice to me, she's not a giver, that's all. She can't help her character.'

'She gave my father me.'

'You were part of a bargain. For his money an heir.'

Hamish pulled across to the slow lane and stopped the car.

'What's the matter? Something wrong with the engine?' Helena watched Hamish get out and stand with his back to her. He reminded her of Hector at his wedding long ago, tall, towering above Calypso, who was a tall girl.

'Did he love me?' Hamish got back into the car.

'He loved you very much.'

'Are you sure? I never really knew.'

'Quite sure. He was very happy about you. You are very like your father, less endearing, though.'

Hamish laughed. 'You are a wicked old woman.'

'I know I am.' Helena nodded. 'Evil.'

119

18

Polly answered the telephone. 'Oh, hullo Monika, how are you? Can you speak louder?'

'Polly, we only have three minutes, can you find Helena, it is urgent.'

'There's a raid on, try to speak louder.'

'*Mein Gott!* I want Helena. She does not answer her phone.'

'She's gone to Max's concert in Liverpool.'

'There are raids there too, *lieber Gott*. What is that noise?'

'A bomb.' Polly crept under the table, taking the telephone with her. 'Sophy and I are under the kitchen table. What do you want Helena for?'

'Richard is ill. I think and *der General* and *der Rektor* thinks she should come, and *Frau Rektor*.'

'I see. I'll try and get hold of her. She will be back in London tomorrow. How ill is he? What? I can't hear you,' Polly shouted.

'It was flu and now pneumonia.'

'Poor old boy. Gosh, that was close.'

'What did you say? Polly, are those bombs?'

'Yes,' yelled Polly. 'I'll do what I can. Don't worry, I promise.'

'We have bombs too in Penzance.'

'Yes, I heard about them.'

'They hit *der* wine merchant, your uncle got his chill trying to rescue his wine.'

'His *what*?'

'His wine. He had tree dozen clarets. They got

121

bomped.' Monika's voice faded. Polly clutched Sophy as she replaced the receiver.

'His claret!' The girls shrieked with laughter.

'You girls got hysterics?' Tony Wood came in from the street. 'It's quite lively tonight.'

'Aren't you on duty?'

'Just on my way, came to see if you were all right. What's Sophy doing here? You all right, Sophy?'

'Yes, thanks. My holidays have started.'

'If we can find Aunt Helena you can travel down with her.'

'I'd much rather go alone, thank you.'

'Safer with Helena. Plymouth has raids too, you have to go through it.'

'People always help. I'd rather be alone –' They all cowered, listening to the sound of a bomb coming down. 'Ouch, that was close.'

'Somewhere near the Brompton Road.'

'Wish I could leave my tin hat with you. Here comes another.' Tony put an arm round each girl. They listened. Not far away an anti-aircraft gun fired, pom, pom, pom – pom, pom, pom.

'And another. What time are you on duty?'

'In half an hour. Must leave you, I'm afraid. I brought you some whisky.'

'How good of you. Do be careful.'

'I'll be all right. And another! I always think of Peter Pan –'

'Captain Hook's trousers tearing.'

'Of course. Goodbye, girls, must be off.' Tony kissed the girls. 'Keep under that table.' He was gone.

'Nice of him to come, it's out of his way. Lovely whisky.'

'I wish Oliver was here. Have you heard from him?' Sophy came as close as she could to Polly.

'Aunt Sarah had a letter, he's in the Middle East. Safer than Walter on the Atlantic run. He says it's awful, sick all the time, non-stop.'

'Polly.'

'Yes?' They huddled together.

'You remember the Terror Run?'

'Of course I do. Yes, let's think of that. The sea, the moon, the camomile lawn.'

'I'm scared. I wish – I must tell.'

'It will be over soon. We will all be back there one day.'

'Polly, on the cliff path I –' The sound of a bomb very near drowned Sophy's voice. It fell close by and Sophy finished her sentence on a high note of fear, '– so I – it was just a push,' but Polly listened to the falling masonry and glass tinkling into the street and failed to hear what Sophy heard, the cry of a man, the sound of seagulls. She was concerned that Sophy wept and trembled in her arms. 'Don't, Sophy, that one was further away, it will be over soon. When the All Clear sounds I'll make some tea and lace it. There may be people hurt out there, we must help them. Tony's whisky will be welcome.'

'I tried to tell you.'

'Of course you did. Naturally. Listen. No guns, no planes. Ah, the All Clear. Pop up the steps and look, while I put the kettle on. I shall have to get hold of Aunt Helena if the telephone's working.'

Later, leaving Sophy to dispense tea to an assortment of bombed-out neighbours with tales of lucky escapes, Polly managed to get through to the hotel in Liverpool where she knew Max Erstweiler was staying.

''Allo. Erstweiler *hier*.'

'Max, do you know where Aunt Helena is? I'm trying to get hold of her. Monika rang up from Cornwall.'

'Monika?' Max's voice conveyed distrust. 'What she want?'

'She wants Helena.'

'What for she want Helena?' Max switched on the bedside light and prodded Helena, asleep beside him. Helena woke, saw Max's finger to his lips, the other hand holding the telephone.

'It is five in the morning.'

'I know it. Can you find Helena? Monika says Uncle

Richard is very ill. She and the Rector and the General think Helena should come.'

'I find her, ein Moment.' Max stuffed the telephone under the pillow. 'It is Richard, is ill, you should go to him.'

'Oh damn.' Helena pushed her hair back and pulled a shawl round her shoulders. She held out her hand for the receiver. 'Helena here. What's the matter? I only just got to sleep. There was a raid after Max's concert. It was a great success, the concert.'

'Aunt Helena, Monika tried to find you, Uncle Richard is very ill.'

'I knew he had flu.'

'Well, now he's got pneumonia.'

'How did he get that?' Helena listened to Polly's voice shouting eerily from London, a garbled explanation.

'His claret? Trying to save his claret? It is my claret. I thought we might run short, can't get rice either now. No, not mice, rice. No.'

Polly's voice suddenly sounded clear and angry. 'While you are waffling he may be dying. I'm putting Sophy on the ten o'clock train. If you can get to Bristol you could join it at Exeter.'

'Sophy?'

'Yes, her holidays have started. She's here but it isn't healthy. I have to work. I can't leave her in the house alone.'

'I'll leave as soon as I can. Can you get through to Cornwall? I can't. I tried last night. Max wanted to tell Monika about the concert,' Helena lied. She put the telephone down. 'Why does one lie?'

'Instinct.' Max was watching her, pink, amply rounded, blonde, the type he liked. 'You look like a Greuze.'

'What's that?' Helena was angrily brushing her hair. 'How inconvenient this is! Oh, do be of some help, find out about trains while I pack. Buck up. Just like Richard to rush out in the rain with flu. I bet all the claret was running down the gutter. Oh, why do I have to behave badly in times of crisis?' Helena wailed with frustration.

'Nimm   deine   Ihre   Arschbacken   zusammen,'
exclaimed Max.

'What's that?'

'A coarse German expression. I will enquire for
trains.'

'I'd forgotten Sophy's holidays, lost my head as well as
my heart.'

'You do not love me.'

'Not at the moment. *Do* go and ask about trains. There
will be some terrible cross-country connection. Hurry
up and do it.'

Sophy from her corner saw Helena puffing from another
platform at Exeter to join the train. She huddled back,
hiding her face with a book, having no wish to endure
Helena's company on the train, which stopped at every
station from Exeter to Penzance. She hid, even though
she suspected Helena had no more wish for her company than she for Helena's.

Crammed into an over-full carriage Helena reproached
herself for neglecting Richard, all too aware that since
the incident in the daffodil field she had discarded her
former life, left the running of her household to her
lover's wife, the care of Sophy to a school, with help in
the holidays from the Rectory. In her mind she saw herself and Max making love under a blue sky surrounded
by golden daffodils, ecstasy in the midst of war. She
ignored the truth, which was that the daffodil season
had long been over, the leaves withered to a dull straw
colour, that there were weeds among the bulbs and that
while slipping off her knickers she had been stung by
nettles. What was true was that the encounter with Max
had produced the first orgasm she had ever experienced
and in return she loved him with an aggressive devotion
he found touching and useful. It wasn't until now that
Richard was ill that she considered his feelings and felt
regret, tinged with guilt, about her new mode of life. She
had no intention of changing it. Another woman, a good

woman, would stand by Richard just because he was boring, just because he had lost a leg, just because he'd been gassed. 'Not me,' said Helena aloud, to confirm the course of her life. 'Not for me.' Her neighbour, a fresh-faced Wren, looked at her in surprise.

'I said there's no tea,' said Helena, 'no tea on this train. No.'

'Oh. Shall I get you a cup at Plymouth? I get off there. There is usually a buffet, unless the station has been disrupted by a raid.'

'It's very kind of you, but I think not, no.' The Wren went back to sleep. Helena planned ahead for her life in London. It was fortunate that Monika was terrified of raids and that Richard loathed London, only visiting it once a year to stay at his club for his regimental dinner, to meet his few remaining contemporaries. Now, with the war, there were no dinners for retired Majors, but opportunity for adultery for their wives. Helena considered the situation with wry amusement.

She had recently met Hector in the street and he had taken her into the Ritz bar. As they sat in the bar he had pointed to the people around them. 'Look at them all, not one with a wife or husband. All hell let loose. War makes people fearfully randy. It may not apply to you, or does it?' He had appraised Helena, sharp-eyed under his eyebrows. She had blushed. 'Well, good luck to you, old girl. Now I'm in the Army Calypso's out every night. She says she goes round to Polly but that's all my eye. She's picked up a friend of Polly's, that's true, Tony Wood, entertaining fellow, and she meets Oliver there. He's in love with her.'

'They were children together.'

'Ceci n'empêche cela! The poor chap's crazy about her.'

'She isn't about him.' Helena knew this in her bones.

'Maybe. Then there's Walter and those twins. Wouldn't blame her there. What a handsome pair! If one had a brougham and they were horses –'

'Those three are over Calypso.'

126

'Really? Nice to know. But look at the choice she has. All the most enterprising Frogs, Dutch, Belgians, Poles, you name it. They'll be around sniffing and God help us husbands when the Americans make up their minds. No, no, this is one hell of an opportunity for licence.' Hector drained his glass and signalled to the barman, 'Same again.'

'No, thank you. You and I are not particularly licentious.' Helena in her role as Max's mistress heard herself making remarks she would never have made until recently.

'No – though – well, what I mean is when I am overseas, as I shall be shortly, I'm not fool enough to imagine Calypso sitting at home, tatting.'

'And what shall you do?'

'I shall be propping up the bar with a popsy, as I'm doing now.'

'Not with such innocence, I daresay.' Helena's martini had gone straight to her head.

'You have your fiddler –'

'How –'

'News gets around, it gets around, good news and true.'

Helena wondered why she had made no denial and decided that she was proud to be pointed out as Max's mistress. It was the only thing that got her through the intolerably boring concerts. 'Are you fond of music?' she asked Hector.

'Yes, but not night and day. I bet you feel the same.' He had stood up to leave, settling his Sam Browne belt at his waist. They had exchanged a glance before parting which Helena was to remember. It said 'Were it not for Calypso' and 'Were it not for Max'. Sitting in the train on her way back to her husband Helena gave a little laugh. The soldier opposite her sized her up, thinking her a bit touched. He was very young, as yet unaware of the extremes a woman of forty's pent-up sexuality could lead to. Helena had tried to conceal her ignorance from Max, but he had noted and played on it, enjoying her pleasure as one would enjoy a volcanic eruption. Not being at a safe distance added spice to his practised palate.

When at weary last the train drew in Helena roused herself, snatched nervously at her suitcase and stepped out on to the platform, half-consciously searching for her old self, her old preoccupations with Richard, her household, her garden, her friends in the neighbourhood. Ahead of her she caught sight of Sophy, a semi-familiar figure walking lopsided because of her suitcase, grown since she had last seen her almost into that stage which is now called teenage but which Helena termed awkward. She felt a spasm of anger as a young man in R.A.F. uniform overtook Sophy and took her heavy case, smiling down as Sophy looked up with laughing profile. Then she saw Sophy wave an arm and break into a run to greet Monika, holding the dachshund on a lead. Sophy and Monika embraced, the dog leapt up barking, the young man carried the case to the car, saluted and went on his way. 'My car, what's she doing with my car?' Helena knew she was being unreasonable as she watched Monika question Sophy and Sophy shake a negative. Monika looked worried, got into the car and Sophy, holding the wriggling dog, followed. Monika started the engine. Helena called out loudly: 'Hey! Monika!'

Monika looked relieved and jumped out of the car, leaving the engine running. 'Sophy said you were not on the train. What a relief you are here.' Sophy looked secretive.

'I joined it at Exeter. I didn't see you.' Helena accepted Sophy's help with her suitcase.

'Nor I you,' Sophy lied.

'Poor Richard will be so glad,' Monika said gently. 'Perhaps you should drive, yes?'

'No, you drive, I expect you can manage.' Helena was ungracious, angry with herself. 'And how is he? Much better?'

'Not better, oh Helena he is not better.'

Helena sighed a sigh of exasperation. 'We'd better be getting along. Can't you keep that animal still, child,' although the animal sat perfectly still in Sophy's arms. Helena met its beady eyes and glanced away from Sophy's black ones. Sophy smiled.

'You must be so worried.' Monika headed the car out of the town.

'Of course I am. Max sent his love,' she added cruelly.

'He has so much.' Monika, used to this kind of attack, rather enjoyed it. 'How was the concert?'

'Splendid. How lovely the sea smells.' Her pre-war self was roused. She consciously tried to get back to Helena, the aunt by marriage of Richard's nephews and nieces, churchgoer, member of the Women's Institute.

'That is where the bomp fell.' Monika slowed the car as they drove through the town. 'Poor Richard unt *der General* were very upset but no people hurt at all.'

'All that lovely wine! I'd asked them to keep it for me. We will win this war, but think what the Germans will have drunk meanwhile. Any news of your son?'

'No.' Monika increased speed. 'None,' choking back her anguish.

'Can I get out before we get to the house? I'll give Duck a run.' Monika stopped to let Sophy and the dog out. 'She loves that dog and so does Richard. You are a good woman, Helena.'

'Oh no I am not. No.'

'Come, Duck, run.' Sophy raced up the hill with the delighted dog, arriving abruptly on the camomile lawn. She ran round it, brushing the turf with her feet. It was the wrong time of year and the scent was faint. She stopped running and looked at the sea, rough and grey, sea horses turning into rollers to crash against the cliffs. She looked along the path, blocked by barbed wire, to the coastguard station once so bravely white, now camouflaged dirty green and brown. 'It's all gone,' she cried miserably to the dog, who whimpered, feeling the wind sharp and cruel on his thin coat.

Helena went upstairs, leaving Monika to manage the

luggage. Richard lay passive, propped on pillows.

'Poor fellow. How d'you feel?' Helena bent to kiss his forehead. 'You've got a temperature. What's the doctor doing about it?'

'Given me M and B.' Richard's voice was weak.

'Hope it works. Who changed the room round?' Helena looked disapprovingly at a change in the order of furniture.

'Monika. Easier to nurse me. She is very good.'

'She called me good just now.' Helena laughed and Richard smiled a conniving smile. 'You'll be all right.' Helena's voice was confident.

'Now you are here.'

Helena felt a pang of guilt. 'Sophy was on the train. We didn't see each other until we arrived. Polly posted her off from Paddington. I was in Liverpool with Max when I heard you were ill.'

'No need for you to bother.'

'Probably not. All the same, it wouldn't look well if I didn't come.'

'What would the neighbours say? I ask you.'

'Are you joking?'

'Of course not.' Richard's voice was hoarse. 'Must think of the General and Monika. Not that she cares.' His voice dropped to a mutter. 'She's used to it. Used to it! I ask you.' He began to cough.

'Shall you get used to it?'

Richard nodded. He looked feeble and unattractive. Helena looked round the room for his leg and, not seeing it, caught his eye.

'She put it next door.'

'Oh.' Helena experienced a rush of friendship for Richard, smiled at him warmly, then sat beside him holding his hand. She felt they had briefly exchanged the truth and grown closer. The dachshund scratched at the door.

'There's your dog. He loves you.'

'Yes.' Richard watched his wife walk across the room to let the dog in. Her walk was different.

'I can't bully you any more,' he said, coughing.

'You never really succeeded.' Helena watched the dog jump on to the bed and settle its head close to Richard's, looking at her down its long nose.

'She's moved the kitchen furniture and you are to sleep in the spare room.'

'Oh.' Helena was surprised into annoyance. 'Why?'

'You might catch my flu.'

'And if I did?'

'You'd stay longer.' He laughed, then coughed, getting very red in the face.

'So that's how it is.' Helena watched him cough, trying to speak between spasms. 'What did you say?'

'A straight swap,' he gasped.

'But it isn't, is it?' she queried.

'No.' He held the dog's absurd nose loosely in his hand, its wet black tip showing between thumb and forefinger, its eyes peering across his veined fist. 'But it's all right.'

Helena was furious, insulted. He was her husband, he should mind.

'You've got bronchial pneumonia,' she said, wondering whether he would die, whether if he did she would mind.

'Not dying, though.' The bout of coughing stopped. He lay back.

'Uncle Richard?' Sophy came in, hurried up to the bed and kissed him, then stood back holding his hand, looking down at him.

Richard's eyes lit up. 'Sophy.'

'Am I glad to see you!' the child exclaimed. Helena was surprised. Sophy had never shown Richard affection.

'Thanks for your letters,' she said. 'They make school bearable.'

'Good,' he said, holding her hand. 'Good.'

He loves her, Helena told herself, loves her. Sophy sensed something and, turning to Helena, said: 'He writes to me about the garden and the birds and what's happening in the village and what the General thinks

131

and the Rector and all that, so that I know it's all here, that I'm not just homesick for an idea. I always end my letters, "Love to the camomile lawn".' She paused and looked at Helena. 'You planted it, didn't you?'

'Yes,' said Helena remembering. 'They all said it wouldn't grow.'

'But it does.' Sophy felt warmth for her aunt, for a brief moment they liked each other.

'You've grown.' Richard held on to Sophy's hand. 'One day –' he began to cough again, a hard, racking cough. 'Bugger this cough, got pneumonia too, doctor says "Being gassed didn't help". The Huns didn't do it to help us. I ask you! Did it to kill us. Sloppy use of the English language.'

'Time you stopped talking.' Monika sailed into the sick room carrying an inhaler. 'Swallow your pills and then you inhale, yes?'

'Whatever you say, my dear.'

His dear! Helena raised her eyebrows.

'He has talked too much.' Monika dismissed Helena gently, Sophy too.

Helena followed Sophy downstairs. 'He doesn't write to me,' she said.

'You don't need letters. You've got so much. Oh, how wizard!' Sophy admired the new arrangement of the kitchen. 'Uncle Richard said I'd like it. You like it, don't you?' She turned to Helena.

'Yes.' Helena looked at the transformed kitchen. 'I admit I do.'

'Much cosier than in Cook's day, quite Viennese, isn't it?'

'Yes.'

'She's enjoying the factory.'

'Who? What factory?'

'Cook.'

'How do you know?'

'We write. She's engaged to the foreman, he's called Terence and is a widower.'

'You do keep in touch.'

'I must. Otherwise I –'

'What?' Helena stopped staring at the unrecognizable kitchen and looked at Richard's niece.

'Nothing.' Sophy patted a cushion which had appeared from another part of the house to soften an upright chair. 'Otherwise I should get lost,' she said to herself, 'disappear.'

19

'I shall have to stop to let Jumbo out.'

'You can't stop on the motorway, Ma.' Iris and James spoke together, knowing best.

'I wasn't born yesterday. I can turn off at the next junction.'

'Junction 17 is two miles on,' James and Iris chorused.

Children! thought Polly. 'Travelling in the war was quite different,' she said. 'There was no petrol except for short runs and the trains were full to bursting. People like Calypso managed to get sleepers. She used to press ten bob into the attendant's hand, look him in the eye and say, "I am the Member of Parliament for Hogmanay" or whatever Hector's constituency was. It worked even when she went to Penzance.'

'He was an M.P. wasn't he – Conservative?'

'Yes.' Polly turned off the motorway. 'All right, Jumbo, I'll let you out in a moment. When he went off to war some other member looked after his constituency. He came back to vote Labour and chuck politics.' She stopped the car, let Jumbo out on to the grass verge. 'Don't take all day,' she said to the dog. 'Hector had more constituents in the Highland regiments than anywhere else.'

'Charging across the desert with bagpipes?' Iris watched the dog defecating. 'He did want to be let out.'

Polly whistled. The dog, who had not finished, ignored her.

'I can't somehow see Calypso in the Highlands.' James snapped his fingers at the dog, now scratching the grass, sending little clods of turf high.

135

'She went once on their honeymoon and once just before Hector went overseas. Catherine came from his place, Hamish's now, of course. Catherine had him up there when he was an infant and later for his holidays. Calypso found it dreary and isolated.'

'Not her style.' Iris pulled the dog into the car. It jumped on to the front seat beside Polly.

'Not her style at all.' Polly drove back on to the motorway. 'Of course Hamish –'

'Hamish behaves as though he had no drop of English blood,' Iris agreed, 'totally Highland.'

'And yet he is Calypso's child.'

'If anyone had told me this would be enjoyable I would have told them to get their head examined.' Calypso, held tight in Hector's arms, rocked with the train. Hector held her, pressing his feet against the foot of the bunk.

'I rather like the rhythm,' she whispered in his ear. 'It says, "Fuck fuck-fucker fuck fuck fuck-fucker fuck." '

He turned his head to find her mouth. 'Improper words.'

'Not for a wife.'

'Another go?'

'Another go. Don't fall out of the bunk.'

'I'll try not to.'

'What time do we get to Euston?'

'Just shut up for a while.'

When she slept he held her in his arms. The train roared south through the night. The engine shrieked eerily.

'Are we nearly there?' she said sleepily.

'No, not yet.'

'We are too big for this bunk.'

'Do you want me to move to mine?'

'Not if you can bear the discomfort.'

If I tell her how happy I am she will laugh, he thought, gritting his teeth against the agonies of cramp.

'Oh, I must stretch, you are squashing me.' She was

136

suddenly fully awake, pushing him on to the floor. 'D'you think there's any whisky left in that bottle?' She pulled a jersey on and sat up.

He had stood up, swaying with the train, to reach up, find the whisky, pour her a drink.

'D'you think the puppy is all right?' Calypso fumbled under the bunk to peer into a basket where crouched a small brindled cairn with a black face. It wagged its tail. 'Yes, he's all right.' She closed the basket. 'He's a lovely present.' She took the whisky from Hector, who watched her sitting swinging her long bare legs, wearing her jersey. Hector poured himself a drink and sat beside her, putting his free hand to cover her warm stomach, feel her hair.

'I shall call him "Highland Fling" but "Hamish" for short.' She tossed back the whisky. 'It's a family name, isn't it?'

'Not for a *dog*,' he shouted at her in sudden rage.

'I didn't mean the dog.' He could not read her expression. 'You are on embarkation leave, aren't you?'

'Darling –' he stared back at her.

'Yes. With any luck. It'll keep me busy. Oh, Hector, do I see a tear?'

'I can't help it – I love you.'

'Is it so painful?' Her wry smile made him laugh.

'Agony,' he said. 'You wouldn't know.'

'Glad I don't.'

'Calypso had a dog in the war.' Polly increased speed.

'I thought she didn't like animals,' said James, who did.

'She liked that dog, horrid little thing. It bit and was never properly house-trained. Hector gave it to her. It slept on her bed.'

'Is that the animal that bit Tony?'

'Must have been, she never had any other dog.'

'So Tony isn't telling tall stories when he says he slept with Calypso,' James remarked.

'Shooting a line, they said at the time,' Polly agreed. 'I hope we aren't going to be late. It's wrong to be late for a funeral. You wait for it all your life and when people are late it seems rude.'

'He won't know, Ma. It's not as though it's a concert. Anyway, the funeral is tomorrow.'

'There was always another concert.'

'Oh really, Ma! Try not to fuss.'

'You can cough and sneeze and cry at funerals but you mustn't be late,' said Polly sadly.

'Oh Ma, just drive carefully or we will be having a mass do.'

Calypso watched Hector pack.

'Shall you grow a military moustache? It would make you very unattractive.'

'Would you mind?'

'I shan't be there to see it.'

'Calypso, darling, will you have Catherine?'

'Who is Catherine? What for?'

'You know perfectly well. Her father bred the puppy, she will look after the baby.'

'And me?'

'Yes.'

'But I don't know yet whether I am having a baby. Shan't know for weeks and weeks.'

'If you do I want you to have Catherine.'

'All right, I will, but only when it's born. Why isn't she in war work? Why isn't she an A.T.T. or a Wren, is she wanting or something?' Watching Hector pack made Calypso disagreeable.

'She's lame.'

'Poor girl. Sorry. But I don't want one of your people spying on me.'

Hector smacked Calypso's face quite hard. 'You fool, do you think I like going off like this, leaving you with no one to look after you? You won't go to your parents because you'd be bored, you won't go to Scotland, you'd be bored there, you insist on staying in London, you may get bombed. I worry.'

'No need to hit me. That's much more of a worry.'

'Don't let's get sour.'

'All right, I'll send for Catherine if anything happens.'

'Hector went off in a filthy temper.' Calypso sat on the edge of Polly's kitchen table swinging her legs. 'All the rush of packing.'

'Shall you miss him?'

'I don't intend to. It's lovely having the house to myself, working when I want, going to bed when I want.'

'With whom you want.'

'I didn't say that.'

'You didn't, of course.' Polly wondered who Calypso intended going to bed with, whether Tony had yet staked a claim.

'If you get lonely you can always come here.'

'Thanks. Any news of Walter?'

'Not for ages and ages.'

'The twins?'

'They are alive. They come up when they get a night off.'

'Always together?'

'Usually one at a time. They get awful nightmares, Calypso. They scream.'

'So would I if I were shot down. It's hard to take in, though. Hector says you look up and if someone's missing from breakfast in the mess it puts you off your nosh; you think it may be you tomorrow. That's what Hector says. It may be quite different for the twins. Hector's experience was in the last war.'

'Like Uncle Richard. Funny that Hector is as old as that. They won't let him near any fighting, will they?'

'He's awfully aggressive, he might be very good at it.'

'Walter says they take ages to get there and they might be torpedoed.'

'Thanks a lot, you're very cheering. I don't know where "there" is, Cairo or Crete or the Suez Canal. Hector won't like being stuck on a ship, he hates inactivity. Polly, d'you hear things in your office, real news?'

'You can read the papers, listen to the wireless.'

'But can one believe one word? Look at Dunkirk. Hector says it was a shameful shambles.'

'Does he? We thought so in our office but we didn't dare say so. Goodness.' Polly looked thoughtfully at Calypso respecting Hector. 'My boss thought we'd be invaded by the end of June, he even knew the date.'

'And what was that?'

'June 24th. I remember because it was Midsummer Day. Why are you laughing?' Polly was startled by Calypso's giggles.

'Nothing, oh nothing. Poor Oliver. I had tonsillitis. I wonder where he is now? He went off in a temper, too.'

'I think we should ring up the old people while we are together. Aunt Sarah's a worrier and I haven't heard anything from Cornwall for weeks. Helena behaves as though they didn't exist.'

'She's having such a good time.' Calypso spoke with admiration. 'I never would have thought it of her, would you?'

'Not in my wildest dreams.'

'We kept in touch by telephone,' said Polly, speaking over her shoulder to Iris and James. 'In the war,' she added, catching James's expression in the driving mirror. 'This drive, this funeral, thinking of Max, Uncle Richard and all of them brings it all back.'

'You seem to remember it all very vividly.' Iris leaned over from the back seat to stroke Jumbo.

'Vivid, yes. London on fire. The House of Commons, the Guildhall, the East End. Some nights we climbed on the roof to watch. Turner couldn't have done better. Other times we hid under the kitchen table.'

'You make it sound beautiful and exhilarating, fun even.'

'It was. One should be ashamed. Before it started we all swore we wouldn't become War Bores like Uncle Richard. Gosh, he was boring. On and on about comradeship, courage, carnage and –'

'Clap?' suggested James.

'If his generation caught clap it wasn't mentioned. Poor old fellow.'

'You never talk about your parents, Ma.'

'I know, I don't know why.' Polly shifted in the driving seat. 'One day they were there, Father in his hospital, Mother doing war work, and the next they were whooshed away by one stray bomb. Walter couldn't get to the funeral, he was at sea. Aunt Helena and Aunt Sarah and Uncle George came. It's an awful thing to say but I simply seemed to forget about them. There was so much going on.'

'Oh,' murmured Iris and James, wondering whether in the event of Polly's sudden demise they would take it so calmly.

Of course they would have objected to what went on, interfered, thought Polly to herself. 'Divine Providence is pretty quirky,' she said aloud. 'We used to telephone. We were rationed to three minutes and had to cram all the news into that.'

'Any news, Aunt Sarah? Any news? How are you and Uncle George?'

'We are well, my dear. How are you?'

'I'm well. Hector's gone overseas.'

'My dear child, are you alone?'

'I'm with Polly at the moment.'

'You shouldn't be alone.'

'I like it. Any news of Oliver?'

'We had a letter. He's in Egypt.'

'How d'you know? I thought they weren't allowed –'

'He said the weather's lovely. Lots of old friends call. They just toot and come in.'

'How naughty of him!' Polly took the telephone from Calypso. 'Not that it does much harm. I've no news of Walter, he's at sea. We are going to ring the Cornish lot.'

'They've got someone they don't like planted on them. I couldn't make out what Monika said, you know her accent. I didn't talk to your uncle, he was out. I know you are busy, but could you get Calypso to go down and see them? Helena has just deserted. This love affair's gone to her head.'

'Not only her head,' said Polly. 'Damn, that's the three minutes.'

They waited patiently to get through to Cornwall. The telephone was answered by Richard.

'Ah, Calypso, just the girl. I want to talk to your Hector.'

'You can't, he's gone overseas.'

'Then give him a message.'

'I can't get hold of him, Uncle.'

'My dear you must, the bloody Army's put a gun under my nose. I ask you, a gun!'

'What sort of gun?'

'Anti-aircraft. It makes us a target. The Hun will shoot us.'

'Surely it's camouflaged?'

'Right under my nose. I won't put up with it. I said so. All the bloody jumped-up joker said was "There's a war on", as if I were not aware. I lost a leg in the last one, I told him. I'm not going to have my lawn ruined in this. Hector could get it moved along the coast.'

'Couldn't they put it on the General's land?' Polly took the receiver and joined the conversation.

'They tried, silly buggers. They tried but he pulled rank, said he was a General. Wouldn't hurt him to have a gun but if they fire the damn thing they will frighten the cow.'

'What cow?'

'Monika's bought a cow, pretty beast, keeps it tethered, says that's what they do in Austria. If they fire, the poor beast might try and run away and strangle itself. It's too appalling to contemplate. Hector could get it moved.'

'The cow?'

'Don't be dense, girl. The gun. If the Huns machine-gunned St Mary's. We are quite unprotected.'

'Was St Mary's machine-gunned?'

'Yes. They say they killed the village idiot but people will say anything these days.'

142

'I didn't know about St Mary's.'

'Supposed to be a top secret. They dropped a bomb on that secret place on Goonhilly Downs, missed of course, made a bloody great crater. We've no defences. The buggers just fly up and down the coast as though it were Bank Holiday, nobody to stop them, all our Army's gone to the Middle East, I hear.'

'You seem to hear an awful lot, Uncle Richard.'

'Monika listens to the German news, it's much clearer than ours. We get jolly good concerts too, no atmospherics. Pretty efficient lot, those Germans, you must grant them that. They wouldn't plant a gun on my front lawn.'

'Is it really on the lawn?'

'Poetic licence. Try and get Calypso to get hold of Hector, there's a good girl. We'll never win the war at this rate, first Dunkirk and now this. Try and –' The telephone crackled then fell silent.

'We've been cut off.' Polly replaced the receiver. 'Could you go down and see what's going on, Calypso?'

'I was thinking of going back to my job now Hector's away to war.'

'Couldn't you go down there first? It sounds as if Uncle Richard is in a fix.'

'All right. We owe it, I suppose. Come, Fling.' She picked up the puppy. 'Goodnight, sweetie, see you soon.'

'Keep in touch. I'd like to know what's going on, and do tell Uncle not to careless talk.'

'Fat lot of good that will do.'

'He will get into trouble if he's too indiscreet listening to the German news.'

'It's Monika. She can't do any harm.'

'Monika is a victim. When shall you go?'

'Soon. It will take my mind off things. Goodnight, discreet cousin.'

'Why do you call me that?'

Calypso went off laughing without answering.

*   *   *

143

'Oh, darling,' said Polly in bed later. 'I am so happy. Will Calypso be all right alone in that big house? Will she be afraid in the raids?'

'She can put out her hand, feel Fling and pretend it's Hector's hairy chest.'

'Perhaps she likes hairy men.' Polly was half asleep.

'She has catholic tastes.'

'Are you speaking from first-hand knowledge?'

'Guesswork and hearsay. Roll over –'

20

'It is good of you to meet me,' Calypso climbed into the car beside Monika, 'when you are rationed for petrol.'

'That's no matter. The General told us what to put on the form for the ration. The General knows all these things.'

'Oh, what did you do?'

'Richard asks for petrol for shopping, yes? Petrol to go to church, yes? Nobody goes much to church. Then to get Sophy to her school. He "forgets" to cancel now she is at boarding school. Then petrol for Max's concerts, that is war work. Petrol for Richard's A.R.P. when he goes to his post, and of course petrol for Richard's leg. That is useful, no?'

'Very.' Calypso was impressed. 'I never thought the General was so fly.'

'War sharpens the intelligence,' said Monika grimly.

'What's this about a cow and a gun?'

'The cow is war work. I buy her from the General. I make the butter and the cheese and we have milk.'

'But what does it eat? Uncle Richard and Helena have no fields.'

'I tie it by the road, it eats what they call "the long pasture". The old men in the pub they tell me that.'

'Is it legal?'

'In Austria they do it. The gypsies do it. The grass is waste if the cow not eat it.'

'Goodness. Where does she sleep?'

'On the lawn or if it rains in the garage.'

'The camomile lawn?'

'The cow does not like the camomile.'

'But we do.' Calypso felt outraged. 'It must make an awful mess.'

'I gather the mess for the vegetables.'

'And where is the gun?'

'On the cliff where you and Oliver were sitting, where Mrs Penrose's husband fell over drunk.'

Calypso asked: 'Who is Mrs Penrose when she's at home?'

'She lives in the village, but she works three days' housework for the Frau Rektor Floyer and three days for me.'

Calypso noted the way Monika referred to Mrs Penrose as working for her.

From outside, the house on the cliff was the same as ever, crouching glum over the sea, but once inside Calypso sniffed. No whiff of Helena's roses and pot-pourri but an aroma of Continental cooking. She did not immediately note other changes as Richard's dachshund sprang, snarling, and pinned Fling screaming to the ground. As she tried to rescue the puppy Richard came and buffeted the struggling dogs with his artificial leg.

'Lay off, you filthy Hun. Can't you see the poor little brute's only a baby? Hullo, Calypso, my dear, good of you to come.' He kissed her. 'We'll have tea by the fire, Monika.'

Calypso, holding Fling out of Duck's reach, followed him to the drawing room.

'You spoke to her as though she was a servant,' she said.

'She doesn't mind. She's Hebrew. Slaves in Egypt and so on. Got to keep my end up. Just look around and see what she's done. I ask you, just look.'

Calypso looked. The furniture was changed round. The pictures re-hung, the old curtains swathed with elegance, the furniture polished.

'Same all over the house,' Richard snorted.

'But it's lovely.'

'That's the trouble. She's got bloody good taste. They say Jews are an artistic race.'

'But –'

'You must see what she's done outside. There's the cow.

146

There are hens. They actually *lay*. She grows vegetables, she knits, she sews, she cooks. I have to speak to her like a servant, she's so bloody competent.' Richard Cuthbertson sat down and began to laugh, his tearful eye spurting. 'She's even got me a new leg, it's got a hinge.' He pulled up his trouser leg and showed his new contraption. 'The old one got a gremlin in it.'

'A new mode of speech too.'

'Parson's twins. Gremlins. Prangs. Burtons. Wizards. Practically incomprehensible.'

'Er – what does er –' Calypso hesitated.

'What does Helena say? Suits her. She's changed too, you may have noticed. She's become flighty.'

'May I go and choose my room, Uncle Richard?' Calypso felt Helena had become thin ice as well as flighty.

'You'll have to ask Monika.' Richard Cuthbertson roared 'Monika!'

'Richard?'

'Where's Calypso to sleep?'

'Might I have the red room?'

'I put you in what was the spare dressing room.'

'Oh.' Calypso followed Monika upstairs carrying the puppy, her suitcase picked up by Monika.

'Richard sleeps here now and Helena there. Max has to have their old rooms because of the piano – he has to have one at night for his inspirations. I sleep here, Sophy in her old room and this is the guest room for guests. You I put in this room, your dog can sleep in the scullery.'

'No, it can't.'

'No? Is it safe? Does it mess?'

'Sometimes. You seem to have been awfully busy, Monika, you seem to have taken an awful lot on your shoulders. You have changed Aunt Helena's house completely, taken over, I mean moved in, moved everything. Apparently you cook, sew, clean, garden, run a farm, run Uncle Richard. It's all very well, but should you? I'm sure it's all very beautiful and in perfect taste but Fling shall not sleep in the scullery and should you have done

all this, Monika, should you? What's the matter?'
Calypso stared at the tears pouring unchecked down
Monika's face. 'I'm sorry, Monika, you poor thing.'

'It is Pauli. If I do not work I go mad. You have no child
so you would not understand, perhaps I am mad
already.' Monika's tears dropped unchecked on to her
jersey, caught like dew in a spider's web. 'I am sorry. I
invented all those jobs for myself. I wanted to thank
Richard and Helena but I have spoilt your childhood. I
am so sorry.'

'It's all right.' Calypso put the puppy down and found
a handkerchief. She wiped Monika's tears. 'It doesn't
matter. I am grown up now.' She stood embarrassed in
front of the older woman. 'Poor you. Is Max as worried?'

'No, he has his work, his success, he has Helena, she
suits, he likes the plump, the phlegm.' She smiled wanly.

'You have Uncle Richard. Blow your nose, do.'

'The poor man. The cow, too, I have the cow. If you like
I move things, put you in the red room, it won't take a
minute to change it round.'

'Oh, Christ, no.' Calypso snatched up Fling, who was
off adventuring. 'I shall be perfectly all right. I haven't
come here to cause trouble. We thought, or rather Polly
thought, Uncle Richard, and you of course, would like a
visit, that you, that I, that, oh blast! I've put my great foot
in it, and honestly Monika I don't usually bother to notice
or care where I put them so you are one up there.'

Monika's mouth twitched. 'You are so beautiful the
feet do not matter.'

'You make me feel awful. I thought I was coming here
to help, or, to be honest, Polly thought of it.'

'You can help. The Floyers' sons come tomorrow, you
can help with them.'

'Paul and David here?'

'Ja. Frau Floyer is too full up with evacuee children, a
new lot arrived last week. I said the boys should sleep
here.'

'Oh goody, how splendid, but a lot more work for you.'

'They make your uncle happy.'

'But you do that, Monika, he is thrilled with what you've done, the cow and everything.'

'I make him comfortable like a good servant.'

'Come and have a drink, Calypso,' shouted Richard from the hall. 'Isn't it time you put the cow away, Monika? Take the dog with you when you go out, he needs a run.'

Calypso accepted a glass of sherry. 'Pretty filthy stuff, I'm afraid, South African, you heard the wine merchant got bombed? Absolute tragedy losing all that claret. Helena should have had it delivered here, silly woman. Had her mind on other things. We shall get bombed now we have that bloody gun. I ask you. What fool would do such a thing? In my day the War Office would have, oh well, they might have done something worse. Hi, Monika, you didn't take the dog. Go on,' he said, opening the door and shooing the dachshund out, 'go on out. Now then, got your drink, good, good. See the look he gave me? Looks like Monika. Long Jewish nose, liquid eyes, reproachful. She looks like the cow too, it's a Jersey.'

'Jerseys don't have –' Calypso spluttered.

'I know they don't, but it's the eyes, the liquid dark eyes. I don't know what will happen when they fire the gun; anti-aircraft's pretty noisy. By the way, careful what you say. The General's taken rather a shine to her, offered to have her with him, I ask you.'

'The cow? Wouldn't that solve –?'

'No, no, Monika. I couldn't possibly allow that. Between ourselves – I can say this now you are a married woman – the General's rather a chap for the girls.'

'An old lecher?'

'So I'm told, only gossip of course, can't stand gossip but can't risk Monika. She worries about that boy in the camp, dead by now if you ask me, Hitler won't be wanting useless mouths. Did you bring your ration book by the way? Give it to Monika if you did. Just thought I'd ask, though we grow so much ourselves nowadays we shall send you back to London laden. I'll show you the gun after dinner and get you to bewitch the officer in charge.'

'I hear the twins are coming '

149

'Yes, their mother has a horde of lousy children crammed in the Rectory, Monika goes over once a week to help the district nurse wash their heads. They are crawling, I ask you. Infesting the village. Now in the last war we had our heads shaved and my batman ironed my uniform when I came out of the front line.'

'Ironed?'

'Lice don't like a hot iron, kills them double quick. I must tell that Pongo fellow, give him a tip or two, he seems pretty green, only a Territorial not the real thing.'

'When shall I see him?' Calypso sipped her sherry and looked round for a handy vase to tip it into.

'If you don't like it,' said Richard, noticing, 'tip it in the soup. Monika makes very good soup. The Pongo is coming to supper. Fellow called Brian Portmadoc.'

'What a grand name.'

'Called after the village where he was born, if you ask me. A Taffy. I'm depending on you to get that gun moved. Charm the fellow, take him to see the General's flower fields, that should do the trick, romantic.'

'Couldn't the twins?'

'No, no, no. Wrong service, wrong sex. There's no love lost between the Air Force and the Army, you should know that. It takes a woman to do this sort of thing.'

'What d'you do in real life?' Walking down the valley to the General's flower fields Calypso edged towards the subject of the gun, which crouched above the sea like an obscene animal covered with camouflage netting.

'Insurance.' Brian Portmadoc, hopelessly ensnared since he set eyes on Calypso, repeated the word sadly. 'Insurance.' Hardly a job to interest a creature of such beauty, married to a romantic-sounding and martial Member of Parliament. 'Insurance,' he said again, studying Calypso's profile.

'What about the windows?' She let her beautiful eyes meet his. He was not bad-looking, rather stubby fingers and short legs but otherwise presentable, the Welsh lilt rather attractive.

'The windows?'

'When you fire your gun they will break. As an insurance man you should know. Cause a lot of ill feeling. Surely you can get it moved? It's awful for Uncle Richard.'

'I have my orders, I didn't choose the spot.' Calypso continued to gaze. 'When it's fired once we have to move it along the coast, so that the Germans think there are lots of guns,' said Brian, embarrassed.

'How silly. Shall we go and see if we can snitch some of the General's violets? Follow me.' Calypso spoke coldly. Brian felt the chill. 'Here we are. I shall sit while you pick a bunch.' Calypso sat on a rock and waved towards the violets planted in long rows. Obediently Brian picked, and as he picked he wondered how he could please this girl. The scent of wet violets roused his senses intolerably. Bending over the flowers he considered furiously how he could please her without getting himself court-martialled.

Calypso, having planted the seed of an idea, was happy to leave it to blossom.

The flower farm, a spread of tiny fields bounded by stone walls, was a delight for Calypso whose visits had always been in barren August. Presently they met the General bullying his work force of old men and boys. She asked to be taken on a tour. Brian fell in behind, listening sulkily to the General showing off his fields of violets, anemones, narcissi and daffodils.

'Help yourself, my dear, any time, take as many as you please. A pity the Scilly Whites are not ready yet.'

'Are you selling?'

'Good gracious, yes, trade's never been so good. We will be sending away trainloads in a few weeks.'

'Doesn't the war interfere?'

'No, less to buy in the shops so people spend on flowers. The more they are bombed the better for trade. They buy them for funerals. From my point of view the war is a bonus. Air raids have their sunny side. I am averaging fivepence a bloom.'

151

'Oh,' said Calypso. 'I shall think of your profits when I'm in a raid.'

'A girl like you must get bunched the whole time.' He put his arm round her waist but she moved away.

The twins arrived in the evening complaining of the journey, the intolerable stops at every station, the crowded train. 'People have become boorish.' They had spent the previous night in London, gone to a show, had a bad meal in a restaurant.

'Did you see Polly?'

'Stayed with her. She sent you all her love.' They put their suitcases in the guest room and went to spend the evening with their parents.

Calypso called her puppy and the dachshund and strolled down to the cliff. Memories of holidays came to mind, summer days spent on the rocks and swimming in the cove. Down there in the dark was the place they all sun-bathed, where she had lain in the sun conscious of Oliver's eyes on her. Here where she stood Oliver had said 'I want to fuck you'. She remembered her feeling of fear and excitement. She stood in the dark, hugging her coat round her, remembering the Terror Run, the games, the laughter, Oliver scared of the drop to the sea. The dogs found a rabbit hole and Duck was frantically digging, lying on his side paddling at the earth with his absurd paws. She watched her puppy, ignorant but eager to join in. The breeze coming off the land brought the smell of ploughed earth and the sound of soldiers' voices by the gun. The war seemed as far away as her childhood, so effectively swept away by Monika's rearrangement of the house. Even the lawn has stopped smelling, she thought resentfully, blaming Monika for the time of year. 'I know it *doesn't smell in winter*,' she muttered. 'Sophy told us.' She called the dogs, who ignored her. She went on her knees to reach into the hole and catch the dachshund, trying to get a grip on its tail. The dog went on digging, the puppy yapped. In the sky a familiar drone. Busy with the dogs, it took minutes to recognize the sound of a German bomber. Above her by the gun orders barked excitedly. The drone grew nearer. She looked up, chilled, listening to the faraway sound of sirens in the town. The plane flew closer and she heard the tearing sound as a stick of bombs dropped screaming. She grabbed the puppy and crouched low by the rabbit hole. The gun fired pom, pom, pom, pom and again, banging a futile threat. The sound of the plane receded and Calypso sat up holding the puppy. The dachshund was still digging, pounding the earth with its paws. She reached in, caught its tail, dragged it out. Carrying both dogs, she started up the cliff. She could hear shouts and see lights. She tried to run, her legs weak, heart pounding. In the house her uncle was shouting.

'Bloody fool, look what he's done! Monika, she's gone. Right through the house, bust the windows, I told him it would happen, look at the mess, I ask you.'

'Uncle, are you hurt? Did it hit the house?'

'Of course it didn't. They can't aim straight. It's that Pongo fellow. The gun frightened the cow, look what she's done. Came bursting through the French windows, she's broken the glass, torn the curtains and now there's the telephone.' He limped to answer the telephone shrilling in the hall. 'Showing a light, am I? What of it? Bloody Boche, nothing better to do than frighten my cow. Of course I'm showing a light. The poor beast broke in through the blackout, broke the window, frightful mess. Nobody hurt, of course not. Turn out the light? Very well, if you insist. Oh, damn your regulations, have a heart. The plane's miles away.'

'Chased by our gallant few.' David and Paul came hurrying in. 'There's a lovely row of craters across the plough. Anyone hurt, any damage?'

'The cow took off through the house.'

'She's all right.' Monika came quietly into the room. 'She is in the kitchen. We must block up the windows; you are showing a light, Richard.'

'God damn it, I know I am. How is my cow? Will this stop her milk?'

153

'No, no, a little cut on her nose, a mess in the kitchen. I clean it up. I will put her in the garage with some hay. Yes.'

Calypso watched Monika lead the cow out of the house, then helped the twins block up the French windows as best they could.

'Hector is afraid of me staying in London,' she said, steadying the steps as David nailed up the torn blackout curtains. 'He wanted me to go to Scotland.'

'They get random bombs there, too.' Paul swept up the glass.

'I shall tell him so when I write.' Calypso suddenly missed Hector. 'I feel sick,' she said, sitting down on the sofa, 'and sweaty.'

'That's fear, we all get it.'

Calypso looked at the twins. 'I didn't realize. I thought it was just me.' She felt admiration.

'Sophy will be sorry to have missed this.' Richard limped in to join them. 'Monika says leave all this mess and come to the kitchen, she has some soup for us. Make a change to have some lively news for the child, my letters get a bit boring.'

'There's someone at the front door.' Paul went and opened it. 'Hullo, Mr Hoskings.' An old man wearing an A.R.P. helmet came into the hall.

'They was trying to bomb Coverack, thought you'd like to know, Major. Any damage here, then?'

'Coverack's thirty miles away, need their heads examined. As for you, young fellow' – Richard Cuthbertson suddenly noticed Brian Portmadoc standing sheepishly behind the air raid warden – 'hope you're pleased with your night's work.'

'Very, very sorry, sir. We shall be moving on now, can't fire it twice from the same place.'

'And how's Jerry to know that?' asked the warden nastily. 'You foreigners coming down here with guns, interfering, ach.'

Calypso showed Brian Portmadoc out.

'What does he mean, foreigner?' Brian asked, aggrieved.

'Anyone who isn't Cornish.'

'I suppose I shan't see you again?' The young man lingered, a prey to mixed feelings, proud to have fired his gun, angry with the air raid warden, infatuated with Calypso.

'Come and see me in London,' she said casually. 'I'm in the book.'

'May I really?'

'Of course. Night, then.' She closed the door and went to the downstairs lavatory and was sick.

'I'm never scared in London,' she said, rejoining the party in the kitchen, 'I must have agoraphobia,' but her uncle, Monika and the twins were not listening. They were gathered round the wireless to hear the news in German with Monika translating.

Presently there was the sound of a car outside and the General came in.

'Hear you had a spot of bother,' he said, looking round the kitchen. 'Nothing serious, I hope.'

Richard regaled him with a list of damage and complaint. The General was wearing battledress with Home Guard insignia.

'Thought if you were in trouble Monika might like to take shelter with me, and anyone else of course. How about you, Calypso?'

'No,' said Richard Cuthbertson, 'let it not be said that the Hun chases my guests away, mustn't allow any hint of defeat. Cow's upset, of course. The only thing I want moved is that infernal gun. Stupid fellow in charge fired the damn thing, even I know it's a million to one chance of his hitting anything in the dark. Just fired it for the hell of it, if you ask me.'

'He did come to apologize,' said Paul. 'Fair's fair, sir.'

'Let's go and see if he's packing up.' David signalled to Calypso, who was watching Monika edge away from the General as he put an arm round her waist.

'Like to come, Monika?' asked Paul. 'Get a breath of fresh air before bed?'

They took Monika round the house and stood on the

155

lawn looking down at the gun. There was activity, sounds of talk of a grumbling nature, a hearty oath. Somebody started a lorry engine. Side lights were switched on, engines revved up and lorries drove away, bumping across the grass.

'It would have amused Sophy.' Calypso took Monika's hand. 'Are you all right, Monika? Hector says we aren't as incompetent as we appear, he talks as though we shall win the war. What do you think of that, twins?' She chuckled.

'We do our best,' they said gravely.

Monika let out a long high cry which echoed down the cliffs, chilling their blood. A howl of anger, frustration, despair.

21

By the time Sophy came home for Christmas the saga of
the gun had grown. Enemy planes, Sophy heard in the
village, had attacked the Scillies, killed several people
and sunk an M.T.B. Some said it was a destroyer but
others said no. Lord Haw-Haw said an M.T.B. The
planes had continued on their way to bomb Helena and
Richard's house and it was not the anti-aircraft gun but
Mr and Mrs Erstweiler who had been the target. Had
not the General said they were German spies? He was
wrong – the village knew. Mrs Erstweiler was harmless, her son a prisoner of war. Not in a real prison camp
but a concentration camp. What's the difference? If
Mrs Penrose worked for Mrs Erstweiler at the house on
the cliff she couldn't be a spy. Mrs Penrose also worked
at the Rectory. All those London kids, disgusting, really.
Mr Erstweiler's a nice gentleman, pity one couldn't
understand his accent. The papers said he was a
famous violinist, so there you are, no spy he, whatever
the General said. Luckily the Floyer twins had run to the
rescue when the bombs fell, nobody hurt bar the cow,
funny Lord Haw-Haw made no mention. They'd swept
on, those bombers, plucky really after being fired at, to
bomb Penzance, did some damage there, Lord Haw-Haw
mentioned that, then on to Plymouth. Getting bombed a
lot, Plymouth.

'I came through Plymouth, the station's a mess,' said
Sophy.

There, now, it just goes to show. Sophy listened at the
post office, at the shop, got hot news at the garage and

best of all the truth, she swore it was the truth, from Mrs Penrose who was entitled to know. Had not her husband fallen over the cliff, pushed by a German spy, just before the war began? Mrs Penrose had a fascination for Sophy, who watched her scrubbing floors on hands and knees, her large bottom high, refusing to use the squeezy mop which Helena had bought on her last visit. Sophy followed Mrs Penrose round the house, watching her dust and make beds and in the kitchen with Monika. While Monika worked silently Mrs Penrose talked, describing her life with Penrose, as she referred to her husband. Penrose had spent his early days at sea before joining the coastguards. Penrose did not like the station on the cliff, Penrose had been happy on the Longships cut off from the drink, for Penrose drank. Never on duty, but when he came off duty he reached for the bottle. Mrs Penrose, having her mid-morning tea, would reach for the teapot in illustration. 'Penrose often went on duty half seas over. No wonder he couldn't be a proper husband, poor soul.'

'What's a proper husband?'

'Never you mind.' Penrose's superiors never knew of his weakness. 'Why, he would walk along the cliff to work as straight and upright as you please. He would sit by the cliff path before going on duty and stare at the sea. He loved the sea, the sea and the drink. He should never have married, he couldn't be a proper husband, could he? Penrose must have been drunk or he would have seen the spy who pushed him over.'

'Did anyone see the spy?'

Nobody, spies were sneaky people who worked unseen. Then thump, push, over he goes, and Mrs Penrose was a widow, not that he was even a proper husband, otherwise –

'What?'

'Well, I'd have kids, wouldn't I? Not that I like kids, look at the worry they cause. You poor dear have all that worry. If Mr Erstweiler, well, if as I say he'd been like Penrose there wouldn't be all this worry over your Pauli, would there? Now,' Mrs Penrose would say, taking her cup to the sink, 'you mustn't keep me here talking. I must get on with my work,' and Sophy and Monika would smile, both too careful to ask the other what she knew or thought she knew of Penrose.

'Are there people like Mrs Penrose in Vienna?'

'Cornwall is not like Vienna,' Monika would answer, 'but Mrs Penrose is a universal character.'

'In the Middle East, will Oliver meet people like her?'

'Surely.' Monika frowned over a cookery book, striving to follow the recipe for Christmas pudding. 'Do you write to him, Sophy? This pudding will be indigestible.'

'No, I don't. I think they are meant to be indigestible. It's just so difficult to imagine them all now. Walter at sea. The twins flying Spitfires. Aunt Sarah told Polly Oliver's in Egypt. I expect he is all right,' said Sophy, who expected all the time to hear that Oliver had been killed and, if he was, whoever killed him would kill her too.

'Child, you look sad, help me with these pies. Christmas is a happy time.'

'I don't think so,' said Sophy, looking at Monika. 'I don't think you do.'

'You must be happy, your aunt arrives this evening.'

'She is not my true aunt and she does not love me.'

'Of course she does, we must make her welcome. And Max comes also, he will be tired after his concerts.'

'A proper husband,' said Sophy, mimicking Mrs Penrose. Monika laughed, thinking of her proper husband in Helena's house in London, and that probably over Christmas he would wake in the night and ask her to accompany him on the piano, a chore which was impossible for Helena.

'I wish they were not coming. It is much nicer here with just you and Uncle Richard.'

'My child –'

'I suppose it will be nice for you, having Max.'

'Of course.'

'Aunt Helena always stops things. You'd think she'd never enjoyed herself.'

159

'Perhaps she has changed,' said Monika drily.

'Like Mrs Penrose, only the other way round?'

'You are very observant.'

'Do you think Mrs Penrose loved her husband, even though he was not proper?' Monika wondered whether this sort of conversation was good for Sophy. 'Are you able to love?' Sophy pressed on.

'Yes, I am able, and so are you.' Monika sang a West Indian song one of the evacuees at the Rectory had brought from the East End.

'It's love and love alone
That caused King Edward to lose de trone.'

'I am sorry you missed Calypso and the twins,' she said.

'I don't mind,' said Sophy, who preferred not to see Calypso so loved by Oliver. 'None of them ever came in the winter before the war.'

Helena came down full of good resolutions, bearing gifts for Richard and Monika, books for the Floyers, a pretty dress for Sophy and a heavy package of gramophone records for Max, who pretended he did not know the contents of the package he carried.

They stepped off the train and stood waiting for a porter, surrounded by their suitcases. Max wore a black overcoat with an astrakhan collar and an Anthony Eden hat; he carried his violin case in his arms, protecting it from the jostling crowd of servicemen hurrying off the train. Helena wore a new fur coat and very high heels, which made her calves bulge. Her hair now waved softly round her face, she smelled expensive. She tendered a cheek to Monika.

'Ah, Monika. Ah, Sophy, you have grown. Is Richard well?'

'Just gone up the street to get some cigs.' Sophy appraised this new Helena. 'You look wonderful,' she said.

'Have to take trouble now our clothes are rationed, though lots of people seem to have no trouble over coupons. Don't you think it's very immoral, Monika?'

'Morality is elastic.' Monika kissed Max on both cheeks as he stood holding his violin case and the parcel of records.

'Let me help,' said Sophy, taking the package.

Max surrendered the records and put his free arm round his wife. 'Ow goes it, *Mein Schatz*?'

Schatz? What is *Schatz*? thought Helena. He never calls me *Schatz*. 'Dear Richard,' she exclaimed, seeing Richard limping down the platform, and broke into a trot to kiss him brightly.

'Well, well,' said Richard, surprised, wiping his tear. 'What's this transformation? Quite the Londoner these days.' Helena took the remark in a kind spirit.

'You are walking better,' she said as they moved towards the car. 'I always thought you made too much of your leg.'

'Absence of. This one's new.'

'What?' Helena stopped in her tracks. 'What d'you mean, new?'

'Monika got me fixed up. Took me to Exeter. Look, it's got a hinge.' He bent down and pulled up his trousers. 'See? I press it and bingo, the knee bends. Shan't be tripping so many people. It's an easier job altogether. I use the old one to poke the fire. I go to bed in this, some-times, just for the hell of it. Wonder what that Bader chap does at night, now he's a prisoner of war.'

Helena said nothing; no use feeling furious, she'd left him alone with Max's '*Schatz*', she'd asked for it.

'D'you mind? You look bothered.'

'Good heavens, no.' She took Richard's arm. 'Why should I mind?' They walked towards the car. 'I should have thought of it myself, it makes me feel –'

'She wrote to the spare part place, sort of St Dunstan's for legs and arms. Imaginative girl, old Monika, thinks of everything, must come from years of looking after an artist. Just wait and see what she's done to the house, we don't even sleep in the same rooms. It's all changed, quite a performance, you'll never recognize it.'

'Oh,' said Helena, angered. 'I can't wait.'

They drove to the house, Richard sitting beside Monika, Helena and Max in the back with Sophy between them. Arrived, Monika said to Sophy, 'Show your aunt her new room, darling.'

Helena cried out with genuine pleasure at the bowls of hyacinths on the hall table and in the drawing room, filling the air with bitter-sweet scent. 'Monika, how gorgeous.'

'I like them for Christmas.' Monika smiled at her. 'I have moved you into the red room, Helena, so that Max can have his piano with him.' She indicated Helena's old room. Where once her dressing table stood was now an upright piano.

'You will be quieter and more peaceful where I have put you. As you probably know, Max likes to play at night.'

'Not the piano.' Helena came into the open. Monika ignored her.

'He calls and I come to accompany him. He is at his best at night. The most inspired. I sleep next door in Richard's old dressing room.'

'Why did you interfere with Richard's leg?' Helena's fury burst out like an angry terrier.

'Are you jealous of something which irritates you profoundly?'

'Yes,' admitted Helena. 'I am. I shall miss it.'

'But he still has it for spare,' said Monika, friendly and calm.

'As Max has you – for spare – his *Schatz*.'

'He always calls me that, it is his pet name for me. Has he yet a pet name for you?' Monika looked amused, ignoring Helena's jibe of 'spare'.

'No.' Wild horses would not make Helena confess to *Kleine Phlegm*. 'This will do very nicely. Thank you, Monika.' She inspected the red room. 'I like this room, it is one of the children's favourites. Any news of Pauli?'

Monika knew Helena hoped to unbalance her. 'No news whatever.'

162

'Oh, curse this war!' Helena put her arms round Monika. 'Curse it, curse it! I am a horrible, selfish creature, Monika, please forgive me.' She held the other woman's shoulders, shaking her to and fro.

'You do no harm.' Monika kissed her lightly. 'We are partners, *nicht*?'

'You are generous.' Helena was briefly humble.

'I try to survive. We shall make a nice Christmas, yes?'

'What have you planned?' Helena sat on the bed looking up at Monika, her eyes clear blue, her hair fair and fluffy, her pink complexion a total contrast to Monika's olive skin and sleek dark hair, drawn back into a knot, accentuating her dark eyes and semitic nose.

'You are beautiful, Monika. You look like Nefertiti.'

'I have a Jewish face even more so than Max.'

'I never thought about Jews before the war.' Helena looked down at her trim ankles as she kicked off her high-heeled shoes.

'You did not have to.'

'I thought they were just other people. Richard's nephews and nieces told me about the Nazis and I became interested when I realized the war was coming. You have no idea how irritating Richard was, he believed everything that boring old General told him. He liked Nazis.'

'He no longer does. The General is very keen on the war, he sends his young workmen to enlist. He is *der Patriot*.'

'I bet they don't want to go,' said Helena.

'He tells them their jobs will be waiting when they come back – if they come back.'

'Do you like him?'

'He tries to be kind. He is useful.' Monika shrugged. 'He does no harm.'

'Like me?'

'Ah, Helena, you and I are friends, yes? We work in a team like the English are supposed to. You make Max happy.'

'Don't you *mind*?' Helena stared at Monika in agitation.

'No,' Monika said lightly, 'I do not mind, so I hope you do not either.'

163

'Richard?' Helena was puzzled. 'Poor Richard.'

'I make him less poor.'

Helena sat looking at her feet. Less poor, she thought, less poor meant richer . . . a caring woman, a new leg, of course he was less poor. She found it hard not to feel resentful. 'What about Christmas plans?' She changed the subject.

'A party in the village hall for the London children. The village children they do not mix, but perhaps Christmas will help? Church. The Rector asks if Max will play his violin if I play the organ. Sophy has helped me make a pudding. The General sent a turkey, he asks us all to go and sing songs on Boxing Day at his house, everybody to choose their favourite tune and for us to sing together.'

'I hope there will be plenty to drink,' said Helena, linking her arm in Monika's and leading her downstairs. 'I never used to drink but since the war I've taken to it. I believe it's the threat of shortage which makes me want it. Tomorrow we die.'

'Of course,' said Helena, all those years later, 'we didn't die. Here we are driving to Max's funeral. Some of us are dead but not me. That was a priceless party!'

'What party?' Hamish lent an ear. Helena's voice was sometimes creaky with age.

'A sing-song at the General's. He had a stroke which did for him in 1948. He made a fortune out of flowers but didn't live to enjoy it.'

'What happened at the party?' Old people wander, thought Hamish.

'Had his stroke in a public lavatory. He wouldn't have planned that. He planned the party so that each of us hummed our favourite tune and the rest of us sang the words if we knew them.'

'Sounds quite a harmless idea.' Helena's laugh made him turn round and look at her. 'What went wrong?' Hamish had a theory that old people liked recalling disasters.

'The General hummed a marching song he'd picked up at the Nuremberg Rally in 1938.'

164

'The Horst Wessel?'

'Yes. As you can imagine Max and Monika were not pleased, especially as only they knew the words.'

'Did that finish the party?'

'It was Sophy's choice which put the kibosh on it.'

'What did she choose?'

'The Internationale. She sang it from beginning to end. She said Oliver had taught it her. I thought the General would have a seizure. She made things worse by saying, "The Russians are our allies and yesterday was Christ's birthday, he was the first Communist." She was at a difficult age. I found out later Max had been giving her drinks. As parties go,' said Helena, enjoying her reminiscences, 'it was a flop, though I remember the evening ended well.'

'That must have taken some doing. How could anyone be so naïve as your General? It's unbelievable.'

'There was quite a strong minority like the General, Conservative people who admired Mussolini for his trains. They didn't want to hear about Abyssinians being thrown out of aeroplanes. Max found it hard to believe the General was really honourable and patriotic. Richard gave us all a nightcap when we got home and we went to bed. It was so funny!' Helena, sitting beside Hamish as he drove down the motorway, chuckled delightedly, tiny tears squeezing out among the wrinkles. 'I shouldn't really tell you.'

'Go on,' said Hamish, driving steadily, 'tell me, do.'

Helena paused in agreeable recollection. Then: 'I undressed and went to bed. I forgot Monika had changed all our bedrooms. I found myself in bed with Max, as though we were in London. When I realized my mistake I was too tipsy to care and presently who should join us but Richard, scrambling in on my other side.'

'A threesome?'

'My dear boy, he had his leg, it was –' Helena paused in recollection.

'His artificial leg? What did you do?'

'Threw it out. Threw it out of the window. I thought he thought I was Monika.'

'And then?'

'Max was furious, told me to go and fetch it. I didn't, of course. I moved in to sleep with Monika. In the morning those two men were asleep in that bed in perfect friendship. I always say one can never know what men will do next.'

'Perhaps they were tired.'

'Drunk, we were all drunk. After today,' said Helena thoughtfully, 'they will be at it again.'

'What do you mean?'

'Side by side in a bed – of clay this time. You won't forget I want to buy flowers, will you, dear?'

'No,' said Hamish, treading on the accelerator.

22

Brian Portmadoc, posted to an anti-aircraft battery in London, telephoned Calypso, inviting her to dinner.

'I'd love to as long as you don't keep me up too late.'

'I won't do that.'

'I am working. They have taken me back in the job I was in before I married.'

'Oh, what's that?'

'Top secret,' Calypso said. 'I'm not allowed to tell you what I do. I don't understand the half of it.'

'Shall I fetch you at your office?'

'Not allowed to tell you where I work. Come to my house.'

Brian arrived bearing flowers.

'How beautiful. How kind.' Calypso held the flowers to her nose and looked at Brian.

'You look beautiful.' He blushed.

'Good,' said Calypso. 'Where are you taking me to dinner?'

'Where would you like to go?'

She thought this tiresome. He should choose a place he could afford, he should say as Hector would, 'We are going to the Savoy or Lyons Corner House.' How could she tell how much money he could afford? Men all looked alike in uniform.

'We could try Soho,' she said. Brian looked grateful. The flowers had been expensive. He found a taxi.

'Hector has hidden his car in the country,' she said, 'otherwise I would drive you. It eats petrol.'

'What is it, a Rolls?'

'Near enough. He doesn't want it bombed, it's his dearest possession.'

'What about you?'

'I am not his possession. I am his wife.' Brian did not know what to say to this.

Difficulty in finding a table in the first restaurant they tried humiliated him and he felt worse when Calypso was effusively greeted at the second and led to a corner table, made much of. She was known and pampered. She knew several other diners. A Frenchman came and talked in French which Brian did not understand until he kissed her hand on departure, saying, 'Alors, à demain.' Other men came up to her during the meal. Brian felt inadequate, that she would prefer to be with someone else, someone smarter, more glamorous.

'Do they all tell you how beautiful you are?' he ventured.

'Some do. I know I am beautiful, now you tell me something I don't know. Tell me about insurance.'

'You are laughing at me.' Brian gulped some wine. 'I would insure every hair of your head,' he said. 'I think it is what they call ash blonde.'

Calypso nodded.

'I would insure your blue eyes and long black lashes.'

'They are real,' she said encouragingly.

'I would insure your nose, your mouth, your teeth, your ears.'

'Good, good. What about my body?'

Brian drank a full glass of wine. The bottle was now empty. 'I don't know about your body,' he muttered, 'I can't –'

'We shall have to correct that. Shall we go? Can you take me home?'

As they left the restaurant she said to the Frenchman, 'See you tomorrow' and 'Let's meet on Thursday week' to two men dining together. Brian took her hand and held it in the taxi. He was afraid to kiss her. When they reached her house she said, 'I must give my dog a run, then you will come in for a nightcap.' The dog jumped

168

with joy when it saw Calypso, then ran excitedly up and down the pavement. 'Hurry up,' she said, 'don't take all night. He came from the Highlands, shouldn't really be in London. Do you notice there are no dogs nowadays, no children, either?' She held Brian's hand like a mother as she watched the dog lift its leg, sniff the railings, trot back wagging, look up at her with beady eyes. 'I hide him under my desk in my office,' she said. 'My boss pretends not to know.'

Brian stood beside her rather drunk, uncertain what to do next.

'Come on in then. Let's correct your ignorance,' she said.

In her bed, his face buried in her hair, Brian said, 'I love you. I love you.'

'I don't know what love is.' She rocked him in her arms. 'I like this, though, you are nice. You don't really love me.'

'I do. If you don't know what love is how can you be sure I don't love you?'

'You have a point. But it won't last, you can't insure it. You can't insure an emotion, it's a pleasure like eating or drinking.'

'It will last with me.'

'That's your affair. I can't help it, can I? Now you should get back to your gun and I must get some sleep.'

She watched him as he dressed, putting on his uniform, doing up his buttons.

'Shall I see you again?' He stood by her bed.

'I expect so. Telephone. Can you let yourself out?'

She listened as he went downstairs, waited until she heard the front door slam. In his basket the little dog whimpered.

'Oh, Fling,' she said, 'I am so lonely.' The dog jumped up on the bed. She lay face down, trying to sleep, then reached out and switched on her radio, twiddling the knobs. Over the air came ghostly voices speaking in German, French and English. She wondered what the hell was going on in the world. What was the time in Egypt, where Oliver was supposed to be? What was Hector doing, and where? She had had no letter for so long and only a B.F.O. address to write to. What could she write about? He would hardly be glad to hear she had slept with Brian Portmadoc and intended sleeping with his French friend. He would get no pleasure on hearing that she quite often slept with Tony when he was not on duty at his fire station. Were most grass widows faithful, were girl friends true? She could write to him, she thought, about her visit to Cornwall and the carryings-on of the older generation, but then she could not, she thought, since Helena and Hector were of much the same age.

She slept and dreamed uneasy dreams which turned to nightmare. She was running through the streets of a town she did not know to escape she knew not what. Her legs would not move, her breath came in gasps, she tried to wake for she knew she was asleep and if she could wake she could tell Hector of her fear. She reached out her hand to wake him, her hand pushing into his hair. Then she screamed, for she felt not his warm cock but something cold and wet. Her terror was so great that she clutched at the hairy thing, which was wet and cold, and it yelped with pain for she squeezed Fling's nose instead of Hector. Instead of Hector to wake her from nightmare there was a frightened little dog.

'Oh,' she said, consoling Fling. 'I did not mean to hurt you. Oh, Fling, my Highland Fling boy, I feel sick.' Sweating and greasy she got up and went downstairs to make tea. When she had drunk it she was very sick indeed and felt so faint she had to lie on the bed until she felt better.

In the morning she telephoned Polly.

'Polly, I haven't seen you since I went to Cornwall.'

'How were they all? Come to supper and tell me about it. Come tonight.'

'I can't come tonight, I'm going out with a Frog friend of Hector's. What about tomorrow, if I'm well enough?'

'Are you ill?'

'I don't know. I've eaten something, I feel sick and

170

nearly fainted just now. Come to think of it, I was sick in Cornwall when they fired the gun. I thought it was just fright. It must be some bug I've picked up.'

'Have you missed the curse?'

'I'm bad at counting.'

'Well, count. I am late for my office. You for yours too, for that matter.'

'I must look at my diary.'

'See you tomorrow. Goodbye.'

'Goodness.' Calypso looked at her diary. 'Goodness,' she murmured, looking at the small pages, 'goodness gracious me. I meant it. But it seemed a sort of joke,' she muttered as she went to clean her teeth, which made her sick again. She telephoned her office and asked leave for the day as she felt ill.

'Seen a doctor?' said her boss briskly.

'Just going to make an appointment.'

'Well, mind you try and get here tomorrow, you know how busy we are. You're the only one who knows that file on –'

'I know, I know. I'll be there.'

'And don't let me catch you lunching in the Écu de France with some Frog.'

'Is that where you're lunching?'

'No. I shall be at my club.'

Calypso telephoned Hector's doctor for an appointment. Then thoughtfully she dialled again: Helena's number. Max answered.

'Listen, can you give me lunch today? Dutch, if you're feeling poor. I'm in need of moral support.'

'Where would you like to meet?'

'Écu de France.'

'It'll have to be Dutch.'

When she left the doctor she took Fling to Hyde Park, walking on the grass, watching him run. Men and women in uniform walked briskly along the asphalt paths, barrage balloons rocked at anchor. Crossing Mayfair she found a post office, found a form. She wrote Hector's name and rank and his alien secret address.

171

She wrote 'Hamish en route Calypso' and handed it to the clerk.

'Better write in English,' he said.

'Why?'

'Looks like code. Is Calypso a ship?'

'No, Calypso is my name.'

'Better put your surname, then.'

The message 'Hamish on the way Calypso Grant' looked chilly. She tore up the form. 'He's not a trunk,' she said to the clerk behind the desk. 'I will write.'

'Please yourself,' he said. Then, finding Calypso pretty, smiled.

She went out into the street. 'It's a commercial undertaking,' she said to herself. 'I shall have to put it in writing.'

Early for her lunch appointment, she strolled through the streets, noting here a gap and there a gap where bombs had struck. Nobody stood to stare or paused as they went by. Calypso paced slowly, with Fling on his lead trotting sedately. At the Écu de France she said to Max: 'I'm feeling generous, I'll stand you lunch.'

'Ta very much.' He switched his gaze to the more expensive dishes on the menu. 'What are you celebrating?'

'A private joke.'

'May I hear it?'

'Sometime, perhaps. What do you think is the best thing to eat?'

They discussed, chose, gave their order.

'Did you tell Helena you were lunching with me?'

'She is out shopping.'

'Who taught you to say "ta"?'

'Isn't it snob?'

'Who taught you, come on Max, tell me.'

'A young woman I know.'

'You are being unfaithful to Helena.'

'And to Monika. I am not a faithful man just as you are not a faithful woman.'

Calypso grinned. 'I went to bed with you, Max, in a

172

purely exploratory fashion. I wanted to find out whether my aunt is on to a good thing, whether you will break her heart.'

'Dear Calypso, would it be too much to ask you to mind your own business?'

'Promise you won't hurt her? Don't let her find out you are sleeping around. We are all very fond of her and Uncle Richard. They are part of our childhood.'

' "Our" meaning you, Polly, Oliver, Walter, Sophy and those twins?'

'Yes.'

'I will not hurt her, I am a sensitive man. Under that British phlegm your aunt is also sensitive.'

'Is she really?' Calypso was thoughtful. 'I would never have known it.'

'There is a lot you do not know, for instance your Hector.'

'What about Hector?' Calypso was instantly on the defensive.

'Your Hector is sensitive.'

Calypso laughed. 'Oh, come on! Hector isn't sensitive, he's a great big hunting, shooting, aggressive politician.'

'And oh so rich.'

'That's why I married him, for his money and in exchange –'

'Yes?'

'In exchange he has a pretty wife.' Wild horses, Calypso thought, feeling the blood rush to her face, wild horses will not make me tell Aunt Helena's lover that I am bearing Hector's child. I am keeping my promise, and he's got to be the first to know. Why should I tell Max, who isn't great shakes in bed anyway, one single thing about Hector's baby? Hector's baby, she thought, not mine, why should it be mine when I don't even like children, what on earth shall I do when I've got it?

She remembered the chugging train and Hector's voice telling her 'You must have Catherine' and again his voice saying curtly, 'She's lame'. The rocking movement of a lame person would lull the baby as she carried it.

'May I come back to your house this afternoon?' Max liked copulating in the afternoon before a rehearsal.

'Sorry, no, I have to write letters. Why not Helena, why not the girl who says "Ta"?'

'Your voice is cruel, your letters can wait.' Max was persuasive.

'How could you know? Will you ask for the bill, please, Max.'

He signalled to the waiter while Calypso fished in her bag for money.

'Did you not enjoy our afternoon together?'

'It was all right, but I think I shall stick to your concerts for Helena's sake.'

'You are very considerate suddenly.' He looked at the bill, which the waiter had put by him folded on a plate.

'Today is a day to be considerate,' she said gravely, as she put money on the bill.

'Shall you perhaps reconsider?'

'I think not. Now,' she exclaimed lightly, 'thank you for your company. Give my love to Helena, see you soon, goodbye.' But as she gathered up her bag a man who had been sitting at another table came across the restaurant. He excused himself to Calypso, drew up a chair, leant across the table and talked to Max in German.

Not understanding a word Calypso watched the two men. The newcomer was large, well dressed and expensive, his shiny hair brushed back in wings. He smelled of cigars, wore a heavy gold watch. Listening, she heard and understood odd words – America – concert – dollars. Monika's name was mentioned. Max was shaking his head, speaking rapidly, gesturing with his hands. His expression lost the look she rather despised of wishing to please and assumed one of pride. He finished what he had to say in English: 'No, I cannot and I will not.'

The stranger turned to Calypso. 'Forgive me, please, Max did not introduce us.' He looked at Max, who stared back, making no effort to do the polite conventional thing. 'I am trying to make Max accept a wonderful offer.'

174

'And what's that?' Calypso was not taken by the stranger, whom she found too opulent.

'I offer him a contract in the States, a passage to America for himself and Monika and he refuses. In America they will be safe and make lots of money. There is no necessity for them to stay where they are in danger. In America Jews are safe.'

'Safe here, too,' said Calypso.

'Only until the Germans come, then they are in terrible danger.'

Calypso opened her mouth but Max laid a hand on hers and said: 'I must speak for myself, Calypso. This man was German. Now he is American, you understand. He is trying to make me run away and I will not. I have run far enough. Here I can work.'

'For less money,' put in the stranger.

'*Ja*, for less money maybe but I work for people who shelter us. I will try to repay their kindness with my music.'

'I've not been particularly kind,' said Calypso.

'Your country has and for that I will pay in the only way I can, with music.' Max sounded pompous, Calypso thought, but his air of pride carried it off. She looked from one man to the other, sizing them up, liking Max.

'Oliver would say you are paying with an idea.'

'Ideas are his speciality.' Max relaxed and laughed.

'Who is this Oliver?' asked the stranger suspiciously. 'A conductor, perhaps? Amateur?'

'A young man who fights the Nazis, fights for the Jews. So do the twins and the other boy Walter.'

'Who are these people? An orchestra?'

'Nothing you would understand. They also have ideals.'

'Do they play the violin?'

'They play with death.'

The prosperous stranger laughed, settling his broad bottom on the chair. 'Listen,' he said. 'England is losing the war. Soon Rommel will be in Egypt. The British Army is retreating. Hitler invades this country after a bit more bombing and then it is goodbye to your talent, goodbye to Jewish refugees. I am here at great risk to find you and others and bring you to the United States. Be sensible, think of your art, your talent, do not waste it. It is no use your listening to this Churchill, who I admit makes good propaganda, but England will starve very shortly. I know you eat a good lunch today but for how long? Do you know what the U-boats are doing, do you hear of the millions of tons which are being sunk? In a matter of months it is all over in Europe, whereas in America I offer you a future. Even to bring your mistress.'

Calypso, watching the two men, became conscious of a Max she did not know. Helena's lover, charming, talented, lighthearted, fairly good in bed, changed into a steely creature who made her shiver. She had seen anger, she had seen rage, everyday emotions compared to what Max was experiencing. He began to speak in a low hard voice in German, staring into the eyes of his enemy, for she guessed that if the stranger had not been an enemy before he was one now. He spoke with bitterness. The stout man tried to interrupt with sneering remarks. Max suddenly spoke in English.

'Now will you go? Get out, leave this country where you are not even worthy to shit, get back to your safe America. I hope the U-boats you so admire will sink you on the way. Get out, get out, you Dung –'

The stranger pushed back his chair and went away. People at neighbouring tables, who had overheard, stared after him then back at Max. Calypso stared back at their disconcerted faces. They looked away. She took Max's hand.

'Have a brandy? Who was that creep?' She signalled to the waiter. 'Brandy, please.'

'A German producer. American now. He makes and breaks in the music world.'

'Well, he didn't frighten you, did he? Here's your brandy, sip it slow.'

'I hate that man. Have I been vulgar, as vulgar as saying "Ta"?'

176

'As I don't understand German I can't say, but you sounded good and rude.'

'Good.' Max's colour was creeping back. He squeezed Calypso's hand. 'Friends?'

'I feel,' she said, 'that I have grown up several years. I was beginning to grow up this morning. Will this scene upset your music, spoil your concert tonight?'

'I shall play better than ever, for me anger works better than an orgasm.'

Calypso laughed, stood up to leave. Max found her a taxi. As she travelled through the streets made shabby by war she mulled a thought, new for her, that she had no need to go to bed with Max because now she was his friend. She wondered whether she could put this into words in her letter to Hector and decided it was too difficult. As she stood on the pavement outside her house paying her taxi, Max drove up in pursuit.

'You forgot your poor Fling. You left him tied up in the ladies' cloakroom.'

'People like me are not fit to have a dog.' She took Fling from him and watched him drive away. 'And as for being fit to have a child, God only knows,' she said to the forgiving dog. She went into the house, where her bicycle was propped against the wall in the hall. How long could she go on riding it without harming the baby? She sat down at her desk and began her letter: 'Darling Hector –'

23

Enduring school, Sophy depended on Richard's weekly letters, a factual account of life in Cornwall. News of the dog, the cow, the hens was far more important than history or mathematics. Every Monday Richard's plump white envelope brought the news which would enable her to survive the week. He wrote about the Home Guard and what the village thought of it, he wrote that the General was bossy. He wrote about the Rectory evacuees returning to London when there was a lull in the air raids, only to hurry back when the raids started up again. He wrote about the wrangle as to whether a mounted Home Guard was feasible in Cornwall, the jealousy of Home Guards who were said to be mounted on Exmoor. He wrote about the Belgian fishing fleet in Newlyn and of how the Cornish fishermen were called up into the Merchant Navy. He wrote of the harvests, the flowers on the General's farm. He told Sophy when Monika made jam and how she saved up the sugar. He wrote about bartering Monika's butter for meat and swapping eggs for fish. He told her which boy had been called up from the village to which regiment, and who was fortunate to be in a reserved occupation. He wrote that Monika and Mildred were shocked that it was possible to buy clothing coupons under the counter from the village shop. He told her which hen was destined for the pot. He wrote about rabbit pie and blackberries, the weather, rain, fog, wind, sun, all recorded in faithful detail, his new leg and Calypso's visit, the gun and the firing of it. He wrote that the pits made by the stick of bombs would become useful ponds; wild duck would come to them.

Sophy put the letters in the locker by her bed to re-read during the week. Every night, homesick and wakeful, she visualized Richard and Monika sitting by the fire, Richard writing his letter, Monika sewing or knitting. She dreamed of summer days when Polly, Walter, Calypso and Oliver had lolled on the camomile lawn, laughing and joking. She treasured the evening she had spent with Oliver in London. Whenever she was cold she remembered the icy streets by St Paul's. She remembered Oliver weeping and her holding his hand when something terrible to do with Calypso had happened. He had let her hold his hand for several minutes before dropping it to blow his nose. Every night before she slept she wished herself back in her bedroom; from there she could climb out along the branch of the Ilex above the camomile lawn and sniff its scent, mixed with the salt smell of the sea. With pain she remembered Oliver loping down the hill to the war.

Once a week she wrote to Richard of her school life, what she was learning, how she hated the cold and the games, what they were allowed to listen to on the radio, the News, *ITMA* and *The Brains' Trust*. Occasionally, if Richard wrote asking permission for her, she was allowed to listen to one of Max's concerts. She longed for the holidays. She never wrote of her unease with Mrs Penrose, nor could she mention Richard's habit of putting his hand up her skirt, which when she was small had not bothered her but now was distasteful, though small cost to keep in touch with the only home she knew. She would find a way round these troubles without causing embarrassment to Richard, who was her only link with Oliver. For Richard would sometimes, among the minutiae of his daily life, write that there had been news of the others. He wrote when Polly and Walter's parents were killed, 'Can't have known anything about it, nice way to go.' He wrote that Sarah had heard from Oliver now fighting in the Desert, 'Jolly good show'. He wrote that Hector, old though he was, forty-four, might also get in on the action, another jolly good show as there was 'No real need for him to take risks'. For Walter on the North Atlantic run he had no praise, 'Foolish fellow not to get over his seasickness, look at Nelson.' He occasionally noted that the Rector and Mildred had heard from the twins, 'Now separated, which only makes sense'. He wrote praising Mr Churchill and criticizing the generals, he wrote that like it or not one had to agree that 'this Hun General Rommel is the best general in the war, he would get defeated though it was hard to imagine how' and that, awkward chap though he seemed to be, 'This General de Gaulle fellow is the only Frog to stand up and be counted.' In those days Sophy grew almost to love him. She forgot in her loneliness the revulsion she felt for his dismemberment, her horror of his smelly breath, the disgust she felt when he touched her, patting her thigh as he had patted stinking old Farticus, now long dead. He did not pat Ducks but fondled his ears, muttering, 'Only good thing to come out of enemy territory.' She wove round Richard's weekly reports the substance which kept her heart alive. She was too young to find it ironic that Richard, whom she had never liked, and who had never liked her, should be the only person to bother to keep her in touch with base.

But when the holidays fell due Sophy travelled to London with her school to be met by whoever Polly persuaded to meet her, spend the night and catch the train to Penzance. By the time Monika met her at the station a metamorphosis would have taken place. She would arrive at the house on the cliff as shy and reticent as ever, finding it possible to talk to Monika and the Floyers but impossible to communicate with Richard. For his part Richard seemed to find this natural and would wait till she was back at school to resume the intimate terms they arrived at on paper.

At the end of an Easter term it was Tony who met her train.

'Hullo, Sophy. Polly is away, she asked me to meet you.'

'Where has she gone?'

'I don't know, somewhere to do with her job. Walter is in London on leave, he's very fed up at missing her. He was still asleep when I looked in before coming to the station. How is school?'

'Horrible. I shall be glad to see Walter. How is he?'

'Tired and fed up. Not only is Polly away but Calypso's gone tripping up to Scotland, so he can't see her either.'

'Whatever for? She hates Scotland.'

'She had all her windows blown in so she went up there while the workmen put them back. Said she had a job to do, something to do with Hector.'

'She'd never put herself out for Hector.'

'You know a lot for your age.' Tony spoke reprovingly. Criticism of Calypso from this child, however apt, was galling. Arriving outside Polly's house he put her suitcase on the doorstep and rang the bell. 'You all right if I leave you? I have to be at my fire station in a few minutes.'

'Yes, thank you.' Sophy watched him go, feeling ungrateful. Walter opened the door.

'I was just going to get breakfast. Are you hungry?' He kissed her heartily.

'I had mine before leaving school.'

'You could do with another. Did he tell you the girls are both away?'

'Yes.'

'Terrible. I get the first leave for ages and no sister, no cousin.' He led the way down to the kitchen. 'Like fried potatoes?'

'Oh yes.'

'And a spot of bacon? Right, you sit down out of the way while I cook. D'you think they'd mind in Cornwall if I came down? There's nothing for me here.'

'They'd love it. I would, anyway. Monika will be pleased and Uncle Richard.'

'Really think so? I don't want to impose. Where is Aunt Helena, somewhere with Max, or don't you know about them?'

'Of course I know. I'm not a baby any more.'

'No,' said Walter, 'you're not, you seem quite a bit bigger. Right then, we'll catch the night train. I haven't been down since those last summer hols.' He dished out fried potatoes and bacon. 'You get stuck into that and then you can bring me up to date with all the changes down there.'

The night train was unbearably crowded. They squeezed into a carriage full of sailors travelling to Plymouth, who filled the carriage with cigarette smoke and drank from beer bottles. Walter pushed Sophy into a corner and squeezed in beside her. The blacked-out train chugged steadily, stopping at dimly-lit stations where the guard shouted the names of the towns. Walter dozed while Sophy sat wakeful, watching the sailors and listening to their talk. She was too uncomfortable to sleep and there was not enough light to read. When she prised a chink in the blind she could see the moon with clouds racing across it. At Taunton more people crowded in, standing in the corridor, smoking, muttering, shifting from foot to foot. Posters in the dim light said, 'Be Like Dad Keep Mum'. Walter fought his way out of the carriage to find a buffet. The train went on again and Sophy became anxious, fearing he had been unable to get on again. Her anxiety was reaching fever pitch when there was a jostling in the corridor and he appeared, elbowing his way, carrying a cup of tea in each hand, stepping over the legs of their fellow occupants.

'Thought this might keep us alive.' Sophy took the cup gratefully. 'Afraid a lot's slopped.'

'Doesn't matter,' she said.

'Filthy stuff, really.' He squeezed beside her. 'It'll be funny to be there without the cousins. We always came together.'

'I'm your cousin.'

'So you are.' Walter put his empty cup under the seat. 'You've always seemed too little to be a cousin.'

'I'm larger now.'

'Much.' He put his arm round her. 'That comfortable? It won't be the same, no Oliver to boss us, no Calypso, no

183

twins. Lovely times, weren't they? Do you remember
those last holidays before this began, d'you remember
the Terror Run? Weren't you bitten by a snake or something and crying in Calypso's arms?' He remembered
Calypso's expression of anxiety and exasperation. The
reflected light from the sea had made her eyes quite a
new colour. 'What did you say?'

'I said I wasn't bitten, it was something else.'

'And that other game we were going to play, we drew
lots. What was it? To kill somebody, something like that,
one of Oliver's barmiest ideas.'

'He said all of us were capable of killing, but he
cancelled it.'

'Well, as things turned out we are at war and doing
our best.' Walter with his arm round Sophy felt dozy.
Their companions in the carriage were snoring, mouths
open, sprawling. Sophy gave a loud sob. 'Hey, what's the
matter? Tell old Walter. 'Ere, 'ere, have a handkerchief.'

'I tried to tell Polly but she didn't take it in. I told her in
an air raid, we were under the kitchen table. I don't even
know if she heard.'

'Tell me, then, I'm all ears.' Walter gave a colossal
yawn, nearly dislocating his jaw. 'I nearly dislocated my
jaw. What did you say?'

'I pushed him over.'

'Pushed who? Pushed over what?'

'The coastguard. He used to hide behind a bush on the
cliff path. He had a pink thing – it looked like a snake –
in his pocket.'

'Oh.' Walter was waking slowly. 'A flasher.'

'What's a flasher?'

'Never mind, go on, ears flapping. I'm awake, tell.
Stop crying, do, you snuffle so I can't hear. Jumped out
from behind a bush, did he?' Walter held her quietly, his
eyes roving over the sleeping sailors.

'He didn't exactly jump, he just appeared from behind
the bushes. You know where they are, near the rocks?'

'Yes, go on.'

'Well, that's what frightened me when we did the

Terror Run, and made me scream.'

'I remember.' He remembered Sophy hysterical, Oliver slapping her face.

'When it happened again I tried to push past him and he went over.' Sophy's voice was almost inaudible. 'He was found in the sea, I was ill and the police came and took Monika and Max off to be interned.'

'What had they got to do with it?'

'Nothing, nothing. Oh, Walter, what shall I do? D'you believe me?'

Walter said nothing, holding her close while the train chugged slowly, the sailors slept and in the corridor a party of soldiers began singing mournfully but in tune.

'They must be Welsh, they are singing in tune.' He rocked her gently, his chin touching the top of her head. What silky hair. Polly said Chinese. He felt the tension slip out of her body and knew she slept. He wondered whether to say anything. The subject is beyond me, he thought.

'You do believe me, don't you?' Sophy spoke sleepily.

'Yes, yes,' he said quietly. 'Yes, yes.'

'Polly didn't.' She slid back to sleep. Walter sat holding her as the train drew into Plymouth. The sailors woke, gathered their luggage and lurched off the train, their places taken by newcomers.

The train carried on, stopping at every station through Cornwall, and still Sophy slept, until at last he heard the cry, 'St Erth change for St Ives', let up the blind and it was early morning. 'Wake up, Sophy, nearly there.' The sun sparkled on Mount's Bay and St Michael's Mount rose from the waves. 'Wake up, wake up, you are home. Gosh, I'm looking forward to this leave.'

'Isn't the sea lovely? I hope Monika's there to meet us.' Sophy combed her hair, tightened the laces of her shoes, looked out at the sea with her oriental eyes. 'I could eat a horse,' she exclaimed.

'Some people pull legs better than others,' Walter muttered to himself as he lifted their suitcases off the rack. 'A word with Polly is what I need.'

*   *   *

'What was so dreadful,' said Polly to Iris and James, driving to Max's funeral all those years later, 'was that I was in Portugal when Walter had his last leave. I never saw him again. If I'd known I'd have got out of it somehow and seen him.'

'But you wouldn't have known he was going to be killed,' said Iris, who had heard her mother say the same thing so often she knew it by heart. 'You couldn't have had last words or anything, as you didn't know.'

'It taught me to treat everybody's leave as perhaps the last. He might have wanted to tell me something. They said he had something on his mind. We only had each other, our parents had been killed by a bomb.'

'I know,' Iris had often heard this too, 'and Helena and Max arrived with a taxi full of flowers from Covent Garden.'

'I bore you as Uncle Richard bored us.' Polly was resentful.

'Oh no, Ma, you don't, it's just –'

But drowning in the North Atlantic three weeks after his leave, Walter had a vivid recollection of Sophy weeping in the train. He opened his mouth to shout for Polly and drowned that much quicker.

24

It was Calypso and Brian Portmadoc who were the first
to hear about Walter. They had dined together. Instead
of inviting him back to her house, as he had hoped,
Calypso said she must go and tell Polly what she had
been doing in Scotland.

'Won't it wait?' Brian longed for Calypso's bed with
Calypso in it.

'No, I have to see her.'

They took a bus which crawled through the blackout.
Calypso rang the bell and waited impatiently. 'I must get
her to give me a key, everyone else seems to have one.'

The door was opened by a slight dark girl with curly
hair.

'Who are you?' Calypso stepped inside, pulling Brian
after her.

'Elizabeth. I'm a friend of Walter's. You must be
Calypso.' The girl was shy and awkward. 'He gave me a
key, he said Polly wouldn't mind.'

'Is she here?'

'She's away somewhere. Walter said –'

'And where is he?'

'He's gone back. He was on leave a few weeks ago but
I –'

'You a girl friend?'

'Well, I was, I –'

'What are you doing here if you're a "was"?'

'We made it up. We talked on the telephone, he said to
come here to Polly. Anyway, what business –'

'Oh, it's no business of mine, I just want to see Polly.'

'Oh.' The girl called Elizabeth looked discomfited by Calypso's hard tone.

'Any clue as to when she'll be back?' Calypso began looking through a pile of letters addressed to Polly on the hall table. 'What's this telegram?'

'I don't know.'

'Might be urgent.' Calypso opened the telegram and read it. 'Oh,' she said, 'Oh,' and looked at Brian and the girl called Elizabeth. 'He's been killed,' she said. 'Why him? Why not somebody nasty? Did you love him?' she asked the girl, who gave a moan, turned and ran upstairs. Calypso watched her go.

'Let's find a drink.' Calypso started down to the kitchen. Brian searched, she stood by the table.

'Weren't their parents killed?'

'Yes. Buck up with that drink.'

'So Polly's alone?' He found some whisky.

'Not exactly alone but no family now. Thanks.' She took a gulp of whisky. 'How bloody, how absolutely bloody.'

'That poor girl.'

'She'll find someone else. What's her name, anyway?'

'Elizabeth.'

'Elizabeth what?'

Above them feet pattered through the hall, the front door opened and slammed shut. They heard high heels clatter away in the dark.

'We shan't know now.' Calypso swallowed whisky in a gulp.

'Was Walter? Did you –'

'No, I didn't. Wish I had. Can't now. Oh, bloody, bloody hell, why him? He never hurt a fly. I think you'd better go, Brian, I'll stay here, she might get back any moment. Awful for her to be alone.'

'Can't I –'

'No. Listen, if I give you my key will you fetch Fling for me? Bring him here. There's a dear. Then I'll be here if she gets back.'

'But I hoped I –'

188

'I know you did, but I wasn't going to anyway. I meant to tell you but you were so nice at dinner. Please, Brian, just fetch my dog.'

'Clothes?' He swallowed, trying to conceal his disappointment.

'I'll manage with Polly's.'

'I've got to go away on a course tomorrow.'

'I know, you told me. Not much luck tonight for either of us.'

When he had gone Calypso re-read the telegram from the Admiralty. She noted it was dated four days earlier. 'How bleak,' she murmured, 'how bleak. Already four days.' She sifted through the letters and found a sheet of paper with a note in Walter's handwriting. 'I've given a key to a girl called Elizabeth, be kind to her for a night or two. Have been in Cornwall, remind me to tell you about Sophy. See you next leave.' Near the letters the girl had left her key. Calypso put it in her bag. She wondered how many girls had loved Walter. He had been secretive about love affairs. She thought of him in Able Seaman's uniform at her wedding, going off with Oliver, drunk. Where now was Oliver and what doing and for that matter Hector, what was he up to?

When Brian came back she thanked him for bringing Fling.

'Can't I come in?'

'Brian, no! Can't you see I want to be alone?'

'But you weren't in love with him.'

'He's part of my life, my cousin. I feel robbed.'

'But you weren't in love, it's not the same. That poor girl who ran off was.'

'I don't know what love is. Just go, Brian. Please. Leave me with Fling.'

When he was gone she fetched some blankets, lit the fire in the drawing room and settled herself with Fling on the sofa. By the light of a table lamp the room looked dusty, deserted by her aunt and uncle snatched by a wanton bomb. In this room there had been parties, children's parties with games, impromptu dances, the rugs

189

rolled up, dancing in Walter or Oliver's arms to the gramophone. She remembered laughter and cries of pain when the boys trod on her feet, cocktail parties as they grew older, windows open on hot summer evenings. Now it was dead and dusty. She would wait for Polly.

Drawing the blankets round her, holding the dog close, she found herself wishing that Hector was there. He could help Polly, he would do it much better than she. She was surprised at her thoughts, and began to think back to the week she had just spent in Scotland and the friend she had made, of some of the things she had been told about Hector, aspects of his life he had been at pains to conceal. She had meant to spend the evening talking to Polly about herself, and was irritated that instead she must stand by for Polly's grief, put her own needs aside. Sleepy, she tried to keep awake, wondering if it would have been better if Hector had been killed or Oliver or the twins. Oliver loved her, she enjoyed his adoration. Hector? She would have his money whether he lived or died. The twins seemed since the war to have lapsed in their adoration and Walter, too. She tried to think of Oliver dead instead of Walter and smiled sleepily, remembering him saying of Hector, 'I hope he gets killed.' She thought she could do without them all. Cuddling Fling close she laid her head back and closed her eyes.

Polly was at her feet when she woke, holding the telegram. Their eyes met.

'I stayed to be here when you got back.' She sat up.

'Thank you.' Polly was very still.

'Where have you been? You are all sunburned.'

'Portugal. Lisbon. It was lovely and hot.'

'Your job?'

'Yes. It won't happen again. It seemed an opportunity. My boss needed me. I'm not supposed to talk about it.'

'Polly, there was a girl here –'

'Elizabeth. He left a note. Elizabeth who? Did she say?'

'No, she ran off crying.'

'In love with him, I suppose. Several girls were, I shall
have to tell them.'

'Why him? Why Walter? Why not Hector or Oliver or
the twins?'

'Not the twins.' Polly gave a gasp, glancing at Calypso.
'Why are you here, anyway?'

'I came to see you. I wanted to talk to you. Then I saw
the telegram and read it and thought I'd wait. You'd be
all alone –'

'Kind of you. What did you want to see me about?'

'I'm having a baby. I wanted to tell you.'

'Hector's?'

'Of course!'

'That's all right, then. I guessed you had morning sick-
ness not food poisoning, didn't I?'

'Yes.'

'Have you told him? He'll be terribly pleased, won't
he?'

'I've written. He should know by now. He wants an
heir. I've got one of his people to be its nurse. I've been
up in Scotland. Hector said if I had a child Catherine
must look after it. She's small, lame, plain and reliable. I
went up there to see her. She will come when I'm ready,
she can look after it.'

Polly listened to Calypso, holding the telegram in her
sunburned fingers.

'Perhaps it will make you happy.'

'But I am happy.'

'That's not happiness that's money.' Polly's voice was
bitterly nasty. She recovered herself quickly. 'Sorry,
Calypso. I must have a bath. D'you think you could ring
them up in Cornwall, and Helena and Aunt Sarah?' She
put the telegram on the table by Calypso. 'I don't think I
can do it, so will you?'

'Of course.' Calypso shook herself free of the blankets. 'I'll just give Fling a run. You go and have your
bath.'

Standing on the doorstep watching her dog trot to and
fro in the early morning street, Calypso found herself

weeping, tears splashing on to the pavement. In the house Polly would be lying in the bath, her sobs drowned by the sound of the water taps. Presently she would appear puff-eyed and grim, refusing to discuss her loss, insist that she was all right and go off to work and snap at anybody who showed her sympathy. Calypso went in to telephone.

'Aunt Helena, it's Calypso. Aunt Helena, Walter's dead. Yes, a telegram. Yes, quite sure. Yes, she knows. No, she's in the bath – well, you know Polly. Yes, I was here. Actually I opened the telegram. What? Not open people's telegrams? Let her read it herself. She did read it herself. I fell asleep and she came home and found it. What has Uncle Richard got to do with it? Oh, your first husband – sorry. It helped to open the telegram yourself? Really? Well, it's too late now. Yes, I'll tell her, she's in the bath. Aunt Helena, I must go now, I have to ring Aunt Sarah. Yes, yes, I will, of course I will. Yes, I'm sure she will. Yes. Goodbye.'

Calypso dialled trunks and asked for Sarah's number in Bath.

'Aunt Sarah? Calypso here. Aunt Sarah, Walter's been killed. Yes, quite sure – a telegram from the Admiralty. Well, you know Polly, she's crying in the bath. Yes, I'm crying here – oh, and you are crying there. In Bath. I suppose that's funny. Well, not funny. Why Walter, why him? Why not someone who could be spared? Yes, I'll tell her. Yes, I'm sure she would like it if you came up. Yes, I've told Aunt Helena, she was angry that I'd opened the telegram. What? I found it and read it, Polly was away. Aunt Helena carried on about opening the telegram about her husband. I'd forgotten she had one. Oh God! Three minutes! Goodbye –'

Calypso slammed down the receiver, wiped her eyes and went down to the kitchen to give Fling some milk. From upstairs she heard the rush of water as Polly pulled the plug in the bath. Hurriedly she dialled trunks on the kitchen extension and asked for the Cornish number.

'Sophy? Is Uncle Richard there? Well, is Monika there? When will they be back? Not till late. Oh God! Sophy, listen, there's bad news. No, no, not Oliver, it's Walter. Walter's dead. Yes. What did you say?'

'He was the sweetest,' Sophy's clear voice all the way from Cornwall.

'Well, darling, will you tell them? Yes, please, Sophy. Yes, course I will kiss her for you. She's – yes, she's in the bath, actually. I heard the water running away just now so – yes – well, goodbye.'

Polly came into the kitchen puffy-eyed.

'Have you told them?'

'Yes. Sophy said he was the sweetest.'

'He was.' Polly tightened her dressing gown belt. 'I must have some coffee and then rush or I will be late for work.'

'I'll get it while you dress.'

'Thank you, but I'll make you late.'

'My office doesn't mind.'

'Mine does. My boss isn't at all obliging.'

'But surely today he –'

'You aren't suggesting I should tell him, are you?' Polly suddenly spat at Calypso, then, seeing her expression, said, 'Right, then. Come to supper tonight and tell me about your baby.'

'Hector's.'

'All right, Hector's.' Polly's face was pinched with misery; she looked almost ugly. 'Not that Hector's baby is much of a replacement.'

'Nobody could replace Walter!' Calypso put her arms round her cousin, feeling her stiff with reserve. 'I would give myself, darling, if it would do any good, but who am I? I love money and a good time, I'm enjoying the war, I find it exciting and frightening. I enjoy the raids, I like all the men taking me out. I like being a grass widow, at least I think I do.' She felt Polly relaxing in her arms. 'But when something like this happens I hate it, Polly, I hate it, and now I shall stop having a good time and blow up into an awful balloon and nobody will want to sleep with

193

me for months and months. D'you think I'll ever get my figure back? Polly, what are you laughing at?'

'You.' Polly pulled away from Calypso, took her face between her hands. 'You're so utterly selfish.' She kissed Calypso gently. 'There. Don't worry. Whatever shape you are all the men will want you. Walter only gave up trying because he thought it was a waste of time. He didn't think he was attractive enough. Think of Oliver –' She kissed her cousin. 'I must go, I hate being late.' She turned and ran upstairs to dress. Calypso followed slowly.

'Can I come this evening? You are so comforting, though I thought I would comfort you.'

'Of course.' Polly was pulling on her stockings. 'Of course you must come. I want to hear all about the baby. What shall you call it?'

'I haven't thought,' Calypso lied, feeling protective towards Hector, who must be the first to know. I'm only a vehicle, she told herself. This boring child is his.

194

25

'Why the fuss?' exclaimed Max. 'What does it matter? A telegram is not private like a letter. Anyway, it was not for you.'

'It's the principle of the thing. When Anthony was killed I saw the telegraph boy coming. I opened the telegram myself. The message was for me. Anthony was my husband, Calypso had no business –' Helena was excited.

Max put his arms round her. 'Helena, where is your calm? The girls do not worry. Calypso has not behaved badly, she –'

'She always behaves badly. I hear she is having affairs all over the place since Hector went overseas. She –'

'Opening the telegram and having affairs are two different things. Maybe she thought she was doing right to open the telegram. You are old-fashioned, my Phlegm, you –'

'Old-fashioned?'

'No, darling, it is my bad English. I am Continental. I do not think poor Calypso behaved –'

'Poor! That girl's rich, not only Hector's money, she's rich in gall. You be careful of her, Max. Before you know where you are she'll be scrambling into bed with you.'

'Ach, Helena.' He stroked her hair, thinking of Calypso's peach-coloured body, relaxed and cheerful before rehearsals. 'She will not make a scramble, as you call it.' No such luck, thought Max. 'What can we do for Polly?' he said, regretfully remembering Calypso's recent refusal to sleep with him any more. 'We should do something. Go and see her, telephone first, she was not thrilled to see us when her parents had been killed.'

'That was different. Poor Polly. What a lovely time we had, the taxi full of flowers. I shall never forget that morning in Covent Garden.' Helena kissed him as she had learned, open-mouthed.

'We telephone presently, my darling.' He pushed her back on the bed. 'We telephone later.' He ran his tongue along her teeth.

'We've only just had breakfast,' said Helena, yielding.

'You still think love is only for between ten thirty p.m. and midnight?'

'Not any more. Come, ruin my make-up. What time is your rehearsal?'

'Shush, *meine Kleine* –'

Later Helena told Sarah on the telephone: 'We rang up but she did not answer. I think she must have gone to work. How much do you think she cares, Sarah?'

'Terribly, I should think. Let's let her be. I offered to come up but she put me off for a few days, said the Floyer twins are coming on leave for two nights. I shall come when they are gone; perhaps it's better for the young to be together. She said Calypso's being very helpful.'

'That will be the day,' said Helena. 'Calypso never helps anyone but herself.'

'Oh, I don't know,' said Sarah, remembering that Calypso had made Oliver telephone when he returned from Norway. 'She's a dark horse. I've known her unselfish.'

Helena, repairing her make-up, wondered whether Sarah had been giving her a small dig. Nobody could call me unselfish these days, she thought, creaming her face. Here am I, making up for lost time, so happy. I must go to Hatchards, she thought, and choose some books for Richard and send something nice to Monika, who looks after him as I should be doing, cares for Sophy in a way I could never manage. How extraordinary it is, thought

Helena, wiping the cream off and starting again, that with all the dreadful news from the Middle East, with Walter dead, with the war spreading all over the world, I should be so happy and Calypso, so different from me, looks as though she is thoroughly enjoying herself. Were it not for Hitler I should never have met Max, were it not for the war Hector would not have decided to marry again. The Jews may be enslaved, thought Helena, powdering her nose, but I am free of boring, boring Richard. If the telegraph boy had not brought me the telegram to say Anthony was killed, what sort of woman would I have become? Certainly not Max's mistress. I still think, Helena told herself, that Calypso was wrong to open that telegram. It was addressed to Polly. Carefully applying lipstick, Helena tried to recall her feelings in 1917 when she grieved for her young husband. She had been wearing a grey herringbone tweed skirt, a white blouse and a woolly cardigan which dipped where she overloaded her pockets. She remembered that she had a cold which weeping made worse, that her period had started the night before she got the news. She remembered being thankful that she was not pregnant. That her mother-in-law wept, exclaiming, 'He was the flower of the flock', she being left with two other sons, both black sheep. Helena stared at her present-day face in the glass. After Anthony's death she had met Richard. A bit unfair when the Great War had left three million surplus women that she should find another husband and now have a lover; a fresh lease in this new war.

A little later, stepping out into the street, Helena met the postman. A bill and a letter in Richard's writing for herself. She put the bill on the hall table then opened Richard's envelope. Richard wrote that, things being what they were and clothes rationed, he was coming to London to visit his tailor and would be staying with Helena in her new house while he had his fittings. This would not take more than a few weeks. He was sure, wrote Richard, that Helena would agree it was wise to buy the best and make the most sensible and lasting use of one's coupons. Also, wrote Richard, it would be nice while he was in London to see a few shows. He hoped Helena would accompany him. It would be an excellent opportunity to attend one of Max's concerts. Since Monika was reluctant to leave Cornwall – there was really no one she could entrust with the cow and the hens – she was giving him her list of shopping and 'I've told her that of course you will be only too delighted to help me with it'.

Helena stood in her hall with the street door open, feeling a fog of intolerable boredom engulf her. How dared he enter her new world? She knew she could not stop him. She re-read the letter. There was no escape. There was a postscript: 'I thought we might go down and take Sophy out from school.' Helena crushed the letter in both hands. 'You might,' she muttered resentfully, 'I won't.' That afternoon she telephoned Sarah again.

'Sarah, could you not come and spend a few nights? You can visit Polly and help me at the same time.'

'What help do you need?' Sarah sounded harassed.

'Richard is proposing himself to stay for weeks. Don't laugh, it's not funny.'

'I'll see what I can do, how long I can be spared.'

'I shall be so grateful,' said Helena. 'He could, he may –'

'I'll come. He won't spoil anything for you, I'll see to that.'

Helena, conscious of the fragility of her happiness, felt a rush of gratitude.

Driving down the motorway with Hamish all those years later she said: 'One did not feel safe at that time.'

'When was that then?'

'During the war.'

'I should imagine not, the bombing must have been pretty frightening.'

'Oh, I didn't mind the bombing, it was my husband –'

'I never knew him.' Hamish was puzzled as he drove fast, pushing a button to squirt water on his windscreen,

switching on the wipers to clear the dust. What had been
wrong with this old creature's husband? Come to think of
it, had she not had two?

'What?' said Hamish, trying to find something to say.
'Why?'

'He barged in at a delicate period. Of course later on
nothing mattered. Max and I were as established as H. G.
Wells and Rebecca West –'

'Didn't he keep trotting off with other ladies?'

'Of course he did. So did Max, but he always came back
to me and Monika.'

'Who was Monika?'

'Monika was his wife, she died. You must have met her.'

'Of course. What did your husband do?' I must get these
relationships straight, thought Hamish. They are of his-
torical interest.

'He bored,' said Helena in her old voice, sitting beside
him. 'He was handicapped by being a bore. Now Max, with
all his faults, never bored anyone.'

'Well, no,' said Hamish, grinning at the road ahead. 'I
never knew him well but I found him a very lively person,
also very courageous.'

'That's what your mother said. She maintained Max
was extremely brave, that he could have taken himself
and Monika off to America and been safe. Extraordinary
of her to think that. After all, they were perfectly safe in
England.'

'Jews,' said Hamish.

'Of course they were Jews, but we won the war. There
was no need for them to bother once they were here.'

'We might have lost it.' Hamish had read history. 'Very
nearly did.'

'It never occurred to me that we would.' Helena stuck
out her jaw. 'Never. People like your father called Dunkirk
a disaster and talked of touch and go in the Middle East,
and Oliver used to carry on about Norway, I believe. That
was a bit of a set-back but apart from the occasional
losses –'

'Singapore? Burma?'

'We got them back. There was no need for the Jews to fuss. Max was no braver than anyone else.'

'Oh.'

'Your mother showed courage, I realize that now. At the time we all thought she was being tiresome and selfish.'

'What did she do that was so special?' Hamish was ever ready to talk about his mother, with whom he had never achieved intimacy.

'At a time when children and pregnant women were being sent to the country she sat tight in London. She refused to go to her parents, she refused to go to Scotland, she paid no heed to anybody, she stayed in the London house quite alone apart from a daily woman, alone except for that dog. She wouldn't budge, said the country in wartime frightened her. She thought Max brave and she ganged up with Polly and called Richard heroic.'

'How interesting. Was he some special kind of boffin, risking his life and limb? Secret war work? That sort of thing?'

'Richard was no *boffin*.' Helena gave a cackle of laughter which ended in a fit of coughing. As she grew mauve in the face Hamish slowed the car and drew on to the hard shoulder. Stopping the car, he patted Helena gently on the back until her wheezes subsided.

'Perhaps you'd better have another swig,' he suggested, and helped her unscrew her flask. Still rather choky she took a swallow.

'Ah, that's better, much. It's comical now but I was angry at the time – yes.'

'I find it very interesting how the English all pulled together in the war and worked.'

'I wouldn't call Richard's behaviour work.' Still chuckling, Helena put the flask back in her bag. 'You'd better drive on, we shall be late for the funeral.'

26

Using the key the girl Elizabeth had left, Calypso let herself into Polly's house. She let Fling off the lead and went into the dining room to take a sheet of writing paper from the desk.

'Darling Polly,' she wrote. 'I haven't told Pa and Ma that I am pregnant. They will want me to go home and I could not bear it. The fuss. The boredom. Help me. Tell them London's safe, that I need to be near my doctor, something plausible. Love. C.' She stuck the note in an envelope and put it on the hall table. 'Come on,' she said to the dog, who was sniffing at a pile of coats on a chair. She looked closer. R.A.F. caps, overcoats, gas masks. 'The twins must be here, how lovely.' She started up the stairs. Outside Polly's room the dog pressed his nose to the door and snuffled. Calypso picked him up and. walked in. Dim light slanted through the cracks in the blackout curtains. In the bed Polly slept, her dark hair covering one cheek, her face serene, long lashes on sunburned cheeks, sad mouth relaxed; on either side of her lay David and Paul, each with an arm across her body.

Calypso held her breath. They looked peaceful, beautiful. They moved gently, enjoying in their sleep a respite from grief and war. She stepped back, closed the door, tiptoed downstairs, clipped the lead on to the dog's collar and let herself out into the street.

For the moment Polly was out of the question. She remembered the night she had come for Polly's help and been interrupted by Richard. She had since been grateful to him. She glanced up at the curtained window, then started walking towards Helena's house. If Polly had discovered what her life was about so, in her way, had Helena. A call was in order. She paced slowly, recollecting the night Oliver had walked her home, his anger, the aridity she had felt, her relief when she heard Hector crash into her bicycle, saving her from difficult talk. Now both were in the Middle East would they meet and speak of her? She put her thumb on Helena's bell, wondering which twin Polly had slept with first. She was smiling when Max opened the door. He came out quickly shutting the door behind him.

'Come on,' he said, taking her arm. 'I am going to the cinema, you come too.' He started walking her along.

'But I came to see Helena.'

'In a bad mood. Better to leave her alone for a bit, *ja*.'

'But I don't want to go to the cinema, I want –'

'You want to see the Marx Brothers in *The Night at the Opera*?'

'I saw it with Hector. It was on in Leicester Square.'

'Now it is in Kensington High Street. Laughter will do you good, you look like you need it. I need it severely.'

Calypso allowed him to propel her along at a brisk clip. 'Why?'

'Ach, Helena is in a foul mood. Your uncle comes to London, she does not want him, she has no talent for living her lives, she wants the compartments separate.'

'So would I,' said Calypso sharply, 'in her shoes.'

'You are grumpy, my Calypso.' He looked at her closely. 'Ach, you are pregnant, *nicht*?'

'How did you guess?'

'It shows in your eyes. Are you sick?'

'I'm in a permanent state of nausea.'

'It will pass. The child is Hector's?'

'Of course it is Hector's.'

'No of course. I might be honoured and who else, one asks? One sees you with others paying court, one hears –'

'Pig.'

202

'I am teasing. Is Hector pleased? He will now have his heir. In Hector's boots I should be delighted. Did you know that at Harrods one can buy boots with rubber soles called "Desert Boots"? You should send some to the proud Papa.'

'He's got some.'

'Well, then, he has an heir en route, he has boots, the brothers Marx will cheer up Mama, she will forget her nausea, we will go back sweet-tempered to Helena and her malaise.'

'Is Uncle Richard coming to London to snoop?'

'*Nein*. He says he comes to buy clothes but I think there is something else, I do not yet know what.'

'Aunt Helena will try to stop him.'

'So. I shall succeed in stopping her stopping him. Come, jump on this bus.'

As the bus careered along Max shouted: 'And Polly, have you seen poor Polly? She must mourn her brother, a lovely fellow, how will she console herself?'

'She has her work.'

'That will not be enough. We must rally round, as you call it, try to blunt the horrors of grief, keep her mind occupied with pleasant things. What can we do for her, what do you suggest?'

'I –'

'A lover is what she needs, a good lover to occupy her, but one does not find him just like that. We must –'

'We must mind our own business,' said Calypso tartly. 'Were you going to volunteer?'

'Oho, it is like that, is it, *das ist sehr interessant*.'

'You –'

'I shut up.' Max smiled wolfishly. 'Come, we get off here for our healing laughter.'

In the cinema Max's immoderate laughter proved infectious and Calypso laughed more than she had when she had seen the film with Hector. When the lights went up she found herself quite feeble and sat waiting for the cinema to empty.

'Thank you, Max, I loved it.' She smiled at him warmly.

'We should have brought Polly, perhaps.'

'Perhaps not.' Calypso grew sober. 'Of course Walter would have adored it –'

'We will go and tell Helena what she has missed.'

'Did you ask her to go with you? I bet not.'

'Mind you,' said Helena to Hamish as they drove, 'Max could be difficult. He used to go off on his own and not tell me what he had been doing. Once he came home from the cinema with Calypso, said he had met her there. I didn't believe him. It was when Calypso was having her baby, she felt sick all the time.'

'So she tells me,' said Hamish drily.

'It was you of course. One forgets. The baby was you, rather a pretty child you were, not that I like babies.'

'Nor does she.'

'She isn't a pram drooler. Where was I?'

'Max and Calypso at the cinema.'

'That's right. They had seen A Night at the Opera and came back to tea. Calypso told me she was pregnant; it was a surprise. Of course I was pleased for your father. I had a soft spot for him.'

'He rather liked you.'

'I believe he did. When Calypso told me I congratulated her. I remember it well, said I supposed she would go and live with her parents. D'you know what she said?'

'No.' Hamish kept his eyes on the road, intending to be punctual at the funeral.

'She said, "Not on your Nelly, not bloody likely." Max was surprised, too.'

'Oh.'

'Her parents, your grandparents, were dim and boring. That was one thing I agreed with Richard. Conventional, puritanical, rather badly off. They had no conception of how to treat a girl like Calypso. She had very little fun. All they ever did was repress and try to prevent her doing almost anything. Put ideas in her head, if you ask me. It was lucky for her she found your father. She might so easily, given her nature, have –'

'What?'

'Become promiscuous.' Helena chuckled. ' "Wild" would have been your grandparents' euphemism. Anyway, she said she had no intention of being bored and did I know what her mother said when she found her reading T. S. Eliot?'

'What had my grandmother said?'

'She said, "Oh, reading that man who doesn't write poetry." Max went into fits. He cried with laughter. I didn't see anything funny. He said of course Calypso couldn't go to your grandparents, it would psychologically upset the baby. Your mother said, "It's not the baby I'm worried about, it's me." Anyway, she stayed in London.'

'Did nobody try to stop her? Surely it would have been sensible to go to the country.'

'She called her mother philistine, she made T. S. Eliot an excuse. Mind you,' said Helena, watching the wide ribbon of the motorway, 'I couldn't say much at that time. I hadn't read Eliot either. I sneaked off to Harrods and bought his poems. That was one good thing about the war.'

'What was?'

'Lots of books. We couldn't buy sanitary towels but there were plenty of books published. People like me took to reading, our minds were loosened as well as our morals.'

'It's difficult to imagine you loose.'

'Well-brought-up girls like Polly and Calypso had such opportunities and I became quite a butterfly.'

Hamish was silent.

'I may look like a chrysalis now,' said Helena angrily, 'but in my forties I flowered. The war even inspired Richard. When he came to London he cramped my style. Your mother egged him on. If left to himself he would have bought his clothes and gone back to Cornwall, but she and Polly encouraged his wild ideas, they were mischievous, those girls.'

'I wish I'd known you all in those days. I've seen photographs, of course.'

Helena snorted. 'Photographs! Polly looking as though butter wouldn't melt when she was selfish, greedy and flouting convention. She got away with it because nobody could believe what she was up to. Her parents would have put a stop if they'd been alive, or at least tried. Your mother did exactly as she pleased, turned a deaf ear to advice and encouraged Richard to make a fool of himself, said he needed a bit of fun.'

'But what did he do? What was so awful?'

'I felt his behaviour reflected on me. I was annoyed with those girls, your mother in particular, and really upset when Oliver's mother took Richard's side.' Helena took another sip from the flask. Glancing sideways, Hamish surmised it held half a bottle of whisky and wondered what Helena would contribute to the funeral.

'I used to take this flask to Max's concerts; it helped me through many an evening.' Helena screwed the top on tightly. 'People thought I had a weak bladder, those constant trips to the cloakroom, ho-ho.'

'When does Uncle Richard arrive? No, no sugar, thanks, Aunt, it makes me queasy.'

'Next week. I have asked Sarah to come up to see Polly. She can help, well, help with Richard. I'm so busy.'

'I'll ask him to take me out to lunch. I'll take him off your hands.' Calypso knew that her aunt knew she knew how unwelcome Richard would be in Enderby Street.

'But you are at that office of yours all day.'

'I'm leaving it this week.'

'Don't they want you any more?'

'It's not that. I'm sick all the time. They are getting a bit cross with me, say it wastes valuable war work time.'

'Oh my dear, is it –' Helena looked at Calypso in alarm. 'I mean –'

'It's Hector's,' said Calypso stuffily. 'Do I have such a wild reputation?'

'No, no, of course not. I was going to say is it wise in wartime to have a baby?'

'Hector wants one, especially if I can grind out a boy. That's what –'

'What a way to talk! Aren't you pleased? Hector will be.'

'Hector doesn't feel sick all the time, he won't swell up like a balloon. His part was easy, it's a part he plays with enthusiasm, he –'

'That's enough, darling, not in front of Max, you'll embarrass him.'

'He doesn't look embarrassed, he's laughing. All right, let's plan how to keep Uncle Richard out of your hair.'

'Oh, Calypso.' Helena began laughing too. 'Richard will enjoy seeing you. He is so fond of you girls, he will be so glad to see you and Polly. Perhaps you could go with him to visit Sophy. I simply haven't got the time.'

'Oh.' Calypso was unbelieving. 'Really?'

'I have joined the Red Cross, that takes up my mornings and –'

'Why the Red Cross, isn't it full of snobs?'

'It's useful for Max. Red Cross charity concerts advertise his name and names are what matter. It doesn't matter if they can't tell one note from another. I can't either.'

'I bet Max knows Sir Thomas Beecham.'

'But not Lady Cunard. So you see, darling, I am busy.'

'Aunt, you have changed.'

'I just have more scope. More tea?'

'No, thank you.'

'She has asked me to call her Emerald.'

'Oh my, you fly high. When does Uncle Richard arrive? I'll meet him.' Calypso watched Max liberally buttering a scone. 'Where d'you get all this butter, Aunt?'

'Monika sends a hamper on the train every week. I send it back empty. It's bit of a nuisance having to go to Paddington to collect it but it's very useful.'

'What else does she send?'

'Cream, eggs, vegetables, fruit. She sent a lobster last week. She hadn't tied its claws properly, I got nipped.'

'Oh, Aunt!'

'Not badly.'

'Isn't it black market?'

'It's my house, my garden, my produce. Monika is my guest.'

'Grey?' suggested Max. '*Le marché gris.*'

'Nonsense, Max, you need the food.'

'I like the food. I shall also meet Richard when he arrives, he will be bringing compôtes and such.'

'I will come with you,' Calypso volunteered.

'I won't have you raiding the hampers.'

'What an idea, Aunt.'

'You should show a bit of enterprise and get Hector's people to send you grouse and venison and herrings.'

'They would go bad.'

'Kippers, then.'

'I'll think about it.'

Richard arrived with several hampers and settled into Helena's spare room, unpacking his ivory brushes, the photograph of his first wife, his toothbrushes, sponge and pyjamas, arranging them in orderly fashion in their new surroundings. Within half an hour he looked, thought Helena, ominously settled.

The following morning he limped out to make a preliminary visit to his tailor, then took a bus to the City and the East End to view the bomb damage.

'Really most impressive,' he said to Calypso, who had turned up at tea time. 'I saw a lot of rubble in France but nothing like this. There's no mud and no dead horses. Those A.R.P. chaps seem efficient at finding the bodies. One misses the smell, a sort of haunting odour of wet dead. What's it been like round your way?'

'I lost all my windows when Parliament was hit.'

'That all? Have you seen the City?'

'No.'

'Good Lord, you live in London and haven't seen it? I'll take you tomorrow, you must see the Docks and the City. I'll take you on a tour. The best way to see it is from the top of a bus. One should walk of course, but with my leg –'

'Even your new one?'

'Not the same as flesh and blood but it will not prevent me from dancing.'

'Dancing!' exclaimed Helena and Calypso in chorus.

Richard smiled with satisfaction. 'I have, or rather Monika has, enrolled me in a course of lessons at a school in Soho.'

'How many lessons?' asked Helena suspiciously.

'Twelve, two a week, so in six weeks I shall – where's she gone?' Helena, carrying the teapot, had left the room, her lips compressed.

'Did Monika suggest this course, Uncle?'

'Yes. Fact is she gets kicked when I dance with her and one gets a bit weary of dancing with a chair.'

'A chair?'

'Yes. I turn back the carpet and dance with a chair. It can't complain if it gets kicked but it's not like dancing with live flesh. But Monika complains about that too.'

'Why?'

'Keeps her awake, scraping noise on the parquet. What with that and the music she loses sleep. She has to get up early to milk the cow, says it can't wait, I ask you, she should train it. Anyway the upshot was she came up with this plan. I paid in advance, start on Wednesday.'

'A brilliant idea, terribly brave.'

'What's brave?' Helena came back carrying the teapot. 'More tea, anybody?'

'Uncle Richard learning to dance is heroic.'

'How long will this pantomime take?' Helena looked coldly at Richard.

'Six weeks, my dear. I told you.'

'My God!'

'I won't be a bother. I have my club, my tailor, Monika's shopping and I'm told there's a place called the Windmill.'

'That's for dirty old men.'

'No it isn't, Aunt Helena. Hector met someone who'd been there. He said it was good clean fun.'

'Did he go himself? No, I can see he didn't.'

'Hector would have no need,' said Richard, looking at Calypso.

'It's naked girls.' Helena sighed.

'You are in no position to talk.' Richard held out his cup for a refill.

'Now, now,' said Calypso, 'don't squabble.'

'Not that one would call you a girl any more,' pursued Richard. 'More in the class of Monika, "*femme d'un certain age*" fits the bill. Now you've abandoned me and taken to this life in London you have beauty –'

'Thanks,' said Helena, interrupting.

'Of course Monika is sensitive. She has a lot to put up with, not knowing whether her son is alive – dead, if you ask me, but women go on hoping – and Max carrying on with you and again, if you ask me, others as well. What d'you think, Calypso?'

'I wouldn't know.'

'Of course you know, fellow's got an eye for the girls and it's not only his eye.' Richard, watching Helena, burst into a guffaw. 'Anyway, who am I to grumble, Monika puts up with it. Life in Cornwall seems to suit her. She did offer to teach me herself but I preferred the chair. A chair does what you want, doesn't try to lead, it bloody goes where you push.'

'What do you do for music? There aren't many dance records in the house.'

'That's a point, clever of you. There's a late-night programme of dance music on the wireless, that keeps her awake too, then she starts thinking about her boy, I daresay.'

'Yes,' said Calypso, 'she probably does.' She remembered Monika's anguish.

'Well, now, suppose I trot round and see Polly? Back from work by now, I expect. I want to ask her to come down and see Sophy. I've never seen a girls' school at close range.'

'I'd ring up first,' said Calypso hastily.

'Really? Like that, is she? My word, you've all changed. I'll probably find Sophy doesn't want to be taken out.'

'Of course she does. I'll come with you. Let's make a day of it, unless you want to go, Aunt Helena?' Helena shook her head. 'Fling will love a day in the country. Let's have a picnic.'

'All right. I'll telephone the school.'

'I'll tell her I'm having a baby. I wonder what she'll say to that.'

'There's a cooked chicken in one of the hampers, the one they called Jane. Sophy was rather fond of it but it's stopped laying so Monika gave it the chop.'

'What brutality.'

'You sure Polly wouldn't like to come too? Take her mind off Walter. The Floyer boys are stationed somewhere near, it might be possible –'

'They've been moved to another station now they are on ops again.'

'Pity, we might have combined – seen them lately, have you?'

'No,' said Calypso obliquely, 'no.'

'They are known as the "High Floyers" in the village. Baptist minister having a dig at the Rector's high churchmanship. Jolly good joke until they got shot down. Perhaps Sophy has some little friends who'd like a blowout. That's what children like when they are at school.'

'She won't be a child much longer.' Helena eyed her husband thoughtfully.

'All the more reason I should do a bit more than just pay the bills. I write, of course, and she writes back, but when she's at home I sometimes wonder –'

'Wonder what?' Helena voiced anxiety.

'Whether she's quite normal. Not a tear when Walter was killed, left a note on the hall table and disappeared on some long walk, it was a shock for Monika and me. "Calypso phoned, Walter is killed." Just like that, I ask you. It was cold of her.'

'I expect she was glad it was not Oliver.' Calypso looked thoughtfully at Helena. 'She loves him.'

'Rubbish, a child doesn't know about love. What she'll mind is if she discovers what she's eating is Jane,' said Richard sarcastically.

'You dolt,' said Helena viciously.

211

27

'Well, one hopes one gave some pleasure.' Richard fumbled for the hinge of his leg through the material of his trousers. 'Sophy's little friends were a lot more forthcoming than she was. She was more interested in the grub than in us, if you ask me.'

'She was glad to see us.'

'You quite sure? I got more change out of her little friends, not that they gave me much information about Sophy.'

'She says she hardly knows them. They aren't in her form. She was sorry for them because nobody takes them out.'

'Really? That shows a proper spirit. I was wrong about Jane. "Is this Jane?" the girl asks, biting into the drumstick, then, with her mouth full, "Can I have a bit of breast?" And then haggled as to who should pull the wishbone. I told you she was cold. Well, we've done our duty.' Richard eased his leg into position and shook open the evening paper. The guard blew his whistle. The train started towards Liverpool Street with a clang.

Calypso pulled down the blackout blind and, leaning back, closed her eyes. Thinking of Sophy's ivory-coloured face, watchful eyes, full-lipped vulnerable mouth, she could not think of her as cold, nor was she unloving, Calypso thought, with a pang of envy.

It had been a crisp blue and gold day and the Backs had looked their best. She and Sophy had walked slowly, following Richard ahead with the two guest girls, one redheaded, one fair. She had told Sophy about her impending child.

'What will you do with it?' Sophy had known instinctively that Calypso could not, would not cope.

She found herself telling Sophy of her visit to Scotland and the plan she had made. Sophy perfectly understood that Hector's castle would receive the baby with joy. She told Sophy about Catherine, the lame woman who would take charge of the infant and bring it up. Walking and talking with Sophy she described the Scottish environment objectively. Sophy needed no explanation or excuse as to why it was not an environment she could bear but would be perfect for Hector's child.

'I suppose Catherine loves Hector?'

'I believe she does.'

'Is it Hector's fault that she is lame?'

'He feels responsible but she says the accident was not his fault, would have happened anyway.'

'Is that true?' Sophy watched her uncle limping ahead. Now and again he touched one of the girls, putting a hand on arm or shoulder.

'She doesn't elaborate.'

'He would feel guilty if he does not love her. What have you arranged?'

Calypso explained that when the child was due Catherine would come. 'I have booked a room in a nursing home in Wimpole Street.'

'And then?'

'Then she will take it up to Scotland and bring it up in Hector's nursery. The place is full of Commandos but there's a comfortable room in the nursery wing, above the kitchens.'

'Won't you have milk?'

'Milk?'

'Won't you feed it? People do. I've learned about it, it's called "breast-feeding".'

'I couldn't bear to.' Calypso shuddered, unconsciously raising her hands to her breasts. Sophy said nothing, watching the figures walking ahead. Then she said carelessly, 'Of course not, they are private. What else?'

Sophy broke into her rare laughter, laughing at

214

Calypso who began to laugh too.

'I haven't told anybody. Hector left me to find out for myself. The bastard. His family are Catholic, all his people up there are Catholic. He's in disgrace for divorcing Daphne, they don't think of me as his proper wife.'

'Will they think the baby is –'

'Blood's thicker than religion in its case, and while they can't take to me they'll love the child.'

'You've never bothered about religion.'

'Of course I haven't, none of us does, look at the twins. Mr Floyer's a parson but you'd never know from their behaviour. It appears Hector's is one of those very old Scottish families who survived Henry VIII's mob. It's rather smart. I am mugging them up.'

'I suppose he thought you might not marry him if you knew.'

'Of course I would have. I married him because he's rich, everyone knows that.'

'I hope he's not going to put his hand up their skirts,' exclaimed Sophy suddenly.

'What?'

'Uncle Richard. That's what he used to do to me. He keeps patting Valerie and stroking Miranda.'

'Then let's walk faster and catch them up.' Calypso increased her pace.

'Didn't he do it to you and Polly?'

'I suppose he did, in a mild form. Oh Sophy, how awful, hurry.'

'It's not awful,' said Sophy. 'It's just boring, but they wouldn't understand. Uncle Richard!' She let out a shout. 'Wait for us.' Ahead of them the two girls turned innocent faces alight with enquiry. 'Calypso wants to see King's Chapel, it's the other way.'

'Then we can have tea in a tea shop if we can find one,' said Calypso to Miranda the redhead.

'That would be nice,' said Miranda. 'Could we go to a lavatory before King's Chapel?'

'I'll wait for you in the Chapel,' said Richard. 'Rest my leg.'

Watching him asleep in the opposite corner Calypso felt affection. He had played his avuncular part. All those two girls had been interested in was gobbling the picnic lunch. Why should he not put his hand up their skirts? she thought indignantly. They wore elastic in their knickers. She had observed the blonde Valerie wrapping a fairy cake in her handkerchief and stuffing it up under her gym tunic.

'Come to me sometimes on your way through London,' she had said to Sophy.

'May I? I would love that. Polly often gets very full up.'

And what, Calypso thought, did Sophy mean by that? What did she know?

'Not bad little friends, those two of Sophy's.' Richard woke suddenly. 'Quite pretty and appetizing in their way. Pity Sophy's growing up so fast.'

'She's going to be a beauty.'

'D'you think so?'

'Yes. Those eyes, like jet. Who was her father, Uncle Richard?'

'Well may you ask! Better not to enquire, I never did. Wouldn't have been much use if I'd wanted to. Her mother was dead by the time I reached her and I was left holding the baby, I ask you. Fortunately I had persuaded Helena to marry me, not that she has ever taken to the child. She is not a child lover.'

'Nor am I.'

Richard laughed. 'Find a wet nurse.'

'I've found a nurse. It can have a bottle.'

'Well then, there's nothing to it.'

'I still have to bear the thing.'

'Strong girl like you.' Richard Cuthbertson snapped his fingers. 'Nothing to it. My poor sister was the runt of the family.'

'Oh? I know nothing about her.'

'Brains though, she had brains, and this mania for travelling, couldn't be content with her own country, always off abroad somewhere. I couldn't keep up with her travels.'

'Did her husband?'

'She didn't have a husband, good Lord, no. Would have tied her down, stopped all that drifting round the world. She came back to base to have Sophy – a British passport matters even to people like my sister – just in time, she was practically born in the docks. She ran it fine.'

'Where had she been?'

'Your guess is as good as mine. By the time I got the letter the child was born and my sister dead.'

'Oh. Was there –'

'Nothing. Padre chap had given her the last rites and she died. If the stupid fellow had stopped to think he might have gleaned a shred of information, but he was high like Floyer, keen on spiritual matters, R.C. now I come to think of it. Supposed he was doing the right thing. Fellow said, "Your sister died in a state of grace." How did he *know*? Said she gasped out "Tell my brother", then kicked the bucket. I've been wondering ever since what the message was.' Richard Cuthbertson lifted the blind and peered out into the darkness. 'Getting into London by the look of it. Indo-China.'

'What?'

'Looks as if she came from Indo-china. Now what's happened? Why are we stopping?'

'Some delay.'

The train sighed, hissed, then all was quiet. Calypso tried to catch the words from a conversation in the next carriage. There was a long pause.

'Life isn't easy, is it?' Richard looked at his niece.

'Not really.'

'I saw you today. I can't help liking little girls, they are so pretty.'

'Uncle Richard, you needn't –'

'I never hurt them. Didn't hurt you or Polly, did I? Now Sophy's growing up, growing away. People say Ruskin was a stinker but I don't suppose he could help himself, probably had only looked at pictures and statuary. "Art" was different in his day, poor fellow was a virgin like as not, then when he married he got the hell of a

217

shock. Were you a virgin when you married?'

'Of course I was.'

'No of course. Bet you got a shock.'

'Actually –'

'Ah, the train's starting. Unexploded bomb on the line, do you think?'

'There haven't been any raids for ages.'

'Nor there have. Funny effect trains have, one finds oneself talking as though one were in limbo, voicing private, er, really private ideas. Just ideas, of course.'

'Of course, Uncle Richard.'

'That's all right, then. The extraordinary thing is that I don't mind it on Monika, actually like it, and she doesn't shave her armpits like you girls.'

'That's Continental.' Calypso began to laugh.

'What are you laughing at?'

'You, Uncle Richard, oh-oh-oh!' Calypso wiped her eyes with the back of her hand. 'Ah-ah-ah oh!' she moaned. 'Oh!'

'I wish I knew what's so funny. You children make a mock of me. I'm just a one-legged misfit in this bloody war.' Richard suddenly felt rage. 'I go to my club and it's full of every conceivable ass in uniform and I am totally useless. Helena has a lover, a well-known violinist, she's sick of her boring one-legged husband. I've never ever been able to make love to her, I ask you. I never liked women until –'

'Monika?'

'Yes. Why am I talking such tommy rot, it's being in a train, what's the matter?' Calypso had moved to sit beside him, putting an arm round his shoulders.

'You're brave, Uncle Richard, you are contributing so much. Look what you've done to my morale. I was depressed. You are wonderful.' Calypso was between laughter and tears.

'No, no.' Richard looked embarrassed.

'Yes, yes, awfully brave. We all love you, you know we do.'

'Rubbish.' Richard grew red in the face.

218

'It's true,' cried Calypso, making it true for herself at least. 'Without you all our lives would be different. Think how you rescued Max and Monika from internment – marvellous.'

'We are getting into the station, let's see if we can find a taxi.' Richard was embarrassed.

Calypso combed her hair and applied lipstick. When the train stopped she took Richard's arm as he limped up the platform.

'Will you be godfather to the baby, Uncle Richard?'

'I don't think I'd be much good. I'm not rich and don't believe in God. Kind of you to ask, though.'

'I mean it.'

'In that case, thank you. I will think about it.'

'Here's a taxi, we're in luck. Get in, quick.'

Richard scrambled in, dragging his leg. The taxi wound its way through dark streets and Richard sat silent. Then said: 'Wish I'd been in those raids, a fellow feels a bit left out.'

'I expect there will be more. Will you drop me at the next corner? I'm practically home.'

'Tell the driver. Thank you for coming with me.'

'I enjoyed it. Goodnight, Uncle. This will do.' Calypso opened the taxi door.

'Goodbye, my dear. She did offer to shave her, er, you know –'

'What? Who?' Calypso was half out of the cab.

'Monika, her pussy, but I said – well, take care of yourself. Enderby Street, driver.'

There were two letters from Hector on the mat. Calypso shut the door and drew the curtains before sitting down to read. That he had not yet heard of the baby was clear. He wrote in his neat script of the people he knew now gathered in Cairo, an old school friend who drove a dog cart to save petrol, of swimming at the Gehzira club, tennis, visits to the pyramids, the ill-feeling emanating from King Farouk, the constant round of parties, the wives who had managed to join their husbands, his doubts as to whether it would be safe for her

219

were she to wish to come. He wrote about the light and the smell and that some day he would love to bring her to Egypt. Then he wrote of his plans for peace and several paragraphs Calypso skipped, of his political views, how they were changing. Then rather stiltedly the letter ended, leaving Calypso wondering whether she missed this man, this political animal, a man as old as her father. At least, she thought, he is interested in women, not pining after little girls. Still in the second letter Hector had not heard of her pregnancy. She frowned. Hector wrote that he planned to buy land in England and plant trees.

Seeing all this desert makes me crave for trees. There was once a forest along the shores of North Africa. The Romans felled the trees and never replanted, hence the soil erosion which caused the desert in which we fight. I write metaphorically. My part in the fighting so far is from an office desk. Perhaps I can remedy this. Back to my dream. I shall plant woods of oak, beech, chestnut and among them flowering cherries. I will plant the cherries in curves and circles so that when some future airman flies over them he will see the name Calypso spelled out in blossom. I was in hospital with a fever when I made this plan. I met your cousin Oliver in a bar yesterday, on leave. He has desert boils, disagreeable but not fatal, love, Hector.

Calypso sat with the thin sheets of airmail paper in her lap. This was a Hector she did not know. There were few trees in Scotland. Pines, birches and rowans. It had been cold on their honeymoon, cold when she had travelled up to see Catherine. She had walked along the track by the river. Catherine, the ghillie's daughter, had limped along, speaking in her lilting voice, stopping to point out the rock that Hector had bullied her into jumping from when he came home from school for the holidays, forcing her to leap so that he could catch her, boasting of his strength. 'There,' she had said, pointing with her sharp chin. 'There we fell and my leg it was that broke.'

'And left you lame,' said Calypso, shocked.

'Aye.' Catherine smiled. 'To remember him by.'

They had stood looking at each other, the older woman's clear blue eyes looking into Calypso's heavily fringed, greenish blue in the Highland light. Then, laughing, the older woman had closed the episode. 'Yon Daphne was no leaper such as you, and our Hamish will love the glens, do not worry. He will stride the hills.'

Sitting alone in battered London Calypso thought not of Hector but of the mountains and rushing streams which were his background, the scudding clouds and driving rain which had turned to snow, of Catherine coming to stir the fire in her bedroom and put another eiderdown over her in Hector's bed, where she felt an alien. She felt grateful that Catherine, like Hector, made no effort to make her love that savage beauty, accepting her as a Southerner, respecting her for not pretending like Daphne to acceptance by Hector's people. By hints and casual references Hector's people had made it clear that, though Daphne was still in God's eyes Hector's wife, in their hearts they regretted it.

Calypso telephoned Polly.

'What are desert boils?'

'No idea. Why?'

'Hector says Oliver has them.'

'Poor Oliver. Ask Aunt Sarah, she is due in London soon. Are you coming round? The twins are here.'

'Not tonight, I'm quite busy.'

'Doing what?'

'Nothing. It takes all my time.'

'Are you all right all alone?'

'I have Fling. I prefer to be alone.'

'That's not like you.'

'Ah, well.' She put down the receiver.

'Pregnancy is making her unsociable,' said Polly to David, who was peeling potatoes for their supper.

'She was always a bit unpredictable,' murmured the other twin. 'A solo artist.'

221

'Not like us,' said his brother. 'But we were fated, born as we were.'

'After all these years I still don't know which of you is the eldest.' Polly paused in her task of laying the able.

'Nor do we know,' said Paul. 'Our parents took the attitude that the first shall be last and the last first. Father living up to his churchy principles and Mother with her idea of fair play.'

'Oh.'

'Rather like you, darling. Will these be enough potatoes?'

Polly blushed, looking from one brother to another. 'I think they are right,' she said. 'You give me a seed of hope.'

'Will you go and see them when we are gone?'

'Gone where?'

'Overseas, darling. The way things are going we are bound to be posted. All the action is in North Africa now. One or both of us may find ourselves in Malta.'

'Oh God, no!' Polly burst into tears.

'As bad as that, is it? We rather guessed.' They faced Polly, who stood in her kitchen apron, an oven glove in her hand, tears streaming down her cheeks.

'Don't cry, sweetheart, think how good the sun will be for us.'

'We can't leave it all to the Pongos. Hector and Oliver have been out there for ages. Nothing has happened to them.'

'Oliver's got boils, Calypso told me.' Polly's tears seemed limitless.

'And Hector has an office job, I know.' Gently they held her, patting her, wiping her tears, stroking her brown hair away from her face. 'There,' they said, 'there. Better now.'

Polly gulped strangled words against David's shoulder, laying her head against him, reaching a hand for Paul.

'It's Walter.'

'That was months and months ago.'

222

'I know, but it's still –'

The brothers exchanged smiles across her tangled hair.

'Come, blow your nose. You may not have to weep for us.'

'When are you likely to go?'

'We have guesswork, that's all. You probably hear more in your office.'

'Hence the tears.' Polly dried her eyes, trying to subdue her fear.

28

Left on her own in Cornwall Monika increased the production of food. To hens she added ducks, letting them stray round the flower garden to eat slugs. She bought two rabbits and put them on the tennis court where, wired in, they lolloped, oblivious of the fate in store. The General came and examined the pretty creatures.

'You realize, Monika, my dear, that you have two bucks. You have been sold a pup.'

'I do not understand.'

'You will never get young with two bucks. You must kill one of these and get a doe.'

The upshot was a rabbit stew such as the General had not imagined possible. He invited himself to come again, to the delight of the villagers who followed his every movement, as reported by Mrs Penrose. Bets were laid as to whether the General would entice Monika into his bachelor household before Richard returned from London or Max visited again. At the Rectory Mildred Floyer remarked to her husband that village gossip might have some foundation and that Monika was strangely naïve.

'She is tormented by fear for her son. Anything that takes her mind off him is a good thing,' said the Rector. 'The W.I. should have gone in for rabbits. They should not wait for Monika to set an example.'

'She is not a member.'

'Why not?'

'Because she is a foreigner, not even of the English variety. Her delicatessens infuriate them.'

'Dear God! Women!' The Rector felt safe to protest to God in his own kitchen.

'She will,' said Mildred, laughing, 'go too far. They are shocked by the fungi, disgusted by the garlic, furious that without a trace of black market she produces so much. They hope she will come to grief.'

'Has she not enough grief?'

'They hope that she will alienate the men as well.'

'You are usually right,' said the Rector. 'Poor woman. We, at least, know more or less what our High Flyers are up to.'

'More or less,' said Mildred. 'Though sometimes it seems to me they perch rather often in Polly's house.'

'They have known Polly all their lives. It was Calypso who struck me as a potential menace before she settled down.'

'And how settled is that, one wonders.'

The Rector did not reply but went to struggle with his sermon, to preach peace which he believed in yet give comfort to the parishioners who had sons at war.

Sophy, home for the holidays, borrowed Mrs Penrose's bicycle to go to Newlyn harbour where, although entrance to the quays was forbidden to anyone without a pass, she had found that a blind eye was turned to a child, especially if the child brought eggs to barter for fish.

Sitting on an upturned lobster pot above a Belgian trawler tied to the quay, having swopped her eggs for a langouste, she listened to the fishermen talking with savage glee of the night's trawl in incomprehensible Flemish. Men drifted in twos and threes to join the group and slap backs, every now and then breaking into laughter. Willy Penrose, a second cousin of Mrs Penrose, came and sat on a bollard.

'What's going on, Willy?'

Willy glanced around, then said: 'They made a funny catch last evening.'

'Oh, what?'

'Not for me to say. Ain't you getting a bit big to be coming into the harbour?'

'What happened, Willy?'

'Cross your heart?' He squinted at her.

'Cross my heart, Willy.'

Willy bent forward, putting a cigarette in his mouth, cupping his hands round the match.

'Jerry plane came down between Land's End and Scillies. Jerry pilot bales out. Belgian picks him out of the drink, ties a rope round his feet then trawls 'im behind. The Belgians ain't fond of Jerries.'

'Oh, Willy!' Sophy stared aghast.

'Crossed your heart, didn't you? No need to believe what I say, plenty don't.'

'Oh, Willy.'

'You stop coming into the harbour where you don't belong to be then. Take your lobster home and don't come again. You're a big girl now, too big to creep in.'

Sophy found her bicycle, put the langouste in the basket and half an hour later, obsessed by the picture of the pilot's body trawling through the sea, skidded on a patch of cow dung and crashed, barking both knees. She was sitting in the road examining her wounds when voices from a nearby cottage drifted through the air. She limped to the cottage and knocked. When a woman opened the door she mutely pointed to her knees. She was led in, sat in a chair, had her wounds painfully bathed, was given a cup of tea and told she would be taken home as soon as Dad came with his car.

'The bicycle.' Sophy shivered from shock.

'Our Tom, go and fetch it.'

A mutinous looking boy went out and clattered the bicycle, propping it against the gate.

'Mrs Penrose's bike, ain't it?'

'Yes, she lent it to me. Is it hurt?'

'Nay.' The boy sat angrily at the kitchen table, putting both hands protectively over a cardboard box.

His mother glanced at him and, continuing the argument Sophy had interrupted, said: 'You take them straight back to that John.'

'Can't. He won't give me back my knife.'

'Do as I tell 'ee.'

'I can't.'

'What you can't is keep those things here.' She looked at Sophy sipping her tea. 'Tom's swapped his knife for guinea pigs, proper pests. I'll throw them out.'

'Do then. I don't want them.' The boy thrust the box towards his mother and slammed out of the house.

'He brings animals home and lets them die,' said his mother.

'Really?'

'Pups, kittens, birds, they all die, as though our lads getting killed weren't enough.'

'Have you got a son in the forces?'

'No, but this war aggravates me. You from Cuthbertsons' up on cliff?'

'Yes.'

'Lost your cousin. Drowned, I suppose.'

'Yes.'

'You have the guinea pigs then. Tom's dad gets angry with all he brings home. 'Tisn't as though the child cared.'

Presently Tom's Dad dropped Sophy, the bicycle and the guinea pigs at the house and Monika put them in with the rabbits. That evening the General called, bringing a bottle of cheap sherry.

'If you don't like it you can use it for cooking.'

'Of course I shall like it. Come and see what Sophy was given today.' Monika led the way to the tennis court.

'There,' she said, pointing proudly.

'By Jove, takes one back, used to keep guinea pigs as a boy. Trouble is they breed faster than rabbits, used to drive my mother mad.' Putting his arm round Monika's waist the General gave it a squeeze.

'Reminds me of Peru,' said Monika, moving away. 'Max did a concert tour of South America and from Lima we went up into the mountains to see the villages.'

'Women wear bowler hats, I hear. Heard about the German plane? Limping home, lucky shot by some ack

228

ack in Bristol I daresay, ditched off Land's End, Belgian trawler picked up the pilot, dead when they got him to Newlyn.'

'How dreadful.' Monika looked at the General in distress.

'Germans, Monika, they were Germans. It was an enemy plane, nothing dreadful about that.'

Monika frowned and went into the house.

'If one didn't know she was worrying about her son one would think she was pro-German,' the General said to Sophy in disgust.

'She doesn't like anyone getting killed.'

'Womanish rubbish. Don't you start. Can't have a war without killing, wouldn't do at all.'

'She didn't want a war.'

'Can't understand her attitude, such a pretty woman, such a good cook.'

Upstairs, face down on her bed, Monika lay wishing Max would come to her for a few days, speak to her in their native tongue, relax for her the constant strain of being an alien in a land at war with her country. She had let them believe her fear of air-raids kept her from London. It was convenient, while Helena created an establishment where Max could invite fellow musicians and get into the English scene, easier for him with Helena. Once acclimatized she knew Helena's ascendancy would weaken. Monika lay listening to the waves breaking against the cliffs. She feared the sea and at times she loathed the English, with their obstinate courage, their patronizing kindness. Her heart ached for Viennese jokes, for the smell of hot chocolate and Continental cigarettes. Max had told her of the bribe to get them to America, a country she liked even less than England. She was thankful he had refused. She opened the drawer of her bedside table and allowed herself to look at a snapshot of Pauli. He frowned in sulky reproach, filling her with guilt.

'Is that your son?' She had not heard Sophy come in. 'I did knock.'

229

'I was a long way away. Yes, that is Pauli if,' she added, 'he is still alive.' Monika put the photograph back in the drawer.

'The General left. Said he'd come back another day.' She exchanged glances with Monika. 'He has a shine on you.'

'What's that?'

'He's falling in love with you, like Uncle Richard.' They laughed. 'Are you very unhappy?'

'An attack of homesickness, that's all.'

'That's enough,' exclaimed Sophy. 'I have it all the time at school. Do you hate it here very much?'

'Only sometimes. What I miss is my mother tongue.'

'Oh.'

'Max says that we must always speak English, learn to think in English, sometimes I rebel. I was thinking just now of the smells of home. Do you understand?'

'Yes, I do. At school I think of the smell of the camomile lawn. What did Pauli smell like? I hope I shall meet him. You won't rush straight back, will you? Will you go and find him, or will he find you?'

'We will never go back. Jews move on.'

'Then he will come here and I will meet him. I wish,' said Sophy, looking out at the scudding clouds, 'I wish they'd all come home. Walter won't. Oh Monika.' She threw herself into Monika's arms, told of the Belgian trawler and what Willy Penrose had said.

Presently comforted in Monika's arms she said, 'Don't let's tell anybody.'

'It would be no use. Only the other side commits atrocities,' said Monika drily.

'But –'

'You think Oliver would not, nor Hector nor the twins?' Monika spoke bitterly. 'They will be given medals. Gongs, as they call them.'

'It's not the same,' Sophy sobbed. 'The fishermen weren't English.'

'But the man who told you was pleased, *nicht*? He approved, *nicht*? He was English.'

'Yes, I suppose – well, Cornish.'

'Then what is the difference? The Nazis are not the only ones.'

'They started it.'

'By the time this is finished none of us will care who started it.' Monika smoothed Sophy's hair. 'Come,' she said, 'help me pack the hampers for our brave family in London.'

'All right.'

'Will you take some eggs to Mrs Floyer for me, and some butter for Herr Floyer? He does not eat enough.'

Sophy propped the bicycle against the porch and walked into the Rectory without knocking. From the kitchen area she heard Mildred Floyer's voice, 'Not so loud,' almost drowned by the sound of children singing a breathless version of Fred Astaire's 'Putting on my top hat', as they tap danced round the big iron boiler of uncertain age and horrible temperament which heated the bath water.

'Monika sent you these eggs and the butter is for Herr Floyer.' Sophy handed over her basket.

'She behaves as though I starve him. He has always been thin, he eats like a horse. Oh, children,' she raised her voice. 'Not quite so much noise, please.' The racket subsided slightly. 'Come into the kitchen, darling. The Herr Floyer will be most grateful, he will probably pass it on to someone he thinks more worthy. Don't tell Monika.'

'Of course not. Your evacuees seem to be flourishing. How are the nits?'

'We have them under control.'

'They all seem very settled.'

'Yes. Some went home, but if the raids start again they will be back.'

'None for ages. Have you heard from Paul and David?'

'Yes, coming on leave, both of them.'

'How lovely.'

'Not lovely, it's embarkation leave.' Mildred Floyer looked anxious.

'Oh, where?'

231

'I don't know. Why is it worse to have them overseas? They are in danger, anyway. It's their second or third tour, I'm losing count.'

'No telephone. A long time for letters. Not being able to imagine the place, I suppose. I try and –'

'Yes?'

'I try and imagine Hector when I see Calypso and Oliver, of course, when I see Aunt Sarah.' And, Sophy thought, at all other times. 'Perhaps they will all meet out there and think of home.'

Mildred stood by the kitchen table holding Monika's basket. 'It's so difficult to realize what's going on. There is so little sign of war. People training, of course, those Commandos round St Ives and now the Americans, but we never actually see anything happening.'

In her mind's eye Sophy saw the body towed behind the Belgian trawler. 'Monika says both sides commit atrocities.'

'What a funny thing to say. She's foreign, of course.'

'Well?'

'Poor Monika. Her son. There seems no way for people like Monika to find out. You'd think the Red Cross –'

'She says the Red Cross have no access to concentration camps.'

'I think, I hope Monika exaggerates. It really is hard to believe that even Hitler – surely our propaganda – I mean that exaggerates too. I am sure when the war is over she will find her Pauli is quite all right and has been doing something useful all the time.' Mildred clutched at her Christian ethics.

'I think he is probably dead.'

'Sophy, what an awful thing to say.'

'Why? He wouldn't be suffering as he is now.'

'Not if he's in a good job.'

'He is a pianist.'

'Well, then, he is probably entertaining the troops. They can't be all that different from us.'

'But he's a Jew, not allowed to work.'

'Oh.' Mildred put the eggs away. 'None of us knows

232

anything and now the boys are off overseas I don't know what to think. We listen to the news but it doesn't really tell us anything, does it? All those names . . .'

'Tobruk, Cairo, El Alamein, Malta,' said Sophy.

'Don't say Malta. I think if they are sent there I shall go mad.' She put the butter on a plate and moved to the larder. 'I can't afford to go mad,' she added. 'I have too much to do, all these children. Tell Monika that I will have the boys here this time. I'd like them to be under their own roof as it's the –' Hopelessly Mildred began to cry. 'Sorry to be so silly.'

'It won't be the last time,' said Sophy stoutly. 'Don't cry, Mrs Floyer.' She handed Mildred a handkerchief.

'I think it's that tune,' said Mildred, 'those children have been singing it non-stop for six weeks. It's on my nerves.'

'It's the best one to tap dance to.' Sophy found herself singing the tune as she pedalled home along the track through the fields. At the top she looked out across the sea, flecked with white horses. Below her the cliff path was overgrown by bracken and brambles. Were it not for the barbed wire there would be no trace of the Terror Run. 'Putting on my top hat,' sang Sophy, pedalling into the wind. 'Tra-la-la my tails.' Her eyes stung in the cold wind, which snatched her voice, to drown it among the gulls lower down the cliff.

233

29

Arriving early and leaving late, Polly immersed herself in her work. She forced herself to listen, to write, to talk of nothing but her work. She surprised the people she worked with by joining them for cups of tea, or lunch, and accepting offers of drinks or meals which normally she would refuse. Once home she turned on the radio or telephoned friends, catching up with people she had let drop. She widened her circle but avoided people close to her, busy filling her life with trivia so that she did not know what might be happening to Helena, Calypso or Sophy. None of this prevented her from waking in that dead hour when it is too early to get up and too late to sleep again, from hearing over and over again the falsely cheerful inanities David and Paul had shouted on the telephone from the air station from which they had flown to North Africa. Both had been drunk and both frightened. They were to be piloted by an American. They were averse to anyone but themselves being at the controls. If Polly had asked herself which she had spoken to last, David or Paul, she would not have been sure, any more than she had been sure of which she had made love with first. To her they were one man, multiplied by one, her lovers. She wanted them both.

For weeks after they left she worried and mourned in agony. Brought up in the conventional mould of her class, nothing had prepared her for the position in which she found herself. She grew thin and short-tempered, she made mistakes at work, she was sent for by her boss.

'Are you ill?' He eyed her with care.

'No, of course not,' she said defensively.

'Worried by something? I don't want to pry.' He looked away.

'No, thank you,' she said stiffly.

'Missing your parents, your brother, it's hard for you –'

'No, I'm glad they – I'm glad they are – well, they would only interfere – I –' She looked at her boss with loathing.

'I think you had better take some leave.' In love with a married man, no doubt. 'Go somewhere quiet. You like Cornwall, don't you?'

'Not there. God, no.'

'Try Dartmoor. Do you know it? No? Well, go and walk on a bit that hasn't got troops training in it. Walk yourself into a coma and see what your subconscious comes up with.'

Polly permitted herself a brief expression of surprise.

'Didn't think of me reading Freud and Jung, did you? Well, go to Newton Abbot, take a taxi and – here, I'll write it down – stay in this pub. Can you ride?'

'Yes.'

'When you're tired of walking you can hire a horse, the landlord has several. I'll bet you come up with the answer after ten days or so. Go tomorrow.'

'Thank you.' She took the slip of paper and left him. He wondered whether she was pregnant, couldn't quite ask her. Married men were just as potent as bachelors.

Polly left the office, leaving her work mates jealous and irritated. 'She's his pet, he took her to Portugal. Why not me? I speak the language.'

'Oh, shut up. She came back to find her brother had been killed.'

'Really? She never said –'

'Somebody who knows a girl friend of his told me, a girl called Elizabeth.'

'Her mother and father were killed, weren't they?'

'Yes, earlier on. Bad luck.'

'I don't know, she's got their money and house. Nice,

in a way. I should like it – my family are always inter-fering with my life.'

'My mother's so busy she never bothers. If my bowels are working and I'm not pregnant she's happy.'

'There.' Polly changed gear as they reached the top of the hill. 'I love this view. The promised land –' The rolling hills of Dartmoor lay ahead stretching to the horizon in the west.

'Why don't we take the road across the moor, and pic-nic up there?' Iris leant over from the back seat. 'Give the old boy a run.' At the word 'run' the mongrel stood up on the front seat, wagging his tail.

'It's longer,' said James, 'but beautiful. Have we time?'

'The funeral is not until tomorrow.'

'We always miss the moor, we are always in such a hurry. Do you know it, Ma?'

'Not really. I spent a few days' leave there in the war. Walking and riding.'

'Sounds nice. Where did you go?'

'It was somewhere between Haytor and Manaton. I'll try and find it. Sit down,' she said to the dog. 'I must concentrate.'

Later, sitting in the sun, their backs to a rock, they ate their lunch, munching brown bread, cheese and pickles, gulping wine. The dog ran joyously in the bracken, leap-ing up to see over the golden fronds, bouncing high. They could see his tail in the waving fern. The autumn sun was warm on their faces.

'This is lovely.' Iris lay back, stretching her legs, lifting her face to the sun. 'Why don't we come here oftener?'

'Always in a rush to reach Cornwall.' James lay propped on his elbow, a mug of wine in his hand. Two years younger than his sister, he had much the same colouring: chestnut hair, but whereas Iris's eyes were brown his were green like Polly's. His teeth too were out of kilter.

'Who did you come here with?'

'I came alone. I was at a low ebb –'

'Why?' James looked interested. His mother seldom spoke of her private life.

'When was this?' Iris enquired casually, afraid of stemming any slight reminiscence.

'I walked,' said Polly in recollection. 'I walked across these moors and clambered over that tor over there. I was trying to tire myself so that I would sleep. I had not been sleeping, it was in the war, I was worried. I had to make a decision.' Brother and sister exchanged a glance. 'I thought –' Polly was speaking now as though to strangers. 'I thought I had to give them up, that I could not marry one and leave the other. I thought that if one of them was killed the decision would be made for me. I was unhappy. Girls like me were brought up to be respectable. The atmosphere of the war shook that, but the shaking hurt. People like Calypso did not seem to worry, but I wonder. I've never known Calypso deeply, she won't allow it. There were dozens of girls who went on being virtuous, but we broke out.'

Polly put out a hand to stroke the dog who had come back to join them. 'Good boy. Having a nice time?' Iris and James said nothing, looking away from their mother across the moor, purple and brown in the distance.

'Then I hired a horse and rode. I could get further into the moor. I rode right across there.' Polly pointed. 'I picked my way round that very rocky tor and not terribly far on the other side there was a moorland farm, green fields fenced in by stone walls around the top of a valley with a stream at the bottom. Emerald fields, blue sky, larks singing, I particularly remember the larks. Then suddenly round a corner came a herd of llamas, white against the sky. My horse reared up terrified, the llamas spat, the horse bolted, I lost my stirrups, the horse jinxed, I fell off.'

'Llamas!' James and Iris were laughing. 'Llamas? Why did you never tell us? What were they doing there?'

'Evacuated from the Paignton Zoo, I heard later.' Polly stroked the dog's head, her eyes on the distant tor, now in sunlight, now in shade, as clouds coming up from the west blocked the sun. 'I was concussed. A farmer found me and brought me back. They put me in the cottage hospital where the people were kind. They didn't know about the llamas, they thought I had D.T.s or something. The doctor found it was true, the llamas were there, only nobody knew, nobody could have foreseen me on a horse, could they?'

'I should have thought –'

'It was wartime. People were so tucked into their little lives they didn't necessarily know what was going on in the next parish. That's why I often think the Germans who say they did not know about the concentration camps may be telling the truth. Anyway –' She gently pulled the dog's ears as he gazed dreamily into her face.

'Anyway?' suggested Iris, almost whispering.

'Anyway,' said Polly, 'I found I could talk to the doctor. I told him my dilemma. He was a nice man, kind.' Polly thought back to the cottage hospital bed. Iris and James exchanged glances of exasperation as she paused. 'He did not give me advice. He sat on my bed and talked about Nepal. He told me about polyandry, he had been on some expedition there. Then one morning he said I was well enough to go back to London and –'

'And?' Iris sighed, drawing out the word.

'He shook hands with me and said, "What you are about to do is not illegal." He had guessed that I would not give up either. So,' Polly looked at her son and daughter for the first time since she began her tale. 'So that's how you two came about. Now,' she said, standing up, 'I must pee, then we must push on.' She walked away behind some rocks.

'I suppose it would be too much to ask which of us is whose child, or whether one or both?' said James to his sister.

'Much too much. There are permutations. I don't believe she knows. We have discussed this often; we will never get any further. I too must pee.' Iris waded away into the bracken. James collected the debris of their meal, packing the remains into the basket. Polly came

239

back, casting her shadow across him as he knelt. He looked at her and her heart lurched at how like he was to the twins. He stood up and kissed her.

'Greedy.' His voice was full of affection.

'That's what they all said.'

'What did they say?' Iris came back, pulling her sweater down over her lean hips.

'That I was greedy and selfish.'

'Good job, too.' Not denying, Iris gave her mother a quick kiss on the cheek, adding, 'We don't think so.'

'There's a storm brewing, look at that sky.' James pointed westward. 'Funeral weather. I wonder who besides us will make it. I suppose,' he said, 'if you had married one of them you would have made everybody miserable.'

'Of course.'

'It's good of you to tell us even a little. I suppose you think now we are middle-aged it's −'

'Middle-aged?' Polly protested. 'Hardly.'

'I'm nearly thirty −'

'I don't know when middle-age is. Look at Helena, nearly ninety, her middle-age must have come pretty late.' Iris packed the picnic basket in among the luggage.

'That generation was tough. Yours, too.'

'Tough, greedy, selfish, all that,' said Polly lightly. 'We were under stress, people react differently under stress. We had an awful lot of fun −'

'And funny adventures. Why did you never tell us about the llamas?'

'It was private.' Polly started the car. 'Private,' and they knew she was not referring to the llamas.

'Was there a great hullabaloo among your stuffy relations?' Iris had often wondered.

'They did not notice for ages. Then it had been going on for so long when they did, other people were so much more interesting. Calypso captured attention, and Monika. Then there was the Rectory's attitude and, oh, I don't know, somehow or other they were all aware and used to it before it occurred to them to be shocked. Nobody was hurt, so why bother?'

'I daresay it was your craftiness.'

'Perhaps it was. Yes, quite likely it was that.'

'A loner?'

'In some ways. Mind you, Calypso is a loner and Sophy turned out a super loner. It was our rebellion against our upbringing.'

'And you had fun.' James, lolling on the back seat, enjoyed the view.

'Yes,' said his mother, 'we certainly did.'

'Look, lightning.' Iris pointed ahead. 'And it's going to pour.'

'Sophy used to tell us about autumn storms when we were young. The wind howling and waves crashing into the cliff and heavy sheets of rain. I hope we don't all catch our deaths and join Max.'

'Wasn't he a great womanizer?' Iris, brought up on a legend, sought the truth.

'Well, I don't know. In trouble some men reach for the bottle; Max reached for the nearest girl, and if the girl was in trouble he was a great consoler. No, I wouldn't say he was a womanizer, just busy.' Polly, driving into the storm, smiled reminiscently.

'Did he ever console you?' James dared question.

'I didn't say so.' Brother and sister smiled at one another.

'It will be interesting to see whether anybody turns up in this ghastly weather. Look at it!'

The rain, slanting from the west, poured on to the windscreen. The dog got down off the seat and crouched under the dashboard while Polly, surprised, suddenly remembered a Sunday afternoon during the invasion of Normandy when Max, finding her alone, had led her to bed and made love to her, assuaging her pent-up anxieties with skill and affection. 'I do this, dear Polly, for the twins' sake. You worry and I worry for Monika and Helena. Worry makes me what you call randy with Monika and Helena. Alas they shut up shop. You open the legs, *nicht*?' Polly, increasing the speed of the screen-wiper, laughed joyously in her sixties.

'What's the joke?'

'I was thinking back to the Normandy landings –'

'The twins were there, weren't they?'

'Indeed they were. I was worried sick.'

'Cause for laughter?' asked Iris, puzzled.

'Max cheered me up. His genius was to make everybody feel better. You should know, you've been to his concerts.'

'You weren't laughing as though you remembered a concert –'

'What else could it be –' Iris muttered so that only her brother could hear. They smiled complicitly on the back seat, amused by their mother and her life.

'And what was Max worrying about? His career rocketed during the war.' Iris tried to visualize the white-haired old man, whose funeral they were about to attend, in bed with her mother.

'He had plenty to worry about. His career went marvellously but the war was agony for him. He worried about Monika worrying, he was nagged by fear for Pauli. He hardly hoped he would ever see him again. He used to talk about him and what a pianist he would be if he survived.'

'How much did people know?'

'Rumours. News trickling through via neutral countries. If we'd known the size of the horrors we couldn't have borne it. Refugees like Max used to hear things from people who got letters through Switzerland or Sweden. Max always played better when he'd heard some ghastly rumour. Sorrow fed his genius, his emotions went to his bow.' Polly paused, peering ahead.

'And his balls.' James filled the pause.

'To be honest, yes.' Polly's mouth twitched. 'This is hardly a suitable recollection of the dead.'

'You so rarely talk to us about your private self, we enjoy it.'

'I thought we were talking about Max.'

'In connection with you.'

'We were all interconnected.' Polly's tone indicated

242

the end of the conversation, such as it was. She kept her eyes on the road and the driving rain, thinking that tapes and records would never replace the tall thin man who had once played for her in the basement kitchen when he had news of the death of a great friend. 'They say he died in a hospital, that is what they say, but I hear they are gassing thousands of people –'

'I cannot believe it,' she had exclaimed in disgust, 'it is too revolting.' He had taken his violin and played so piercingly sadly that she had wept for his friend, whose name he had not told her, and on that occasion it was she who had reached for him.

'You sound a caring group,' said Iris, Polly's daughter, who concerned herself with good works to assuage her conscience, which had nothing to be guilty about, she having been born good.

'Not caring enough, as was proved with Calypso. Not that it wasn't her fault, a more secretive character it would be hard to come by.'

'I wonder whether she will turn up by the grave?' James spoke enquiringly.

'Hamish is driving Helena down, so it looks unlikely,' said Iris.

'Hamish wants the glory of bringing the head-mistress,' said her brother, who had offered and been refused. 'Besides, he has the best car.'

30

Helena looked forward to the end of Richard's dancing lessons. A gleam at the end of the tunnel of boredom now shaped her days. True, he despatched the empty hampers from Paddington and fetched back the full ones. True, he was out every day lunching at his club, where he watched men younger than himself now high ranking, men he had served with in the Great War. True, he stayed out most days until dark, but he always came back in time for tea at five and stayed in from then on to talk to her, if she would listen, to Max, if he was home, and tirelessly to Max's musical friends, who frequently stayed to supper, sampling the pâtés, compôtes and cooked meats with fresh vegetables with which Monika stuffed the hampers. Her ample supply of eggs and butter assured Helena of many a convivial evening, when all her soul longed for was to be alone with her lover.

'You are impatient, my Helena.'

'He's got his new suits, he's shopped for Monika, he should go home.'

'He is enjoying himself. He is out all day, I am not. Why don't you come nicely to bed now? I have a rehearsal about three, there is just time.' Max held her against him, stroking her back, kissing her neck, glancing at his wristwatch over her shoulder. One forty-five. 'Come, meine dumpling.' He nuzzled her neck. 'You smell nice.'

'He might suddenly come in. He comes back and goes out again.'

'So he goes out again. Let me in.' He pushed her back on to the sofa.

'Max!' Her token protest. 'Really!'

'*Ja, ja,* relax and enjoy –'

'There's the telephone, oh –'

'So let it ring, we make symphony to its ringing. The telephone has no soul but I try and conduct. There, that was good, *nicht?*'

'For you.' Helena wept with fury.

'*Du bist nervös.*' Gently he held her. 'Where is your phlegm?'

Helena pulled down her skirt. 'I wish you wouldn't call me that, it makes people laugh.'

'People don't know.'

'Sometimes you forget and call me – er – call me that in front of your friends.'

'*Kleine.* Jewish refugees do not know what it means. They think I call you heroine, they think phlegm is like spirit of Dunkirk or Rule Britannia or some such, *nicht?*'

'All the same –' Helena kissed his ear, relenting.

'I must go. They will be waiting for me at the rehearsal.' He kissed her briskly. 'If I bring some few friends is there food? I make an omelette. Ludwig's wife makes omelettes with dried egg, Eno's salts to make the egg powder rise and salad dressing with medicinal paraffin. He has never been so healthy.' Max smoothed his hair, straightened his tie, bent to kiss her while buttoning his flies.

'Richard collected a hamper this morning,' she said stiffly.

'Good. *Auf Wiedersehen.*' On the doorstep he met Richard. 'My dear fellow, would you be amused to come to my rehearsal? I go this minute.'

'Delighted,' said Richard, and turned to walk with him. 'D'you know, I saw General de Gaulle in Piccadilly walking past the Ritz, looked lonely, poor chap, carries that big nose high.'

Resentfully Helena watched them, heads together in interested talk until they turned the corner. It annoyed her that they were friends. 'Damn, damn, damn!' she shouted in her empty drawing room. She plumped up the sofa cushions and went to unpack the hamper, arrange a cold supper. Max never came back from rehearsal without two or more friends. If he calls me 'phlegm' tonight I shall hit him, she told herself, or deny him my favours. She was laughing when the doorbell rang. She opened the door to her sister-in-law.

'Sarah, my dear, how lovely.'

'I telephoned. You must have been out.'

'No, no, I heard it, we were, I was in the lavatory. Come in, come in.'

'I was wondering if you were visible.'

'What d'you mean, visible. Here I am.'

'I meant busy,' said Sarah, who had wondered whether Helena had been in bed with Max. 'Are you busy?'

'I was seeing about supper. Max has taken Richard to his rehearsal. Oh, Sarah, d'you think he will ever go home?'

'Why ever not?'

'He's enjoying himself. He says he's seeing the war at first hand.'

'I thought he came up to see his tailor and shop.'

'Can you stay to supper? He's finished with his tailor, he's done his shopping, he's been to the cinemas and the Windmill, he's nearly finished his dancing lessons but he shows no signs of leaving. I tell you he is enjoying himself.'

'Isn't that a good thing?' Sarah, having followed Helena to the kitchen, helped her unpack the hamper. 'What a lot of goodies!'

'Monika's clever. Doesn't think me much of a cook, sends lots of cooked stuff. She's right, of course. Could you carve those things and put them on a dish? I never know how many people Max will bring home. It's a good thing the hamper came today. Richard fetches and sends back the empties, at least he does that chore.'

'What are these?' Sarah searched for a knife.

'Chickens, rabbits, mix them up. There's a pâté too. We are rather short of drink, though.'

247

'I brought you a bottle.'

'Oh, Sarah, wonderful! So hard to get.'

'What is the poor old boy doing then?'

'Getting on my nerves. Just joint those things, here's a dish. He goes to his club and counts generals. He knew a lot of them in his youth. Then he prowls the streets.'

'What d'you mean, prowls?' Sarah exclaimed anxiously.

'He prowls about clubland, Sarah, and Whitehall, he's like a child. He's thrilled if he sees General Eisenhower or Brooke or Alexander, anyone in the news. This morning he saw General de Gaulle. I heard him tell Max.'

'Seems quite harmless to me.' Sarah looked relieved.

'He's your brother, you know he is harmless. It's me that's suffering. I want him to go home. He assumes that just because I bought these houses he has the right to live in them.' Helena began to cry stormily. 'I want to be alone with Max. God knows I seldom am, he's dreadfully sociable, always asking people here. If I can't be alone with him at night when can I be? Don't laugh, Sarah, it's not funny.'

'It is, though. What about Monika? I thought Richard and she –'

'So did I, but she sends all this food, she keeps the Cornish house going far better than I ever did and she seems very matey with the General, the Floyers and the village.'

'Why don't you ask her to come up?'

'God, no. Besides, she can't leave the hens and the cow. No, Sarah, he's got to go, he's ruining my life.'

'I'll try and think of some ploy. By the way, I have to see Calypso. She won't go near her parents, they are worried stiff.'

'No need, she's another who's enjoying the war.'

'She's pregnant.'

'Ceci n'empêche cela.'

'Really?'

'From what I hear. Never in. Lunching, dining,

dancing with French, Poles, Americans, Belgians, Australians. She was even seen with a Sikh, it will be a black man next.'

'There are no black officers.'

'Just as well. She's no longer working so she has all the time in the world and that delightful house.'

Parting with her lunch companion, a Free French officer with the pseudonym of a Paris Métro station, Calypso rode on the top of a bus towards Kensington noting, from her elevated viewpoint, Uncle Richard walking along Knightsbridge with Max, limping nimbly beside the violinist who was restricting his usual stride to accommodate the older man. The bus rocketed along Kensington Gore. She got out at the Broad Walk to give Fling his walk across the parks. The giant avenue of elms was touched by misty green almost invisible against the pale sky, still cold from winter. On the north side of the park barrage balloons bobbed sulkily. She headed across the grass past Watts's 'Physical Energy' to the Serpentine, where the ducks hopefully congregated to be fed by nannies and children long since evacuated to the country. She appreciated the wide stretch of grass, bare since the outbreak of war, empty of pekinese, dachshund and poodle. Fling barked at a squirrel, sleepy from the long winter, exploring a paper bag. The gardens looked blousy and unloved, park chairs tipped over and in need of paint, restless bits of paper scurrying in the chill wind. Nostalgically she doubled back to the Round Pond but nobody raced toy boats, no model yachts sailed. Some vandal had thrown a park seat into the water; a row of gulls perched along the back. Here, once, Oliver had pushed her in. She had sat waist deep in icy water screaming, while Walter, infected, had pushed in Polly, then given her Nanny a shove as she leaned to the rescue, hoping not to get her feet wet. Calypso remembered the row when they got back to Aunt Sarah's house, followed by hot tea and crumpets. The gulls rose shrieking and drifted west. A soldier wandered along, meeting no girl, having no tryst. She walked faster, making for the Dutch garden. There, pacing between the pools, peering to see whether coot or duck were yet nesting, busy in their tiny world of reeds, Fling leaned to catch sight of his whiskery reflection and jumped back barking. Hands in pockets, she turned back to the Serpentine to walk along the north side, watching mallard in pursuit of duck skitter along the water, then rise high in flight across to St James's Park, their quacks diminishing in the evening sky. Down in the Dell she stood by the railings. A moorhen walked jerkily from the bushes and rabbits hopped slowly across the grass, impervious to the war. Hector had told her to be careful Fling did not squeeze in and give chase; he had once had a lurcher who had leapt the railings and caused havoc. She walked up to the Row, shabby and sad, robbed of its railings. Hector had been angry, asked questions in the House, unfashionably blamed Lord Beaverbrook for the desecration of London's parks and squares by the uprooting of railings made from the guns of the Peninsular War and Waterloo. She thought of dancing with him in the '400', held close against him, feeling his cock rise in desire against her body. Now, standing by deserted Rotten Row, she felt an answering pang. She stared in disgust at the growing mountain of rubble from bombed buildings heaped on the Guards' football ground. Were there bones of people unaccounted for in the rubble, precious furniture, objets d'art? She crossed Hyde Park Corner dodging the traffic and, tired now, walked down past the Palace into the maze of streets round Petty France. Near the Underground she was amused to see Polly wheel her bicycle from an office building and pedal towards Knightsbridge. She looked at the ugly block which housed Polly's secret work. Her own job had been two doors down. Both were sworn not to disclose the whereabouts of their offices. We could have met for lunch, she thought, and mockingly remembered the many documents marked Top Secret which often contained information equally available in the *Daily Mirror*.

The telephone was ringing as she put her key in the door.

'Hullo,' she said. 'Hullo.'

'Telegrams.'

'Yes?'

'Calypso Grant Mrs?'

'I am Calypso Grant. Yes, please read it – yes, I've got that. Yes. No – yes, a confirmation copy. Yes, please. Thank you.' She replaced the receiver and bent to take Fling off his lead. In her haste to reach the telephone she had left the door open. In the street the plane trees dappled shadows on the pavement, a tug hooted on the river. She closed the door and listened to the silence in the house. Then she went into the cloakroom and was sick. She splashed her face with cold water and rinsed her mouth, expelling the haunting taste of bile.

'What the hell was he doing?' she said to the dog. 'I thought he was safe in Cairo.' She dried her face, looking round the cloakroom. Umbrellas, a shooting stick, Wellington boots, an old country hat, a Spy cartoon of his grandfather on the wall, a faint whiff of hair oil and tobacco. She sat on the bottom stair. Fling sat beside her, pressing his rough little body against her legs. She leant her head back against the banisters, waiting for strength to flow back. When she opened her eyes it was night. She felt a peculiar fluttering sensation in her belly. 'Ah,' she said grimly, 'It's you, is it? He won't be here to welcome you and I don't much want you.'

31

'What a good party.' Sarah helped Helena clear the table. 'Feeding nine of us. It reminds me of pre-war, delicious food.'

'I couldn't do it without Monika.' Helena carried a tray to the kitchen, stepping carefully down the precipitous basement stairs. If the houses survived the war she intended a drastic remodelling. She navigated a chair in the passage where the men had heaped their overcoats, brushed past Ludwig's cello case propped against the umbrellas. She cursed Ludwig's instrument, also his wife Irena who had a way of sitting cross-legged on the floor which annoyed her. 'Let someone else have the chairs, I am so small I take no room.'

Sarah joined her in the basement. 'That's the lot. Let me wash up, you dry.'

'All right.' Helena reached ungraciously for a tea towel.

'What's the matter?' Sarah turned on the hot tap.

Helena did not answer but stood waiting for the wet plates.

'Cough up. What's the matter?' Sarah handed her a plate.

'It's difficult to explain. I'd rather not try.'

'Very well.' Sarah washed the plates, stacking them to drip. 'I have to telephone George. There might be a letter from Oliver. We worry. There's been so much fighting in the Western Desert.'

'The telephone's in the drawing room. It will be a good excuse to get them to leave early.' Helena brightened.

'Don't do that. They are enjoying themselves.'

'But you want to talk privately.'

'I'll go back to Polly's, it's only a step. I don't want to break up your party.'

Helena sighed, wishing that Sarah would break it up, wishing the party over. She blamed herself for not objecting long ago to Max inviting his friends to eat her food, drink her drink, sprawl in her drawing room. When first she had bought the houses she had welcomed his friends, but now she felt differently. She did not grudge them the food, she grudged them the long hours they stayed, discussing their music, behaving, as many of them gratefully told her, as though they were at home in Vienna, Prague, Berlin or Budapest. They treated her with affection, apparently unaware that she wished them, their music and their laughter gone, so that she could have Max to herself, be in bed with him, feel his whip-thin body against hers and rejoice in the miracle which had befallen so late in life.

'I'll trot round to Polly's, then. Back in a few minutes. Are you all right, Helena? You look funny.'

'No, I'm not all right,' Helena shouted.

'Why not? Are you ill?'

'No. I wish they'd all go. I never seem to see Max now Richard is here. I'm never alone with him. I thought –'

'If you become possessive you will lose him. Try and be like Monika, let him off the lead.'

'Like Monika?'

'They've been married years. She never tries to change him. If you listen to those people you'll find they are all her friends too.'

'Then why isn't she here?'

'I should think that's pretty obvious.'

'Because I am?'

'You and air raids. Although I don't know her, I think she is doing what she can for him, taking care of Richard, sending up food, running your house.'

'I wish Richard would go back to her.'

'You'd still have all the friends.'

254

'I suppose so.' Helena groaned.

'They are his life, like his violin. You can't have just the one thing –'

'Bed?'

'You've got to realize he is more than bed if you want to keep him.'

'You mean go to all the concerts, listen to all his friends for ever?'

'If you want to keep him,' Sarah repeated.

'I love him.'

'Then think on it. I'm going round to telephone from Polly's. Shan't be long.'

Helena sat by the kitchen table listening to the talk and laughter from the room above, trying to catch Max's voice from among the many, hearing Richard's laugh, sharp cries of appreciation from the women, feeling anguish. Could she ever fit in with this cosmopolitan crowd, she who was tone deaf? Was love enough? Irena found her. Irena so small, who took up so much room with her ebullience, her brilliance, her enthusiasm.

'Helena, what you do sitting alone?' she cried.

'Nothing.' Helena was ungracious.

'Come up, we miss you, do not leave us.'

'You don't need me,' she said grumpily.

'But we do. You are our cement, we cannot do without you.'

'*I am tone deaf*,' Helena said to Irena in a hard flat voice, hoping to shock her into throwing her out of Max's life, his music, his love. She felt at that moment that Irena or any of Max's friends was capable of casting her out. She would go meekly to the square house on the cliff, back to her former life. She felt desperate facing Irena. Irena laughed.

'You are ridiculous.' She cried with merriment, not questioning Helena's statement, laughing so that Helena laughed too, recognizing her curmudgeonly jealousy for what it was. They linked arms and climbed the stairs, jostling each other in the narrow space. In the hall they met Sarah coming back from using Polly's telephone.

'Any news?' Helena asked, not caring in her happiness whether there was news or not.

'George had a letter from Oliver. He read it to me. He says Hector –'

At that moment the telephone in the drawing room rang and its news blotted out any news Sarah might have.

Richard, answering the telephone, exclaimed: 'Mildred old thing, you all right? Your voice sounds –' The telephone crackled and Richard held it away from his ear with an expression of unbelief.

'She wants to speak to you.' He handed the receiver to Max. 'Called me maladroit. I ask you, what's got into her? Says Monika –'

Max took the receiver. 'Max *hier*.' Everyone in the room listened, trying to make sense of Max's responses. 'When – where? The cliff – 'ow did she? What pigs? We never eat pigs. The General he say *that*? Crazy old *Dummkopf*! Where is she now? The coastguard – I come at once to kill that man. I get the first train.' He replaced the receiver, eyes blazing. 'She threw herself over the cliff,' Max shouted, 'my lovely Monika. Why have you left her so long?' he yelled at Richard. 'I have to work, you are my friend, you should look after her.'

'Is she dead?' asked Helena, bravely asking the question on everyone's mind.

Irena burst into stormy weeping and threw herself into Ludwig's arms. 'Monika is *tot*.'

'No,' cried Max, 'but I kill that swine General, that mother-fucking Nazi.'

'What happened? Stop shouting Max, tell us.' Helena peered up into his face, gripping his hands.

'You bloody English!' Max shouted, distraught.

Helena smacked his face, reaching up on tiptoe. 'Tell us what happened instead of abusing us, you great oaf.'

'It is your hampers, your *verdammt* hampers of food. She puts in pigs.'

'Are you mad?' cried Helena, getting excited. 'Chickens, rabbits, butter, eggs: you know perfectly well she has no pigs.'

'Guinea pigs, my Phlegm, she has been breeding guinea pigs. We have been eating them and your swine General says Monika is a spy, a foreigner, a Jew, and eating habits in England do not permit guinea pigs –'

'I kept guinea pigs as a boy,' Richard broke in. 'Charming little –'

'Shut up,' said Helena.

'Wogs eat songbirds,' Richard continued.

'Shut up,' said Helena. 'Max, try to be calm and tell us.'

Max sat down suddenly on the sofa, clutching his head.

'And the Frogs eat frogs, but guinea pigs, I ask you, that's a bit steep,' Richard carried on.

'Shut up, I tell you.' Helena silenced him. 'Now Max, please, try and tell us what Mildred –'

'She said –' Max took a deep breath. 'She said some fool gave Sophy those pigs. She gives them to Monika, *ja*, *und* Monika breeds them with her rabbits which we eat, probably we eat them tonight?' He looked round the room.

'Delicious,' said Ludwig calmly, stroking Irena's shoulder, holding her as tenderly as he held his cello. 'Delicious and original.'

'And?' Helena resented Ludwig's interruption.

'She gives this *schrecklich* old man supper. He asks what it is he eats, so gourmet, so unlike the filthy rations. Monika tells him and then –' Max's voice rose again, 'this disgusting old man abuses her and Monika cracks, runs out and throws herself over the cliff.'

'Oh no, no, no,' moaned Irena and another girl, 'oh, no, no, no,' in chorus.

'But,' said Max slowly, 'she sticks on a ledge and the Floyers and the coastguards they pull her up.'

'Is she hurt?'

'How do I know? Mildred says she has the breakdown.'

'We'd better catch the midnight train. Quick – somebody go and find a taxi, hurry. Max, I will come with you.' Helena, suddenly calm, British and practical, took charge.

257

'I'll come along too.' Richard limped out of the room.
'Won't take a minute to pack. Most of my stuff is ready,
I –'

But nobody listened. Sarah, aghast at the whole scene,
took her leave and started back to Polly's house, not
wishing to get involved in such foreign turmoil. As she
reached the corner of the street Irena and Ludwig were
waylaying a taxi which was disgorging its passengers.

'Sorry, luv,' said the taximan. 'I'm shot to bits, dead
tired, going 'ome.'

'This is *sehr important*,' begged Irena.

'Sorry, luv, not tonight.'

'It is only to Paddington,' pleaded Irena.

'Sorry, luv –'

'It is for the exiled King of Greece,' cried Ludwig. 'He
lives here. It's of vital importance he catch the train –'

'King of Greece?' The taximan was incredulous.

'Top secret,' said Irena, lowering her voice. 'So urgent.
So secret.'

The taxi driver opened the door. Irena and Ludwig
sprang into the taxi and waved to Sarah as they drove
past with gleeful faces. Sarah, while disapproving, was
impressed by their ingenuity.

Driving with Hamish to Max's funeral, Helena remembered her dinner party.

'Did you ever hear the saga of the guinea pigs?' she
asked Hamish.

'Yes. That is one aspect of your war which has
impressed me.' By his tone Hamish made clear the
impression was not a good one.

'When you consider the horrors of war, it's remark-
able that it was guinea pigs which gave Monika a breakdown. Max blamed me. He wasn't really loyal over those
guinea pigs and yet it was during that period I became
really fond of Monika.'

'How was that?'

'If you really love somebody,' said Helena in her
steady old voice, 'you see the people they love through

258

their eyes. Monika would have bought him flowers if she were here and I not.'

'Would she?'

'Yes. He hated chrysanthemums. I can't buy those. They made him sneeze.'

'Me too.'

'Lilies? A bit banal. Why not violets? On the way to the night train he saw a flower barrow being trundled along the street, stopped the taxi and bought a basket of violets for Monika. Nearly made us miss the train.'

'Oh.'

'Silly really,' Helena chortled, 'when you think they'd been grown in Cornwall. Come to think of it, they may have been grown by the old idiot who had upset Monika, made her try to kill herself.'

Hamish was silent, visualizing the scene.

'We were pretty crazy that night. We were in such a rush to catch the night train we left the door unlocked.'

'Were you robbed?'

'No. Sometime during the night Sophy turned up. She'd run away from school. We never found out why.'

'Poor kid.' Hamish's experience of Sophy was of a later date. 'She doesn't strike me as the running away kind,' he said thoughtfully.

'How well do you know her?' Helena enquired, glancing at Hamish's profile, finding him handsome. I may be old, she thought, but I dearly love a good-looking man.

'I wouldn't say well, not well at all.' He thought back to the year he was sixteen when, in the South of France, in a mutual friend's house, Sophy had gathered him into her bed and relieved him tenderly of his virginity, setting him a standard for the future. He had thought himself in love with her. There had been no pain in their relations. 'Was she unhappy?' he asked Helena. 'Was she in pain?'

'Waste of time worrying about what that child felt. I never asked her. She's just the same now, doesn't have any feelings. People say she is enigmatic but I wonder whether there is anything there.'

Disliking his passenger Hamish said: 'Perhaps you never bothered to find out.'

Helena was silent, rebuked by Calypso's son. She liked men to approve of her. Max had given her this luxury; from now on she must live with less approval, less of everything. 'It would be nice if I could find violets,' she said. 'He loved violets.'

'Wrong time of year,' said Hamish, hoping to hurt, thinking of Sophy. 'No violets.'

Sophy's flight was unpremeditated. Suddenly she could bear no more. The insidious horror had begun towards the end of the previous term, started again on her return to school, grown over the weeks to unbearable proportions. If she had known what it was about she might have fought back, but she could do nothing about sniggers from her peers, nothing to protect herself from the sarcastic innuendoes of mistresses, nothing against the prick of snide remarks, nothing against the incomprehensible envy, disgust and veiled accusation which wrapped her in a frightening fog. Instead of doing history prep she took her pocket money, put on her outdoor shoes and overcoat and caught a bus to the station. Her money bought a single ticket to Liverpool Street and from there she walked, arriving outside Polly's house in the early hours footsore, hungry, elated at having escaped her prison. She looked forward to telling Polly how she had crossed London through the blackout, alone.

No one answered the bell. She stepped back in the street to look up at the windows. The ground floor was shuttered; she could see by the light of the moon that the upper floors had curtains drawn. She remembered Polly writing, 'Sometimes I go to Bletchley.' This must be one of those times. Her elation evaporated. She was too exhausted to walk on to Calypso in Westminster. Helena was only round the corner. She made her way to Helena's house. She hoped Richard or Max would open the door, be there to protect her from Helena's disapproval.

Arriving, she stood hesitating to ring the bell. How could she explain to Helena a mystery with undertones of indecency and disgustingness? She pressed the bell. She was poised for flight should Helena appear, but as at Polly's nobody answered, nobody came. She leant against the door in defeat. It swung open.

Coming off duty from his fire station, looking forward to a few hours' sleep, Tony Wood, passing Helena's house, noticed the front door open and a light showing. He went to investigate.

'Hullo? Hullo? Helena? You there? Your front door's open, anything wrong?' There was no answer. Puzzled, he put his tin hat and gas mask on the hall table, shut the door, investigated. Strong smell of cigarettes and liquor, signs of a party, cushions crushed, chairs awry, music sheets loosely stacked on a side table, no people. He went down to the kitchen, found Sophy standing petrified with terror, a glass of milk in one hand, a piece of meat in the other.

'Christ,' he said, 'what the hell are you doing here? Where's Helena?'

Sophy leapt into his arms, clutching him round the neck, gasping incomprehensible sentences. 'Couldn't stand any more – nobody here – hungry – walked from Liverpool Street – they said – I can't – it was horrible – I'll never go back – please, Tony – please help – I won't – I can't – I had to run away.' Her thin arms clutching him in a vice reminded him of a terrified cat up a tree.

'Steady on,' he said. 'It's all right, calm down, let a chap breathe.' He tried to prise her from his neck but she clung tighter, her face pressed into his neck, her hair stuffed up his nose. He held her taut body, patting her back, stroking her. 'Calm down, try and tell me what it's about.' He managed to free his face from her hair. 'There, now, let's find somewhere to sit.' He led her to the drawing room, sat her on the sofa, put his arm round her. 'Try and tell me what happened, poor child, tell now –' But she's not a child, he thought, she's a girl and

261

a bloody attractive one. 'Oh,' he said, 'been in trouble with some man, been writing notes to a boy? My sister had that trouble at her school. Is that it?'

'No!' Sophy screamed, pulling away from him. 'No. They said – they thought – they – they – it wasn't men, they said – they said I was – I was in love with Miss Stevens.'

'A woman? One of the mistresses?'

'Yes.'

'Silly cows.' Light glimmered in Tony's perplexed brain. A schoolgirl pash.

'How could I be in love with a *woman*?' She looked up at him, her eyes enormous in her white face, her expression one of profound disgust.

'It happens.'

'A woman in love with a woman? I can't believe it.' She looked incredulous.

'Perhaps she fancied you?' Tony suggested.

'Oh God.' Sophy shuddered. 'Revolting.'

'Men love men,' Tony found himself saying.

'That's different.' Sophy pulled away from him. 'That's all right, I know that happens, but women, ugh.'

Tony laughed, pulling her towards him. 'Try and forget it, it's over now.'

'Not if they send me back.'

'I don't suppose they will.' But Tony thought: They probably will. Helena wants her out from under her feet.

'Oh God,' Sophy began to cry. 'Oh God, if they knew what it's been like.'

Tony kept quiet, holding her against him, letting her cry, handing her his handkerchief to mop the tears which spilled the fear of the indefinable from her system. He guessed she would tell him no more, that probably she couldn't.

'It's not against the law,' he said, 'what women do. Chaps, that's different. Found out and you go to prison.'

'Why?'

'I've often wondered,' said Tony, who frequently found his own sex attractive. 'The laws of sex are rather obfusc.'

262

'I wish I knew about sex. Nobody tells one anything and what the girls at school say is patently untrue.'

'I long to know.'

'I shan't tell you, you'd laugh. Oh God,' she said suddenly, 'I'm so tired.'

'Bed then.' He took her hand and led her upstairs. 'You'd better get into Helena's bed. She's vanished somewhere, and Max too.'

'Don't leave me.' Panic sounded again.

'OK, but go and wash and get undressed.' He yawned, fatigue catching up with him from long hours on duty. Sophy took off her school jersey and skirt and laid them on a chair. He watched her as she stood with her back to him, thin legs in black lisle stockings protruding from grey school bloomers. He counted the knobs on her spine before she turned round, breasts showing small under her wool vest.

'D'you think I could borrow one of Aunt Helena's nighties?'

'Sure.' He yawned again.

She searched in a chest of drawers. 'Gosh!' she exclaimed. 'What undies, silk, look!' She held up a pair of pink camiknickers. 'Wow, what a change falling in love with Max has made. She used to wear liberty bodices and, oh, look at this.' She held up a brassière.

'Buck up, find a nightdress.'

'D'you think I could borrow this?' Sophy whispered as though in church as she held up a white satin nightdress trimmed with lace. 'It's awfully bridal.' She began to giggle. 'Aunt Helena, of all people. She's so old.'

'Hurry up, Sophy, I'm whacked.'

'All right.' She disappeared into the bathroom carrying the nightdress. Tony scrubbed his hand over his jaw feeling the bristles. From the bathroom he heard small exclamations, the sound of taps being turned on and off, the clatter of glass on the glass shelf. 'Hurry up,' he called, 'I'm half dead.'

Sophy came out of the bathroom on a choking wave of scent, her black hair brushed, wearing the white nightdress. She held it up on one side like a ball dress. He stared at her, taking in long arms and legs, black eyes, black hair, the shadow of her small bush through the white silk, her hand outstretched.

'What do you think this is?' She reached out to him. 'She's got gallons of Chanel 5 in there and Elizabeth Arden make-up. What d'you think it can be?' She handed him a Dutch cap. 'What is it for?'

'You'd better put it back where you found it.'

'Oh, is it medical?'

'You could say that.'

'Something like a truss? For a bosom?'

'Buck up and get into bed. Put that thing back first, though.'

'All right.'

'Now get into bed and go to sleep.'

'Don't leave me.' She was afraid again.

'I'll be downstairs.'

'Can't you wait until I'm asleep? Mrs Floyer does. Kiss me goodnight like her.'

'Who's she?'

'Our Rector's wife, the twins' mother.'

'I'm not the Rector's wife,' said Tony through gritted teeth.

'She sits on the end of my bed.'

Tony sat on a chair at a safe distance, feeling her school skirt and bloomers bunching under him.

'Won't you kiss me?' She held out her arms.

He bent over her and kissed her mouth. 'You stink,' he said.

'I didn't mean to use so much.' She lay back in the bed. 'Why don't you lie here, if you're so tired?'

'For Christ's sake go to sleep,' he yelled at her, exasperated.

'Sorry.' She closed her eyes and, as he watched, relaxed suddenly like a cat and slept. Presently he stood up and looked down at her full mouth, short thick lashes. He pressed his hand against his genitals, grunting with anger and need.

Downstairs he stood by the telephone, the receiver on the table, dialling with one hand while he fingered his flies with the other. He got no answer from Polly and the telephone rang disregarded in Calypso's house. 'Bloody little sexual hazard,' he cried out loud. 'Under age, too,' he muttered in anguish. 'Miss Stevens, indeed. What about me?' He lay face down on the sofa, blotting out the feel of Sophy's mouth against a cushion while he wooed sleep.

32

Sarah, hoping to find Helena's daily help, rang the bell in Enderby Street. She was surprised when Tony Wood, dishevelled and sleepy, opened the door.

'Who are you?' she asked. 'You were not at the party last night.' She sounded aggrieved.

Tony explained himself, brushing his hair back with his fingers, straightening his loosened tie.

'I am a friend of Helena's. I met her through Polly and Calypso.'

'My nieces.' Sarah eyed him with chill.

'Then you must be Sophy's aunt. She's upstairs.'

'Sophy's at school.'

'She's asleep in Helena's bed, or was when I last looked. She ran away.'

'Perhaps you can explain. Do you mind if I come in?' Sarah crossed the threshold. Tony hastily buttoned the top of his trousers and reached for his coat.

'Has there been a fire?' Sarah sniffed the atmosphere in the drawing room, wondering what a fireman was doing in Helena's house. 'Where's Helena's daily?'

'I don't think she comes today. Would you like some coffee or something?'

'I will make you some,' said Sarah, taking charge. 'Open the windows and get rid of this fug. While I make coffee you can explain.'

Guiltily Tony obeyed, throwing wide the windows, letting in the chill air. He joined Sarah in the kitchen.

'Why did she run away? Is the child in love with you or –' He could see the phrase 'something silly' freeze on her respectable lips.

'I wish – I mean, no. She came here because she couldn't find Polly. She –'

'I must have missed her. I got in late from Helena's party. Perhaps you had better tell me what you know.'

'Do you know where Helena is?'

'By now she should be arriving at home in Cornwall.'

As she made coffee Sarah gave Tony a bare account of Helena's departure with Richard and Max, but not all the reasons for it. In his turn Tony told of finding the lights showing, the door open and Sophy in the kitchen. He did not tell her why Sophy had run away.

'Why did she run away?'

'I think she'd better tell you herself, she was very upset last night. She doesn't want to go back.'

'Wouldn't have run away if she wanted to stay,' said Sarah crisply. Tony recovered his equilibrium. He had not, he told himself, done anything. Well, not much.

'Helena will be put out,' said Sarah.

'Yes. Thank you.' He took the cup she tendered.

'I'll see what I can do. I have to go and see Calypso. I can take Sophy with me.'

'I tried to phone her in the night; she didn't answer. I tried Polly's number first.'

'Polly's away. I sleep very deeply. I am staying in her house.'

'Oh,' said Tony neutrally. 'Oh.' They sat on either side of the table. Tony drank coffee. Sarah watched him, wondering where he fitted into the scheme of things, whether he was trustworthy.

'So you are a friend of my nieces?'

'Yes.' She sounded coldly inquisitorial. Next she would be enquiring whether he went to bed with them. He felt disinclined to tell her that whereas he and Polly had slept together they no longer did, that when he had last invited himself into Calypso's bed she had refused him on the feeble pretext that she had not enjoyed herself the last time. As for Sophy, it was a case of thought more than deed. At some later date he hoped he would rectify the situation. He smiled at Sarah, putting on the charm.

268

'You must be Oliver's mother.'

'Yes.'

'How is Oliver?' Blast his guts, he thought, remembering Oliver snitching Calypso from under his nose, so confident, so handsome.

'Oliver? Did you say Oliver?' Sophy came eagerly into the kitchen. 'Aunt Sarah, how are you, how is Oliver?' She hugged Sarah. 'I am glad to see you,' she said sincerely.

'Go and put a dressing gown on, then I'll make you some breakfast. You'll catch cold in that thing.'

'Isn't it beautiful? Aunt H has got some terrific clothes. Where does she get the coupons?'

'I don't know, darling. Go and wrap up.' Sarah was startled by the transparent garment.

Tony carried his cup to the sink. He wondered whether Sarah, who had followed Sophy from the room, believed he had left Sophy's virtue intact. It would seem unlikely. Helena's silk nightdress made her look much older than she was, more desirable. He called up the stairs, 'I have to go, Sophy. I'll ring up and find out how you are. Where will you be?'

'With Aunt Sarah at Polly's.' Her cheerful voice came down the stairs. 'Or with Calypso.'

'Thank you, Mr Wood. We'll let you know.' Sarah leant over the banisters. He knew that she suspected him of malintent. 'I will take care of her now.' She was dismissive.

'I will be off, then,' he said. 'Goodbye.'

'Goodbye,' said Sarah. 'Thanks again.'

Tony walked down the street feeling empty. For a few hours Sophy had turned to him; now she had her robust tweed-suited aunt. Oliver's mother, rather a dragon.

'When you are dressed,' said Sarah to Sophy, lying in the bath, 'we must go to Calypso. There's been a letter from Oliver. I gather something has happened to Hector.'

'If he's dead Oliver will be delighted.'

'What a dreadful thing to say.'

269

'But it's true,' said Sophy. 'Nothing would please him more.'

'Sophy!' Sarah was shocked.

'It doesn't please me, though.' She reached for her school vest and bloomers. 'And I hate these clothes,' she said viciously.

'Can you tell me why you ran away? Is it serious? What happened? What did you do?'

'Nothing happened. I didn't do anything. It's serious to me. I am not going back.' Sophy's face was closed. Sarah was realistic enough to know that Sophy would sooner part with her back teeth than oblige with information. Quietly she thanked her God who voted Conservative and was on the side of the Allies that she was not blessed with a daughter. She sat watching Sophy put on her school skirt, tie, jersey and sensible shoes, obliterating the brilliant image that had appeared in the kitchen.

'We can catch a Number Eleven bus if we walk to Sloane Square,' she said.

'Of course.' Sophy looked as pleased as though Sarah had said Pumpkin Coach.

Presently they stood on Calypso's doorstep and pressed the bell. Inside the house Fling barked furiously, running to the door, his nails clicking on the tiles. Nobody came.

'She must be out.'

'I'm sure she's in.' Sophy rang the bell again, holding her thumb hard on the button. Fling barked crazily, choking with excitement. Sophy pushed open the letter flap and tried to peer in. The door opened suddenly.

'Hullo,' said Calypso. 'Come in.' She picked up the dog with one hand and scooped letters off the mat with the other. 'Come in,' she repeated. 'Nice to see you.' She kissed her aunt and Sophy and began sorting the letters vaguely. 'Mostly bills,' she said, laying them down. 'Shut up, Fling, be quiet now. He's made a mess, mind where you put your feet – he hasn't been out yet.'

'I don't suppose he could last, it's long after ten.'

Sarah, prepared to lavish sympathy, was furious with herself at her implied reproach.

'I'll clean it up presently. Mrs Welsh doesn't like him. I thought you were at school, Sophy.'

'I've run away.'

'I don't blame you. I was asked to leave mine, accused of flirting with the gardener, I ask you, as Uncle Richard would say. A spotty youth. It was an insult to my intelligence. I was about as ignorant as a newborn baby.' Calypso made a faint choking sound, thinking of her ignorance so brilliantly enlightened by Hector. 'Come to the kitchen. I'll make tea or something.' She walked down the hall, her body unbalanced by her pregnancy.

'I had a letter from Oliver, darling.' Sarah watched Calypso fill the kettle, wondered when the child was due.

'Told you Hector was dead, I suppose? He must be pleased.'

'Oh no, darling.' Sarah was shocked.

'How are his boils?'

'What boils?' Sarah was caught off balance.

'Oliver's. Hector wrote that Oliver had desert boils. Didn't he tell you?'

'No.' Sarah wondered how to get through the barrier of indifference Calypso wore. 'I came, I came,' she said bravely, 'to see whether there is anything I can do.'

Calypso watched the kettle. 'Thanks, Aunt Sarah, there's nothing at all.'

Sarah asked: 'When did you hear? Why haven't you –' She paused.

'Why haven't I told you all? Rather be alone, I suppose.' She spooned tea into the pot and poured from the kettle. 'Except that I'm not alone, there's this bloody baby. I can't wait to get my body back to myself. Roll on the ninth month.'

'Naturally you are upset.' Sarah flinched at her inadequacy.

'Why can't they tell the truth? What's the use of "missing believed killed"? They only say that because they

271

haven't found the body. They didn't find Walter's. They only say it to prolong the agony.' Calypso blazed with anger. 'D'you like milk and sugar?' Her expression snapped back to normal.

'Just milk, please.' Sarah sat on a kitchen chair, her back stiff. 'It's the most terrible shock when you are in love with –'

'I don't know what love is,' Calypso said. 'Sugar, Sophy? I married Hector for his money. I've got his money. He made a generous will, everything to go to the baby after me. I can marry again if I want to and still keep the money for my life. The child is provided for separately.' She sipped her tea, smiled wryly. ' "Separate" being the operative word. Once this lump and I are separate everything will be OK. That about wraps it up. There isn't any "in love", Aunt.'

'I'll go and clear up that dog mess and give him a run.' Sarah stood up, too horrified to speak.

'His lead's on the table.' Calypso watched her aunt leave the room with the dog, then grinned at Sophy. 'She can walk him round Parliament Square and cool down,' she said. 'Why don't you stay with me, Sophy, love, while they get used to the idea that you won't be going back.'

'D'you think they will let me?'

'Yes, I do. Monika tried to kill herself. Tony rang me up before you came. Don't worry, she didn't succeed. Aunt Helena will be busy smoothing things down in Cornwall. I'll take charge. Aunt Sarah can't have you in Bath, she is dreadfully busy with her W.V.S. You stay here for a while and amuse me.'

'If only I could.'

'You can, we'll fix it. Have to get you some clothes, you can't go around looking like that.'

'Coupons?'

'Mrs Welsh has an inexhaustible supply at a pound each from the *Marché Noir*.'

'A pound! Gosh!'

'I'm rich, so what's a pound?'

'What did you say about Monika? Aunt Sarah said she was ill.'

'She would. I daresay she is ill. All Tony knows is that she tried to jump over the cliff. I think the war is affecting people's minds. Do you know what Hector's letters have been about? Trees, planting trees, "designing" is the word he used, designing woods. You'd think he had no interest in anything else.'

'She wouldn't fall far,' said Sophy, who wasn't listening. 'The Army have blocked the Terror Run with barbed wire.'

Sarah, her equanimity recovered, came back into the kitchen with the dog.

'What does Oliver write about in his letters, Aunt Sarah?'

'Oh, darling, he writes that the desert is cold and gritty, that he is bored, that he is tired, that he is –'

'Frightened?'

'He doesn't say so but no doubt he is. He can't write what one wants to hear because of censorship. It's all so horrible.' Sarah sat down and stared at her niece anxiously.

'Hector wrote about trees. Before that he wrote about politics, that the whole Army will vote Labour next time and so would he and that he was going to give up politics. Well, it doesn't matter now.'

'He's only missing, darling.' Sarah spoke gently.

'Believed killed,' Calypso replied steadily. The two women stared at each other, then Calypso said brightly: 'I've asked Sophy to stay with me. She can keep me company. Will you deal with her school, say she's not coming back?'

'Helena should deal with the school. Perhaps Sophy should go back, I don't know why she left.'

'I do,' said Calypso, who had been told by Tony. 'She can't possibly go back. Why not leave it to me?'

'But –'

'They won't know I'm only twenty, they won't know it's me. I can be awfully toffee-nosed. I will deal with them, tear them off a strip. I will enjoy having Sophy here, she will take my mind off things.'

'If you think –' Sarah began weakly.

'I do, Aunt Sarah, I know. This will be good for us both. Sophy will care for me, won't you, Sophy?'

'Yes.'

'Well, for the moment. Just for a short time –' Sarah in her country tweeds looked worriedly at Calypso wrapped in a lace dressing gown which did nothing to hide her shape. 'If I could have her I would.' She stood up, feeling she must leave. 'I shall talk to Helena and Richard.'

'The bulge and I will be very glad to have her,' said Calypso.

'I'll see you to the bus,' said Sophy.

'Can't I get you to a taxi?' Calypso kissed her aunt, mentally speeding her off.

'No, a bus, Number Eleven.' Sarah kissed Calypso. 'Look after yourself, darling.' She felt inadequate, shut out.

'I will. And Sophy.' Calypso was cool and firm.

'I wish I knew whether I was doing the right thing.'

'Don't worry, Aunt. Don't fail to tell us news of Oliver.'

'I'm sure he writes to you oftener than me.'

'Oh, no,' cried Calypso, waving from the doorstep, 'of course not.' She waved again, then gathered the letters from the table where she had laid them, among them one from Oliver.

'I bet he's gleeful, the bastard,' she muttered. Slitting the thin air mail letter open she read: 'Now that you are a widow, my darling, we can start making plans for our future in case I survive this bloody fucking war. I calculate we can live very comfortably on your late lamented (not by me) husband's money while I write my first novel, after which all will be plain sailing into the sunset. Talking of fucking, we are very deprived here in the desert so get set to make up for lost time when –' She screwed up the letter and threw it onto the floor. 'The shit,' she muttered, 'shit, shit, shit.' She watched Fling pounce on the letter and tear it to shreds, growling and shaking it like a rat. Coming back into the house Sophy said: 'What is he eating?'

'A letter from Oliver.'

'He told Aunt Sarah about Hector. I suppose he is pleased.'

'Don't sound so desolate. Oliver may get killed, and the twins, and that will be the end of our lot, not that Hector belonged –' Her voice trailed.

Sophy asked: 'Has Oliver really got boils?'

'So Hector said. Let's go and light the fire in the drawing room.' Calypso led the way up the stairs. 'I hope Mrs Welsh has laid it.' She struck a match, held it to the paper, watched the flame creep and take hold. 'Don't tell me about school if you don't want to. I can guess. Was Tony kind?'

'Very, but he said I stank.' Sophy described Helena's bathroom, her soaps and scent. 'I used too much. He kissed me goodnight.' She touched her mouth unconsciously. Calypso smiled.

'He will fall in love with you.'

'Nobody will do that. The girls at school call me –'

'What?'

'Eurasian. They say none of their brothers –'

'Bugger their brothers. You don't need that kind of girl's brother. Sophy, you are lovely, beautiful, didn't you know?'

'Me?' Sophy stared at Calypso in astonishment. 'You are just trying to be nice.'

Calypso grinned. 'Nice is not a word much applied to me. I am going to dress. You read these while I have my bath, then we will go shopping and buy some clothes for you.' She handed Sophy a batch of letters and left the room.

Sophy held the letters, turning them this way and that. Letters from Hector, written on air mail paper. She began to read, unfolding them carefully, refolding each one as she finished it. When she had read them she laid them on a side table and sat staring into the fire, where Calypso presently found her.

'I wish someone would write letters like that to me.'

'About trees,' Calypso scoffed. 'What was he thinking

about, what did he mean by it? There's nothing, absolutely nothing about the war or what he's doing. The nearest we get is Oliver's boils.'

'Perhaps he didn't want to think about the war. The letters are all about after the war and things he wants to do for you, with you –'

'I haven't read them properly.' Calypso was defensive.

'He wanted to plant a forest with your name spelled with wild cherry trees.'

'You make it sound poetic. It is wasted on me. Let's go shopping. I don't want to talk about Hector, Sophy. He isn't like that, he's a tough who gets drunk and –'

'So do Oliver and the twins, so does Uncle Richard, so did Walter.'

'Was Tony drunk last night?'

'No.'

'You were lucky.' If he had been drunk, thought Calypso, Sophy wouldn't be sitting there looking so virginal. 'It's the war. Everybody's drinking, even Aunt Helena.'

'Really?'

'Yes, she is. People say it's fear. I think it's because people think there's a shortage. They soup it up in case the next person wants it. The war's driving us to drink. At the moment. It makes me sick. As soon as I am delivered of this lump I shall go on a bender.'

Filling in the time before the funeral Sophy walked along the cliffs in the wind, which stung her eyes. She remembered the time spent with Calypso while here in Cornwall Richard and Helena had cared for Monika, each solicitous for a different reason, Richard because he was truly fond, Helena because she wanted to get back to London. Max had travelled to Cornwall whenever he could leave London, deeply concerned for Monika. He would come and sit with Calypso, bringing presents of books or flowers, and talk about life in Vienna before the war and on rare occasions of Pauli, his son, hinting with perplexity at a stormily aggressive character who might or might not, if he survived, become an artist, a youth who somehow frightened his parents into an excess of guilt, giving the impression of some dire force which made him unlovable. Then he would pause, rub his hands together, shake his shoulders, laugh and change the subject. Similarly Calypso rarely mentioned Hector, and Polly, who came often after work, never mentioned the twins except casually and jokingly as the High or Hoi Floyers.

As she strode along the path, neatly signposted by the National Trust, Sophy remembered those months in London as months of happiness. Calypso taking her shopping, buying her pretty clothes, teaching her how to care for her hair and nails. Max, Brian Portmadoc, Tony Wood and other friends of Calypso and Polly came to spend evenings, talking, joking, cooking supper in Calypso's kitchen, sharing bottles of wine which one or other would bring. They had all, Sophy thought, shied away from anxious subjects like Hector, Pauli, Oliver and the twins and turned to her as a person they could share communally in safety without awkwardness. They had taken her to the cinema and out to lunch. Once or twice Max had taken her to a concert, several times Tony had smuggled her into a pub. She walked Fling in the parks with Brian. It was generally understood, though not underlined, that presently, when Monika was well again, when Helena came back to London, Sophy would go back to Cornwall and help with the cow and the hens, go to day school perhaps. The attitude seemed to be that there was no hurry, things would work out, meanwhile forget beastly school, have fun, grow up. Ah, thought Sophy, walking over the short cliff grass in her green gumboots, those were the days when I grew up, when we chattered and gossiped and phoned occasionally to the old people, Helena, Sarah, Uncle Richard and Monika, none of them, except perhaps Uncle Richard, as old then as I am now.

They had discussed war news, shortages, the unexploded bomb which had lurked for months under

Knightsbridge while the buses trundled over it, the flooding of London by the Americans, who got noisily drunk and were so helpful and polite, giving nylons to the girls, nylons, nylons. Sophy tramped over the cliff, hearing the gulls' high-pitched crazy cry, as they had always cried over the grey sea. She tried to remember what Calypso had said to her school, that nightmare place, and failed. We were all in love, she thought, stopping on the headland, looking out to sea, Uncle Richard with Monika, Max with Monika and Helena, Polly with the twins, Helena with Max, I with Oliver. Oliver and all the men with Calypso, who said she didn't know what love was.

Sophy wondered what Calypso looked like now she'd had a stroke, recovered, they said, except for her face. It was some years since she had seen her. She wondered whether she dyed her hair, and what she would look like with her face twisted, though someone had said it was twisted only a little. I remember, Sophy told herself, I shall always remember what she looked like when the news came that Hector was a prisoner of war and not dead at all.

33

Turning back towards the house, the wind nudging her along with threats of winter stinging her ears, she could see across the fields the church tower rearing above the squat little village, protecting as it had for centuries the bones of the dead, among which lay Uncle Richard, the Floyers and Monika, where tomorrow they would lay Max with whom she had spent the day that Calypso was given the news that Hector was no longer missing but a prisoner of war.

With the wind bringing colour to her high cheekbones, Sophy remembered that day, or thought she did, for she knew well enough that memory plays false, that mind and emotion build on memory. The picture which is not clear at the time becomes lucent with recollection.

Max had taken her to a rehearsal of Yehudi Menuhin. She had sat listening to the talk, watching Menuhin and other musicians, and then the unearthly sounds of Menuhin's violin drew her up to a new plane of existence. She was aware that Max had left the hall to talk to a stranger. Coming back he sat beside her, held her hand until the music stopped, then said, 'We must go', and led her out. He had not said goodbye to any of the people. He had said, pushing her into a taxi, 'Stay with me, try not to talk.' On the way to Enderby Street he had held her against him, sitting taut, just holding her until they arrived, fumbling for money, paying the taxi, not speaking, pushing her ahead of him into Helena's house. He had told her in the drawing room or Helena's bedroom that in the concert hall the man who had access to information, no one knew exactly how, told him that Pauli had died in the concentration camp. 'I have lost my son. What can I say to Monika? Why did we not stay? Why did we run away?' He had rocked her in his arms, holding her against his bony body. She had responded, holding his head against her breast, consoling him with all the emotion set in train by Menuhin, and then Sophy delved back into that traumatic afternoon in Helena's bed, to the tender love-making of a deeply sorrowful man. She had lain beside him as he slept, glad of what he had done. He had woken, kissed her. 'Did I hurt you, child?'

'Very little,' she had said honestly.

'I am glad you were there,' he said, consoling her.

'I am glad, too,' she had answered, comforting him.

Sophy, remembering the comfort of Helena's bed, the hardness of Max's ribs, was glad that she had been there while he endured the agony of his loss – not unexpected, no deaths were unexpected. Later they shared the bath, using Helena's bath essence, wrapping themselves in her enormous white towels with 'H' stitched on the corners in red. They dressed and walked from Enderby Street to Calypso's house. Max had held her hand all the way. On the cliff-top Sophy smiled, for now he was dead she was the only one left who knew that they had been lovers. She had happened to be there at the right moment for him to reach for.

In the dusk they had stopped to stare at a bombsite, each noticing, neither commenting on the weeds growing in the cracks of what had once been a house. They had reached Calypso's house as it grew dark, letting themselves in. Fling had rushed to greet them and Calypso had called from upstairs, 'Is that you?'

She was sitting in the middle of the sofa, heavily pregnant, legs apart, holding the telegram. Sophy remembered Calypso's eyes and she remembered Max's face as he read the telegram held out to him.

'What joy,' he had said, kissing Calypso, who put her arms round him, laying her face against his. His eyes catching Sophy's had signalled 'No', and neither of them had breathed a word about Pauli.

Max had said: 'Bubbly, *nicht*?' being very keen on using what he called 'English argot'. They had trooped to the basement to raid Hector's precious cellar and Calypso had telephoned Aunt Sarah, her parents, Helena and Richard. Polly had come round with Brian Portmadoc, Tony Wood and a Frenchman who knew Hector. There had been quite a party. Probably, Sophy thought, it was the best thing for Max, who did not break the news until weeks later to Monika, waiting until she was quite well, no longer likely to throw herself over the cliff, as she had tried during the guinea pig scandal. It must have been about here, Sophy thought, peering over. There was the ledge she had fallen on. If it had been anyone other than Monika one would think she had known she couldn't fall far. As she peered over, aware of the sea, the wind, the crying gulls, measuring the drop to the ledge, one of the many impertinent cliff foxes poor Ducks used to chase zigzagged along the slope. Sophy felt a rush of tears for the dog, for Max to be buried tomorrow, for her virginity given him so carelessly. Lucky, she thought, that she didn't conceive a replacement for Pauli, and she remembered what she had long forgotten, Calypso's glance exchanged with Max, the way they had smiled complicitly, then Calypso's change of tone.

'Perhaps he'll stay long enough in prison to get the news that I am pregnant.'

'You make him sound like a shop,' Polly had said with implied reproach.

'He is very distant,' Calypso had answered. 'Hard to imagine when he isn't here.'

Sophy climbed the last bit of cliff, arriving breathless on the camomile lawn. She looked at the house, quiet now, its rooms empty, the windows sightless. The Ilex tree stood as it always had, protecting the eastern side; the branch she had climbed along as a child darkened the drawing room. Here Helena had sat in her deck chair, here Oliver, Walter, Polly, the twins and Calypso had lolled chatting on the summer evenings of their youth. Here she had stood whistling and calling Ducks when he had gone hunting the cliff foxes when Uncle Richard lay ill with pneumonia. He had fretted for his dog. She had spent hours whistling and calling, her voice mingling with the gulls. On the third evening the dog had appeared, paws sore with digging, coat ingrained with earth, eyes bunged up with sand, so tired he crawled to Sophy's feet and lay feebly wagging. She had carried the dog into the house, given it water, tempted it with food and carried it up to Uncle Richard, who gasped for breath against his pillows. Coughing, he had said, 'Give him to me, put him here.' The dog had lain in the crook of his arm, his long nose on the sleeve of Richard's striped pyjamas, his eyes closed in exhaustion and Richard had slept for the first time for days. Monika had sat up with him, sending her to bed, anxious for Richard who was iller this time than ever before, not responding to the M and B pills prescribed by the doctor.

Mildred Floyer had come to sit with Richard. Sophy had listened to the two women discussing penicillin, which could save Richard but was only issued to the forces. Unable to sleep, she came down to the kitchen to join them drinking cocoa.

'He was so anxious for the dog, he will get better now he is found.'

'One hopes,' Monika had said. Monika, who no longer had hope for Pauli, no longer flushed at the mention of guinea pigs. Monika, who had in her sorrow strength to lavish on Richard, who loved her, had said, 'He may try to get better now, perhaps he will try for the dog's sake.' She had asked to be allowed to sit with Richard and they had agreed. Mildred left to get a little rest, her face etched with anxiety for the twins in Italy now, for the war had taken its turn for the better and the German armies were moving back, albeit slowly.

Standing on the lawn Sophy remembered Richard and sitting by the bed listening to his breathing, his snorts

282

and snuffles. Repelled by the sickroom smell she sat bolt upright, unable to relax, watching Richard's grey face, his mouth slackly open, his every breath an effort. He opened his eyes and said: 'I'm buggering off.'

'What?'

'Come over here.' She got up and stood by the bed.

'Dog's done for too.' His breath whistled.

'What?' She could barely hear him for the fear she felt.

'Can't move his legs, poor little brute.'

She had felt the dog, picked him up, put him on the floor where he rolled over, his eye catching hers, listless.

'Put him back.' Richard coughed, fighting for breath, gasping, wheezing, his face a dull purple.

She eased the dog back into place. 'He's not old,' she had said defensively, feeling the dog criticized.

'But done for.'

'I'll get the vet as soon as it's light.'

'No good, both dying.' Richard's eyes on her face, the dog staring, daring her to move it again, its teeth bared.

'He loves you,' she had said, adding after a pause, 'we all do.'

'Love,' Richard gasped, an expression of weary contempt on his face. 'Used to love Helena.' Sophy had leant close to hear. The dog growled, threatening to snap. 'Love Monika now. Your mother said she loved, Priest said she said.' His chin sank on his chest. 'Some Chink, I ask you. A coolie, shouldn't be surprised, lucky we're winning the war, the Huns would see you're not pure Aryan.' His voice had trailed into a coughing fit. She remembered holding the glass of water so that he could sip, and hating his breath. He gripped her hand.

'I ask you, Sophy. It is Sophy?'

'Yes,' she had said. 'Yes, it's Sophy,' repelled by him.

'Come closer.'

Holding her breath so that she need not breathe the odour she feared, she had leant closer.

'See that they bury him with me.'

'At your feet?'

'In coffin. Promise.' His anxious eyes close to hers

283

echoed the dog's expression. 'I ask you –' His grip on her hand faded, his chin sank on to his chest, she could hear the bedside clock ticking where Monika had moved it on to the chest of drawers. She stared at the dog and the dog stared back. She closed Richard's eyes, able to touch him now without dread. She remembered waking Monika and that Monika had lifted the dog from the bed, saying in a matter of fact voice, 'Put him in his basket,' that she had carried the dog to its basket in the dressing room, reached for something to cover it and the nearest thing was a pair of trousers. She had pulled the artificial leg away and wrapped the trousers over the animal.

Sophy remembered standing where she stood now the morning Richard died. She had wept for the dog, who was dying. She had run back into the house where Monika was telephoning the doctor and Helena and found the dog dead. It was Max who helped her smuggle it into the coffin where Richard lay in a dark suit, his wispy hair brushed neatly back, his face wearing the mortician's idea of dignity. Ducks joined his master, his lip curled in a snarl, body stiffly bent. Max tucked him in beside Richard and called to the undertaker to put the lid on the coffin. Standing on the lawn, looking up at the house, Sophy wondered how large a tip had been pressed into the undertaker's hand, how Max had ensured the dog's burial would remain secret. When she stood by the grave with Helena, Monika and Mildred Floyer, Mr Floyer reading the burial service, his surplice flapping in the wind, the coffin resting in the deep pit, Max had caught her eye across the open grave and smiled. The old devil, Sophy thought, turning to look at the sea, where later strange shapes which were bits of Mulberry Harbour were towed past in the spring of 1944. How Uncle Richard would have loved the Normandy invasion, she thought, even though both the High Floyers were wounded and several men from the village never came home. He would have gloried, watching American bombers fly over the coast to bomb France. Without his enthusiasm the war had become dull, something to be finished as quickly as possible, for Richard had represented the audience. All the rest of us, she thought, who had gathered in 1939 on the camomile lawn, played small parts. She bent to look at the texture of the lawn. It was amazing it had survived. She ran her palm over it, sniffing the elusive scent evocative of other times, other loves. Someone tapped on the glass of the French windows. She had thought the house empty and was startled. The light, tempered by racing clouds, shone in her eyes. She could see a shadowy figure behind the glass, who tapped again then backed out of sight.

Sophy crossed the lawn and stared in at Monika's meticulously furnished drawing room, all trace of Helena obliterated. When Max bought the house in the fifties Helena had finally settled in London. She tried the windows, found them locked and walked round to the front door.

'I'm in the kitchen,' Calypso called, 'making tea.'

'Oh.' Sophy felt mixed emotions: anger at being disturbed in her nostalgic trip, gladness at hearing Calypso's voice.

'Come along, darling, it's only me.'

The two women embraced, each hiding her face against the other's cheek.

'You still use Mitsuko,' said Sophy.

Calypso stood back, holding Sophy's shoulders, smiling.

'Not a grey hair. Not even a rinse! How many years?'

'What are you doing? The funeral is tomorrow.' They spoke together.

'I thought I'd collect my thoughts. I haven't been here for years.' Sophy returned Calypso's crooked smile.

'Doesn't show much, does it? I thought I'd come the night before the wake. I've got a carload of booze. Any idea who's coming?'

'The neighbours, I suppose, friends, other artists. Hamish is bringing Helena, you know.'

Calypso laughed. 'At her age, crikey.'

'She enjoys funerals, she's strong. She was at Richard's, Monika's, both Mr and Mrs Floyer's. She even turned up at General Peachum's.'

'Seems excessive. Were you at all of them?'

'No, no, only Monika's and Uncle Richard's. Felt I owed it. Why didn't you come?'

'I was abroad. Besides, if you mean what I think you mean, I don't know that I –'

'I always imagined you qualified.'

Calypso chuckled. 'I expect Polly will come, don't you?'

'Yes.' Sophy watched Calypso search for cups, find sugar, warm the pot. 'I wanted to look round the house.'

'I'll come with you, unless you want to be alone.'

'No.'

'I suppose it will be sold now, Pauli won't want it.'

'I am sure he doesn't.'

They left the kitchen, strolling through the hall – 'D'you remember Monika's hyacinths?' – into the dining room. 'Those holiday breakfasts, Uncle Richard crumpling The Times.'

'Monika made this room look lovely.' They stood in the drawing room.

'Helena had no real idea.'

'The bedrooms were always comfortable.'

'Cold in the winter.'

'Not since they put in central heating.'

Companionably they climbed the stairs. Sophy noticed that Calypso dragged a leg.

'This room had the finest view.' Calypso opened a bedroom door.

'Uncle Richard died in it.'

'Oh Sophy, look, did you know?'

Propped on stools Max lay in his coffin. Calypso crossed herself. Sophy took her hand.

The afternoon light was kind to Max. He seemed to be listening, his springy white hair swept back, arched nose, mobile mouth, bottom lip slightly pouting, brow lined but serene, paper-thin eyelids hiding the black observant eyes.

286

'I never realized he was so beautiful,' Calypso whispered.

'Because he was busy making us feel beautiful.' Sophy spoke in a normal voice. 'No need to whisper,' she said.

'He doesn't look his age. He's as old as Aunt Helena.'

'Not quite.' Sophy bent to kiss the still face. Calypso watched her.

'I couldn't do that,' she said. 'I couldn't even kiss Hector goodbye. What are you laughing at?' She turned on Sophy, who had sat back on the bed giggling.

Sophy told her of Max smuggling the dog into Richard's coffin. Calypso let out a yelp of laughter.

'The old rogue.'

'He had compassion,' said Sophy.

'What a philanderer,' Calypso grinned.

'But faithful to Monika and Helena,' said Sophy.

'If you like a *ménage à trois*,' said Calypso.

'They did. Country wife and town wife. They were happy.'

'Mistress,' said Calypso.

'If you must split hairs,' said Sophy, who had never married.

'Shall we make that tea?' They went downstairs. 'I will gee up the kettle. I wonder why they haven't closed the coffin, why he's alone, why the house is empty –'

'We'd better stay and keep him company.'

'I don't want to,' said Calypso. 'I've got a room at the Queen's.'

'I shall, then. Somebody should until Pauli comes –'

'Of course that's why it's open. I'd forgotten Pauli.' Calypso made the tea.

'People do.' Sophy watched Calypso pour water into the pot.

'He isn't one of us, is he?' Calypso poured. 'Lapsang Souchong sounds better but doesn't taste as good as Earl Grey.' She handed Sophy her cup. 'Sugar?'

'No, thanks.'

'Come and spend the night at the Queen's. I'll pay.'

'No, thank you, Calypso.'

'Come to dinner, then, we have so much to catch up on – do. It's so many years.'

But Sophy refused. 'No, thank you, love.' She had so very nearly married Hamish. What would Calypso have been like as a mother-in-law?

'Tell me something.' Calypso sipped her tea, reading Sophy's thoughts.

'What?' Sophy was wary. 'I always think you know everything.'

'Did Hamish want to marry you?'

'I was there when he was born –'

'That's no answer.'

Sophy laughed. 'I am nearly old enough to be his mother.'

'You haven't answered me.' Calypso was watchful. 'You would have been rich, didn't that tempt you? I like being rich, always have.'

'So you always said. You said, too, that you didn't know what love was. You lied.'

'Oh?' Calypso was non-committal. 'What makes you think that?'

'When Hamish was born you gave yourself away.'

'How?'

'Your voice.'

'I don't remember saying anything. I remember yelling a lot.'

'When you saw him, when you looked at him you said, "His balls are as big as Hector's" – your voice.'

'I'd never seen a new-born baby, it gave me a shock.'

'You sounded as if you loved Hector.'

'You are fanciful.' Calypso sipped her tea, watching Sophy. 'You still haven't answered my question.'

'It wouldn't have worked.'

'So he did want to marry you.'

'He was only a baby.'

'Too young to know his own mind?'

'Of course.'

'He has never married anyone else.'

'There's time enough,' said Sophy stoutly.

Calypso laughed. 'What a birth that was, put me off having another.'

'You didn't want another.'

'Right. Hamish is enough. We might have got on, you and me. You could have provided me with a grandchild. Hector would have liked that.'

'Cousins.'

'Not too close. Walter was too close and Oliver.' Calypso let Oliver's name hang in the air. 'Does he ever come to England?'

'I wouldn't know.' Sophy's neutral voice was steady. It would be unbearable if Oliver turned up.

Both women sat thoughtfully holding their teacups in the kitchen which had become so exclusively Monika's.

'You were extremely plucky when Hamish was born. I've never really thanked you. I didn't see you after I was whisked off to hospital. What happened to you?'

'Brian put me on the train to Penzance.'

'Not Max?'

'No, Brian. They had arrived together to find you. Max went with you to the hospital.'

'Oh.'

Calypso and Sophy remembered the solitary air raid, the bomb which had demolished Calypso's house, trapping them in the basement, the shock bringing on premature labour, the long hours while rescue workers frantically dug.

'How Fling barked!'

'How I yelled. You must have been terrified.'

'I was until the baby came out.'

'You wrapped him in glass cloths.'

'There was nothing else.'

'You found Mrs Welsh's apron, you used that.'

'So I did.'

'It was wonderful when they got us out.'

'Wasn't it!'

'Even more wonderful when Catherine came and took him off to Scotland so that I could be free. I wonder who sent for her?

'I did.'

'Really? Clever of you.'

'I telephoned her and she came right away. She was furious. She said you'd been irresponsible.'

'So I was.' Calypso laughed, not minding the criticism. 'But there was no need to fuss. I was quite all right.'

'It was Hamish she was worried about,' said Sophy drily. 'Not you.'

'Hector's baby,' Calypso agreed. 'So long ago it doesn't seem real, does it?' She stood up. 'Sure you won't come to the Queen's? It's comfortable.' She gathered her bag, put on her coat not expecting a reply. 'See you tomorrow in church. Goodbye, love.' She laid her cheek against Sophy's in token affection. Sophy watched her get into her car and drive out of sight, then went and stood by the drawing room window and looked out. She folded her arms, hugging herself, remembering how in the bomb-blasted kitchen in London she had held new-born Hamish screaming his objections to this horrible world. She had crouched, holding the infant, listening to the curses of the rescuers as they dug through the rubble to reach Calypso, buried they knew, injured they thought, unaware that she had Sophy with her, unaware that she had given birth to Hamish. She had crawled about the kitchen still amazingly intact. The ceiling had not completely collapsed until after they were rescued. She had seen the telephone, tried it, found it wonderfully working, said to the operator, 'Get me through to Scotland.' She supposed the number had been written up somewhere, or had she asked Calypso? She could not remember. Catherine had answered – she could recollect Catherine's voice, clear from the Highlands – 'I can hear him greeting.' She had wrapped Mrs Welsh's apron more tightly round the sticky, screaming baby and, crouching beside Calypso, had waited for release.

'D'you think they will get us out?' Calypso had been wonderfully resilient.

'Of course they will.' Sophy listened to the picks and shovels, the grunts of the men trying to reach them, guided by Fling's high-pitched barking.

'Hector will kill me for this' – Calypso had sounded pleased, crouching in the shattered kitchen – 'when he gets to know. I really believed he was dead.'

'I know. I wonder what it's like to be a prisoner of war. At least he's safe.'

'He still writes about trees,' Calypso had complained. 'Nothing about his camp or me.'

'If he wrote love letters he would not want someone other than you to read them. I expect he feels private. I would.'

'D'you think that's it? I hadn't thought.'

'Of course. For flowering trees read whatever he says when he tells you he loves you.' Calypso had laughed.

'Clever Sophy. Guess what he says when he loves me.'

'I couldn't. I know, though, that he loves you.'

'He loves my rump and, well no, I can't tell you what he says, you would be shocked.'

'Perhaps.'

'I'll whisper. We mustn't let the baby hear what its pa says.' She whispered in Sophy's ear. Both girls were laughing when the first of their rescuers broke through, bringing with him a shower of rubble. There was so much laughter at that time, Sophy thought, and Hector had not been safe in a P.O.W. camp but winding his way down Italy in an intricate escape. She had been back in Cornwall when he got home to Calypso. Hamish had grown up in Scotland. Hector had joined the Labour Party and taken up forestry. Calypso had lived on, beautiful, remote, adored. Hector had died some time in the fifties. Calypso had not remarried and Oliver presumably went on loving her, for though he had married she had never heard he was happy.

Looking out at the grey unfriendly sea, Sophy remembered the last period of the war, living with Monika, helping with the cow, the hens, the garden, Mr and Mrs Floyer, village activities, and of how she had longed to be back in that dreadful school for the sake of the brief moments passing through London when she had felt part

291

of Helena's, Polly's or Calypso's lives, with news of Oliver, glimpses of the twins, moments with Max, talk of Hector, a feel of belonging, of being part of the group which had dined on the lawn on one of the last days of August 1939, sitting round a table lit by candles, with the moon rising over the sea.

I was alone then, she thought. I'm alone now. Oliver, bane of my life.

34

'Curious that they have both died in that house.' Helena had not spoken for some miles, Hamish thinking her asleep.

'Who, what both?' he blurted in surprise.

'My husband Richard, my lover Max are "both".' Helena's accent was tart. 'I sold it to Max after Richard died. I am said to have smothered him with a pillow. It has become folk lore. I wasn't sorry when he died, though.'

'Oh.' Hamish had heard the legend. 'Oh.' He felt uncomfortable.

'I could not have smothered him, I was in London with Max. Richard smothered me until I bought my present houses. Sound investment, though not thought so at the time. I paid two thousand pounds for the two.'

'It's unbelievable. As little as that?'

'Richard said they were jerry built. They will last me out.' Helena paused, thinking of her houses. 'I like risks,' she said. 'Polly's was hit by a doodle bug, only her bed survived. Your mother was caught in a raid, too.'

'So she tells me. Brought on her labour.'

'She can be boring about it. She had Sophy with her to make herself useful. One could say she was the midwife.'

'I never knew that.' Hamish thought, I must remember to quiz mother about Sophy being there. Helena may be inventing.

'If anyone smothered Richard it would have been Sophy. She was with him when he died,'

'Why on earth should she?' Hamish was surprised at the amount of ill feeling the old woman could arouse.

'Richard wasn't what you'd call safe with little girls, though I thought at the time Monika had weaned him. Perhaps she had, perhaps I am wrong about Sophy.' Helena stared thoughtfully at the road ahead. 'Mind you, she was secretive as a child, still is. When Richard died she was in her teens, revenge perhaps. Something odd happened in the early days of the war.' She paused then went on, 'Well, what does it matter, it's so long ago. I was busy with Max. Falling in love left me no room for anything else. You wouldn't know, perhaps.'

Oh, wouldn't I, thought Hamish, grimly remembering Sophy's body, silky hair, slant-eyed tenderness. What a bloody old woman Helena is, he thought. What possessed me to come to this funeral anyway?

Helena was speaking again. 'I may be wrong. At the time nobody else thought so, it was only a hunch so –'

'What was only a hunch?' Curious in spite of himself, Hamish questioned his passenger.

'Just that one of the coastguards fell over the cliff. I wondered whether Sophy might have pushed him.'

'Jesus Christ!'

'Not Jesus Christ. Sophy. It was only an idea. The child had some sort of seizure. I thought if she'd given the man a push it would account for it. Then Max and Monika were interned and of course one couldn't think of anything else.' Helena laughed her old person's laugh. 'The war kept us all busy, even if we didn't actually take up arms like your dear father and all those boys, Oliver, Walter, David and Paul, beautiful young men. Oldish now, of course, except Walter who had no time to deteriorate.'

'But Sophy –' Hamish betrayed himself, Helena noted.

'Sophy was much younger. Far too shy to push anyone over anything. That I even thought such a thing shows the state war got us into, not that I didn't enjoy the war, I would be a liar to deny it. Sophy wouldn't hurt a fly,' said Helena with force, not wishing to hurt Hamish, Calypso's son. 'Sophy had a vein of something which attracted people. Even before her sort of looks became *comme-il-faut* Max was –'

'Max?' Hamish was unaware of the jealousy in his voice but Helena noted it, confirming her suspicion that Hamish loved Sophy. I must not be garrulous, she admonished herself.

'Max was fond of the child, said she would have a success with some types of men.'

'Did he really?' Hamish felt relief. Helena smiled. Not you, my lad, I shall not tell you what I never told anybody, that I found black asiatic hairs in my bed and minded when I never minded any of the other women. She cried out, sitting in Hamish's car on her way to Max's funeral.

'I *mind*! God, how I *mind*!' Helena's voice was strong.

'What?' He felt her pain embarrassing.

'Max dying.' She sighed, lying.

'Let's see if we can find violets,' Hamish said, repenting his anger, but Helena's grief was not to be assuaged.

She said bitterly: 'Just because I am very old does not mean I have forgotten about loving.'

Hamish drove on in sulky silence, wishing that curiosity to see something of his mother's contemporaries had not lured him to come to the funeral.

'I trust this performance will not be the most fearful cock-up,' said Helena, using an expression that had been a favourite of Max's, who had learned it from the twins. 'Cock-up,' she said, looking at Hamish's profile, 'was one of his expressions.'

'Whose?' Hamish felt he would never get used to his passenger's use of the English language.

'Max's. He was so keen to learn English slang. He learned "cock-up" and "pull your finger out" from David and Paul and used them in the wrong context.'

'When was that?'

'In bed. I never undeceived him. I overheard a woman at one of his concerts tell a friend with considerable indignation that he had lured her into bed then said,

"This is a cock-up, isn't it." Ah-ha-ha-ha.' Helena laughed merrily. 'He tried so hard to be English. Ah-ha-ha-ha.'

Glancing at Helena Hamish suddenly saw the years fall away. 'You sound as though you had fun.'

'We did, we did, a lot of fun. Max and I, Max and Monika, Monika and I. We had many a good laugh.'

'I've never understood Monika's attitude,' said Hamish, who held the rather puritanical views of some cradle Catholics.

'Quite simple,' said Helena. 'We were fond of each other. Once Monika took to country life she reigned in Cornwall. I was his town wife. We travelled with him in turns. It wasn't anyone's business but ours. After Richard died it worked very well. When poor Monika died I carried on. Max needed two women just as Polly –'

'Polly?'

'I was going to say needed two men. She was greedy, she wanted, got and kept the twins. My word, if you'd seen her as a girl!'

'What was she like?'

'Pretty, reserved. Gave the impression she was conventional, that no one should dare question her life. On the whole nobody did. Her sheer effrontery silenced her critics and gained the admiration of her peers. It came in useful when she decided to have James and Iris.'

'Do you know which twin is Iris or James's father? I often wonder.'

'I presume they do too. I have never asked because I do not think Polly knows herself.' Helena laughed her ah-ha-ha-ha laugh, appreciating Richard's niece Polly, and added, 'It worked, it still does. There you are, dear boy, two cases of it takes three to make a marriage. Why don't you try it?' she asked cheerfully.

'The Church, my upbringing.'

'None of us allowed our upbringing to interfere with our mode of life.'

'Well –'

'Your nurse Catherine! Your mother! My! My! Your

296

mother converted to annoy your father, who had lapsed. Then, like Saint Paul when he fell off his horse or whatever he did, found she liked it. Your father was flummoxed.'

'He didn't mind.'

'He was like putty in her hands.'

'He adored her. They had awful rows,' said Hamish, remembering his childhood.

'When he was drunk, only when he was drunk. He blacked her eye.'

'My mother can't have liked that.' Hamish was shocked.

'You'd be surprised what people put up with when they are in love.'

'Are you suggesting my mother was in love with my father?' Hamish's tone of disbelief delighted Helena.

'Of course she was. She never let on.'

'My God!' Hamish whispered. 'My God!'

'Why do you imagine she never remarried?' Helena left her question to penetrate Hamish's mind. I can't bear dense men, she thought, how can I endure life without Max? She fumbled in her bag for her flask and unscrewed the cap. After drinking she said in a new tone of voice: 'If you see a suitable pub please stop, so that I can refill my flask and go to the lavatory.'

'And if I die in the attempt I shall find you violets.' Hamish felt a surge of gratitude towards Helena for her betrayal of Calypso. 'I won't tell her you told me,' he said.

'Much better not,' Helena agreed, casting her mind back to the return of Hector, escaped from his P.O.W. camp in Italy, and Calypso's efforts to conceal her joy.

'She tries to protect herself, unsere Calypso,' Max had told her. 'She pretends she cannot love, it is her camouflage.'

'If your father had not loved your mother so helplessly he would have returned to the Church,' said Helena thoughtfully.

'How come? I'm not with you.'

297

'It would have changed her idea of him, he couldn't risk that.'

'If I fail to find violets what other flowers did Max like?'

'We will find violets,' said Helena, liking Hamish, Calypso's son, who reminded her of Hector, his father. Then, feeling warmth for Hamish, she said: 'As you know, your mother had quite a reputation for sleeping around.' Hamish winced. 'But I never heard a whisper after your father came back from the war. Max said she stopped looking at any other man because she found she had the best of both worlds.'

'When she joined the Church?'

'Tcha! She married the world of money, found it held a world of love. The Church was for you, I imagine, as much as for Hector. Let's call it a sauce.'

'My parents being the goose and the gander?'

'There's a pub about a mile ahead, we can stop there,' said Helena. 'Your Church had a thumping Requiem Mass for your father when he died. I went with Max and Monika – most impressive. Calypso manoeuvred it. You were there, quite a nice little boy, same hair as your father's.'

'I can't think that there was any manoeuvre,' said Hamish defensively. 'The Church isn't like that.'

'But Calypso is.' Helena snapped her bag shut as they drew up at the pub. 'Oh, look,' she said, 'that's Polly's car. She's driving Iris and James down. Hoot.'

Hamish obediently tooted his horn, pulling in beside Polly's car. James came out of the pub.

'Hullo,' he said, kissing Helena's cheek as she got out of the car. 'Mother and Iris are in the loo.'

'Good.' Helena drew herself up straight. 'Get this filled.' She handed her flask to Hamish. 'I like Vat 69. We can all arrive together.'

Hamish and James watched her enter the pub.

'She's got hollow legs,' said Hamish.

'We wondered whether there would be anything to eat. We stocked up at that mini-Fortnums in Tavistock.

We spent the night there.' James was amicable.

'Great-aunt Helena has been reminiscing,' said Hamish.

'So has Mother.' James grinned. 'That is what happens at funerals.'

'Any cats out of bags?'

'Not exactly, more a tiny clarification.' James walked with Hamish into the pub. 'About our backgrounds.'

'Our stable backgrounds,' said Hamish. 'What will you drink?'

'Nothing, thanks, I'm driving the last lap.'

Hamish ordered himself a whisky and asked the barman to fill Helena's flask with Vat 69.

'Considering our backgrounds,' said James, 'yours and ours, I'd say we were remarkably stable.'

'What are you on about?' Hamish was not particularly fond of James, preferring his sister who had tact.

'We have two fathers, you have none,' James asserted with pride.

'I had one to start with.' Hamish was huffy. 'He died. They weren't divorced or anything. Yours never married your mother.'

'How could they?' said James angrily.

'Now, now,' Iris had come up behind them. 'For God's sake, let well alone. The less we disentangle relationships the better. You forget I am married and have two small children who will soon be asking questions.'

Hamish laughed, for indeed he forgot Iris was married and had two children, her husband and style of life being so respectable and happy no attention was ever attracted.

'And what shall you tell them?' Hamish sipped his drink, smiling at Iris, who was less beautiful than her mother, far less beautiful than Calypso.

'I don't think they are going to be interested,' said Iris, 'it's all so long ago. We are only interested on occasions like this when the funeral stirs up Mother's memories.'

'And Helena's,' said Hamish.

'Yes, I daresay. Poor old thing, but when she's gone –' her voice trailed.

'There's my mother, there's Sophy, your – er – your fathers. Are they coming, by the way?'

'They may not be back in time, they are in Vichy. I don't think they can make it.'

Hamish remembered that Paul and David seldom turned up at family gatherings, using their arthritis as an excuse.

35

Pauli Erstweiler drove up to the house in his Mercedes.
He slammed the door of his car. Sophy heard his heavy
steps in the hall. He paused by the hall table then went to
look at his father, who had been in England while he,
Pauli, had been in the concentration camp. She could feel
Pauli's bitterness sweep into the house with him, wrap its
icy silence round her like a shroud. She shrank back into
the nearest room and stood behind the door. She heard
his heavy tread come down the stairs, heard him lift the
telephone, dial, speak, ordering the undertaker to close
the coffin. Then: 'Thank you. *Ja, Ja.* Two-thirty tomorrow.
What?' He listened. 'Yes, yes, the house will be for sale.
Do you know of a buyer? Tomorrow then, thank you,
tomorrow will do,' his heavy accent.

He went into the drawing room, his tread the tread of
ownership. He lifted the lid of the piano, played a few
blurred chords with fingers crushed by the camp guards,
their music expunged from his life. He let the lid slam and
again heavy footsteps to the door, the door opening, slamming shut, the car door slamming, the engine revved, the
crunch of tyres, the sound of the wind drowning the sound
of the car, rain sheeting against the window.

Poor Pauli, so full of bitterness, she had thought, lying
in his arms. How can you love when you are filled with
hate?

How could he believe he would have been a musician
when he had no love? He had made himself a millionaire,
they said, wheeling and dealing in tanks, planes, guns.
She went back to stand by Max, lying silent, his music

301

stilled, his grief for Pauli over. There had been such joy over Pauli's survival. She remembered the skeletal young man, Monika and Max's joy turning to fear, pain, sourness.

'He needs love,' Monika had said.

'He needs love,' Max, too, had said.

'He needs rest,' the Floyers had said, 'and peace.'

'He needs a good smack,' Helena had said.

They had watched Pauli grasp at life and use it, careless of the hurt he inflicted, greedy, cruel, selfish, worldly.

'He was a cruel, selfish young man,' she said to Max lying in his coffin. 'I made a fool of myself trying to wake love in him. Calypso was right when she called him "the sow's ear". He is still those things. Calypso when she first met him had said, "He is not one of us." Polly had said, "He is not the Jew the twins fought for," and Helena sized him up immediately, saying it would have been better for Max and Monika if he had died, leaving them with their memory of him unscarred.'

Gently Sophy stroked Max's face with her finger, feeling the cold cheek, the mobile mouth. It would have been better to bury Max without Pauli's arrogant presence.

Made restless by the wind, uneasy by Pauli's abrupt visit, she wandered the house, refurnishing it in her mind as it had been in her childhood. She went up to her bedroom and, looking along the branch of the Ilex tree, she remembered the years when she had dreamed of Oliver, Oliver who loved Calypso. She tried to pin down a time when she had not loved him, or the time she had ceased to love him, and failed. She could not remember when she had last seen him, or where it had been. Long years ago, another life, she thought, moving into Uncle Richard's room. Poor old man, too ill to wipe his tear. Why did I not do it for him, why let him die with a smeared cheek? she reproached herself.

'Sophy.' Calypso's clear voice. 'Are you still here? Are you mad?'

'I thought I'd better stay with him tonight.' Sophy went to meet Calypso on the stairs.

'Morbid, but please yourself. Can you give me a hand? I've brought the booze for tomorrow. Can you help me unload the car?'

Sophy followed Calypso out. 'Goodness, champagne.'

'He liked bubbly. D'you remember he called it bubbly? D'you remember when we heard Hector was not killed we celebrated?'

'I remember well.'

'So I thought,' said Calypso, moving towards her car, 'we'd have bubbly tomorrow, he'd like that.'

'He would.'

'Guess who I saw in the town – Pauli.'

'He's been here. I hid.'

'Don't blame you, he's a right sod. I think he's a changeling. When you think of Monika and Max you think he can't be theirs.'

'Almost.'

'Not almost. Quite. Quite not theirs. D'you know – can you carry all that, it's heavy – d'you know he made a pass at me once.'

'I slept with him.'

'How *could* you? What *possessed* you?'

Sophy laughed at Calypso's astonished expression. 'I thought I'd teach him how to love,' she said wryly.

Calypso put down the case she was carrying and let out a shout of laughter. Momentarily she looked as she had long ago before the war. 'But darling, you love Oliver, you always did, nobody else ever mattered.'

'As a child. How did you know?' Standing in the rain and wind, holding the champagne, Sophy grasped at her privacy, trying to protect it.

'We all knew.' Calypso pushed open the front door. 'Your enigmatic little face, your eyes. Where shall we put it?'

'In the kitchen.' Sophy, carrying the case of champagne, led the way, glad to turn her back on Calypso. 'In the larder it's cool, let's put it there.'

'Oliver's such an ass. Have you seen him lately?'

'Not for years.'

'Both his wives. Awful.'

Sophy said, 'Are there more cases like this?' wishing to drop the subject of Oliver.

'Yes, in the car. He got over me years and years ago when the penny dropped,' Calypso persisted.

'What penny?'

'The penny that said Hector.'

'I always knew you loved Hector.'

'No, no, not love. He suited me, nobody else did.'

'That's your version.' Sophy sniffed.

'When we've finished unloading I'm going to take you off to dinner.'

'I thought I'd stay the night here.'

'Why?'

'Max is all alone. He always needed one of us there.'

'Very well, we will have bacon and eggs and I'll keep you company. You can't stay here alone, Pauli might come back. Why d'you think he came?'

'To look at Max. I heard him tell the undertaker to close the coffin and that the house is for sale. It's his now.'

'Doesn't let the grass grow. Not that it matters, it will never be the same. I always think of it as Richard and Monika's. In the war when Brian fired the gun.'

'Monika and Max's. Latterly Max alone, with Helena visiting.'

'Of course, but our roots are on the lawn. D'you think it smells now?'

'Faintly.' Sophy smiled at Calypso, glad she had come back.

'Let's finish unloading, then we can have a bottle with our supper. He would approve.'

'I don't like leaving him in the dark.'

'Candles, then. Electric light wouldn't look right. Wish I had some holy candles.'

'The only time he used holy candles was during power cuts. He'd make a dash to the Oratory. Helena was shocked.'

'I'm sure the Church wouldn't mind.' Calypso rummaged in a cupboard. 'Here we are, pity they are red.'

'The light is much the same.' Sophy took them from her and led the way upstairs. 'We'll use the candlesticks we had at his first dinner party here before the war.'

'D'you remember that?'

'Yes, the full moon. You held Oliver's hand.'

'You noticed?' Calypso laughed.

'And Uncle Richard toasted absent friends, meaning Pauli,' said Sophy.

'And the lawn smelt delicious after the heat of the day and Max looked us all over.' Calypso struck a match to light the candles.

'Aunt Helena wore a long dress and kicked Uncle Richard when he was tactless about Pauli.' Sophy set the candlesticks by Max's head.

'And Monika's eyes were huge as she sat thinking about Pauli left behind in Auschwitz. Why do you think they left him behind?' Calypso, lighting the last candle, stood with the lighted match looking across at Sophy.

'A friend they trusted had sworn he could get him out and send him to join them. It didn't come off. The friend ended in a camp too.'

'Ow!' Calypso dropped the match which had burned her fingers. It fell on to Max's chest.

'Look out, you'll set fire to him.' Sophy snatched at the match. 'You've singed his suit.' She brushed at the dying match.

'Horrid smell, pooh.' Calypso blew on her fingers. 'Monika was very clever,' she said thoughtfully, looking across Max's body at Sophy. 'She and Helena ended by adoring each other. Attraction of opposites? Mutual interests? She was clever. Good, too.'

'Also artful. When the guinea pig scandal was on she moved into the General's house.' Sophy smiled in recollection.

'But he started it, horrid old thing,' Calypso exclaimed. 'What d'you mean "moved in"?'

'She packed a small case, walked across the cliffs to his house and put it to him that as the press were on to the story, as an English gentleman it was up to him to protect her, give her asylum.'

305

'Oh my, how crafty.'

'She knew and he knew he'd look pretty silly if the press got the story, so he stifled them. I thought it quite fly of Monika.'

'I bet Max put her up to it.'

'No, no. Max, Helena and Uncle Richard arrived here to find her holed up with the General.'

'I never knew.'

'No one did. She put him on his mettle to do the English gentleman bit,' said Sophy.

'Always putting his arm round our waists for a squeeze. How did you find out?'

'David and Paul's mother. She said she thought it a just punishment for his pro-Nazi views.'

'Oh, yes. One forgets.' Calypso looked thoughtful. 'Used he not to make passes at Monika too?'

'Yes, he did, but never after the guinea pig affair. I wish you could join in this conversation.' Sophy looked down at Max. 'I don't think the burn will show.'

'Let's open a bottle. We'll remember even more after a drink or two.' Calypso moved towards the stairs. 'If we weren't so old we'd be off on a moonlight run. My goodness,' she said, catching hold of Sophy's hand, 'we were an ignorant lot in those days.'

'Very.'

'Who did you sleep with first? Who was your first lover?' Calypso bit her tongue, seeing Sophy's face close blankly shut. 'Mine was Hector,' she plunged on. 'Nobody believed it but Hector was my first, and it didn't take me long to find he was the best, too.' She watched Sophy relax warily. 'They thought I grew stuck-up when I married, perhaps I did. Being rich went to my head.' The danger's passed, she told herself. 'Let's crack a bottle,' she said, moving down to the harsh light of the kitchen, where she looked quite old but a lot more human since her stroke than the girl on the camomile lawn.

36

Too early for the service, Sophy strolled in the church-yard in her green gumboots, the wind whipping her skirt round her knees, her head wrapped in a shawl.

Among the local Penhaligans, Boscences, Penroses, Tremaynes and Tredinnicks she sought the Floyers, Uncle Richard and Monika. She read the Floyers' names, the dates of their births and deaths. Rector of this Parish R.I.P. Someone had planted the grave with daffodils. In spring they lay under a yellow duvet. Others had planted colchicum. Now, in the rain, the Floyers rested under a shocking pink spread which reached across to neighbouring graves as their spirit had envel-oped the parish. Sophy marvelled that they had never criticized or interfered with their sons and Polly. Their acceptance of an unusual situation had silenced waspish tongues as effectively as foam suffocates fire.

Richard Cuthbertson lay apart, his grave planted with spring and autumn cyclamen, fluted pink heads thrusting up through marbled leaves.

'Uncle Richard, salute, and Ducks.' Sophy ran her hand over the cool leaves. Richard, tap dancing with the Rectory evacuees round the hot water boiler, had over-heated and caught a chill leading to pneumonia and death. 'Putting on my top hat –' Where, when the time came, would they put Aunt Helena? It seemed a pity to disturb the cyclamen so well established.

Sophy, holding the shawl close under her chin, observed the pit dug ready for Max, dark earth piled to one side, a pit which already held Monika, now lined with plastic grass. Was there room for three? Sophy suppressed a smile as she walked back past the Penhaligans, Boscences, Penroses, Tremaynes and Tredinnicks. Which among the many Penroses was the Penrose who had not been a proper husband, who had exposed himself to a terrified child, who had fallen or been pushed over the cliff? In the church porch Sophy took the shawl off and shook the rain from it. The lingering memory of a man's shout flipped away with the raindrops as she looked across the fields to the cliffs and the grey Atlantic raging in from the western approaches. Replacing the shawl, Sophy moved into the church, her eyes adjusting to the semi-darkness.

The church was a blaze of colour, red, yellow, pink, orange, dahlias, lilies, chrysanthemums, michaelmas daisies, blue, green, pink and white hydrangeas, stooks of corn, stacks of vegetables, pots of jam, sacks of potatoes, bunches of carrots, vegetable marrows, pots of chutney, baskets of fungi, strings of onions, ropes of garlic, oranges, bananas. Harvest Festival tomorrow.

Outside the wind screamed and battered. The rain slanted vicious rods from bulging clouds. Rainbow weather.

In front of the altar two coffin stools waited to receive Max. Sophy sat at the back of the church to wait the hour. Soon they would all be gathering, the friends, the colleagues, the lovers, the curious, to bury the alien, the refugee, the man who had made this place his own, who had earned the right to rest among them. After nearly fifty years even Monika was forgiven her alien ways, vide the ropes of garlic, the baskets of fungi, mute testimony of quasi-acceptance. Sophy sneezed, breathing in the pungent smell of chrysanthemums, the earthy reek of potato sacks. Feeling chilly, she moved to the space under the tower where the bell ringers gathered, and danced a jig to whip up her circulation, her gumboots slapping on the stone floor. When she heard voices in the porch she sat down again, panting, well back in the shadows.

308

Three or four pressmen gathered, pushing back the hoods of their parkas.

'Won't take long, there's to be a memorial service in London. Only worth a paragraph or two.'

'Depends who comes. Won't be many celebrities, this weather.'

'Never know. There are two coppers to direct the traffic. I saw several faces in the pub worth a mention.'

The village came in twos and threes, middle-aged women with umbrellas, men in sober suits. They sat at the back near Sophy.

'Looks lovely this year.' They viewed the harvest decorations with pride.

'I see Lorna Tremayne's put three jars of her pickle by the font. That's not like her.'

'She'll take un back after service. She'm so mean she won't give you the drips off her nose if so be you might want them.'

'Parson will have to look sharp if he wants 'em for the hospital.'

'Mrs Floyer always made a list, no flies on Mrs Floyer. New parson needs a wife.'

'He'm too high. Higher than High Floyer ever was.'

'Ah. Miss them when they're gone, new chap don't seem to have what it takes.' The voices dropped to an inaudible whisper and suppressed laughter shook the row.

More footsteps in the porch. The pressmen asked for names. A posse of well-wrapped women followed by their consorts in overcoats and hats, pausing a moment to give their names to the press, then moving in to find a seat, settle their haunches, look around, wave discreetly to friends, admire the Harvest Festival flora, peer at the vegetables.

A group of young people carrying musical instruments came in a shy rush, the girls tossing back long hair, the young men ill at ease in formal clothes.

'His master-class,' said a well-informed woman in front of Sophy.

'There's to be music then. Ah.'

Polly, followed by Iris and James. How fat Polly had grown; she looked funny wearing a brown hat, handing James her umbrella to shake, settling with her son and daughter in the third row from the front.

An elderly man, rather shaky on his pins, with a large healthy consort. Sophy recognized Brian Portmadoc. Another vaguely familiar figure, hair trained from a low parting to cover his baldness, asking fussily, 'Where shall we sit? Which side shall we go?' By his voice Sophy knew him. Tony Wood, brave fireman, true friend.

'Doesn't matter, it isn't a wedding, sit where we can. Here will do.' Tony's friend: he had finally settled for a male lover. They ran an antique shop in Brighton.

Two identical figures, bald heads with a frill of white hair, both paunchy, both lame, both heavy on their feet. They looked about them, spotted Polly, Iris and James. Polly looked up and waved.

'I didn't know you were coming.' Polly looked delighted, smiling her contagious toothy smile.

'Move along a bit. We came by train. You'll have to sit in the next row, James.' Inflexion of parental affection.

'No, no, it's all right, nicer all together.' Affection there, too.

'Bit of a squeeze.' Paul sat down smiling.

'How was Vichy?' Iris welcoming.

'Did you do anything about a wreath?' David vaguely anxious.

'Of course I did. Shush –'

People came in a steady stream. The young musicians put up their music stands, one or two notes tentatively played on the organ, a scrape on a violin, a twang from a cello. Sophy, breathing in the damp smell of autumn flowers, dreamed of camomile, the dry aromatic smell of her youth. In the porch the pressmen stood aside to allow Helena, wafting into the church in an aura of whisky, to walk steadily up the aisle to the front pew, where she sat alone on the left hand side close to the coffin stools. The whispering in the church stopped; all eyes were on Helena, boring into her back. Swiftly behind her Calypso in white overcoat, black hat, gloves, stockings and shoes, her lovely face composed, Hamish beside her lightly holding her elbow. They sat immediately behind Helena. Hamish leant forward to put a cardboard box beside her. Helena nodded her thanks.

The church was full, every pew filled except for the front pews, where Helena sat on the left, the right-hand pew empty, waiting for the chief mourner.

Above the whispers of the congregation the wind bumped and buffeted the church, whining round the finials on the tower, growling over the lead roof. Helena took the flask from her bag, unscrewed the top, tipped a liberal swig into her mouth, swallowed. 'Shall I ever be warm again –'

The congregation stood. Slow steps on the gravel path grated.

'I am the resurrection and the life, saith the Lord –'

The new parson's bass voice, carrying through the gale, led the coffin up the path to the church. The newsmen drew aside as he stood for a moment in the porch, a giant wearing a black cloak billowing out in the wind to display its red lining.

'We brought nothing into this world and it is certain we can carry nothing out.'

The words rolled out in splendid cadence.

'You carry my love,' Helena muttered mutinously, and Calypso drew in her breath while Hamish glanced quickly at her, wondering whether his mother prayed and what her prayers might be. She always looked particularly beautiful in church.

'I mind, God how I mind.' Helena watched them steady the coffin on to the stools. She did not hear the Rector's sonorous voice, she did not listen to the service or the music played by Max's pupils. Max's spirit was not in the coffin, far too ornate, chosen by Pauli, Pauli who had followed the coffin into the church and now sat across the aisle alone in the right hand pew. How could he be Max's son, how could he have been conceived by Monika, so lovely, so sweet, so good without being

311

boring? Helena turned to stare at Pauli, who looked ahead. What business deal was he dreaming up, this financial wizard spawned by Max? 'I bet you are never frivolous in bed,' Helena muttered, for yes, it may have taken time, but she and Max had had many laughs. 'What shall I do without his jokes?' her old heart cried.

The service rolled inexorably on. Automatically Helena stood, knelt, sat and behind her, her mind straying as it always did at Mass, Calypso thought of food and sex and of Hector. The texture of his skin, his nutty smell, his laughter, his passion, his rages. Max had made jokes too. Briefly she paid attention. Max would enjoy the sight of Helena and Polly, Sophy hiding at the back of the church and herself attending his funeral and goodness knows, thought Calypso, how many more of us in here lay with him. Hector always said Max would impregnate this corner of Cornwall with a shot of musical spunk. She wished she could in decency lean forward and ask Helena for a swig from that flask. She took Hamish's hand and squeezed it, enjoying his quick smile, so like Hector's.

'Soon be over.'

'Yes.'

Helena was glaring at Pauli, Pauli risen from the dead to hate, make money, hate again, make more money. He had no love for Monika and Max, no understanding and, quite extraordinarily, no music. Max, unable to understand his lost son found again, had wept and Monika had nearly thrown herself over the cliffs, blaming herself for the accidents of fate.

'Not again, mein Schatz, you cannot do it twice. For the guinea pig was enough.'

Helena smiled broadly at the parson, remembering Max's voice, the easing of tension, the laughter. Without being drunk I could not get through this, she thought.

The parson, seeing her broad grin, hesitated in mid flow, missed a beat but carried on bravely, glad that his training enabled him to perform without much thought. He was glad too that he had put on warm socks. It would be cold by the grave.

How Helena hates Pauli, thought Calypso. How could Sophy have slept with him? Wish she had married Hamish, being older wouldn't have mattered. The trouble with Sophy was that she thought a bit of love was a cure-all. What was it Hector said? 'She's deliberately wasting her gifts.' Oh Hector, my darling, you did not waste yours, the woods you planted spell my name in spring. I wonder whether Pauli has provided any food to soak up my champagne. I should have thought of it sooner, not in the middle of the service. Her reverent expression pleased the Rector, who looked past Helena, resting his eye on Calypso with approval. Wonder what he's like in bed, thought Calypso from force of habit. Did parsons need a little boost, as Max had before rehearsal? How he laughed in the cinema. What had been the film? She frowned, trying to remember.

'Was Max a Protestant?' Hamish whispered as they knelt.

'Haven't the foggiest,' Calypso whispered behind clasped hands. 'He must have been born something.'

'If he was a Catholic this is all wrong.'

'Too late now. Shut up.'

'I'll ask Helena. Helena,' he leant forward, his head on a level with Helena's as she sat in front of him, having found that kneeling hurt. 'Aunt Helena, was Max a Protestant or a Catholic?'

'Jew. Why do you ask?' Helena's voice rang clear.

'This funeral service. Surely –'

'Not practising. He didn't practise religion, only the violin. Women too, of course.'

'Hush,' whispered Hamish.

'You started it, hush yourself.' Helena stood up as the choir prepared to sing.

'*O God our help in ages past.*'

She cleared her throat, recognizing the words. There would not be many more ages, she thought with satisfaction, as she picked up the cardboard box and prepared to follow the coffin to the grave. He never minded that I am tone deaf, she consoled herself, he thought it funny.

Oliver, drenched from his long walk from the station, wished he had not come. First the shock of finding Penzance harbour, where water had always lapped in greeting by the train, filled in to form a car park. Now, arriving late, crushed in the crowd at the back of the church, having to endure the spectacle of Polly grown fat and stodgy, flanked by children who must be at least thirty. Calypso, squired by a younger version of Hector, looking so preserved. Preserved for what? He had heard she had had a stroke. She looked trim 'tiré à quatre épingles', the epitome of everything he disliked: classy bitch preserved in money. Well, that was what she had wanted, she had been honest about it. What a fool one was in youth. And there the twins, couldn't be anyone else. Those godlike giants grown stout, bald, lame. Probably had piles, all pilots had piles he had heard. Couldn't put that in his novel, not very well. Well, why not, anything goes these days. Stupid idea, though, to think he'd get copy from Max's funeral. Funerals in books and plays were vieux jeux. That fearfully old woman, could it be Helena? Must be, must be about a hundred, mummified, what a survivor and glaring at that fellow in the other pew. Pauli, of course. Pauli risen from the heap. Well, I never, so that's Pauli. Well! Oliver remembered Max telling him of his own and Monika's dodgy escape from the Nazis and the dismal failure of Pauli's expected follow-on. 'We shall always feel guilty. We shall always feel we should have died with him.' Well, he hadn't died. That looked like a vicuna coat. Do people still wear vicuna coats? I must check, though none of my characters wears that sort of clobber. Oliver gingerly moved his legs in their damp cord trousers, hunched his shoulders in his heavy storm-proof parka, wished he'd put on another sweater. The woman in front of him wearing gumboots, with a shawl round her head sneezed. She wasn't dressed like all these respectables. None of them wore gumboots. High-heeled leather boots, plastic boots towards the back here with zips. No, no good for the novel, thought Oliver, so I'll sit back and enjoy the music when it comes. Those pupils of Max look ready to play their hearts out, not that one would hear very well with the bloody gale blowing.

'What are they going to play?' he asked a neighbour. 'D'you know?'

'Mozart, I believe, and Bach while they go to the grave. We could move up the church when the front pews empty.'

'Thanks.' Oliver realized he had not been attending to the service. A white haired man was finishing the reading:

'– and all the trumpets sounded for him on the other side.'

Oliver felt furious. Trumpets. How did they know? How outrageous! They are fooling us, how do they dare think of trumpets? There is earth. I saw it in Spain. I saw it in the desert, earth, earth, no bloody trumpets, just holes in the ground. I don't write these illusions, I write about uncomfortable things, that's what sells. Oliver felt a jet of pleasure douse his bitterness, glad that from callow boy he had evolved to successful writer.

The church part of the service was ending, the splendid parson in his theatrical cloak preparing to lead Max out to his grave. It would soon be possible to move up closer to hear the music. Oliver, looking over his half-moon spectacles, watched the procession form, Pauli behind the coffin, broad, plump, Monika's eyes, lardy cheeks, no trace of Max's whippy body or humorous face. Helena shrunken, all her weight in the middle, carrying a cardboard box, her blue eyes vague, hair faded to dust colour. Calypso in vivid white coat, eyes shaded by black hat, Hamish a new version of Hector. The twins stoutly limping with sticks and their middle-aged children. Polly in spectacles, her hair a sort of quasi-henna. Elizabeth, surely that woman was the girl Elizabeth who had loved Walter and married Brian Portmadoc. Walter would laugh at this crew. And there Brian talking to Tony Wood, must be, couldn't be anyone else, and all these people, who were they? Where did

315

they come from? Oliver felt hysterical laughter rise in his chest as the procession passed him. Soon he would be soothed by violins and cellos. A man he recognized as probably the best music critic in the business laid his hand on Helena's arm.

'Dear Helena. Just to say I am so sorry that Max, that – so sorry about Max's death.'

'There's a lot of it about.' Helena focused old eyes on the man for an instant and walked steadily out into the porch. Calypso, Hamish and the twins closed round her. Forgetting the violins and cellos Oliver followed the little group, pushing his spectacles further up his nose, pulling his collar round his ears. The rain had stopped and shafts of afternoon sun struggled through the hasty black clouds.

'There will be a rainbow.' A boy's voice broke through the sound of shuffling feet.

'Mind where you put your feet, never mind the rainbow.' An anxious mother snatched at her son as he trampled on to wreaths and sheaves of expensive flowers heaped near the path by undertakers' minions, their beauty blinded by cellophane wrapping. 'You clumsy lout.'

The woman in gumboots sneezed despairingly, 'Aaachoo, aaachoo.'

'D'you need a handkerchief?' Oliver offered.

'Got one, thanks.'

They were lowering Max into that bosom of green plastic.

'*Man that is born of woman hath but a short time to live.*'

Good Lord, thought Oliver, the sneezer is Sophy. What a surprise.

'*– of whom may we seek for succour but of –*'

When had he last seen Sophy? Years and years. He racked his brain. She sneezed again, pressing her handkerchief over her nose to drown the sound. The parson's rich voice rolled on and from the church a burst of Mozart.

'– I heard a voice from heaven saying unto me "Write" –'

All very well, thought Oliver, saying 'Write' like that. Writing is damned hard work without voices from heaven interfering. And now the Lord's Prayer. Oliver muttered with others, resenting as he always did the 'Lead us not into temptation' bit. If God were God, supposing he existed, he wouldn't do anything so damn stupid.

'The grace of –'

Oliver looked across the grave at Helena. What was she up to? What was that box?

'Be with us all evermore. Amen.'

'Amen,' said Calypso and Hamish, crossing themselves. Of course, he'd heard she'd gone over to Rome, old Hector was some sort of Papist.

'Amen.' Helena opened the cardboard box and with a hand bony and veiny with age, mottled with brown death marks, began dropping its contents into the grave: violets, their scent, as they fell down on to the coffin, filling the wet air.

Hamish and the twins threw token clods of earth then followed Calypso and Polly, who walked slowly on either side of Helena to shake hands with the parson in his cloak, and wander towards the cars.

Oliver came up behind Sophy, took hold of her elbow.

'Can you give me a lift?'

'Of course.' Sophy looked at Oliver, startled, her oriental eyes taking him in, stooped, thinning hair, spectacles, very tall, very thin, wet, perfectly recognizable.

'I walked from Penzance.' He held her arm.

'A long way.' She moved away from him.

'They've filled in the harbour,' he said angrily.

'Yes. A very long time ago.'

Pauli standing by the gate. Impossible to avoid him.

'Sophy. You will come back to the house, of course.' A command.

'Well – I –' Sophy looked distressed.

'You must come. Calypso has provided drinks, Polly food.'

'This is Oliver Anstey.'

'I have of course heard of you. You will come too. Helena will be there, I suppose –' Pauli had authority, confidence.

'Yes, we'll come.' Sophy walked quickly to her car, followed by Oliver.

'He looks so pleased,' she burst out.

'What Uncle Richard would call a bounder.'

'The camp *didn't* do him good.' Sophy burst into nervous giggles. 'Oh my God, my feet are freezing. I must change my shoes.' She pulled off her boots and sought shoes. 'They're on the back seat. Oh, thanks.'

Oliver stared at her. 'You haven't changed. All the others –'

'We've grown old.' She was keeping her distance.

'It's not that, it's –'

'Aunt Helena is drunk, we'd better get to the house.' She started the engine. 'I think I've caught a cold.'

'I noticed you sneeze.'

'Inviting her to her own house –'

'Is it still hers?'

'She sold it to Max years ago but she was constantly here. She just happened to be in London when he died.'

'So it's not Pauli's?'

'Technically, but –'

'What?'

'He doesn't belong. Max was ours, not Pauli's.'

'You don't like him?'

'I don't think he likes us.' Sophy stalled the engine. 'Damn.'

'Listen.' Oliver put a hand on her arm. 'Roll down the window.'

A lull in the storm, a burst of sound from the church as violins and cello reached their climax. Oliver put a finger to catch the tear rolling down Sophy's cheek.

He licked his finger. 'How salt your tears are.' She started the engine and drove following the procession of cars. 'I suppose we have to go to this wake.'

'I want to see that Aunt Helena is all right.' Sophy was anxious.

'Aunt Helena is made of sterner stuff than us, she's tone deaf. D'you know,' Oliver leant back in his seat, stretching his legs, 'a friend of mine watched her read the whole of *War and Peace* during a performance of *The Ring*.'

'Bully for her. Where on earth shall I park? I'd no idea so many people would come. Look at all those cars.' Sophy sounded desperate.

'Leave it here. Let's walk.' Oliver was calm.

They left the car by the side of the road and, climbing a stile, approached the house from the cliff path.

'I haven't been here since our last holidays before the war. Where was it we ran?' Oliver peered over the edge.

'The path was wired up during the war and became overgrown. This path is a new one.'

'I had vertigo. I was terrified.'

'I was frightened too. I ran to show off, to gain attention.'

'Let me give you a hand.' He helped her up the bank on to the lawn. 'Does it still smell?'

'Of course.' Her voice was distant. She was looking towards the house. She let go of his hand and he watched her run across the lawn to the French windows, tapping on them for admittance, slipping in, a little dark shadow as James let her in, leaving him outside. Oliver felt a rush of emotion and wondered what it could be. Fear. Am I afraid? he questioned. In which case what am I afraid of? She ran off, she left me. Why the hell did she do that? He stood on the lawn while the wind rose again, lashed him, clouds covered the brief sun and the rain poured down aslant. Hamish opened the French windows and waved a champagne bottle.

'You'll get soaked. Come in, for heaven's sake, come in and have a drink before it's all gone.' Hamish had had a few drinks and his careful nature was expanding.

319

'Is Sophy married?' Oliver peeled off his wet anorak.

'Good Lord, no, of course not. Not for want of –'

'I wondered. I've been abroad so long I'm out of touch. Oh, thanks.' Oliver accepted a glass thrust into his hand by a stranger.

'I'm a great admirer of yours. I've read all your books.' Hamish beamed at Oliver, pinning him against the window. 'I suppose you can't come home because of tax –'

'Tax?'

'Income tax.' Hamish still beamed.

'I'm not that kind of a writer. Surprised you can read.' Feeling suddenly hurt, Oliver wished to wound. 'Are you Calypso's son?'

'Yes. Yes I am.' Hamish looked wounded.

Oliver felt perverse pleasure. 'Saw your father run over by a tank in the war. Didn't kill him, though. I was upset at the time, seems a joke now. I liked your father, a man of imagination. When Calypso married him I thought, we all thought –'

'Thought what?' Hamish stared at Oliver through an alcoholic haze. The rush of champagne on an empty stomach was having a malign effect.

'We thought she was wrong to marry for money –'

Hamish aimed a blow at Oliver and hit the curtain beside him. As he strove to regain his balance Oliver put out a hand to steady him.

'Now, now, what's going on?' Calypso appeared beside them. 'Are you two squabbling? Can't have that.'

'He said –' Hamish tried to speak.

'I said you married for money,' said Oliver.

'So I did.' Calypso spoke lightly. 'Wisest thing I ever did. Married for money. Then fell in love.' She looked from Oliver to Hamish.

'Why did you never tell me?' Hamish suddenly roared at his mother. 'Why did you keep it so bloody secret? Why did you never let on? Why did you let me suffer?'

'You are drunk. Go and eat something oily, you are making an exhibition.' She waved Hamish away. 'Have you got any children, Olly?'

320

'No.'

'But you married.'

'Twice.'

'Twice. Goodness, I'd forgotten. Are you married now?'

'No.' Oliver's eyes searched the room.

'Are you happy?' She watched him. He looked lean but had worn well.

'Are you?' His eyes came back to her face. 'What's happened to your face?'

'I had a little stroke. Yes, thanks, I am happy. Well, as happy as it's possible to be. Where do you live?'

'Abroad.' Oliver was noncommittal.

'All right, don't tell me.'

'Polly's grown very fat and respectable.'

'Spread. She's happy, too –'

'Who is the father of –'

'James and Iris? I've never asked. Why don't you? We don't dare.' Leaving him apart Calypso moved back into the crowd, most of whom now held glasses of champagne. Oliver stood by the window watching the pattern of the party, two moving circles, the nearest moving up to and round Pauli, greeting, not lingering. The second circling round Helena sitting in an armchair, Polly and her children posed protectively, filtering, without seeming to, the guests who wished to speak to her. Calypso in white moving through the crowd. Corks popping and laughter from the kitchen where the twins opened bottles to fill glasses carried on trays by the young musicians who, offering with shy smiles, received congratulations on their performance, thanked with the kindness of youth the compliments of the old.

'Fancy you turning up.' Tony Wood shook Oliver's hand. 'Remember me, Tony Wood? We first met on the doorstep of Polly's house.'

'Yes, I remember.' Time had done something terrible to Tony Wood.

'We've all changed, of course. Old age has crept up on us.' Tony noticed Oliver's expression with malicious pleasure.

321

'Yes, indeed.'

'Have you seen Sophy? Helena wants her.' Iris kindly enquiring.

'No.' Oliver realized that what his eye sought was Sophy. 'She was here. We came back from the church together.'

'Oh, did you?' Tony Wood's bright eyes investigated. 'What an exquisite girl child she was, one almost –'

'Almost?'

'Succumbed. Ah, here you are, have you met Peter? Peter and I have a shop in Brighton, antiques and objets. Peter, this is Oliver Anstey, you love his books.'

'Do I, darling?' pouting at Oliver.

'Yes, you do. What about another drink and some of that lovely nosh Polly brought?' Peter allowed himself to be led away by Tony. Oliver elbowed his way after them through the crowd. 'Didn't think then you'd become a writer.' Tony looked at Oliver over his shoulder.

'Didn't think you'd turn into an elderly poof.'

'Oh, screw you.' Tony let out a high gleeful laugh.

Oliver paused to listen to Pauli, who had succeeded in buttonholing a stranger.

'If I add a wing for a restaurant and build a pool it will sell very well as an hotel in this situation.'

'Oh,' said the stranger. Oliver stopped to listen. 'Of course.'

'My father's name will attract people. He had his master-classes here, you know.'

'Yes, very wonderful.'

Pauli waved his twisted fingers. 'As I say, the situation above the sea is unique now the National Trust try to buy the whole coast. One heats the pool, it goes without saying.'

'Of course,' the man agreed, smiling.

Oliver thought the man did not look like a friend of Max. Was Pauli merging business with funeral meats?

'Dig up the lawn, pave it with those warm-coloured slabs, have a terrace.' Pauli gestured out towards the lawn saturated and discoloured by the storm.

'Put fake plastic chairs and tubs of flowers.' Oliver shouldered into the conversation. 'Something that doesn't smell.'

'Admirable suggestion,' Pauli thanked him, 'and of course garages, a sauna, haute cuisine, it goes without saying. One gets planning permission.'

'It will make a nice property,' said the man. 'How much are you thinking of asking?' He refrained from looking Pauli in the eye, glancing casually out at the water-logged lawn.

'I must cost it.' Pauli was thoughtful.

Oliver moved to join another group, thinking he must say goodbye to Helena, feeling sickened, wanting to leave.

'Has anyone seen Sophy?' Polly's voice, not much changed. 'It's getting late. Helena wants her before she leaves. I can't see her anywhere.'

'I'll look upstairs.' Oliver ran up the stairs two at a time.

Sophy was standing by the window of what had once been her bedroom, looking out through the branches of the Ilex tree which shivered and creaked in the gale.

'Sophy, Helena wants you,' he said harshly.

'What does she want?' Sophy looked likely to take flight.

'Are you leaving tonight?' He came close to her, moving slowly, as though she were a nervous animal.

'Yes, very soon.' She moved towards the door. 'Why are you here? You were not at the other funerals.' She was wary.

'I thought I'd get some ideas for the book I'm writing. It was stupid of me.' She hadn't grown much, he thought, compared with the other girls. She was a very small woman. 'Why are you up here?'

She looked away from him. 'I used to climb along that branch.'

'In your pyjamas, and eavesdrop.'

She glanced at him sidelong. 'What does Helena want?'

323

'You jumped down and I caught you. Will you give me a lift? I came by train. We could have a meal at the Red Lion in Truro.' He followed her onto the landing.

'They've pulled it down. It's gone.' She sped down the stairs.

'Oh no!' He hurried after her in distress.

'Oh yes.' She had reached the hall.

'Pauli is going to dig up the lawn.' He caught her arm.

'It belongs to him now.' Her voice was expressionless. 'You should not have come back,' she said, looking at him with pain. 'It's worse for you.'

'The lovely harbour's been turned into a bloody great carpark.' Oliver's anger grasped at lesser sorrows. 'We used to step off the train and hear the water slopping against the quay.'

'I know, I know.' Gently she took his hand away from her arm. 'I must go to Helena.'

'She planted the lawn –' He gripped her arm again.

'I know, I know. Please, Oliver –' She turned and went swiftly to find Helena, slipping through the crowd like an eel.

'What do you want me for?'

Helena gripped her hand. 'Listen, Sophy, bend down close.' Helena spoke urgently into Sophy's ear. Oliver, joining them, heard her say, 'Promise you'll do that for me.'

'Of course I will. Have you told your lawyer, put it in writing?'

'Of course I have. I'm not senile yet. I hope to die first.'

'That's all right, then.' Sophy stayed close to Helena, surrounded by Polly, David, Paul, Iris and James.

'What's the secret? Don't keep moving away, you used not to be so elusive.'

'She wants her ashes dug into Max and Monika's grave.'

'Good Lord.' Oliver was taken aback.

'It seems reasonable.'

'What about Uncle Richard?'

'He's got his dog, didn't you know? It's what Max and

Monika would want. Uncle Richard wouldn't want her.'

'Good Lord,' said Oliver again.

'It's obvious, it's right. Uncle Richard would be the first to – what are you laughing at?'

'It's so peculiar.' Oliver looked at Sophy. 'We were such an ordinary lot of people at that dinner party.'

'You remember it, too?' she said. 'Max's first appearance.'

'So conventional,' Oliver insisted. 'We were.'

'Calypso's conventional.' Sophy spoke defensively.

'What will that splendid parson say?'

'I shan't tell him.'

'How then will you manage?'

'I shall be planting rosemary or something on Max and Monika and just pop Helena's ashes in too. No need to say anything or tell anyone, just do it. You can come and help if you like.' Sophy was defiant. 'You used not to be so conventional.'

'Oh, but I was, that was my trouble,' said Oliver, staring at Sophy, suddenly realizing what he had been like as a young man. 'If the Red Lion's gone, how about oysters somewhere near the Helford River. We could –'

'I don't know.' Sophy was in retreat again, he noticed.

'You don't know what?'

'I don't know anything any more. This was my home. It's gone, it's crumbling away.' She looked near tears.

'We'll go somewhere we've neither of us ever been.' She was edging away from him. 'You are upset.' He felt inadequate. Sophy sneezed violently.

'I've caught a chill. I must go.'

'I'm coming with you. We can't go before Helena. I'm still conventional enough to know that.'

'Poor Helena.' Sophy looked distraught. 'She's getting up, she's leaving.'

Oliver was holding Sophy by the wrist.

'Let go,' she whispered.

'No, I won't.' He tightened his grip as she twisted to get free.

'You are hurting me.'

'No I'm not. Look, she's gathering herself up to go.'
Oliver held Sophy, who gave in and stood quietly. 'Look,
she's having a last swig. I didn't know Helena drank.
That flask must hold half a bottle.'

'She doesn't really drink. This is a special occasion.'

'I'll say!' Hamish was standing beside them. 'I refilled
it on the way down and I found her violets. Wasn't that
marvellous? I mean, violets in October! She didn't want
anything else for Max.' Hamish sounded amiably drunk.

'I will drive Helena.' Calypso came up to Hamish. 'You
had better sit in the back.'

'What about my car?' Hamish was truculent.

'I've arranged for your car. You don't want to get
breathalysed, do you? Here she comes.'

They watched Helena making her progress out of the
house.

'Where's your wife?' Sophy snatched her hand free.

'What wife?' Oliver grabbed it back.

'I thought you were married.' Sophy, not wishing to
make a scene, left her wrist in Oliver's hand.

'I married twice, Calypso look-alikes, neither worked.
Haven't been married for years. What about you?'

'No, no.' Sophy sounded miserable.

'Lovers?'

'Yes, yes.'

'I heard rumours about various –'

'I daresay you did,' she said stiffly. Then – 'Will you
let me go. We aren't children.' She twisted her hand.

'Sixty and more, and you?'

'Fifty and more. Oh, look.' Her wrist in Oliver's grip,
Sophy watched Helena.

Helena's progress was slow. She shook hands or
kissed the guests saying, 'I am glad you came, it was nice
for Pauli. Thank you.' She said the same thing to each
person so that the words 'nice for Pauli' became the
most important: 'Thank you. Nice for Pauli.' She walked
quite steadily, flanked by Polly and Calypso, through the
crowd of guests all preparing, as she was, to say goodbye
to the inheritor, Max and Monika's son, stout, prosperous,

326

able to pull off a business deal in any circumstances, his soul uncluttered by musical nonsense.

Not much nonsense about Pauli, thought Helena, as she reached him and stood looking up into his face.

Holding Sophy's wrist, drawing her close to him, Oliver watched Helena, as did all the guests, making ready to leave, to thank their host, to say goodbye, to condole once again on the loss of his father, to reach their cars, to drive away sighing with relief, to catch their train, to return to normality, to life, to forget this brief interlude until the next, the next funeral, maybe one's own.

Helena was speaking now. It was amazing that such an old woman should have such a clear voice. Her voice in the wet evening air – it had stopped raining, there would be a beautiful sunset – carried to all the guests in the house, on the steps, in the drive.

'Goodbye, Pauli, I am sorry –' she hesitated. 'I forget what I was going to say,' she said, looking at him carefully, searching for some small trace of Max and finding none. She turned away, assuming vagueness, taking Calypso's arm and walked to the waiting car.

I am sorry, thought Helena, that so petty a thing as his intention to dig up the camomile lawn should make me wish he had died in his concentration camp, never come back, been made into a lampshade. 'I cannot help my thoughts,' she said much later to Calypso. 'They rage.'

As the guests dispersed a flight of starlings homing to roost blackened the sky, the sound of their wings muffling all other sound. Oliver tucked Sophy's hand into his pocket and walked her to the car.

Watching them go Polly said to the twins, 'I hope the old boy hasn't left it too late.'

In Calypso's car Helena turned to Hamish in the back. 'Run after them, dear boy, and give them this.' She handed him her silver flask. 'It will help them over those awkward moments.' Then, seeing him hesitate, for his baser nature hankered after the flask for himself, she added, 'And look sharp about it.'

So Hamish obediently ran, catching up with Sophy's car as she started the engine. He watched her drive off without a backward glance, then plodded back to Calypso and Helena.

Sophy drew into the side of the lane and sat staring ahead. From time to time she sneezed, her whole body shaken by the spasms. Oliver watched from the corner of his eye. He felt immensely tired, drained of anger and resentment.

The funeral guests drove past, their tyres hissing on the wet road, spattering the windscreen with mud.

Polly, her family all talking at once, the dog barking, a sudden cacophony of cheerful noise which Oliver took to be their norm and briefly envied as he watched other cars bearing Max's friends, colleagues, neighbours. Then Calypso in her white coat glimpsed in profile driving serenely. Helena beside her, old, exhausted, spent. Hamish on the back seat, mouth slightly open, face blank.

Finally Pauli's Mercedes nipping along, lights on, indicators blinking, horn sounding in frenetic haste. Then the procession was over, leaving the sound of the wind, the sea in the distance, gulls crying, fresh rain tapping on the glass.

Oliver looked at Sophy's profile, tiny face, high cheekbones, immense black eyes, full mouth. She threw up her nose to sneeze, her thin fingers clutching the steering wheel, a tear forced from the corner of her eye.

'Oh.' She laid her head on her hands on the wheel. 'Oh my God.' He counted white hairs among the black, observed the wrinkles round her eyes and mouth. Picking up Helena's flask he unscrewed the cap, swallowed a mouthful of whisky and said: 'You?'

'No, no thank you.' She did not look at him.

'Once,' he said, staring ahead at the empty road, 'you hid behind the curtains of the red room and I took you to bed to warm you. You smelt of soap. Rather nice soap. I wonder what it was.'

'Rose geranium.' Sophy turned her head away in protest.

'When you were still asleep I put you back in your own bed, d'you remember?'

'No.' She shook her head. 'No.'

'Liar.' He gulped some more whisky. 'A funny little girl you were.'

'Over forty-five years ago,' Sophy whispered.

'So now we have whatever's left to catch up. What d'you say to that?'

'We can't.' She turned to look at him in despair.

'Why not?' He stared at her, letting her see his thin lined face, receding hair, bright, slightly squinting eyes.

'I am terrified,' she said.

'What makes you think I am not afraid too?' Again he offered the flask. 'I am just the same inside,' he said defiantly, 'as I was then.' He forbore to say he might be wiser. He wondered whether she would refer to Calypso. She took the flask, tipped it, swallowed a mouthful. He watched her throat working.

'I don't feel anything any more,' she said, averting her eyes. 'I don't know you now. I am old and so are you.'

'I admit there's a considerable gap in our relationship.' Still he watched her and she did not answer. 'If you are thinking of Calypso,' he said tartly, 'it was like loving Greta Garbo or Marilyn Monroe. It wasn't real, it was a sort of measles.'

'A very long attack,' she said sharply.

'All right, a very long attack.' Oliver was patient, which went against his nature, holding back annoyance.

'You slept with her.'

'How do you know?'

'I guessed.'

'Just once. She made it clear she didn't enjoy it. It was humiliating.'

'Oh.' Sophy sneezed. 'I am sorry to keep sneezing like this. I must have caught cold in the churchyard.' Her voice was brittle. 'Looking at the graves.'

'I was beginning to think you were allergic to me,' he said grumpily.

'Not that.' Her emphasis was inadvertent.

329

'So you feel something?' he pressed her.

'Terribly hungry. I couldn't eat anything at the wake.'

'All right, then, let's go and find some oysters. There must be somewhere we can eat on our way.'

'We have no *way*,' she cried in pain. 'We know nothing about each other. There's an enormous forty-year gap.' She turned to look at him again.

'Then start the bloody car and let's see what we can do about filling it,' he yelled, losing patience.

Choking with sudden laughter, Sophy switched on the engine, wondering whether what she felt was real or just the whisky.

'We risk making ourselves the object of ridicule,' she said as she changed gear.

'It's a risk I am prepared to take.' Oliver was content that she had used the plural.

Driving towards Helston Sophy uneasily remembered the old adage: 'Be careful what you wish for, for it will surely come true.'

THE END

THE HISTORY OF VINTAGE

The famous American publisher Alfred A. Knopf (1892–1984) founded Vintage Books in the United States in 1954 as a paperback home for the authors published by his company. Vintage was launched in the United Kingdom in 1990 and works independently from the American imprint although both are part of the international publishing group, Random House.

Vintage in the United Kingdom was initially created to publish paperback editions of books bought by the prestigious literary hardback imprints in the Random House Group such as Jonathan Cape, Chatto & Windus, Hutchinson and later William Heinemann, Secker & Warburg and The Harvill Press. There are many Booker and Nobel Prize-winning authors on the Vintage list and the imprint publishes a huge variety of fiction and non-fiction. Over the years Vintage has expanded and the list now includes great authors of the past – who are published under the Vintage Classics imprint – as well as many of the most influential authors of the present. In 2012 Vintage Children's Classics was launched to include the much-loved authors of our youth.

For a full list of the books Vintage publishes,
please visit our website
www.vintage-books.co.uk

For book details and other information about the classic authors we publish, please visit the Vintage Classics website
www.vintage-classics.info

www.vintage-classics.info